At the Court of F
and Other Malayan

SIR HUGH CLIFFORD, G.C.M.G., G.C.B.

At the Court of Pelesu
and Other Malayan Stories

HUGH CLIFFORD

Selected and Introduced by
WILLIAM R. ROFF

KUALA LUMPUR
OXFORD UNIVERSITY PRESS
OXFORD NEW YORK
1993

Oxford University Press, Walton Street, Oxford OX2 6DP

*Oxford New York Toronto
Delhi Bombay Calcutta Madras Karachi
Kuala Lumpur Singapore Hong Kong Tokyo
Nairobi Dar es Salaam Cape Town
Melbourne Auckland Madrid*

*and associated companies in
Berlin Ibadan*

Oxford is a trade mark of Oxford University Press

Selection and Introduction © *Oxford University Press 1966
First published as* Stories *by Sir Hugh Clifford
by Oxford University Press, Kuala Lumpur, 1966
Reissued as an Oxford University Press paperback 1993*

ISBN 967 65 3028 X

*Printed by Peter Chong Printers Sdn Bhd., Malaysia
Published by Oxford University Press,
19–25, Jalan Kuchai Lama, 58200 Kuala Lumpur, Malaysia*

CONTENTS

Acknowledgements	vi
Editor's Acknowledgements	vi
Introduction	vii
CONCERNING MAURICE CURZON	1
THE EAST COAST	10
IN THE DAYS WHEN THE LAND WAS FREE	23
AT THE COURT OF PĚLĚSU	40
THE STORY OF RAM SINGH	93
WAN BEH, PRINCESS OF THE BLOOD	110
THE WEEDING OF THE TARES	135
THE FATE OF LEH, THE STROLLING PLAYER	143
UMAT	155
ON MALAYAN RIVERS	170
AMONG THE FISHER-FOLK	186
UP COUNTRY	201
'OUR TRUSTY AND WELL-BELOVED'	210

ACKNOWLEDGEMENTS

The publishers wish to thank the following for permission to reproduce copyright material: The representatives of the Estate of the late Sir Hugh Clifford, Hope Leresche & Steele; John Baker (Publishers) Ltd. and The Richards Press *In Court and Kampong* ('The East Coast', 'In the Days when the Land was Free', 'Among the Fisher-Folk' and 'Up Country') and *Studies in Brown Humanity* ('The Fate of Leh, the Strolling Player', 'Umat', 'On Malayan Rivers' and 'The Weeding of the Tares'); Ernest Benn Limited *A Corner of Asia* ('At the Court of Pĕlĕsu' and 'The Story of Ram Singh'); William Heinemann Ltd. *Bush-whacking and other Asiatic Tales and Memories* ('Wan Beh, Princess of the Blood'); Methuen and Co., Ltd. *A Freelance of Today* ('Concerning Maurice Curzon'); John Murray (Publishers) Ltd. *Malayan Monochromes* ('Our Trusty and Well-Beloved').

EDITOR'S ACKNOWLEDGEMENTS

Information for the introductory essay has been derived from a number of sources, the most important being: *Henry Clifford V.C., His Letters and Sketches from the Crimea* (London, 1956); W. Linehan, 'History of Pahang', *Journal Malayan Branch Royal Asiatic Society*, XIV, 2 (1936); and J. de V. Allen, 'Two Imperialists', *Journal Malayan Branch Royal Asiatic Society*, XXXVII, 1 (1964). In addition, I am indebted to J. de V. Allen for supplementary information concerning Clifford properties in England.

Clifford's own footnotes to the stories have been retained.

W.R.R.

INTRODUCTION

DESCRIBING Maurice Curzon, the fictional hero of his novel *A Freelance of Today*, Hugh Clifford wrote in 1903 that

> circumstance had combined to well-nigh denationalise him, to make him turn from his own kind, herd with natives, and conceive for them such an affection and sympathy that he was accustomed to contrast his countrymen unfavourably with his Malayan friends. This, be it said, is not a wholesome attitude of mind for any European, but it is curiously common among such white men as chance has thrown for long periods of time into close contact with Oriental races, and whom Nature has endowed with imaginations sufficiently keen to enable them to live into the life of the strange folk around them.

Amongst those whom chance thus threw into close contact with 'Oriental races' in the latter part of the nineteenth century was Hugh Clifford himself, who in 1883, at the age of seventeen, came out from a somewhat sheltered boyhood in England to join the Civil Service of what were then styled the Protected Malay States. He was to remain there, except for brief intervals, for almost twenty years, throughout the larger part of the formative period of British colonial rule. And because, like Maurice Curzon, he was not only 'a thorough Anglo-Saxon, clean-bred, and a good specimen of his race', but an unusually imaginative and sensitive man, strongly drawn—often despite himself—to the strange folk around him, the mark left on Clifford by Malaya and the Malays was deep and enduring. It found expression in the corpus of writings which stands to his name. During his years in the peninsula, and later as a senior British official in other colonial territories which moved him less, he wrote four novels and some eighty short stories and descriptive pieces, the great majority set in Malaya. It is from these stories that the present collection has been assembled in the belief that whatever their short-comings as fine literature and however unacceptable many of the basic assumptions underlying them must appear today, they form an important and sometimes moving record of the early days of colonial rule, and of one side of that ambiguous phenomenon, the colonial relationship.

Hugh Charles Clifford was born in London on 5 March 1866, the eldest son of Colonel Henry Clifford and a grandson of the seventh Baron Clifford of Chudleigh, in Devon. His mother, Josephine, was the only daughter of Joseph Anstice, who before his untimely death from tuberculosis in 1836 (at the age of twenty-eight) had been a brilliant student at Oxford (where he took a double First in Classics and Mathematics) and a young and more than usually promising professor of classical literature at King's College, London. Josephine herself had literary aspirations, and as a young woman contributed regularly to the periodicals edited at that time by Charles Dickens, and received, it is said, much encouragement from the great man. Perhaps this side of Hugh's ancestry helped later to stimulate his own urge to express himself in words. On his father's side, less noted artistically despite Colonel Clifford's penchant for sketching the field of battle, Hugh belonged to one of the leading Roman Catholic landed families in England, and could if he wished trace his descent back to the time of Henry II in the twelfth century. He numbered among his forebears in the direct line Sir Lewis de Clifford, Ambassador to France for Richard II, and Thomas, first Baron Clifford of Chudleigh, who was Principal Secretary of State and Lord High Treasurer to Charles II in the 1670's and gave his initial 'C' to the group of Ministers known as the CABAL.

Though in later years, as a result in part no doubt of the Test Act and other penalties visited in England upon Roman Catholics, the Cliffords had withdrawn somewhat from public life, they continued to represent an important section of the Catholic landed aristocracy, and to supply a steady stream of younger sons to the Church and (in the nineteenth century) the Army. One of Hugh's uncles became Roman Catholic Bishop of Clifton, and his father, the third son of the seventh Baron Clifford, served with distinction on or beyond the boundaries of Empire in the eighteen forties and fifties—in the Kaffir Wars in South Africa, in the Crimea (where he earned the VC at the Battle of Inkerman), and in the Opium Wars in China. The later part of his career, during Hugh's early boyhood, was spent mainly on the Staff in England, where he rose to the rank of Major-General and was created a Knight Cross of St Michael and St George by a grateful Queen.

The heartland of the Clifford family lay in the West Country, especially Devonshire and Somerset, and it was here that a large part of Hugh Clifford's childhood was spent—in the great manor houses and one-time Royalist castles belonging to his own and allied families. These ancient houses had, and in many cases still have today, certain pronounced characteristics which it is perhaps worth dwelling on for a moment, for the light they may shed on Hugh's later imaginative response to Malaya and the Malays. Unlike most Church of England manors, in and looking on to the villages of which they were an integral part, the great Roman Catholic houses of the West were inward-looking enclaves somewhat set apart from the life around them, and filled with a strong aura of medieval and often romantic unworldliness. Facing into their own high-walled parks, full of chapels, crucifixes and religious statuary, they gave to the world as many priests and nuns as men of action, and held a distant, if firmly paternal, castle-and-cottage relationship with their extra-manorial dependants, which seemed to partake of an earlier and simpler vision of society than that of the late nineteenth century. It is hard not to see in this a shaping influence upon Hugh's later romanticization of Malay life, with its 'court and kampong' dichotomy and its supposedly medieval system of values, and upon his own strong bent for benevolent paternalism and mistrust of material progress.

Hugh Clifford received his formal education not, as might have been expected, at one of the great English public schools, but at a private tutoring establishment run by a friend of the family. Exactly how long he spent here is not known, but it is clear that it served him sufficiently well to enable him to pass the entrance examination for Sandhurst in 1883. He seemed destined to follow in his father's footsteps and make a career in the Army. What deflected him from this course is not recorded—perhaps the death of his father in the same year affected the decision, perhaps he thought the army insufficiently romantic or idealistic. At any rate, he decided instead to go East and join the Civil Service of the Malay States, of which territories his father's cousin, Frederick Weld, as Governor of the Straits Settlements, was now High Commissioner. Accordingly, in the autumn of 1883, the young Hugh Clifford arrived in Malaya to take up a position as a Cadet in the Residency of Hugh Low in Perak, the first state to come under protectorate rule.

INTRODUCTION

The reasons for direct British intervention in the internal affairs of the western Malay states in the preceding decade had been of several kinds: a desire to exploit the economic resources of the hinterland of the Straits Settlements; a desire to secure the peninsula as a British sphere of influence against possible intrusion by other European powers; and changing attitudes in London about the value and function of colonial possessions. One of the principal arguments advanced by the men on the spot however—by those entrusted with actually carrying out British policy and introducing modern forms of administration—was of a rather different kind. It related to the great benefits which, it was profoundly believed, could be and ought to be brought to the benighted peoples of the earth. The 'unregenerate' Malays—a term much favoured by Victorian colonial administrators—clearly qualified for the assistance and the blessings of British rule, not least because in the mid-nineteenth century the typical Malay state was held to be manifestly a morass of misrule, inefficiency and social injustice, of a kind at which a good administrator could only shudder. It was widely believed, among men of this stamp, that for reasons of enervation by climate and a natural heritage of political corruption, 'Oriental races' were simply incapable of ordering their affairs competently, and that in consequence it could only be of benefit —to themselves and to mankind—to do so for them. Clifford's own connexion, Frederick Weld, spoke for many of his kind when he wrote in 1880: 'I doubt if Asiatics can ever really be taught to govern themselves. Good government seems not to be a plant congenial to the soil.' But lest we should be tempted to think the colonial protectorate simply a device for heedless exploitation, it may be remembered that a system of obligations was also held to be involved, for as another defendant of the system remarked, alien rule 'places upon the colonizing powers a grave responsibility for honest and efficient administration of the affairs of people whose development has reached the limit imposed by inexorable natural laws'.

Hugh Clifford certainly came out to Malaya possessed of ideas roughly of this kind, and to some extent he subscribed to them for most of his life. At the same time, he discovered, as did a number of others of his generation in the Malay states, that the Malays, though they might not be 'civilised', though they might require 'regeneration', were an extraordinarily attractive people, and that it was a source of endless fascination and reward to live among them. His first appointment was, as has been remarked, in Hugh Low's Residency in Perak, not too many years after Low's predecessor in office had been murdered by local chiefs for attempting to press British intervention too far and too fast. The British, accordingly, had learnt to deal more gently with the people they had come, ostensibly, to advise, and Low himself was a model of tact, humanity and respect for the susceptibilities of the Malays. Hugh Clifford, then, spent his first two or three years of service at the feet of an admirable teacher, became in addition an accomplished Malay linguist, and entered with all the enthusiasm of a young man into the task of learning to understand 'the strange folk around him', in the interests of bringing them the enlightenment of the West. In the course of this apprenticeship, and of his subsequent years as sole or senior British official in the wilds of Pahang, Clifford found in himself a strong natural sympathy with all classes of the Malay people, and the beginnings of a nagging doubt about the wisdom of wrenching a medieval society (as he liked to think of it) into the modern world: a doubt which, despite his passionate desire to dispel the dark cruelties of feudal rule, continued to possess him until the end of his working days—

indeed, did so increasingly as the infelicities of the twentieth century began to leave their mark on the rural society he loved so much. During these years also, he came to discover the frightening fascination of living completely immersed within a culture alien to his own, and coming to accept in some measure an alien system of values. It is this twin impulse—the need to look more closely at what may be called the moral effects of colonial rule and the need to explore the innermost character of the people he was set to govern and of his relationship with them—which underlies much of Clifford's writing. That he was unsuccessful in resolving the problems which thus arose is less remarkable than that he saw them to exist.

Clifford's association with Pahang, which was to last for sixteen years, give him his most intimate insights into Malay life, and provide him with the material for a large number of his stories, began in 1887. In January of that year, at the age of twenty, he was sent on a special mission to Pekan to persuade the ruler of Pahang, Bendahara Ahmad, to accept some measure of British control. Pahang at this time was accessible by land from the west coast only with extreme difficulty (Clifford was one of the first officials to make the journey) and was cut off by sea for several months of the year by the northeast monsoon. For many years it had been warred over by rival Malay factions, and the unsettled state of affairs which resulted, compounded by boundary disputes and uncontrolled land concessions in the interior to European entrepreneurs, prompted the British to seek to bring the state within its sphere of influence. In the nature of things, this was no easy task, as previous attempts had shown, but it was one into which a young and idealistic propagator of Western enlightenment might throw himself with enthusiasm. After painstaking and protracted negotiations, in which the Sultan of Johore played an important and probably decisive role, Bendahara Ahmad agreed to receive at his court a British political agent, with consular powers. To this post Clifford himself was appointed in October 1887, remaining in it until events forced the acceptance by Pahang of a full British Resident a year later. These two years, from January 1887 until November 1888, spent as a solitary British official at the court of a Malay ruler, thrown entirely upon Malays for companionship and solace, seem to have been crucial in Clifford's life. As he was to write later, in the story 'Up Country',

> The free, queer, utterly unconventional life has a fascination which is all its own. Each day brings a little added knowledge of the hopes and fears, longings and desires, joys and sorrows, pains and agonies of the people among whom ones lot is cast. Each hour brings fresh insight into the mysterious workings of the minds and hearts of that very human section of our race, which ignorant Europeans calmly class as 'niggers'. All these things come to possess a charm for him, the power of which grows apace, and eats into the very marrow of the bones of the man who has once tasted this particular fruit of the great Tree of Knowledge.

Something of the flavour of Clifford's life in Pekan is conveyed in the story 'At the Court of Pĕlĕsu', which contains in addition a thinly disguised account of the events which heralded the ultimate absorption of Pahang into the protectorate system at the close of 1888. Shortly after this, Clifford was invalided home to England on sick leave, but he returned to Malaya in 1891 and was posted once more to Pahang, where, under the new dispensation, he became Superintendent of Ulu Pahang and later Acting Resident, stationed in Kuala Lipis. Here again, as in Pekan, he found himself living in intimate and pleasurable contact with Malays for many months on end, furthering his already considerable knowledge of Malay life and of that of the aboriginal peoples who inhabited the interior of the state. But Pahang, though its ruler had accepted, albeit somewhat reluctantly, the fact of British control (and had been rewarded with the title Sultan for his pains), was not yet at peace. A number of the senior Malay chiefs, unable to acquiesce in the deprivation of powers which British rule brought in its train, rose in rebellion, and the next few years were spent in what Clifford called, with a certain amount of distaste, 'a heart-breaking little war'. Though the irony of this mode of inaugurating a rule of peace did not escape him, he himself played an important part in the suppression of the rebellion, displaying in the course of it marked personal courage, as the Malay *Hikayat Pahang* testifies. Later, when some of the dissident chiefs continued to harry Pahang from outside its borders (a passage of arms of this kind is described in 'The Story of Ram Singh'), Clifford was entrusted with the task of leading a punitive expedition to Trengganu and Kelantan, of which he later wrote a long and rather wry account in *Bushwhacking and Other Sketches*.

By the end of 1895, Pahang was at peace, and in the following year, after several times acting in that capacity, Clifford was made British Resident of the state. He was to remain there for the rest of his service in Malaya, except for a brief period spent as Governor in North Borneo and Labuan, a post from which he asked to be released. But the old glories had departed, and the new order, which he himself had done so much to usher in, was in full if unexciting cry. 'Bushwhacking' was exchanged for the more prosaic, and from Clifford's eminence less time-consuming, tasks of day-to-day administration, and encouraged perhaps by the success of his colleague Frank Swettenham's *Malay Sketches*, he turned to writing as a means of reliving the past and reflecting on the directions taken by the present. His first book, *East Coast Etchings*, published in 1896, was followed in rapid succession by *In Court and Kampong* (1897), *Studies in Brown Humanity* and the novel *Since the Beginning* (1898), *In a Corner of Asia* (1899), and *Bushwhacking and Other Sketches* (1901). Though most of the stories in these collections are frankly and unpretentiously descriptive, many illustrate clearly the preoccupations which now troubled Clifford's mind. A thorough Anglo-Saxon, clean-bred and a good specimen of his race, strapped from childhood into the conventions of the English upper-class and the Roman Catholic Church, he had found himself drawn to 'herding with natives, and conceiving for them such an affection and sympathy that he was accustomed to contrast his countrymen unfavourably with his Malayan friends'. He became much concerned with the problem of what we should call today 'race relations', and in 1903-4 attempted to deal imaginatively with this subject in *A Freelance of Today* and in the novella 'Sally: a Study', depicting respectively an Englishman who tried to become a Malay and a Malay who tried to become English. And added to the considerable crisis of the spirit which reflections of this kind aroused, he began to have serious doubts about part at least of the very ideology of Imperialism which explained and justified his own presence in Malaya. Though he remained convinced, as he wrote in the preface to *In Court and Kampong*, that 'the only salvation for the Malay lies in the increase of British influence in the Peninsula', he could not suppress the fear that by reducing the land 'to a dead monotony of order and peace' the British had helped to destroy much that was good and valuable in Malay life.

Clifford was not a great writer—as his friend and mentor

Joseph Conrad said in reviewing one of his books, 'One cannot expect to be, at the same time, a ruler of men and an irreproachable player on the flute'—but his vignettes of nineteenth-century Malaya sometimes possess an accuracy of observation, and an emotional identification, which lift them well above the general run of 'outpost of empire' tales. In addition, they have one characteristic which makes them singular for the time: the majority of their thinking and feeling characters are natives of the peninsula—Malays for the most part, Aborigines, Chinese, Indians—observed, so far as Clifford was capable, with sympathy and insight. An incorrigible romantic, he used many of his stories to celebrate an age that was either past or fast disappearing—the days, to use one of his own titles, when the land was free, or the first halcyon days of British rule when the Malay peasant welcomed the Union Jack as a liberator from the despotic rule of arbitrary chiefs, and when it was still possible for a British colonial administrator to divest himself of his robes and live among and of the people of 'that dear land which has claimed me for its own'.

In 1903, Clifford was parted from Malaya, as he then thought for good, and transferred by an unromantic Colonial Office to become Colonial Secretary of Trinidad and successively Governor of Ceylon, the Gold Coast, Nigeria, and again Ceylon. It was a bitter separation, but if Clifford had left Malaya, Malaya had not left him, and he continued for many years to publish stories about the peninsula and its peoples. Few are as vivid or as well-told as those written in the fastnesses of Pahang in the 1890's, but one, though wholly fictional, is oddly prophetic and moving. 'Our Trusty and Well-Beloved', first published in 1913, tells the story of Sir Philip Hanbury-Erskine, G.C.B., G.C.M.G., who, after half a life-time spent rising to the top in other outposts of empire, realizes 'his only steady ambition' and returns as Governor to the land where he had spent his unregenerate youth. In its way absurdly romantic and inarticulate, the story nevertheless depicts, as Maurice Curzon had done earlier, one of Clifford's dearest dreams.

Fourteen years after this piece was written, and twenty-four years after he had left Malaya, Sir Hugh Clifford, G.C.B., G.C.M.G., returned to the peninsula as Governor of the Straits Settlements and High Commissioner for the Malay States. He was greeted with every honour, and made triumphal and emotional visits to his old haunts. But he was getting old, and the illness which had been foreshadowed in some of his earliest writings was already upon him. Though he retained the affection and the respect of the Malayan peoples he had once tried to serve, 'even', as one biographer has written, 'when the onset of cyclical insanity led to eccentricities of behaviour', neither he nor Malaya had gone unchanged. In October 1929 he was forced to cut short his tour of duty and retire to England and obscurity. He died in hospital on 18 December 1941.

Monash University
Victoria   WILLIAM R. ROFF
June 1965

CONCERNING MAURICE CURZON

MAURICE Curzon let the folds of the mosquito-net fall around him, stretched himself upon his mattress and set himself to think out the *pros* and *cons* of his friend's proposal. Lying thus, in spite of his Oriental surroundings, and of the native garments which formed his sleeping-kit, he looked what he was—a thorough Anglo-Saxon, clean bred, and a good specimen of his race. His long, spare figure was lithe, active and hard; his eyes were blue, their light colour being intensified by the rich brown tint to which the Eastern sun had burnt his skin; they looked out upon the world with a direct gaze simple and honest. His hair was fair, and both it and his short beard were curly and crisp. The air of latent energy which inspired the whole man ,even in repose, marked him for a white man of the white men—a masterful son of the dominant race; yet circumstance and inclination had combined to well-nigh denationalise him, to make him turn from his own kind, herd with natives, and conceive for them such an affection and sympathy that he was accustomed to contrast his countrymen unfavourably with his Malayan friends. This, be it said, is not a wholesome attitude of mind for any European, but it is curiously common among such white men as chance has thrown for long periods of time into close contact with Oriental races, and whom Nature has endowed with imaginations sufficiently keen to enable them to live into the life of the strange folk around them.

Maurice was one of the many victims of competitive examinations. At school he had been ever foremost in the playing-fields, where his energies found unlimited scope, but as a scholar he had been a subject for tears. It was not that he lacked brains, for he could acquire anything which had the good fortune to interest him, as he had since acquired the Malayan language; but school-books had few attractions for him, and his father had considered himself fortunate when the opportunity presented itself to obtain a clerkship in an Oriental banking-house for the muscular young scamp.

'It is a thousand pities to waste the fellow upon such a poor career,' he had said discontentedly, 'but needs must when the devil drives. Confound him! why wasn't he born fifty years earlier? I am sure that he would have carved out a path for himself if he had had a chance. Well, I can only hope that he will stick to his stool better than he has stuck to his books.'

And Mr Curzon shook his head sceptically. Also he fell to abusing competitive examinations—a system which would have robbed India of Clive—forgetting in his wrath that the East has progressed since the days of the early heroes, and conceivably stands in need now of a different class of man from that which so gloriously fulfilled England's requirements when British rule in India was in its strenuous youth.

So Maurice Curzon, nothing loth to escape from bondage, betook himself to Singapore, and there the magic of the East gripped him, as it ever grips boys of strong imagination—the victims it has marked for its own. Instead of making himself socially agreeable to the men and women with whom he should have taken his pleasure, and suffering his life to run as nearly on the lines of a little country town at home as a thermometer ranging between 85° and 90° in the shade would permit, Maurice took to prosecuting inquiries into the mysteries of native life on his own account, the which is a dangerous pastime. Instead of working hard at the ledgers all day and dreaming by night of some time becoming a bank manager, and of transacting gigantic financial operations with unvarying skill and success, he too often added up his columns of figures with an amazing disregard for accuracy, and counted the hours that would set him free to go off 'slumming', as his fellows termed it, in the least savoury alleys of the native quarter. Also he dreamed of freedom, and longed for some chance to occur that should deliver him from the slavery of the office-stool and take him far away into untrodden places. The wonder of the East awoke a gipsy spirit within him. The magic and the mystery of Asia possessed him. He heard its music—that blended discord and harmony of strange tongues of men and beasts and insects; he smelt it in a thousand scents, half fragrant, half repulsive, wholly enervating and voluptuous; he saw it, filled with figures of men and women, quaint or picturesque, with trees and plants and shrubs of a new form, with flowers and birds and beasts that hitherto had existed for him only in hot-houses or in captivity. But more than aught else he seemed to be by instinct conscious of an unknown life underlying it all—of the throbbing of emotions that he could not understand; of a whispered suggestion hinting the existence of an unmapped country; of marvels closely hidden, yet marking their presence, as it were, by means of a cryptogram to which he might find the key; of an atmosphere of mystery that fired his imagination. Often he seemed to be standing, holding his breath, on the brink of some portentous discovery, his ears strained to catch the murmured sound that might perhaps be the master-word of a great enigma, his brows puckered by the effort of peering so eagerly into the luminous Darkness, in which, as behind a veil, moved dim figures secret and wonderful.

Two years of this dual existence, unsatisfactory alike to Maurice and to his employers, ended in an offer being made to him to accompany a prospecting expedition, in the capacity of interpreter, into one of the least-known native states of the Malay Peninsula. The post opened up no career and made no pretence of permanency, but with the recklessness and the invincible hopefulness of youth Maurice jumped at the chance and quitted his stool in the bank, to the intense satisfaction of himself and his superiors. The only person who viewed this step with extreme disapproval was Maurice's father, who waxed blasphemous over the letter in which the young man airily announced the decision at which he had arrived.

The expedition lasted for the best part of two years. Then the mine was abandoned and the party broke up. Maurice found himself in the possession of a fair sum of ready money, part of which he spent in a tour through the Malay Archipelago, by which he sought to enlarge his experience of native life, and later he rented cheap lodgings in Kampong Glam, and, like the excellent Mr Micawber, waited for something to turn up.

Maurice had waited now for several months with such equanimity as he could command, but as yet nothing of any kind *had* turned up. He had been horribly bored by this period of idleness; he had pined for the forests and for the free, wild life which he had learned to love; while his rapidly-emptying purse had filled him with forebodings. He had fully made up his mind to ship before the mast, and thus to earn his bread without the aid of his relations, whenever he should find himself at his last dollar, and it had been in the hope of expediting this necessity, since he found the continued suspense unendurable, that he had set himself resolutely to gamble with all his available capital upon the race-meeting which took place that autumn. But Fortune, who, as befits a lady, is often in a contradictory mood, smiled upon him with unvarying persistence. Back what horse he would, it seemed that he could not go wrong, and now on the evening of the last day of the meeting a heavy bundle of greasy paper money lay beside him on his mat, and he had the satisfaction of knowing that several thousands of dollars stood to his credit with the Sporting Club, which had charge of the lotteries.

Yet that afternoon, as he walked away from the crowded bar below the grand stand and threaded his way through the throng of natives of many nationalities in the direction of his lodgings, this knowledge had rendered him very little satisfaction indeed. The possession of a substantial sum of ready money only served to emphasise the fact that he was, as he termed it, completely 'at a loose end'. The utter aimlessness and the inactivity of his life irked him sorely; the gipsy in him urged him to move on and out, yet he knew not whither to turn; the nostalgia which calls the jungle-lover back to the wilderness was strong upon him, yet he did not dare to again allow his finances to fall into the deplorable condition from which Chance had so recently rescued them. The mob of eager, excited, boisterous, perspiring Englishmen which filled the bar that he had just quitted had offended his fastidiousness. The noise, the bear-fighting and the peals of facile laughter had stirred up that feeling of repulsion within him which was too often inspired by contact with his countrymen since he had learned to look upon them through the eyes of the Oriental, to whom many of their ways appear at once vulgar and repulsive. Looking at the sunset flaming above the squalid town, the restlessness that was never far from him had seized upon him anew, and Maurice Curzon had discovered that he was profoundly unhappy and ill at ease. It was just then that he had been attracted by the sight of a crowd in the centre of the street, and, pushing his way through it, he had discovered that its centre was a little native policeman blubbering frankly and a gaily-dressed and excessively truculent Malay, in whom Curzon recognised Raja Tuakal, a chief with whom he had struck up a close friendship during his term of service with the prospecting expedition. The latter seemingly was in trouble for bearing arms, and the representative of law and order was having a very bad time of it, to the huge delight of the native spectators, when Maurice's appearance upon the scene put an end to the dispute. Silver speedily dried the policeman's tears and quieted his sense of duty, whereupon Maurice bore Raja Tuakal off to his lodgings, hoping thereby to keep him out of further mischief. And now, just when he was ripe for almost any adventure, prepared to embark upon any speculation, provided that it would take him far away from the haunts of white men and would afford a reasonable prospect of adding to, rather than devouring, his small capital, Raja Tuakal had come forward with his proposal, which, let common sense say what it would, was undoubtedly fascinating to a man of Maurice's temperament.

None the less Curzon was sufficiently cool-headed to realise the momentous nature of the decision which he was about to make, and he understood the nature of the risks which the enterprise would entail far more accurately than his Malay friend could do. He saw that if he tried to run a cargo of arms into Acheh he ran the chance of having two European Governments upon his back. The exportation of warlike stores from the British Colony was strictly prohibited, and it would be his individual task to evade the English port officials before he could put to sea with his contraband goods. If he failed he would inevitably make acquaintance with the interior of the central gaol, and this, for a white man in the East, is one of the least attractive experiences that Asia can offer to the exile. But the British port authorities, after all, constituted merely the first line of defence, and when their vigilance had been eluded the fleet of Dutch gunboats prowling up and down the west coast of Sumatra would present a new and far more serious difficulty. If aught went amiss at this second stage of the proceedings, the best that the adventurers could hope for would be that they might not be taken alive. The fury which the discovery of a white man in the act of aiding the natives against them would occasion in his Dutch captors would be like to express itself in a most unpleasant manner; and even if he escaped unmaimed from the hands of the gunboats' crews, the civil power, into whose custody he would pass, would certainly show him a very scant measure of mercy. Moreover, the British Government would, of course, decline to interfere on his behalf, wherefore capture would probably mean a lifetime spent in a Dutch prison, which, if men speak truly, is an even less desirable residence than its English counterpart.

With this knowledge to aid him, Maurice Curzon conjured up a series of quite surprisingly unpleasant pictures, for, boyish adventurer though he was, he had a strong imagination, and was not altogether a fool. True, the prospect of an adventure that was wild and risky, nay, the grim shadow of danger itself, had for him an unholy fascination, and in so much he stood convicted of folly before the tribunal of commonsense. Yet, with all his limitations, he was guiltless of that more egregious madness which drives men to charge stupidly at Impossibility, as poor Don Quixote flung himself against the windmills.

Raja Tuakal's scheme could not, he thought, be classed as belonging to those things which are impossible of achievement. Cargoes of arms and ammunition had frequently been run into Acheh by natives without mishap, and what man has done man may do. The risks which faced Maurice were ugly to look at, but he solaced himself with the thought that the breach of the law which he contemplated was of the nature of a political, not a criminal offence, and curiously enough many men cannot bring themselves to believe that a like disgrace attaches to the one as the other. Had he regarded the proposed adventure as a dishonourable undertaking he would not have given it a second thought, but to him it appeared solely and purely in the light of a gamble in which he was about to stake his personal safety and liberty against the chance of meeting with new and thrilling experiences, and of incidentally making a pile of money. It was a game, he told himself, a great game, in which he was to be pitted against a skilful and immensely powerful antagonist. The very magnitude of the risks made all fair to his thinking. In his secret heart he already knew that he would surely end by falling in with Raja Tuakal's wishes, though he still made belief to dally with the idea, and told himself that his mind was not yet made up.

And how, in truth, could the issue remain doubtful, for as he lay thinking the restless longing for action and excitement which for so many weeks had spurred him to desperation, rowelled him afresh? The prospect of dangers which craft and courage might surmount sent the blood leaping through his veins, and set his pulses beating their battle-drums. How more than good it would be to taste again the free life of the jungle, with that added spice which would come, he thought, from the lust of battle, himself in the forefront of the fight! The anticipation sent a thrill of delight pulsing through him. What a chance to come to a man in these ordered days of peace, monotony and dulness! It was not in flesh and blood to resist a temptation so alluring when personal risk and the dread of perils were the only deterrents to bid a man cry 'Halt!'

From *A Freelance of Today*, London, 1903.

THE EAST COAST

IN these days, the boot of the ubiquitous white man leaves its marks on all the fair places of the Earth, and scores thereon an even more gigantic track than that which affrighted Robinson Crusoe in his solitude. It crushes down the forests, beats out roads, strides across the rivers, kicks down native institutions and generally tramples on the growths of nature, and the works of primitive man, reducing all things to that dead level of conventionality, which we call civilisation. Incidentally, it stamps out much of what is best in the customs and characteristics of the native races against which it brushes; and, though it relieves them of many things which hurt and oppressed them ere it came, it injures them morally almost as much as it benefits them materially. We, who are white men, admire our work not a little—which is natural—and many are found willing to wear out their souls in efforts to clothe in the stiff garments of European conventionalities, the naked, brown limbs of Orientalism. The natives, who, for the most part, are frank Vandals, also admire efforts of which they are aware that they are themselves incapable, and even the *laudator temporis acti* has his mouth stopped by the cheap and often tawdry luxury, which the coming of the Europeans has placed within his reach. So effectually has the heel of the white man been ground into the face of Perak and Sĕlangor, that these Native States are now only nominally what their name implies. The alien population far out-numbers the people of the land in most of the principal districts, and it is possible for a European to spend weeks in either of these States without coming into contact with any Asiatics save those who wait at table, wash his shirts, or drive his cab. It is also possible, I am told, for a European to spend years on the West Coast of the Peninsula without acquiring any very profound knowledge of the natives of the country, or of the language which is their speech-medium. This being so, most of the white men who live in the Protected Native States are somewhat apt to disregard the effect which their actions have upon the natives, and labour under the common European inability to view matters from the native standpoint. Moreover, we have become accustomed to existing conditions, and thus it is that few, perhaps, realise the precise nature of the work which the British in the Peninsula have set themselves to accomplish. What we are really attempting, however, is nothing less than to crush into twenty years the revolutions in facts and in ideas which, even in energetic Europe, six long centuries have been needed to accomplish. No one will, of course, be found to dispute that the strides made in our knowledge of the art of government, since the Thirteenth Century, are prodigious and vast, nor that the general condition or the people of Europe has been immensely improved since that day; but, nevertheless, one cannot but sympathise with the Malays, who are suddenly and violently translated from the point to which they had attained in the natural development of their race, and are required to live up to the standards of a people who are six centuries in advance of them in national progress. If a plant is made to blossom or bear fruit three months before its time, it is regarded as a triumph of the gardener's art; but what, then, are we to say of this huge moral-forcing system which we call 'Protection'? Forced plants, we know, suffer in the process; and the Malay, whose proper place is amidst the conditions of the Thirteenth Century, is apt to become morally weak and seedy, and to lose something of his robust self-respect, when he is forced to bear Nineteenth-Century fruit.

Until the British Government interfered in the administration of the Malay States in 1874, the people of the Peninsula were, to all intents and purposes, living in the Middle Ages. Each State was ruled by its own Sultan or *Raja* under a complete Feudal Syatem, which presents a curiously close parallel to that which was in force in Mediæval Europe. The *Raja* was, of course, the paramount authority, and all power emanated from him. Technically, the whole country was his property, and all its inhabitants his slaves; but each State was divided into districts which were held in fief by the *Orang Bĕsar*, or Great Chiefs. The conditions on which these fiefs were held, were homage, and military and other service. The Officers [*sic*] were hereditary but succession was subject to the sanction of the *Raja*, who personally invested and ennobled each Chief, and gave him, as an ostensible sign of authority, a warrant and a State spear, both of which were returned to the *Raja* on the death of the holder. As in Europe, high treason (*dĕrhaka*) was the only offence which warranted the *Raja* in forfeiting a fief. Each of the districts was subdivided into minor baronies, which were held, on a similar tenure, from the District Chief by a *Dato' Muda*; and the village communes, of which these baronies were composed, were held in a like manner, and on similar conditions, by the Headmen from the *Dato' Muda*. When war or any other public work was toward, the *Raja* summoned the Great Chiefs, who transmitted the order to their *Dato' Muda*. By the latter, the village Headmen and their able-bodied *raayat*[1] were called together, the free-holders in each village being

---

[1] *Raayat* = Peasants, villagers.

bound to the local *Penghulu*[1] by ties similar to those which bound him to his immediate Chief. In the same way, the *Raja* made his demands for money-grants to the Great Chiefs, and the *raayat* supplied the necessary contributions, while their superiors gained the credit attaching to those who fulfil the desires of the King. Under this system, the *raayat*, of course, possessed no rights, either of person or property. He was entirely in the hands of the Chiefs, was forced to labour unremittingly that others might profit by his toil; and neither his life, his land, his cattle, nor the very persons of his womenfolk, could properly be said to belong to him, since all were at the mercy of any one who desired to take them from him, and was strong enough to do so. This, of course, is the weak point in the Feudal System, and was probably not confined to the peoples of Asia. The chroniclers of Mediæval Europe tell only of Princes and Nobles, and Knights and Dames—and merry tales they are—but we are left to guess what was the condition of the bulk of the lower classes in Thirteenth-Century England. If we knew all, however, it is probable that their lot would prove to have been but little more fortunate than is that of the Malay *raayat* of to-day, whose hardships and grievances, under native rule, move our modern souls to indignation and compassion. Therefore, we should be cautious how we apply our *fin de siècle* standards to a people whose ideas of the fitness of things are much the same as those which prevailed in Europe some six centuries agone.

Those who love to indulge in that pleasing but singularly useless pastime of imagining what might have been under certain impossible circumstances, will find occupation in speculating as to whether the Malays, had they remained free from all extraneous influence for another thousand years, would ever have succeeded in evolving a system of Govern-

[1] *Penghulu* = Headman.

ment in any way resembling our own, out of a Feudal System which presents so curious a parallel to that from which our modern institutions have sprung. Would the Great Chiefs have ever combined to wrest a Magna Charta from an unwilling King, and the *raayat* have succeeded in beating down the tyranny of their Chiefs? No answer can be given; but those who know the Malays best will find reason to doubt whether the energy of the race would ever, under any circumstances, have been sufficient to grapple with these great questions. The *raayat* would have been content, I fancy, to plod on through the centuries 'without hope of change'; and, so far as the past history of a people can be taken as giving an indication of its future, it would seem that, in Malay countries, the growing tendencies made rather for an absolute than for a limited monarchy. The genius of the Malay is in most things mimetic rather than original, and, where he has no other model at hand to copy, he falls back upon the past. An observer of Malay political tendencies in an Independent Native State finds himself placed in the position of Inspector Buckett—there is no move on the board which would surprise him, provided that it is in the wrong direction.

Such changes have been wrought in the condition of the Malay on the West Coast, during the past twenty years of British Protection, that there one can no longer see him in his natural and unregenerate state. He has become sadly dull, limp, and civilised. The gossip of the Court, and the tales of ill things done daringly, which delighted his fathers, can scarcely quicken his slackened pulses. His wooings have lost their spice of danger, and, with it, more than half their romance. He is as frankly profligate as his thin blood permits, but the dissipation in which he indulges only makes him a disreputable member of society, and calls for none of the manly virtues which make the Malay attractive to those who know and love him in his truculent untamed state. On the East Coast, things are different, and the Malay States are still what they profess to be—States in which the native element predominates, where the people still think boldly from right to left, and lead much the same lives as those their forbears led before them. Here are still to be found some of the few remaining places, on this overhandled Earth, which have as yet been but little disturbed by extraneous influences, and here the lover of things as they are, and ought not to be, may find a dwelling among an unregenerate and more or less uncivilised people, whose customs are still unsullied by European vulgarity, and the surface of whose lives is but little ruffled by the fever-heated breath of European progress.

As you crush your way out of the crowded roadstead of Singapore, and skirting the red cliffs of Tanah Merah, slip round the heel of the Peninsula, you turn your back for a space on the seas in which ships jostle one another, and betake yourself to a corner of the globe where the world is very old, and where conditions of life have seen but little change during the last thousand years. The only modern innovation is an occasional 'caster', or sea tramp, plying its way up the coast to pick up a precarious profit for its owners by carrying cargoes of evil-smelling trade from the fishing villages along the shore. Save for this, there is nothing to show that white men ever visit these seas, and, sailing up the coast in a native craft, you may almost fancy yourself one of the early explorers skirting the lovely shores of some undiscovered country. As you sprawl on the bamboo decking under the shadow of the immense palm leaf sail—which is so ingeniously rigged that, if taken aback, the boat must turn turtle, unless, by the blessing of the gods, the mast parts asunder—you look out through half-closed eyelids at a very beautiful coast. The waves dance, and glimmer, and shine in the sunlight, the long stretch of sand is yellow as a buttercup, and the fringes of graceful *casuarina* trees quiver like aspens in the breeze, and shimmer in the heat haze. The wash of the waves against the boat's side, and the ripple of the bow make music in your drowsy ears, and, as you glide through cluster after cluster of thickly-wooded islands, you lie in that delightful comatose state in which you have all the pleasure of existence with none of the labour of living. The monsoon threshes across these seas for four months in the year, and keeps them fresh, and free from the dingy mangrove clumps, and hideous banks of mud, which breed fever and mosquitoes in the, Straits of Malacca. In the interior, too, patches of open country abound, such as are but rarely met with on the West Coast but here, as elsewhere in the Peninsula, the jungles, which shut down around them, are impenetrable to anything less persuasive than an axe.

These forests are among the wonderful things of the Earth. They are immense in extent, and the trees which form them grow so close together that they tread on one another's toes. All are lashed, and bound, and relashed, into one huge magnificent tangled net, by the thickest underwood, and the most marvellous parasitic growths that nature has ever devised. No human being can force his way through this maze of trees, and shrubs, and thorns, and plants, and creepers; and even the great beasts which dwell in the jungle find their strength unequal to the task, and have to follow game paths, beaten out by the passage of innumerable animals, through the thickest and deepest parts of the forest. The branches cross and recross, and are bound together by countless parasitic creepers, forming a green canopy overhead, through which the fierce sunlight only forces a partial passage, the struggling rays flecking the trees on which they fall with little splashes of light and colour. The air 'hangs heavy as remembered sin', and the gloom of a great cathedral is on every side. Everything is damp, and moist, and oppressive. The soil, and the cool dead leaves under foot are dank with decay, and sodden to the touch. Enormous fungous growths flourish luxuriantly; and over all, during the long hot hours of the day, hangs a silence as of the grave. Though these jungles teem with life, no living thing is to be seen, save the busy ants, a few brilliantly-coloured butterflies and insects, and an occasional nest of bees high up in the tree-tops. A little stream ripples its way over the pebbles of its bed, and makes a humming murmur in the distance; a faint breeze sweeping over the forest gently sways the upper branches of a few of the tallest trees; but, for the rest, all is melancholy, silent, and motionless. As the hour of sunset approaches, the tree beetles and cicada join in their strident chorus, which tells of the dying day; the thrushes join in the song with rich trills and grace-notes; the jungle fowls crow to one another; the monkeys whoop and give tongue like a pack of foxhounds; the gaudy parrots scream and flash as they hunt for flies;

> And all the long-pent stream of life
> Bursts downwards in a cataract.

Then, as you lie listening through the long watches of the night, sounds are borne to you which tell that the jungle is afoot. The argus pheasants yell to one another as the hours creep by; the far-away trumpet of an elephant breaks the stillness; and the frightened barking cry of a deer comes to you from across the river. The insects are awake all night, and the little workman bird sits on a tree close by you and drives coffin nails without number. With the dawn, the tree beetles again raise their chorus; the birds sing and trill more sweetly than in the evening; the monkeys bark afresh as they leap through the branches; and the leaves of the forest glisten in the undried dew. Then, as the sun mounts, and the dew dries, the sounds of the jungle die down one by one, until the silence of the forest is once more unbroken for the long hot day.

Through these jungles innumerable streams and rivers flow seawards; for so marvellously is this country watered that, from end to end of the Peninsula, no two hills are found, but there is a stream of some sort in the gut which divides them. Far up-country, the rivers run riot through long successions of falls and rapids, but as they near the coast, they settle down into broad imposing looking streams, miles wide in places, but for the most part uniformly shallow, the surfaces of which are studded with green islands and yellow sandbanks. These rivers, on the East Coast, form the principal, and often the only highways, many of them being navigated for nearly three hundred miles of their course. When they become too much obstructed by falls to be navigable even for a dug-out, they still serve the Malays of the interior as highways. Where they are very shallow indeed they are used as tracks, men wading up them for miles and miles. A river-bed is a path ready cleared through the forests, and, to the Sĕmang,[1] Sakai,[2] and jungle-bred Malay, it is Nature's macadamized road. More often the unnavigable streams serve as guides to the traveller in the dense jungles, the tracks running up their banks, crossing and recrossing them at frequent intervals. One of these paths, which leads from Trĕngganu to Kĕlantan, crosses the same river no less than thirty times in about six miles, and, in most places, the fords are well above a tall man's knee. The stream is followed until a *Ka-*

---

[1] *Sĕmang* = Aboriginal natives of the Peninsula, belonging to the Negrit family.
[2] *Sakai* = Aboriginal natives of the Peninsula, belonging to the Mon-Annam family.

naik—or taking-off place—is reached, and, leaving it, the traveller crosses a low range of hills, and presently strikes the banks of a stream, which belongs to another river basin. A path, similar to the one which he has just left, leads down this stream, and by following it he will eventually reach inhabited country. No man need ever lose himself in a Malay jungle. He can never have any difficulty in finding running water, and this, if followed down, means a river, and a river presupposes a village sooner or later. In the same way, a knowledge of the localities in which the rivers of a country rise, and a rough idea of the directions in which they flow, are all the geographical data which are required in order to enable you to find your way, unaided, into any portion of that, or the adjoining States which you may desire to visit. This is the secret of travelling through Malay jungles, in places where the white man's roads are still far to seek, and where the natives are content to move slowly, as their fathers did before them.

The Malay States on the East of the Peninsula are Sĕnggora, Pĕtani, Jambe, Jaring, Raman, Lĕgeh, Kĕlantan, Trĕngganu, Pahang, and Johor.

Sĕnggora possesses the doubtful privilege of being ruled by a Siamese Official, who is appointed from Bangkok, as the phrase goes, to *kin*—or eat—the surrounding district.

The next four States are usually spoken of collectively as Pĕtani, by Europeans, though the territory which really bears that name is of insignificant importance and area, the jurisdiction of its *Raja* only extending up the Pĕtani river as far as Jambe. It is said that when the Raja of Pĕtani and the ruler of the latter State had a difference of opinion, the former was obliged to send to Kĕlantan for his drinking water, since he could not trust his neighbour to refrain from poisoning the supply, which flows from Jambe through his kingdom.

Uneasy indeed must lie the head which wears the crown of Pětani!

All the States, as far down the coast as Lěgeh, are under the protection of the Siamese Government. Kělantan and Trěngganu still claim to be independent, though they send the *bunga ěmas*—or golden flower— to Bangkok once in three years. Pahang was placed under British Protection in 1888, and Johor is still independent, though its relations with the Government of Great Britain are very much the same as those which subsist between Siam and the Malay States of Kělantan and Trěngganu.

The *bunga ěmas*, to which reference has been made above, consists of two ornamental plants, with leaves and flowers, fashioned from gold and silver, and their value is estimated at about $5000. The sum necessary to defray the cost of these gifts is raised by means of a *banchi*, or poll-tax, to which every adult male contributes; and the return presents, sent from Bangkok, are of precisely the same value, and are, of course, a perquisite of the *Raja*. The exact significance of these gifts is a question of which very different views are taken by the parties concerned. The Siamese maintain that the *bunga ěmas* is a direct admission of suzerainty on the part of the *Raja* who sends it, while the Malay Sultans and their Chiefs entirely deny this, and hold that it is merely *tanda s'pakat dan běrsahabat*—a token of alliance and friendship. It is not, perhaps, generally known that, as late as 1826, Pěrak was in the habit of sending a similar gift to Siam, and that the British Government bound itself not to restrain the Sultan of Pěrak from continuing this practice if he had a mind to do so. From this it would seem that there is some grounds for the contention of Trěngganu and Kělantan that the *bunga ěmas* is a purely voluntary gift, sent as a token of friendship to a more powerful State, with which the sender desires to be on terms of amity. Be this how it may, it is certain that Sultan Mansur of Trĕngganu, who first sent the *bunga ĕmas* to Siam in 1776, did so, not in compliance with any demand made by the Siamese Government, but because he deemed it wise to be on friendly terms with the only race in his vicinity which was capable, in his opinion, of doing him a hurt.

Direct interference in the Government of Kĕlantan and Trĕngganu has been more than once attempted by the Siamese, during the last few years, strenuous efforts having been made to increase their influence on the East Coast of the Peninsula, since the visit of the King of Siam to the Malay States in 1890. In Trĕngganu, all these endeavours have been of no avail, and the Siamese have abandoned several projects which were devised in order to give them a hold over this State. In Kĕlantan, internal troubles have aided Siamese intrigues, the present *Raja* and his late brother both having so insecure a seat upon their thrones that they readily made concessions to the Siamese in order to purchase their support. Thus, at the present time, the flag of the White Elephant floats at the mouth of the Kĕlantan river on State occasions, though the administration of the country is still entirely in the hands of the *Raja* and his Chiefs.

The methods of Malay rulers, when they are unchecked by extraneous influences, are very curious; and those who desire to see the Malay *Raja* and the Malay *raayat* in their natural condition, must nowadays study life on the East Coast. Nowhere else has the Malay been so little changed by the advancing years, and those who are only acquainted with the West Coast and its people, as they are to-day, will find much to learn when they visit the Eastern sea-board.

Until British interference changed the conditions which existed in Pahang, that country was the best type of an independent Malay State in the Peninsula, and much that was to be seen and learned in Pahang, in the days before the appointment of a British Resident, cannot now be experienced in quite the same measure anywhere else. Both Trĕngganu and Kĕlantan have produced their strong rulers—for instance, Baginda Umar of Trĕngganu, and the 'Red-mouthed Sultan' of Kĕlantan—but neither of the present *Rajas* can boast anything resembling the same personality and force of character, or are possessed of the same power and influence, as distinguished Sultan Ahmad Maatham, Shah of Pahang, in the brave days before the coming of the white men.

In subsequent articles, I hope, by sketching a few events which have occurred in some of the States on the East Coast; by relating some characteristic incidents, many of which have come within my experience; and by descriptions of the conditions of life among the natives, as I have known them; to give my European readers some idea of a state of Society, wholly unlike anything to which they are accustomed, and which must inevitably be altered out of all recognition by the rapidly increasing influence of foreigners in the Malay Peninsula.

From *In Court and Kampong*, London, 1897.

IN THE DAYS WHEN THE LAND WAS FREE

IN 1873 the people of Pahang who, then as now, were ever ready to go upon the war-path poured over the cool summits of the range that forms at once the backbone of the Peninsula and the boundary between Pahang and Sĕlangor. They went at the invitation of the British Government, to bring to a final conclusion the protracted struggles, in which Malay *Rajas*, foreign mercenaries, and Chinese miners had alike been engaged for years, distracting the State of Sĕlangor, and breaking the peace of the Peninsula. A few months later, the Pahang Army, albeit sadly reduced by cholera, poured back again across the mountains, the survivors slapping their chests and their *kris*-hilts, and boasting loudly of their deeds, as befitted victorious warriors in a Malay land. The same stories are still told 'with circumstance and much embroidery', by those who took part in the campaign, throughout the length and breadth of Pahang even unto this day.

Among the great Chiefs who led their people across the range, one of the last to go, and one of those whose heart was most uplifted by victory, was the present Mahraja Pĕrba of Jĕlai, commonly called To' Raja. His own people, even at that time, gave him the title he now bears, but the Bĕndahara of Pahang (since styled Sultan) had never formally installed him in the hereditary office of which he was the heir, so by the Court Faction he was still addressed as Panglima Prang Mamat.

On his arrival at Pĕkan, the Panglima Prang, unmindful

of the fate which, at an earlier period, had befallen his brother Wan Bong, whose severed head lay buried somewhere near the palace in a nameless grave, began to assert himself in a manner which no Malay King could be expected to tolerate. Not content with receiving from his own people the semi-royal honours, which successive To' Rajas have insisted upon from the natives of the interior, Panglima Prang allowed his pride to run away with both his prudence and his manners. He landed at Pĕkan with a following of nearly fifty men, all wearing shoes, the spoils of war, it is said, which had fallen to his lot through the capture of a Chinese store; he walked down the principal street of the town with an umbrella carried by one of his henchmen; and he ascended into the King's *Balai* with his *kris* uncovered by the folds of his *sarong*! The enormity of these proceedings may not, perhaps, be apparent; but, in those days, the wearing of shoes of a European type, and the public use of an umbrella, were among the proudest privileges of royalty. To ascend the *Balai* with an uncloaked weapon in one's girdle was, moreover, a warlike proceeding, which can only be compared to the snapping of fingers in the face of royalty. Therefore, when Panglima Prang left Pĕkan, and betook himself up river to his house in the Jĕlai, he left a flustered court, and a very angry King behind him.

But at this time there was a man in Pahang who was not slow to seize an opportunity, and in the King's anger he saw a chance that he had long been seeking. This man was Dato' Imam Prang Indĕra Gajah Pahang, a title which, being interpreted, meaneth, The War Chief, the Elephant of Pahang. Magnificent and high sounding as was this name, it was found too large a mouthful for everyday use, and to the people of Pahang he was always known by the abbreviated title of To' Gajah. He had risen from small beginnings by his genius for war, and more especially for that branch of the science which the Malays call *tipu prang*—the deception of strife—a term which is more accurately rendered into English by the word treachery, than by that more dignified epithet strategy. He had already been the recipient of various land grants from the King, which carried with them some hundreds of devoted families who chanced to live on the alienated territories; he already took rank as a great Chief; but his ambition was to become the master of the Lipis Valley, in which he had been born, by displacing the aged To' Kaya Stia-wangsa, the hereditary Chief of the District.

To' Gajah knew that To' Kaya of Lipis, and all his people were more or less closely related to Panglima Prang, and to the Jĕlai natives. He foresaw that, if war was declared against Panglima Prang by the King, the Lipis people would throw in their fortunes with the former. It was here, therefore, that he saw his chance, and, as the fates would have it, an instrument lay ready to his hand.

At Kuala Lipis there dwelt in those days an old and cross-grained madman, a Jĕlai native by birth, who, in the days before his trouble came upon him, had been a great Chief in Pahang. He bore the title of Orang Kaya Haji, and his eldest son was named Wan Lingga. The latter was as wax in To' Gajah's hands, and when they had arranged between themselves that in the event of a campaign against Panglima Prang proving successful, Wan Lingga should replace the latter by becoming To' Raja of Jĕlai, while the Lipis Valley should be allotted to To' Gajah, with the title of Dato' Kaya Stia-wangsa, they together approached the Bĕndahara on the subject.

They found him willing enough to entertain any scheme, which included the humbling of his proud vassal Panglima Prang, who so lately had done him dishonour in his own capital. Moreover the Bĕndahara of Pahang was as astute as it is given to most men to be, and he saw that strife between the great Chiefs must, by weakening all, eventually strengthen his own hand, since he would, in the end, be the peacemaker between them. Therefore he granted a letter of authority to Wan Lingga and To' Gajah, and thus the war began.

The people of Pahang flocked to the interior, all noisily eager to stamp out of existence the upstart Chief, who had dared to wear shoes, and to carry an umbrella in the streets of their King's capital. The aged Chief of Lipis and his people, however clove to Panglima Prang, or To' Raja, as he now openly called himself, and the war did not prosper. To' Gajah had inspired but little love in the hearts of the men whom the Bĕndahara had given him for a following, and they allowed their stockades to be taken without a blow by the Jĕlai people, and on one occasion To' Gajah only escaped by being paddled hastily down stream concealed in the rolled-up hide of a buffalo.

At last it became evident that war alone could never subdue the Jĕlai and Lipis districts and consequently negotiations were opened. A Chief named the Orang Kaya Pahlawan of Sĕmantan visited To' Raja in the Jĕlai and besought him to make his peace by coming to Pĕkan.

'Thou hast been victorious until now,' said he, 'but thy food is running low. How then wilt thou fare? It were better to submit to the Bĕndahara, and I will go warrant that no harm befalls thee. If the Bĕndahara shears off thy head, he shall only do so when thy neck has been used as a block for mine own. And thou knowest that the King loveth me.' To' Raja therefore allowed himself to be persuaded, but stipulated that Wan Lingga, who was then at Kuala Lipis, should also go down to Pĕkan, since if he remained in the interior he might succeed in subverting the loyalty of the Jĕlai people who hitherto had been faithful to To' Raja. Accordingly Wan

Lingga left Kuala Lipis, ostensibly for Pĕkan, but, after descending the river for a few miles, he turned off into a side stream, named the Kichan, where he lay hidden biding his time.

When To' Raja heard of this, he at first declined to continue his journey down stream, but at length, making a virtue of necessity, he again set forward, saying that he entertained no fear of Wan Lingga, since one who could hide in the forest 'like a fawn or a mouse-deer' could never, he said, fill the seat of To' Raja of Jĕlai.

It is whispered, that it had been To' Gajah's intention to make away with To' Raja, on his way down stream, by means of that 'warlike' art for which, I have said, he had a special aptitude; but the Jĕlai people knew the particular turn of the genius with which they had to deal, and consequently they remained very much on their guard. They travelled, some forty or fifty strong, on an enormous bamboo raft, with a large fortified house erected in its centre. They never parted with their arms, taking them both to bed and to bath; they turned out in force at the very faintest alarm of danger; they moored the raft in mid-stream when the evening fell; and, wonderful to relate, for Malays make bad sentinels, they kept faithful watch both by day and by night. Thus at length they won to Pĕkan without mishap; and thereafter they were suffered to remain in peace, no further and immediate attempts being made upon their lives.

To' Raja—or Panglima Prang as he was still called by the King and the Court Faction—remained at the capital a prisoner in all but the name. The Bĕndahara declined to accord him an interview, pointedly avoided speech with him, when they chanced to meet in public, and resolutely declined to allow him to leave Pĕkan. This, in ancient days, was practically the King's only means of punishing a powerful vassal, against whom he did not deem it prudent to take more active measures; and as, at a Malay Court, the *entourage* of the Raja slavishly follow any example which their King may set them, the position of a great Chief living at the capital in disgrace was sufficiently isolated, dreary, humiliating, and galling.

But To' Raja's own followers clove to him with the loyalty for which, on occasion, the natives of Pahang are remarkable. The Běndahara spared no pains to seduce them from their allegiance, and the three principal Chieftains who followed in To' Raja's train were constantly called into the King's presence, and were shown other acts of favour which were steadfastly denied to their master. But it profited the Běndahara nothing, for Imam Bakar, the oldest of the three set an example of loyalty which his two companions, Imam Prang Samah and Khatib Bujang, followed resolutely. Imam Bakar himself acted from principle. He was a man whom Nature had endowed with firm nerves, a faithful heart and that touch of recklessness and fatalism which is needed to put the finishing touch to the courage of an oriental. He loved To' Raja and all his house, nor could he be tempted or scared into a denial of his affection and loyalty. Imam Prang Samah and Khatib Bujang, both of whom I know well, are men of a different type. They belong to the weak-kneed brethren, and they followed Imam Bakar because they feared him and To' Raja. They found themselves, to use an emphatic colloquialism, between the Devil and the Deep Sea, nor had they sufficient originality between them to suggest a compromise. Thus they imitated Imam Bakar, repeated his phrases after him, and, in the end, but narrowly escaped sharing with him the fate which awaits those who arouse the wrath of a King.

At each interview which these Chieftains had with their monarch, the latter invariably concluded the conversation by calling upon them to testify to the faith that was in them.

'Who,' he would ask, 'is your Master, and who is your Chief?'

And the three, led by Imam Bakar, would make answer with equal regularity:

'Thou, O Highness, art Master of thy servants, and His Highness To' Raja is thy servants' Chief.'

Now, from the point of view of the Běndahara, this answer was most foully treasonable. That in speaking to him, the King, they should give To' Raja—the vassal he had been at such pains to humble—a royal title equal to his own, was in itself bad enough. But that, not content with this outrage, they should decline to acknowledge to the Běndahara as both Master and Chief was the sorest offence of all. A man may own duty to any Chief he pleases, until such time as he comes into the presence of his King, who is the Chief of Chiefs. Then all loyalty to minor personages must be laid aside, and the Monarch must be acknowledged as the Master and Lord above all others. But it was just this one thing that Imam Bakar was determined not to do, and at each succeeding interview the anger of the Běndahara waxed hotter and hotter.

At the last interview of all, and before the fatal question had been asked and answered, the King spoke with the three Chieftains concerning the manner of their life in the remote interior, and, turning to Imam Bakar, he asked how they of the upper country lived.

'Thy servants live on earth,' replied the Imam, meaning thereby that they were tillers of the soil.

When they had once more given the hateful answer to the oft put question, and had withdrawn in fear and trembling before the King's anger, the latter called To' Gajah to him and said:

'Imam Bakar and the men his friends told me a moment since that they eat earth. Verily the Earth will have its revenge, for I foresee that in a little space the Earth will swallow Imam Bakar.'

Next day the three recalcitrant Chiefs left Pĕkan for their homes in the interior, and, a day or two later, To' Gajah, by the Bĕndahara's order, followed them in pursuit. His instructions were to kill all three without further questionings, should he chance to overtake them before they reached their homes at Kuala Tĕmbĕling. If, however, they should win to their homes in safety, they were once more to be asked the fatal question, and their lives were to depend upon the nature of their answer. This was done, lest a rising of the Chieftains' relations should give needless trouble to the King's people; for the clan was not a small one, and any unprovoked attack upon the villages, in which the Chieftains lived, would be calculated to give offence.

Imam Bakar and his friends were punted up the long reaches of the Pahang river, past the middle country, where the banks are lined with villages nestling in the palm and fruit trees; past Gunong Sĕnuyum—the Smiling Mountain—that great limestone rock, which raises its crest high above the forest that clothes the plain in which it stands in solitary beauty; past Lubok Plang, where in a nameless grave lies the Princess of ancient story, the legend of whose loveliness alone survives; past Glanggi's Fort, those gigantic caves which seem to lend some probability to the tradition that, before they changed to stone, they were once the palace of a King; and on and on, until, at last, the yellow sandbanks of Pasir Tambang came in sight. And close at their heels, though they knew it not, followed To' Gajah and those of the King's Youths who had been deputed to cover their Master's shame.

At Kuala Tĕmbĕling, where the waters of the river of that name make common cause with those of the Jĕlai, and where the united streams first take the name of Pahang, there lies a broad stretch of sand glistening in the fierce sunlight. It has been heaped up, during countless generations, by little tributes from the streams which meet at its feet, and it is never still. Every flood increases or diminishes its size, and weaves its restless sands into some new fantastic curve or billow. The sun which beats upon it bakes the sand almost to boiling point, and the heat-haze dances above it, like some restless phantom above a grave. And who shall say that ghosts of the dead and gone do not haunt this sandbank far away in the heart of the Peninsula? If native report speaks true, the spot is haunted, for the sand, they say, is 'hard ground' such as the devils love to dwell upon. Full well may it be so, for Pasir Tambang has been the scene of many a cruel tragedy, and could its sands but speak, what tales would they have to tell us of woe and murder, of valour and treachery, of shrieking souls torn before their time from their sheaths of flesh and blood, and of all the savage deeds of this

> race of venomous worms
> That sting each other here in the dust.

It was on this sandbank that To' Gajah and his people pitched their camp, building a small open house with rude uprights, and thatching it with palm leaves cut in the neighbouring jungle. To' Gajah knew that Imam Bakar was the man with whom he really had to deal. Imam Prang Samah and Khatib Bujang he rated at their proper worth, and it was to Imam Bakar, therefore, that he first sent a message, desiring him once more to answer as to who was his Master and who his Chief. Imam Bakar, after consulting his two friends, once more returned the answer that while he acknowledged the Běndahara as his King and his Master, his immediate Chief was no other than 'His Highness To' Raja'. That answer sealed his doom.

On the following day To' Gajah sent for Imam Bakar, and made all things ready against his coming. To this end he buried his spears and other arms under the sand within his hut.

When the summons to visit To' Gajah reached Imam Bakar, he feared that his time had come. He was not a man, however, who would willingly fly from danger, and he foresaw moreover that if he took refuge in flight all his possessions would be destroyed by his enemies, while he himself, with his wife and little ones, would die in the jungles or fall into the hands of his pursuers. He already regarded himself as a dead man, but though he knew that he could save himself even now by a tardy desertion of To' Raja, the idea of adopting this means of escape was never entertained by him for an instant.

'If I sit down, I die, and if I stand up, I die!' he said to the messenger. 'Better then does it befit a man to die standing. Come, let us go to Pasir Tambang and learn what To' Gajah hath in store for me!'

The sun was half-mast high in the heavens as Imam Bakar crossed the river to Pasir Tambang in his tiny dug-out. Until the sun's rays fall more or less perpendicularly, the slanting light paints broad reaches of water a brilliant dazzling white, unrelieved by shadow or reflection. The green of the masses of jungle on the river banks takes to itself a paler hue than usual, and the yellow of the sandbanks changes its shade from the colour of a cowslip to that of a pale and early primrose. It was on such a white morning as this that Imam Bakar crossed slowly to meet his fate. His dug-out grounded on the sandbank, and when it had been made fast to a pole, its owner, fully armed, walked towards the hut in which To' Gajah was seated.

This Chief was a very heavily built man, with a bullet-shaped head, and a square resolute jaw, partially cloaked by a short sparse beard of coarse wiry hair. His voice and his laugh were both loud and boisterous, and he usually affected an air of open, noisy good-fellowship, which was but little in keeping with his character. When he saw Imam Bakar approaching him, with the slow and solemn tread of one who believes himself to be walking to his death, he cried out to him, while he was yet some way off, with every appearance of friendship and cordiality:

'O Imam Bakar! What is the news? Come hither to me and fear nothing. I come as thy friend, in peace and love. Come let us touch hands in salutation as befits those who harbour no evil one to another.'

Imam Bakar was astonished at this reception. His heart bounded against his ribs with relief at finding his worst fears so speedily dispelled, and being, for the moment, off his guard, he placed his two hands between those of To' Gajah in the usual manner of Malay formal salutation. Quick as thought, To' Gajah seized him by the wrists, his whole demeanour changing in a moment from that of the rough good-fellowship of the boon companion, to excited and cruel ferocity.

'Stab! Stab! Stab! Ye sons of evil women!' he yelled to his men, and before poor Imam Bakar could free himself from the powerful grasp which held him, the spears were unearthed, and half a dozen or their blades met in his shuddering flesh. It was soon over, and Imam Bakar lay dead upon the sandbank, his body still quivering, while the peaceful morning song of the birds came uninterrupted from the forest around.

Then Khatib Bujang and Imam Prang Samah were sent for, and as they came trembling into the presence of To' Gajah, whose hands were still red with the blood of their friend and kinsman, they squatted humbly on the sand at his feet.

'Behold a sample of what ye also may soon be,' said To'

Gajah, spurning the dead body of Imam Bakar as he spoke. 'Mark it well, and then tell me who is your Master and who your Chief!'

Khatib Bujang and Imam Prang Samah stuttered and stammered, but not because they hesitated about the answer, but rather through over eagerness to speak, and a deadly fear which held them dumb. At last, however, they found words and cried together:

'The Bĕndahara is our Master, and our Chief is whomsoever thou mayest be pleased to appoint.'

Thus they saved their lives, and are still living, while To' Gajah lies buried in an exile's grave; but many will agree in thinking that such a death as Imam Bakar's is a better thing for a man to win, than empty years such as his companions have survived to pass in scorn and in dishonour.

But while these things were being done at Pĕkan and at Pasir Tambang, Wan Lingga, who, as I have related, had remained behind in the upper country when To' Raja was carried to Pĕkan, was sparing no pains to seduce the faithful natives of the interior from their loyalty to their hereditary Chief. In all his efforts, however, he was uniformly unsuccessful, for, though he had got rid of To' Raja, there remained in the Lipis Valley the aged Chief of the District, the Dato' Kaya Stia-wangsa, whom the people both loved and feared. He had been a great warrior in the days of his youth, and a series of lucky chances and hair-breadth escapes had won for him an almost fabulous reputation, such as among a superstitious people easily attaches itself to any striking and successful personality. It was reported that he bore a charmed life, that he was invulnerable alike to lead bullets and to steel blades, and even the silver slugs which his enemies had fashioned for him had hitherto failed to find their billet in his body. From the first this man had thrown in his lot with his

IN THE DAYS WHEN THE LAND WAS FREE 35

kinsman To' Raja, and, unlike him, he had declined to allow himself to be persuaded to visit the capital when the war came to an end. Thus he continues to live at the curious little village of Pĕnjum, on the Lipis river, and, so long as he was present in person to exert his influence upon the people, Wan Lingga found it impossible to make any headway against him.

These things were reported by Wan Lingga to To' Gajah, and by the latter to the Bĕndahara. The result was an order to Wan Lingga, charging him to attack To' Kaya Stia-wangsa by night, and to slay him and all his house. With To' Kaya dead and buried, and To' Raja a State prisoner at the capital, the game which To' Gajah and Wan Lingga had been playing would at least be won. The Lipis would fall to the former, and the Jĕlai to the latter as their spoils of war; and the people of these Districts, being left 'like little chicks without the mother hen', would acquiesce in the arrangement, following their new Chiefs as captives of their bows and spears.

Thus all looked well for the future when Wan Lingga set out, just before sun-down, from his house at Atok to attack To' Kaya Stia-wangsa at Pĕnjum. The latter village was at that time inhabited by more Chinese than Malays. It was the nearest point on the river to the gold mines of Jalis, and at the back of the squalid native shops, that lined the river bank, a wellworn footpath led inland to the Chinese alluvial washings. Almost in the centre of the long line of shops and hovels which formed the village of Pĕnjum, stood the thatched house in which To' Kaya Stia-wangsa lived, with forty or fifty women, and about a dozen male followers. The house was roofed with thatch. Its walls were fashioned from plaited laths of split bamboo, and it was surrounded by a high fence of the same material. This was the place which was to be Wan Lingga's object of attack.

A band of nearly a hundred men followed Wan Lingga

from Atok. Their way lay through a broad belt of virgin forest, which stretches between Atok and Pĕnjum, a distance of about half a dozen miles. The tramp of the men moving in a single file through the jungle, along the narrow footpath, worn smooth by the passage of countless naked feet, made sufficient noise to scare all living things from their path. The forests of the Peninsula, even at night, when their denizens are afoot, are not cheerful places. Though a man lie very still, so that the life of the jungle is undisturbed by his presence, the weird night noises, that are borne to his ears, only serve to emphasise the solitude and the gloom. The white moonlight struggles in patches through the thick canopy of leaves overhead, and makes the shadows blacker and more awful by the contrast of light and shade. But a night march through the forest is even more depressing, when the soft pat of bare feet, the snapping of a dry twig, a whispered word of warning or advice, the dull deep note of the night-jar, and the ticking of the tree insects alone break the stillness. Nerves become strung to a pitch of intensity which the circumstances hardly seem to warrant, and all the chances of evil, which in the broad light of day a man would laugh to scorn, assume in one's mind the aspect of inevitable certainties.

I speak by the book; for well I know the depression, and the fearful presentiment of coming evil, which these night marches are apt to occasion; and well can I picture the feelings and thoughts which must have weighed upon Wan Lingga, during that four hours' silent tramp through the forest.

He was playing his last card. If he succeeded in falling upon To' Kaya unawares, and slaying him on the spot, all that he had longed for and dreamed of, all that he desired for himself and for those whom he held dear, all that he deemed to be of any worth, would be his for all his years. And if he failed?—He dared not think of what his position would then be; and yet it was this very thought that clung to him with such persistence during the slow march. He saw himself hated and abhorred by the people of the interior, who would then no longer have reason to fear him; he saw himself deserted by To' Gajah, in whose eyes, he was well aware, he was merely regarded as a tool, to be laid aside when use for it was over; he saw himself in disgrace with the King, whose orders he had failed to carry out; and he saw himself a laughing stock in the land, one who had aspired and had not attained, one who had striven and had failed, with that grim phantom of hereditary madness, of which he was always conscious, stretching out its hand to seize him. All these things he saw and feared, and his soul sank within him.

At last Pĕnjum was reached, and To' Kaya's house was ringed about by Wan Lingga's men. The placid moonlight fell gently on the sleeping village, and showed Wan Lingga's face white with eagerness and anxiety, as he gave the word to fire. In a moment all was noise and tumult. Wan Lingga's men raised their war-yell, and shrieking 'By order of the King!' fired into To' Kaya's house. Old To' Kaya, thus rudely awakened, set his men to hold the enemy in check, and himself passed out of the house in the centre of the mob of his frightened women-folk. He was not seen until he reached the river bank, when he leaped into the stream, and, old man that he was, swam stoutly for the far side. Shot after shot was fired at him, and eight of them, it is said, struck him, though none of them broke the skin, and he won to the far side in safety. Here he stood for a moment, in spite of the hail of bullets with which his enemy greeted his landing. He shook his angry old arm at Wan Lingga, shouted a withering curse, took one sad look at his blazing roof-tree, and then plunged into the forest.

When the looting was over, Wan Lingga's people dispersed

in all directions. Nothing, they knew, fails like failure, and the Lipis people, who would have feared to avenge the outrage had Wan Lingga been successful, would now, they feared, wreak summary punishment on those who had dared to attack their Chief. Wan Lingga, finding himself deserted, fled down stream, there to suffer all that he had foreseen and dreaded during that march through the silent forests. His mind gave way under the strain put upon it by the misery of his position at Pĕkan. The man who had failed was discredited and alone. His former friends stood aloof, his enemies multiplied exceedingly. So when the madness, which was in his blood, fell upon him at Pĕkan, he was thrust into a wooden cage, where he languished for years, tended as befits the madman whom the Malay ranks with the beasts.

When he regained his reason, the politics of the country had undergone a change, and his old ambitious dreams had faded away for ever. His old enemy To' Raja, whom he had sought to displace, was now ruling the Jĕlai, and enjoying every mark of the King's favour. Domestic troubles in the royal household had led the King to regard the friendship of this Chief as a matter of some importance, and Wan Lingga's chances of preferment were dead and buried.

He returned to his house at Atok, where he lived, discredited and unhonoured, the object of constant slights. He spent his days in futile intrigues and plots, which were too impotent to be regarded seriously, or as anything but subjects for mirth, and, from time to time, his madness fell upon him, and drove him forth to wallow with the kine, and to herd with the beasts in the forest.

At last, in 1891, he resolved to put away the things of this world, and set out on the pilgrimage to Mecca. All was ready for his departure on the morrow, and his brethren crowded the little house at Atok to wish him god-speed. But in the night the madness fell upon him once more, and rising up he ran *amok* through his dwelling, slaying his wife and child, and wounding one of his brothers. Then he fled into the forest, and after many days was found hanging dead in the fork of a fruit-tree. He had climbed into the branches to sleep, and in his slumbers had slipped down into the fork where he had become tightly wedged. With his impotent arms hanging on one side of the tree, and his legs dangling limply on the other, he had died of exhaustion, alone and untended, without even a rag to cover his nakedness.

It was a miserable, and withal a tragic death, but not ill fitted to one who had staked his all to gain a prize he had not the strength to seize; one whom Fate had doomed to perpetual and inglorious failure.

From *In Court and Kampong*, London, 1897.

AT THE COURT OF PĚLĚSU

I

A SCENE within a few miles of the seashore on the eastern side of the Malay Peninsula. A river measuring near two miles across, its waters running white in the aching midday heat, their glaring monotony relieved by a number of islands smothered in vegetation, every leaf motionless in the hot, still air, each frond of the coconut palms stretching impotent arms heavenward in a mute prayer for coolness. On the right bank, extending up and down stream for something over a mile, the closely packed thatched roofs of a large Malayan village, many of the houses straggling far out over the water, on piles fashioned from the straight black trunks of the *nibong* palm. A background of foliage, showing here and there above the thatch; in the foreground, moored about the feet of the piles, a medley of mat-roofed boats of many sorts, shapes, and sizes, crowds of dug-out canoes, and a jumble of bathing-rafts, the latter connected with the dark doorways of the houses by rickety bamboo ladders; and all things casting shadows against the white sunlight as hard as if cut out of black paper.

Such, nearly forty years ago, was the capital of the independent native State of Pělěsu, which at that time was inhabited by a Malayan king of the old school; a big native population of chiefs and courtiers; many traders and tillers

AT THE COURT OF PĚLĚSU 41

of the soil; by half a hundred Chinese merchants, doggedly bent upon the acquisition of wealth, in defiance of local lawlessness; and by Mr. John Norris, British political agent.

The capital city of the Sultan of Pělěsu was a somewhat squalid place. It mainly consisted of one long, irregular lane running parallel to the river-bank, the houses on the one side having a double frontage, abutting respectively on the shore and on the water, while the occupants of those facing them could obtain access to the river only by means of a few narrow landing-places, which were almost edged out of existence by the encroachments of the hovels on either hand. The street was unmetalled; but the red and dusty earth had been beaten smooth and hard by the passage of innumerable unshod feet, save where the escaping rain-water had worn for itself deep channels in the course of its rush riverward. This main thoroughfare was lined on either side by Malayan houses and Chinese shops, each built without much reference to the alignment of its neighbours, and matching them only in the wattled bamboo and palm thatching of which all were alike constructed, and in the air of slovenly neglect that pervaded every one of them. At the eastern end of the town, in an open space facing a drunken-looking landing-jetty, a brick mosque, glaringly whitewashed, refracted and redoubled the pitiless heat of the sun. Near the centre of the village, and standing a little back from the road behind a fence of split bamboos, in the middle of an untidy compound, was a whitewashed, green-shuttered house, two storeys high, and of European design. A quarter of a mile farther up river a much larger stone and plaster building of obviously Chinese construction showed its bare windows and its slate roof over an eight-foot wall of stone, patched here and there with a yard or two of bamboo fencing, the whole grown upon by creepers like drapery.

From the main street a number of narrow and crooked

lanes elbowed their way through the pack of dwelling-houses, and led through palm groves, fruit orchards, and untidy, shady compounds to the grazing-grounds and croplands situated behind the town.

The mosque, the neglected European bungalow, and the big stone building were all alike the property of the King, the two former serving to mark a period of his reign during which, after a short visit of ceremony to a neighbouring British colony, he for a space had devoted to public works some portion of the funds which were more commonly employed in ministering to his personal pleasures and to the adornment of the constantly changing inmates of his kaleidoscopic harem. The third and largest building was of older date, and represented the attempt of a Chinese craftsman to construct a palace for a monarch, one of whose modest titles was *Shah 'Alam*, or Lord of the Universe.

Both the bungalow and the old palace were inhabited by wives of the King and by their numerous retinues of parasitic hangers-on. The rank of these ladies was such that the King had not thought it politic to divorce them, but their faded charms had long ago ceased to hold his fickle affection in any semblance of bondage. Occasionally the monarch paid a ceremonial visit to one or the other of them, and from time to time they sent him presents of carefully prepared food, in brass trays covered by brilliant yellow cloths, borne by many maidens, and shaded from the sunlight by the silken spread of state umbrellas. For the rest, they occupied positions of dignified humiliation, and in impotent wrath and jealousy watched from afar the triumphs of their supplanters the female favourites of the moment.

For his part, the King resembled the gentlemen whose names sometimes appear in the police reports inasmuch as, like them, he had no fixed place of abode. The standards of

AT THE COURT OF PĚLĚSU

civilisation, represented respectively by the white man's bungalow and by the palace of Chinese design, made no appeal to him; and instead he led a peripatetic existence, dividing his time, as the passing fancy dictated, between the houses occupied by his numerous concubines. These favoured creatures were accommodated, each with a female retinue of her own, in one or another of half a dozen rather squalid huts abutting on the river and opening on to the main street, which differed in no respect from the shops and hovels that adjoined them. All of these dwelling-places belonged, of course, to the King; and in any one of them he might or might not be found at any given hour of the day or night. Sometimes two or more of these houses were built side by side, and were so arranged that the King could make his way from one to the other unobserved by the curious public. This well suited the royal convenience, for, having entered the doors of one of these rabbit warrens, wherein no other man was suffered to set foot, the King was apt to be lost to the sight of his loyal subjects, and to be cut off from intercourse with all tiresome and importunate people, for days or even weeks at a time. During these not infrequent pauses in his autocratic administration the affairs of his country were suffered to take care of themselves, and the State itself was left to drift placidly to destruction.

An indolent European monarch may perhaps seek comfort in the reflection, '*Après moi le deluge!*'; but the fact that he has realised that a flood of troubles is impending implies that he has devoted some scant measure of thought to the affairs of his kingdom. Even so languid a mental effort as this, however, presupposes a keener interest in the condition of his subjects, and a more lavish expenditure of energy than the typical Oriental ruler of the good old days could ordinarily be persuaded to spare from his more intimate pleasures, so long as his harem and his opium-pipe continued to be sufficiently well stocked. Thus it came to pass that in some parts of the East, at the time of which I write, a quite unspeakable state of things endured decade after decade, without let or hindrance, all in authority being apparently convinced that the prevailing conditions would last for ever. Then, upon a certain day, the deluge would precipitate itself, as though the sea had been upset, and evil-mannered native kings and hopelessly rotten social and political institutions would suddenly be found jostling one another on the surface of the flood.

In the State of Pĕlĕsu at this period the storm, which had long been brewing, was very near to its breaking. To the observant eye there were many signs and portents that could not be misread; and, indeed, it needed no gift of prophetic vision to recognise in Mr. John Norris, political agent, the stormy petrel, the forerunner of the tempest.

II

Jack Norris was, at this time one of the score or so of obscure Englishmen who, unknown for the most part to their stay-at-home fellow-countrymen, occupied outposts somewhere just beyond the British border. They were set there to see fair' in places where fair dealing formed no essential part of the local polity; and they represented, in some sort, the foremost skirmishing line of the mighty army of Great Britain's Empire. A few decades ago they were often cast as bread upon the waters, and if any native potentate were so imprudent as to mistake their loneliness for impotence, Great Britain occasionally moved one ponderous step forward over their mutilated remains.

Political agents of this type, who forty years ago were

AT THE COURT OF PĚLĚSU

attached to little one-horse courts in Further India, are by no means to be confused with those senior and distinguished members of the Indian Civil Service who reside in the capitals of the great Feudatory Princes of Hindustan, and who, in the envious estimation of their juniors combine the dignity of Solomon with the wealth of Croesus. Instead, such outpost billets were poorly paid, because pay in the East is largely a matter of age and of seniority in the public service, and these jobs were usually allotted to, comparatively speaking, junior men. The reason for this is plain. Men who had already made their mark could not be spared for side-show work of this description, which, on the other hand could not be entrusted to people of proved incapacity. These posts always represented an opportunity; they had in them an element of adventure, and a spice of danger was rarely lacking. Wherefore, they were eagerly scrambled for by the boys with pluck and brains.

It is a curious trait in the character of the Englishman that, for him, the prospect of danger casts a certain glamour over things which, viewed from the standpoint of common sense, are obviously objectionable on that and other grounds. This glamour, I may add, has a nasty trick of wearing thin when actuality takes the place of the merely prospective; but given an Englishman with his back to the wall—or so our national vanity assures us—it is ordained that he should fight as it is given to few men to fight. The political agent in Further India, from his position as a solitary white man in a hostile environment, where as a rule he was totally unsupported by even a show of force, had his back to the wall as a more or less permanent arrangement; wherefore, when he eventually found himself in the inevitable tight place, he could usually be depended upon to show good sport.

The State of Pělěsu had long been a thorn in the side of

the Government that presided over the neighbouring Crown colony and the adjoining British protectorate; and little by little the evil deeds of the King gathered sufficient weight to turn the slow wheels upon which runs the administration of one of the most ponderous nations of the earth. Treaty negotiations were started for the purpose of establishing some sort of control over Pĕlĕsu and its irresponsible ruler; but as the State was more than ordinarily inaccessible, and the King a skilful procrastinator, this was a stage of the proceedings which occupied many months. The Government, therefore, looked about for a junior officer possessed of a good knowledge of the natives and of the vernacular, a tough constitution, and a slender stipend; all of which qualifications were found united in the person of young Jack Norris. Accordingly, he was sent to Pĕlĕsu; and when after an incredibly long period of gestation, the treaty was at last born into the world he was left there to act as the political agent, for whose presence in the King's capital one of its articles provided.

He was lodged in a big, rambling native hut which had formerly been occupied by one of the concubines of the King. This building abutted on the main street, and the *balai*—or reception-room—which composed that side of the house rested on terra-firma. The rest of the premises straggled out over the river, on half a hundred crazy wooden piles. Opening out of the *balai* was a large square apartment filled for the most part by a platform raised some two and a half feet above floor level, and surrounded on all sides by a narrow gangway. This room had been used by its former occupant as her boudoir, the raised dais serving the dual purpose of sitting-room and bed; and here Jack now squatted to eat his rice, to yarn with his own people, or to receive those of his native visitors who could be given a more or less public audience. Adjoining it, upon the left, was the room which

Norris used as his bedroom and study, and at the back was a big oblong apartment, devoted to the use of his native followers. Behind this again was a large kitchen, in which food always seemed to be in process of preparation; and a back door and ladder-way led to the bathing-raft of the establishment, which was moored to the piles that supported the kitchen floor of split bamboos.

Norris spent most of his time in his bed-sitting-room, which was oblong in shape, and looked through two narrow windows on to the river, flowing by and under it. The furniture was not elaborate. The plank flooring was covered with straw-coloured matting, fashioned from the woven fronds of the *mĕngkuang* palm; and a small mat and pillows, spread beneath an enormous set of chintz bed curtains—looped up by day—filled one side of the room. Mosquitoes were rarely seen, and nearly a decade was still to run ere men would learn to connect the bite of these insects with the causation of malaria and other tropical fevers. Accordingly, Norris did not use a net, and the ample bed curtains were designed to insure a measure of privacy and also to exclude the daylight when, as often happened, the eccentricities of local aristocratic society forced him to turn day into night.

Near the bed half a hundred books were tumbled together upon the floor, some of them written in the crabbed Arabic script which the Malays have adopted for the transliteration of their own beautiful and elaborate language; and close to the mat-head there stood a green earthen-ware jar, which was used for the reception of Jack's cigarette-ends and other rubbish. Below the window stood a writing-table littered with papers, and two cane-bottomed chairs were set close to it. In one corner of the room two leather portmanteaux were placed against the wall with some of Jack's clothes and his toilet requisites laid out neatly upon them. These, with the writing-table and the chairs, were the only concessions to European civilisation anywhere visible in the queer household of which this young Englishman was the master.

His native followers consisted of about thirty Malays—some of the very best ruffians in the Peninsula—who had come to Pĕlĕsu at the heels of Jack Norris, with whom they had foregathered in various places while he was serving within the borders of the British protectorate. Two of them were men of *raja* rank, and all of them had known the good old days, when the Malayan world had been wont to go forward in the bad old way, ere European ideas of right and wrong had begun to make matchwood of native notions concerning the fitness of things. They all loved war, or thought they did, which produces often much the same results; and they were united in traditional contempt for the people of Pĕlĕsu and in an unshakeable faith in themselves and in Jack Norris.

Such was the position of things at the Court of Pĕlĕsu when the north-east monsoon began to break in the autumn of a certain year, threatening presently to close the ports on the China Sea and to cut off all communication with the outside world for a period of at least five months.

III

A week or two before the mouth of the Pĕlĕsu River finally closed for the year, Jack Norris lay stretched upon his mat one evening with a cigarette between his lips and a book in his hand. He was a short, swarthy youngster of about one-and-twenty years of age. He was thick-set and very powerfully built, with sturdy legs and arms on which the biceps stood up in knots. His features were rather broad and flat, his straight mouth shut like a trap, and there was a dogged strength in every hard line that early responsibility and exposure to the sun-glare of the East had drawn upon his ugly face. He was clothed after the manner commonly adopted by Europeans in the Malay Peninsula during their hours of ease. He wore a short linen jumper with sleeves cut short above the elbow, drawers of the same material that did not quite reach to his knees, and an ample *sarong*—or native waist-cloth—which might be huddled up about his waist, or be suffered to fall to his ankles, or to cover his bare feet, if the mosquitoes or sandflies were troublesome.

The room was dimly lighted by a stinking kerosene oil-lamp, which stood on the mat-covered floor at Norris' elbow. One or two Malays—members of Jack's household—squatted at one end of the room near the curtained doorway, chewing quids of areca-nut and talking together in low murmurs. Through the narrow slits of window the moonbeams strove to penetrate, in defiance of the greasy lamplight, and the insistent hum of insects varied by the occasional, clear note of a nightjar, was borne upon the almost motionless hot air.

The surroundings in which he found himself had grown so familiar to Jack Norris that Thackeray's brilliant description of the fête at Gaunt House—whereat dear Becky scored her glittering, short-lived triumph—which he was re-reading for perhaps the hundredth time struck for him no incongruous note with his environment. One-half of his mind unconsciously assimilated the trivial talk of the Malays near the doorway, while the other conjured up the scenes evoked by the familiar words of his book.

Presently someone came to the door and spoke a few words in a low voice to one of the Malays seated near it.

'There is a Chinaman here who would come into your presence, *Tuan*,' the latter reported, turning to Norris.

'Bid him enter,' said Norris, sitting up, arranging his *sarong* decently over his crossed legs and laying his book aside.

The curtains of the doorway were put apart, and an old Chinaman entered. He saluted Norris and then seated himself cross-legged on the floor near the foot of the sleeping-mat. He was a long-boned, sunken-cheeked, deeply wrinkled old creature with a skin like ancient parchment, and with a slender pigtail, composed almost entirely of black silk, hanging from the sparse grey hairs at the back of his shaven scalp. His shoulders were bowed to a permanent stoop, and there hung about him that peculiar odour of roasted coffee and chocolate which, combined with a strange closeness of the atmosphere that clings to him denotes the confirmed opium-smoker.

'What is the news?' asked Jack, speaking in Malay, and employing the usual native interrogative greeting.

'The news is good,' rejoined the visitor, speaking in the same language, and making use of the conventional reply, which is as empty of meaning as is the 'Quite well, thank you' of the confirmed invalid.

A pause followed, during which the Chinaman shifted uneasily and glanced over his shoulder at the Malays seated near the door. Then he drew himself along the floor, edging closer to Norris, and said in a hoarse whisper:

'There is something that I would say to you, *Tuan*.'

'Speak on,' said Norris. 'These men are mine own people. Have no fear.'

'But that which I would say must be said to you alone,' objected the Chinaman; and Norris signed to the Malays with an upward jerk of his chin, native fashion, to withdraw. The Chinaman, satisfied that he and the white man were alone, crept a little nearer.

'I come to you craving aid,' he said in the same hoarse and agitated whisper. 'I am exceedingly troubled. I have a wife.'

'*Kasihan*!' (You have my sympathy!) said Norris, with all the ready cynicism of the young bachelor.

'She is a very good woman, the mother of my children, and she is, moreover, virtuous.'

'*Aja'ib*! (I am astonished!) In Pĕlĕsu such women are very rare,' said Norris, who knew much that was unprintable on the subject of local morals.

'That is true,' said the Chinaman gravely. 'It is indeed strange that she is what she is; the more so because she is endowed with great beauty, and the King himself has conceived for her a devouring passion. It is in this wise. She was married to me some four years ago, and she has borne me two men-children, and we are happy, living together in love. Does it seem strange to you, *Tuan*, that a woman who is young and beautiful should love me, whom the years have stricken? Even to me it is strange; but no man can account for the ways of women; and this woman, who is my wife, loves me indeed, and she will have naught to do with the King or with his presents. You know, *Tuan*, the habits of the King. He spends many days and nights in the house of his concubine, Che' Layang, the which adjoins my own dwelling. Now, upon a certain day the King, peeping through the crannies of the wattled walls which divide the two buildings, beheld the woman, my wife, playing with her sons, and forthwith he was stricken by 'the madness' on her account. Since that time he has sought many means wherewith to seduce her from me. First, he sent an aged crone of his household to make known to her the King's desire for her; but immediately upon hearing the so-evil words of this aged crone, my wife raised such a tumult of railings that the hag fled in terror. None the less, she and others, witch-folk like herself, tried to insinuate certain love philtres into my wife's food; but we detected the magic, and threw the food into the river. Later, the King sent to my wife gifts of gold and diamonds and fine garments, which were borne to her by the hands of certain of his armed Youths, who chose for the purpose an hour when they knew me to be absent from my house. But my wife received these Youths with scorn and with reproaches, many and pungent; and the gifts of the King she cast forth into the mire of the street, so that the fine silks were soiled, the jewellery was covered with dirt and a great shame was put upon the King.

'Thereafter my wife stuffed rags into the crevices in the wall through which the King was wont to pry upon her, and, moreover, she placed boarding over them; but in the nighttime the rags were removed and the boarding torn away.

'All these happenings occasioned a great anxiety within me and filled me with terror; for behold, *Tuan*, I love my wife, who is the mother of my sons, and also I value highly the life that quickens me.

'You ask why the King has not seized her by force, as he seized the young wife of Che' Ahmad of Pulau Aur and the wife of Chi On, the Keh trader. *Tuan*, it is not without reason that men name you the *pĕn-awar puteh* (the white antidote); and but for that medicine many a man had suffered death and worse in this land of Pĕlĕsu since your coming. And I also, but for your presence here, had surely lost my honour and perhaps my life too. It is fear of you, and of those who sent you hither, which causes the King to employ stealth and stratagem where, in past days, he was wont to use force. Now, therefore, come I to you, weeping and wailing, secretly and by night, praying that you will aid and protect me—me and the woman, my wife, and the men-children, my two little sons. Both she and I are British subjects; for though we have long resided in this land of Pĕlĕsu, our parents are of Hong-Kong where also we ourselves were born. Thus we are to be reckoned among the number of your own people, and we trust in you with a thousand, thousand hopes.'

'Shall I speak to the King on your behalf?' enquired Norris.

'No, no, I pray you!' cried the Chinaman, who was obviously aghast at the mere suggestion. 'Were you to do so, I very certainly would forthwith die at his hands. Even if he knew that I had visited you and had spoken to you of this matter he would, without doubt, cause his Youths to do me in.'[1]

'If that be so, you tie the hands of the man from whom you are seeking help,' said Norris. 'I cannot aid you if you are afraid for me even to speak to the King. The better course, therefore, would be for you and all your house to quit Pĕlĕsu and to seek refuge in the colony.'

'That, also, I cannot do,' said the Chinaman. 'My business and all my stock-in-trade and other possessions are here in Pĕlĕsu, and, lacking the wherewithal to support life, my children and my wife, strangers in the colony, would die of famine. That may not be. Also, the mouth of the river closes to-morrow or the day after; who can tell when the winds of the monsoon will descend upon us? No I cannot leave Pĕlĕsu now; but perhaps when once more the mouth of the river is open to traffic, if life still remain to us I shall so have ordered my affairs that I shall be able to remove to the colony without sustaining too ruinous a loss. For the moment, I ask nothing of you, *Tuan*, for I have sought you only that you might know the nature of my trouble and the danger in which I stand. Mayhap that, knowing this you will make shift to aid me, should the occasion arise.'

'That will I promise, and willingly,' said Norris. 'But remember the proverb of the Malays: *Be economical ere thy substance be consumed, and watchful ere thou art stricken*. It would be best for you to go forthwith to Singapore, no matter how

---

[1] The Malay idiom is almost an exact translation of the modern slang phrase.

great your loss of money. Failing that, it would be well for you to suffer me to speak to the King.'

'I dare not, *Tuan*,' the Chinaman cried earnestly. 'Did you do so, I should forthwith be as one already dead.'

'It is enough,' said Norris discontentedly. 'Have no fear; I will hold my peace. Nevertheless, I foresee that evil things will result from this inaction. And now return to your dwelling, and if trouble assails you, come you to me in the hour of your need.'

The Chinaman salaamed, rose, and withdrew. The Malayan language provides no stereotyped idiom for use as an expression of gratitude. When one is thanked by a native, it is silently and by deeds, not with verbal profusion, as amongst ourselves. Of the two methods, the former, rarely though it be employed, is, perhaps, of the greater worth.

When Che' Ah Ku, the Chinaman, had departed, Norris called Raja Haji Hamid, the chief of his followers to his side, and the two sat talking far into the night.

Raja Haji was a man who, on the other side of the Peninsula, had won for himself an astonishing reputation for courage, for invulnerability, and for many other qualities which, judged from any ordinary standpoint, could by no stretch of the imagination be accounted virtues. It is on historical record that, when he was fighting against the British during the early seventies of last century, the news of his arrival in the war area, with five ragged cut-throats at his heels, acted with such galvanic force that it caused several hundreds of 'friendly' Malays discreetly to desert from our standards and to seek safety in the neighbouring British colony of Malacca. With the poverty of imagination commonly manifested by natives in such circumstances, they alleged that filial duty demanded their immediate presence at the bedsides of ailing mothers, the victims, apparently, of some sudden epidemic.

Raja Haji had at that time been one of the most reckless and untamed scions of a particularly lawless royal house, which for centuries had played ducks and drakes with the affairs of the native State over which it ruled. He had attained to the prime of his manhood ere ever the British Government had intervened to reduce things in that State to the dull monotony of order, and he had therefore had uncounted opportunities of acquiring at first hand a knowledge of the seamy side of Malayan human nature, which was as curious as it was profound. Norris also knew something of the same subject, but when matters of difficulty arose he generally sought the counsel of this hoary old villain who loved him and who looked upon the politics of Pĕlĕsu as a game of skill in which he and Jack, as partners, were ranged against the King and the people of the land.

'I, too, have peeped at the woman Chik, the wife of Ah Ku the Chinaman,' he said now; for advancing years had in no wise dimmed his eye for the detection of feminine charms. 'I have peeped at her whenever occasion offered, and indeed she is very fair. But it is not by reason of her beauty that the desire of the King is so hot for her. There be many others as good to look upon as she, but a madness of longing is kindled within him because she alone of all the people of this land dares to deny herself to him. That, to him, is something wholly new and strange, and in any case it would prove a very inflammable fuel to pile upon the fire already alight in the heart of any masculine person. Men say that the King has made use of all manner of love potions, but they profit him not with her. It is very clearly to be seen that that ancient man, her husband, is a master of occult arts, and that he has cast a glamour over her. How otherwise should she be faithful to one so ugly and so old? None the less, *Tuan*, it is certain that trouble will arise. Balked desire in the heart of one whose desires have ne'er been balked is like gun medicine. At the appointed hour the explosion must come. Moreover, it was but yesternight that I dreamed that the King invited you and me to eat *durian* and sundry other fruits of globular shape; and little skill is needed to interpret the meaning of that vision. The fruit are cannon-balls and musket bullets, and the dream is a warning that battle is imminent. Well, it is long since I bathed me in the fumes and the bullets of war, and indeed, I am *kĕtageh*—craving that to which habit has accustomed me—as the opium-smoker craves for his drug. It will be to me a very pleasant thing if war results with these so-called men of Pĕlĕsu. It stirs within me memories of past days in mine own native land. Listen, *Tuan*, I recall . . .'

And forthwith Raja Haji plunged into a long, tangled tale of deeds of wrong and rapine (in which he had had a triumphantly outrageous share) wrought in the days whereof he still cherished such glowing recollections. With these blood-stained things he was wont to regale Norris for hours at a time.

It is only by dwelling among Malays in intimacy and good fellowship that a European can really learn what manner of men they are. Jack Norris, who on his first arrival in Pĕlĕsu, had believed himself to know as much about natives as any white man in the peninsula, had very soon discovered that as yet he was still merely stumbling over the ABC of his study. It had been at once a humiliating and a stimulating disillusionment; but the past year and a half had taught him much, and daily he was acquiring little odds and ends and shreds of knowledge, which would gradually piece themselves together until he would eventually become a master of his subject.

IV

At six o'clock one afternoon Jack Norris awoke from sleep. It was part of the peculiarity of his position as a lonely white man, living and working among a courtful of Malayan chiefs and notables, that he was forced to accommodate himself to any hours they might choose to keep. Time, as Europeans understand it, had no meaning for any of his associates, and presently it came to have hardly more significance for him. He very rarely found himself in bed before six or seven o'clock in the morning, and his hour of rising was proportionately late. Sometimes, before turning in, he would take his gun, and, followed by two or three of his Malays, would put in an hour or two of snipe-shooting in the rice-fields and grazing-grounds lying at the back of the town. Sometimes his first waking hours in the afternoon were spent in a similar fashion, till the darkness drove him homeward to a dinner that was in reality his breakfast.

On this particular evening the meal was served shortly after seven o'clock. It consisted of enormous quantities of rice and a fine variety of curries, pungent and appetising. Jack ate this food in the company of Raja Haji Hamid and Raja Uteh, the latter a withered old sprig of Sumatran royalty, who hid the heart of a lion under a lamb-like exterior. The meal was eaten native fashion, Jack and his two friends squatting around the brass trays which held the curry-bowls, each with a piled plate of rice in front of him. They ate in silence, messing the curry into their rice with their fingers, and then conveying big kneaded masses to their mouths.

White men, who do not know, are wont to entertain a strong prejudice against this practice of eating with the fingers; yet its adoption is a necessity, no less for one who would support life for a prolonged period on a rice diet. To do this it is essential that an enormous quantity of rice should daily be consumed, but owing to the aeration of the boiled grain if a spoon be used, no normal stomach can cope with the mass required. The fingers are needed to express the air from the rice, in such a fashion that all which passes into the mouth is solid food—not grain saturated with oxygen. Experience had very early forced the acceptance of these practical if prosaic facts upon Jack, who had now been living upon native diet for the best part of two years; and for the rest, a remark of Raja Haji Hamid had disposed of his last scruple in the matter.

'The fingers of my right hand,' the Raja had said 'have never entered the mouth of any other human being. Can you say as much of your spoons and forks, *Tuan?*'

The meal ended, Norris sat for a while smoking and talking with Raja Haji and Raja Uteh, then went back to his room and wrote up his official diary and passed an hour or so lying reading on his sleeping-mat. The latter was his only substitute for an easy-chair.

At about nine o'clock he rose up, exchanged his native kit for a white duck tunic and trousers, put shoes on his feet and a cap on his head, and sauntered out into the main street. He carried a revolver under the skirt of his coat, and a serviceable Malayan broadsword, with a wooden sheath, in his hand. Two or three of his followers, marking his exit, armed themselves with daggers and spears, and hurriedly fell in behind him. In those days in Pĕlĕsu no prudent or self-respecting person ever ventured forth without his weapons, and even at night-time men slept with their daggers under their pillows.

Jack walked a few hundred yards up the street and then entered a Chinese shop, bowing his head to pass beneath the lintel of the low door, over which was inscribed in black Chinese characters, sprawling down a gilt board, the grandiose legend, *The Dwelling of Divine Repose.* Facing him as he

AT THE COURT OF PĚLĚSU

entered, the wall between two narrow doorways was occupied by the usual tawdry altar, supporting the picture of the Sage with his two attendant demons, before which many joss-sticks were smouldering. Norris, nodding to the Chinese shopmen, who greeted him with grave courtesy, passed through the doorway on the right, and proceeded to grope and stumble along a dark and narrow passage, which was more like a subterranean gallery in a mine than any part of an ordinary dwelling-house.

The place was redolent of a thousand odours peculiar to the Chinese; but Norris had subdued his nose long ere this, and the smells inseparable from native houses had almost ceased to annoy him.

Arrived at the end of the passage, Jack pushed aside a dingy curtain which cloaked a doorway on his left, and entered a small dark room, the sanctum of Su Kim, the Chinese trader, to whom the place belonged. It was more than half filled by a raised sleeping-platform or opium-bench, which served its owner indifferently as bed, chair, and table. Su Kim, who occupied it, sat up to greet Norris, but he continued to fill with great care a long bamboo pipe with the opium which he was toasting at the end of a slim steel skewer over a small lamp that stood on the mat beside him. The faint smell of the drug filled the room, as the opium swelled into big brown blisters, or subsided like a bubble, as Su Kim cooked it.

He was an old man, and his creased and wrinkled body was bare to the waist. His legs were cased in a pair of ample black silk trousers, very full and loose and to the belt which secured them were attached an oblong money-pouch, ornamented by much beadwork, and a bunch of silver hooks and prods such as the Chinese use for tickling and picking at the insides of their ears. Indulgence in this practice causes the majority of these people to be slightly deaf.

Against the walls of the room small octagonal tea-poys, or stools were ranged and a little terracotta teapot, surrounded by a dozen tiny china cups without handles, stood on a wooden tray on Su Kim's bunk.

To the European eye this Chinese trader's sanctum was a sufficiently squalid place, yet it was one of the recognised social centres of the King's capital. Here nightly it was the custom of the principal chiefs and notables to look in for an hour or so, to meet, gossip, and exchange news. This evening Norris found that he was the first of its habitues to reach this place of general rendezvous, and as he seated himself on one of the stools and took the cup of tea which his host offered to him he opened the conversation in the usual way.

'What is the news?'

'The news is good,' replied Su Kim mechanically. 'But I have something to tell you, *Tuan*, before other folk come hither. Have you heard of what befell Che' Ah Ku and Li Tat on the night of the King's feast? Men tell you that Li Tat is dead, and that the King has seized all of which he died possessed, claiming the same for a debt. It is even so; and now that we are alone I will tell you of Li Tat's death. We Chinese traders of Pĕlĕsu were all bidden to a feast, spread for us in the *Balai* of the King; and, as in duty bound, we all went. Che' Ah Ku and Li Tat were invited to eat from the same tray of food, but Ah Ku, fearing evil, ate nought save only the rice, and so escaped death. But Li Tat, unsuspicious of harm, ate unwarily. From childhood he had served the King with fidelity, and on many occasions he had earned his gratitude; wherefore he had no fear. Thereby, *Tuan*, he showed himself to be a person lacking in wisdom and discretion, for he had waxed rich, and the King desired to become his heir. No sooner had he returned to his house than a devastating sickness smote him, by reason of the said food, and even before his eyes had closed in death came the Treasurer of the King, with seals and tumult and armed men, and seized upon all his stores of money and rubber and merchandise. Now, therefore, we others—Chinese traders who have amassed dollars one or two—have much anxiety in our hearts; but above all, Che' Ah Ku is faint with fear, for it is certain that he is doomed to die, though he cannot guess in what manner death will fall upon him.'

'Are you sure of the truth of these things?' asked Norris.

'Alas! yes, all men know them to be true,' replied Su Kim. 'But peace, *Tuan*. Someone comes this way.'

Presently the curtain was once more put aside, and a big-limbed, imposing-looking Malay, with a face like a handsome tom-cat, stepped into the room. On his head was a kerchief twisted into a fantastic peak; he wore a bright green satin coat and short, coarse silk knickers, barred with all the hues of the rainbow. Over the *kris* stuck in his girdle a cotton *sarong* of Bugis manufacture was draped, hiding the dagger completely, and covering its owner's body from the waist to a point a little above the knees. This garment was dark blue in colour, and a shining surface had been imparted to it by hard friction with a shell.

This man was the Dato' Běndahara Sri Stiawan, a member of the royal house, and a cousin of the King, whom Norris knew well for a truculent, bullying fellow with a loud voice, a boisterous manner, the avarice of a Jew, and the heart of a mouse.

The conversation now turned to indifferent topics, and every moment more and more chiefs and notables filtered through the doorway and joined in the talk and the tea-drinking. The Ungku Muda, a little-loved brother of the King, and a friend of Jack's, was among the last to arrive, and presently the whole party, including Norris, adjourned to the *Balai*, or Hall of State, a large building consisting of a solid roof supported upon substantial carved timber columns, open to the air on three sides, and adjoining the palace on the fourth, its floor being raised some six feet above the level of the ground. It was here that the greater portion of the night was ordinarily spent by the elite of Pĕlĕsu, for the Chinese merchants were encouraged to spread their gambling-mats in this part of the royal precincts, a percentage of all stakes won from the gaming public being a perquisite of the King, who, for his part, caused sweetmeats to be served to the assembled notables at frequent intervals. Occasionally the King himself would condescend to visit the *Balai*, and even to stake a few dollars on the turn of the Chinese dice; but in any event this was the great news mart of the capital, and Norris, whose business it was to keep abreast of all that was going forward in Pĕlĕsu, found it necessary to be one of the most constant frequenters of the place.

This evening he had been seated cross-legged on the mat-strewn floor of the *Balai* for perhaps an hour, and a first relay of sickly Malayan sweetmeats—all sugar and egg—had just been served when of a sudden the breathless quiet of the hot Malayan night was rent and shattered by peal after peal of shrill screaming such as only the throat of a woman in misery or in pain can produce. Jack started to his feet, moved by that instinct which invariably prompts a white man who finds himself alone among natives, to take the lead in any moment of emergency; but the Dato' Bĕndahara put forth a shaking hand and begged him to be seated.

'Have patience, *Tuan*,' he said. ' 'Tis but the howling of a dog; and, moreover, the custom is known to you. None may leave the King's hall when food has been served until he hath partaken thereof.'

In Malaya *custom* is a mighty tyrant: '*Let our children die, rather than our customs,*' says the native proverb. Very reluctantly, therefore, Jack resumed his seat; but forthwith he poured water over his fingers, dipped them in the nearest dish, swallowed a mouthful of the cloying stuff, and with a perfunctory 'I ask your leave to depart' addressed to the Dato' Bĕndahara, swung himself over the edge of the verandah on to the ground beneath, and set off at a run down the village street.

The night had been dark a few minutes earlier, but now a ruddy moon was lying just above the horizon on a bed of fleecy clouds. A broad lane of light lay along the surface of the river, ribbed with the countless ripples of the water, and the huts bordering the path down which Norris ran were black and shapeless masses that cast impenetrable shadows across his way. A few hundreds of yards down the street a small knot of awed and silent natives stood pressing one against another, half in and half out of the moon-light. In the shallow ditch that separated the huts from the pathway a black heap was dimly discernible, and the outcry of a moment before had now sunken to the continuous inarticulate moans and sobs of a woman in sorrow.

As Jack drew nearer this black heap resolved itself into the body of a man, lying with limbs flung wide in all the *abandon* of death or of insensibility, and the form of a woman thrown prostrate across it, her head and hands beating the earth in the reckless, unrestrained grief of the Oriental. When she caught sight of Norris, her cries broke out once more with redoubled energy, the shrieks running up the scale till they culminated in a note deafeningly shrill which at each repetition stabbed Jack's nerves with a pang of physical pain. The man was Che' Ah Ku and the wailing woman was Chik, his wife.

'What thing is this?' cried Norris; and forthwith the silence of the little group of Malays was replaced by a clamorous chorus of divergent explanations.

'He smote his head against the lintel of his door.'

'He hath fallen in a fit.'

'The madness of the pig (epilepsy) hath come upon him.'

'An evil spirit hath laid hold upon him.'

'He is possessed by a devil.'

'He hath missed his footing, and, falling to the earth, hath done himself some hurt.'

By this time Jack Norris was kneeling by the side of the unconscious Chinaman, and, as the tumult of futile explanation ceased, his fresh young voice, speaking with the perfect Malay accent for which he was famous, fell upon the ears of the crowd and hushed their noisy vapourings into the chill silence of fear.

'This man hath been stabbed,' he said. 'Stabbed at the very door of the King's house. Where are the King's Youths, who keep watch and ward here by day and by night? How comes it to pass that this night alone they are not at their post? How doth it befall that they witnessed nothing of what has happened? Moreover, why hath no man aided this woman to carry her husband into his house?'

There was not a native present who entertained the slightest doubt concerning the origin of Che' Ah Ku's mishap. All were convinced that he had been stabbed by the King's Youths at the instance of their master; but in Pĕlĕsu men who desired that their days should be long in the land knew better than to say all that they thought. Jack Norris' plain speaking smote them with terror, for even to listen to such truths might well be accounted a crime. Also, in a sense, it was shocking by reason of its very novelty. It was to them like the thing that should only be uttered in a whisper being of a sudden shouted through a megaphone; and, filled with uneasiness, his hearers one by one slunk away discomfited.

Raja Haji Hamid with a knot of Jack's own Malays had by now come upon the scene, and, aided by them, Jack carried the still unconscious Ah Ku into his house and laid him on the opium-bench in the inner room. He had been badly mauled. A *kris* stab had pierced his upper lip, splitting it from the nostril to the gums and knocking away four of his front teeth. The point of the blade had come out in the centre of Ah Ku's left cheek. A second stab had struck him in the forehead, above the left eye, but though the concussion had evidently been violent, the steel had failed to penetrate the bone of the skull. This wound was very clean and well defined, and Jack's keen eyes had no difficulty in detecting that it had been made with a *kris mělela*—a dagger with a raised ridge running down the centre of the blade—such as few save the King's Youths were wont to carry. Ah Ku had fallen backward when he was stabbed, and several heavy blows on the chest from a wooden club, or from some similar blunt instrument, had been dealt him, probably as he lay upon the ground, and for the purpose of administering to him the *coup de grace*.

Jack pulled off his coat, rolled up his sleeves and washed his hands carefully in a bowl of *sam-shu*—raw Chinese spirit. Then he drove all the onlookers out of the room except Raja Haji Hamid, and set to work to do what he could to mend Che' Ah Ku. He washed and dressed the wounds on Ah Ku's cheek and forehead, put a couple of horsehair stitches into the severed lip, and applied a compress to the injured chest. He plied his patient with stimulants, and eventually had the satisfaction of restoring him to consciousness. Then, having charged Chik to tend him carefully and to administer rice gruel at regular intervals, he returned to his own house. His surgery was, it must be confessed, of a sadly amateurish character, but that war-worn warrior, Raja Haji, had acquired a good deal of rough-and-ready experience, and between them they made a more creditable job of Che' Ah Ku than might have been expected.

Next day their patient was better and as soon as Jack had dressed his wounds a statement was made, and taken down in writing, which, in any better ordered community, would amply have sufficed to hang one or two of Jack's most intimate acquaintances, who were leading members of the King's bodyguard. Ah Ku, it appeared, had been sent for that evening by the King's Treasurer, on some trivial pretext connected with the estate of the late Li Tat, and had been detained by him until the dark hour had come which precedes the rising of the moon. He had then been dismissed, and as he groped his way homeward he had been struck by the fact that the main street, contrary to its wont, was strangely empty. Suddenly, as he drew near to the entrance to his house, four or five armed men had leaped out upon him from the shadows cast by the overhanging roof of the adjoining building, which was the dwelling-place of one of the King's concubines; but Ah Ku, despite the darkness, had identified, by their voices and gestures, at least three of his assailants. The latter, in their excitement and hurry, had done their work clumsily enough; but they had not ceased their attack until their victim had fallen into a state of unconsciousness, which they had probably mistaken for death.

V

The weeks that followed proved to be a weary time for Jack Norris. He tended Ah Ku with the most anxious care, and was rewarded by seeing the wounds heal up, though they left monstrous and unsightly cicatrices behind them. None the less, the old man's strength waned daily, and Jack presently was forced to realise that his patient had sustained some severe internal injuries, the treatment of which was a task altogether beyond the reach of his homely doctoring. The decline, though persistent, was very gradual, and Jack watched, with intense and growing anxiety, the race which the ebbing vitality of Ah Ku was running against time—the time that must elapse ere the breaking of the monsoon would reopen communications with the outside world.

Jack felt that if only Ah Ku could be made to hang on to life until the first ship of the season arrived at the mouth of the Pĕlĕsu River, if he could thereafter be sent to the neighbouring British colony, his scarred face and wrecked body would tell their tale with an eloquence that is denied to mere written depositions. His appearance, Jack was convinced, would be all that was needed to complete the long and heavy indictment already standing to the discredit of the King of Pĕlĕsu, and would be held to justify the Government in taking one more forward step at last. So Jack fought with death, doggedly and fiercely, day and night, heart and soul, as a man strives to stay the passing of one who is very dear to him. His cheeks began to grow pale and lined under his deep sun-tan, his eyes to burn with an unnatural brightness from anxiety and want of sleep; but still he carried on the struggle, Chik aiding him with a tireless devotion.

The King shut himself up in his rabbit warrens, and once only—and then by chance—did Jack get word with him during all those weeks. The monarch had come out into the main street, which was an immediate signal for all who were in sight to squat reverently in the dust, and for traffic to be forthwith suspended. Jack, who happened to be in a Chinese shop close at hand, was quick to seize his opportunity in a way that made evasion impossible. The King, in melancholy accents, his gentle voice vibrating with tenderness and compassion, enquired anxiously after Jack's patient, expressed his admiration of the skill and kindness which the white man had lavished upon this unfortunate, and uttered some copybook maxims on the subject of the extreme naughtiness of assault and battery. Jack grinned rather grimly with that tight-shut mouth of his, and in equally dulcet tones, and with an elaborate air of deference and respect, dropped into the ear of his royal friend a few sentences that burned like fire. He spoke in that subtle Malay language which lends itself so readily to the framing of soft-sounding phrases, that convey so much more than the mere words express. Had the terms of which Jack made use been analysed, no man could deny that they were at once courteous, harmless, and commonplace enough; but none the less, both Jack and the King knew that the former had made against the latter an accusation of murder as unequivocal in character as the charge addressed to a criminal in the dock.

After this the King went to bed and apparently stayed there, for, if one might believe his messages, he was invariably asleep, or too sick to rise from his couch, when Jack sought an interview with him. Speech with the monarch being thus rendered impossible, Jack wrote him a letter pointing out that Ah Ku, a British subject, had been attacked and left for dead in the main street of the King's capital, and within a few yards of one of the royal residences; that no one had been punished for this cold-blooded crime; and that, as soon as the mouth of the river opened to traffic, the wounded man and his family would be despatched to Singapore, there to lay the tale of their wrongs before the Governor of the colony. No reply was received to this communication, but Jack was neither surprised nor perturbed by the King's silence. He was convinced that his adversary would go to considerable lengths in order to prevent the transfer of his victim to the colony; but Jack was determined to vindicate the right of a British subject to come and go as he pleased. Moreover, he was resolved to avoid any act that might be regarded as an attempt to spirit Ah Ku away, and it was to this end that he had given formal written notice of his intention to remove him from Pĕlĕsu.

Meanwhile the atmosphere in which the political agent found himself living began to grow somewhat sultry. The folk who thronged the Court of the King of Pĕlĕsu learned to look askance at Jack Norris seeing in him now the almost openly declared enemy of their monarch. The timid shunned him. Those who were bolder cocked arrogant eyes in his direction or were as nearly insolent as they dared. His followers shared in their master's disfavour and once or twice some of them were hustled in the street or the market-place by sundry of the King's Youths. Jack lived in terror lest the latter should succeed in picking a quarrel with his people in which event the little band of adventurers might perhaps be wiped out and the rights and wrongs of the story never come to light. But discipline was good in Jack's household and he was ably seconded by Raja Haji Hamid and by Raja Uteh, who appreciated the situation as justly as he did. None the less this protracted period of waiting and inaction was trying, and required a fair measure of nerve.

One night Jack went to the King's *Balai* as he had been wont to do before Ah Ku had met with his misadventure; but the looks with which he was greeted by the assembled *rajas* and chiefs were not encouraging.

The Bĕndahara Sri Stiawan who was the senior man present turned to him almost as soon as he was seated and growled out sulkily:

'How fares it with that Chinaman whom you are tending?'

He knew Ah Ku's name as well as he knew his own, but he spoke of him contemptuously as 'that Chinaman' because he wished to be offensive.

Norris was somewhat nettled by the Běndahara's manner and by the changed, unfriendly faces that surrounded him, and in the pride and naughtiness of his heart he told himself that he would make these men of Pělěsu 'sit up and snort'. There was in this resolve a measure of calculation superadded to the natural hot-headedness of youth, for Jack felt that his life was not oversafe at this time, and his knowledge of Malayan character taught him that in bluff and in an ostentatious scorn of the dangers by which his path was beset lay his best chance of prolonging his insecure lease of life. Accordingly, he cast a dare-devil look at the Běndahara and spoke, selecting words which no native would dare to employ, and adopting a manner which he knew would send a tremor through his large audience.

'Try to think for yourself,' he said. 'How should a man fare who has been stabbed with daggers?'

He heard the men near him gulp and draw in their breath at the word; for it was the official contention at the Court of Pělěsu that, no matter what might have befallen Ah Ku, it was beyond all things certain that he had not been the victim of an assault. To utter any other opinion was, in the estimation of the courtiers, felony, high treason, or worse.

'Who says that Ah Ku was stabbed?' cried the Běndahara in dismay.

'I say it,' replied Norris calmly. 'Moreover, all men say the like who dare speak that which it is in their bellies to speak. Ah Ku was stabbed with knives close to the door of the King's house, at the spot where certain of the King's Youths are wont every night to sit.'

'How do you know that he was stabbed?' cried the Běndahara. 'There was a lath of bamboo projecting from the thatch, and men say that Ah Ku stumbled and fell against it.'

'Ah Ku does not measure five cubits in height,' Norris answered, with a grin. 'Moreover, a horizontal lath doth not make a perpendicular wound. Think once again, *Ungku*. Mayhap you will find some still better explanation.'

And thereupon Jack laughed aloud, while his audience shuffled uneasily, and the Běndahara scowled at this stranger who, with so light a heart, gave utterance to such inconvenient and uncompromising things, and who seemed quite unawed by the danger by which all men knew him to be surrounded.

'Then I say that it was a devil that did this thing,' exclaimed the Běndahara, his voice rising almost to a scream.

To his Malayan audience there was nothing outlandish or preposterous in this explanation. To their thinking, the line dividing the natural from the supernatural, the normal from the supernormal, is none too rigid a boundary.

'In very truth it was a devil,' Jack assented. 'But mark my words. The devil who wrought this thing went on two legs, and was armed with a *kris mělela*—a dagger with a ridged blade. From whom, think you, did he borrow that weapon? Or did it perchance fall from the scabbard of one of the King's Youths, who are wont to sit together by night at the very spot where the deed was done? What profits it to seek explanations from the rim of the platter to its centre, when all men know the truth? You and I be men, full grown, *Ungku*, and endowed with all our faculties. Is it good, then, to play a game of make-believe like children? But try to remember this: Though this thing was done in the dark, it hath come forth into the light of day; and it may be that many in this land of Pělěsu will live to pay the price of that night's work, nor will it greatly avail them if they seek to make Satan bear the burden of their evil-doing. I crave your leave to depart.'

And Jack dropped over the edge of the verandah, leaving a flustered, discomfited, and disgruntled assembly behind him.

This was one of several such encounters that thrust themselves upon Norris at this time. The knowledge that his life hung by a thread—that his death was ardently desired by a potentate who had long been accustomed to destroy his fellow-creatures with as little scruple as a cook breaks eggs—had the effect of making him doubly reckless. Though he was very much alone, though he had no man of his own race at hand to advise, aid, or protect him, he found the excitement of this precarious existence unusually stimulating, and he learned actively to enjoy the risks which he now ran almost hourly.

Thus the days slipped by until the monsoon broke, and a vessel was at last reported as having entered the mouth of the river.

VI

Norris set off down stream as soon as he learned that the ship had arrived. He travelled in a long, narrow, beautifully modelled dugout, taking the steer-oar himself, while sixteen of his men, all dressed alike in white jumpers and knickers, and dark blue *sarongs* and headkerchiefs, bent to their paddles, to the accompaniment of a perfect tumult of shrill whoops and yells. The boat tore through the water in a succession of long, smooth leaps and in less than an hour Jack found himself climbing up the port side of a villainous little steam-tramp and being received by the Malay skipper and by the Chinese *chin-chu*, or supercargo folk, at whose hands she ran strange risks and suffered many and terrible things almost every time

AT THE COURT OF PĕLĕSU

she put to sea. As he boarded her, he saw the Panglima Dalam—the King's Chamberlain—and a number of the royal bodyguard scrambling into a boat moored on the starboard side; and from this he inferred that the ruler of Pĕlĕsu had already done his best to prevent the ship from accepting Ah Ku and his family as passengers.

This suspicion was soon confirmed, for the Malay captain and the Chinese supercargo both flatly refused to run the risk inseparable from an attempt to remove from Pĕlĕsu persons whom the King was resolved to retain within his own jurisdiction. Norris, however, had anticipated this, and he proceeded calmly to explain that if the refusal were persisted in, the good ship *Bang Ah Hong* would shortly forfeit her licence to carry passengers, and would meet with other inconveniences and disasters exceedingly unpleasant to her owners. After some further arguments, therefore, the captain of the vessel gave in; and when Jack had exacted a promise that the ship should not put to sea until he gave her permission to do so, he at once set off up stream to return to the capital.

Arrived at his destination, Jack made a round of afternoon calls. In the first place, he visited the Ungku Muda, the King's brother, who was on friendly terms with Norris and on exceedingly bad ones with the ruler of Pĕlĕsu. To him Jack explained that it was his intention, on the following morning, to remove Ah Ku and his family from Pĕlĕsu, and to send them by sea to Singapore.

'In the name of Allah, refrain!' cried the Ungku Muda in dismay. 'The King will never permit it. If you persist you will be slain, and when you are dead I, too, shall perish at the hands of the King. You are to me the wall of my stockade, and behold, you would demolish it!'

Norris laughed, and suggested to the Ungku Muda that if that was his view of the situation, his best course would be to hold himself in readiness to lend a hand in the removal of Ah Ku, since, if the attempt failed, it looked as though they both ran a chance of being dead men ere long. The *raja*, however, was not a courageous person, and he evidently found Jack's proposal quite extraordinarily unattractive. He therefore beseeched Norris to abandon his reckless project, and, moved even to tears, loudly bewailed the evil fate which he foresaw was like to engulf himself and all connected with him.

'What can one do?' said Norris philosophically. 'My word has gone forth and may not now be recalled. I have told the King that I will send Ah Ku and his wife and children to the colony, and behold, the time has come to act! I ask leave to depart.'

He left the Ungku Muda mourning the cruelties of his fate with weak outcries and the futile wringings of slack, irresolute hands, and betook himself to the compound of the Bĕndahara Sri Stiawan.

'There will be trouble—bad trouble—if you attempt this thing,' said the Bĕndahara. 'In my opinion, it is quite certain that you and yours will inevitably be slain. I therefore pray you to give me a writing that will survive you, telling all who may read it that I, *Tuan*, was ever your friend.'

The cynical selfishness of this suggestion set Norris laughing, though he saw scant reason to question the soundness of the Bĕndahara's opinion concerning the probable course of events. Though he was outwardly calm, he was tingling with excitement and the humours of the situation pleased him.

'There will be no need of a writing, *Ungku*,' he said sardonically. 'If you are indeed my friend, all men will know it, should trouble beset me, for your deeds doubtless will prove it.'

'But I am an impotent person, a man devoid of power and authority,' whined the Bĕndahara. 'It is not possible for me actively to aid you; but before Allah, *Tuan*, I am your friend, near to you in heart as the quick is near to the nail.'

'He who is not for me is against me,' translated Norris; and so saying he took his leave of the Bĕndahara.

His next visit was to the big raft moored on the other side of the river, in which dwelt the Ungku Tumĕnggong, yet another leading chief of royal blood. This worthy, however, was famed throughout Pĕlĕsu for his prudence, and, having scented trouble in the air, he had most opportunely departed up stream to snare turtle-doves, and was not expected to return for some days.

Finally, Norris went to see Tungku Indut, the eldest son of the King, a young man of considerable force of character, who chanced at this time to be at enmity with his father. To him also Jack stated that it was his intention to remove Ah Ku and his family from Pĕlĕsu at dawn on the morrow.

'Have you well considered this business?' enquired the prince.

'Yes,' replied Norris gravely. 'I have weighed it with care.'

'And your mind is made up?' asked Tungku Indut. 'And that, though you are aware that the King will certainly resist your action, it may be even with force?'

'Yes,' returned Norris. 'My mind is made up, and my word has gone forth.'

'Then, if you will follow my advice, remove Ah Ku by night, and secretly, so that no man may know the hour of his departure.'

'That I cannot do,' rejoined Norris. 'I am no thief, carrying off by stealth aught that is the property of the King, your father. Ah Ku and his people are British subjects, and all such are free to come and go as it pleases them. That is a right which none may deny to them. At day-break to-morrow I take them forth, and I have come hither to tell you of my intention, that all may be open, and so that no man may be able to say that I acted with chicanery or deceit.'

Tungku Indut sat in silence for a few moments gloomily pondering upon the situation. Then he spoke.

'Then there is no further word to be said. You must do that which you hold to be right; but be warned *Tuan*. There will very certainly be trouble, and with your life you will pay the penalty that overtakes those who oppose the King.'

So Norris returned to his boat and paddled through the darkness, which had now fallen, to the bathing-raft moored at the back of his house. He had eaten no food since dawn, but his hunger was not yet to be appeased, for two chiefs were awaiting him, who had come as messengers from the King. They brought word that the Sovereign was expecting him—that he had, indeed, been waiting for a considerable time—and that he desired urgently to have speech with him.

In spite of their whispered protests, Norris bade all his men remain in the house, and went alone to this interview with the hostile King. He knew that the capital of Pĕlĕsu was, at the moment, in an exceedingly excited state, and that the ruler of the kingdom would welcome any pretext that would serve to precipitate a quarrel, the result of which might be the murder of Jack and of his people. Any chance row that might seem to be wholly unconnected with politics would, Jack knew, be regarded by the King as a godsend, and this of all things Norris was determined to avoid. Moreover, the bravado, as many of the natives would judge it, of this unattended visit to the King, suited his reckless humour, and might in itself prove useful as a practical demonstration of the fact that he was not in the least afraid. Nor was he, for the excitement of the situation still thrilled and stimulated him, so that as yet he had no time for fear.

The King was awaiting Jack's coming, seated upon a mat

spread on the ground in the open air in front of the whitewashed bungalow, of which mention has already been made. The cleared space between the house and the fence and all the approaches to the building were thronged with men squatting humbly on the earth, after the manner of Malays when in the presence of royalty; and the moonlight revealed the fact that one and all were armed to the teeth. Moreover, the people of the neighbouring hamlets, Jack noted, had been summoned to the capital, a thing in itself so unusual that nothing further was needed to show that mischief was intended. Convinced of this, and knowing well the character of the people with whom he was dealing, Jack judged that the assumption of an air of light-hearted indifference to danger was at once the wisest and the safest attitude for him to adopt in the presence of this multitude of enemies.

'*Hai*, Merah!' he cried laughingly to one burly native of the King's bodyguard, against whom he brushed in passing. 'You and your fellows are in force to-night.'

The man, squatting at his feet, scowled up at him sulkily, and those near turned to witness the encounter.

'Yes, we be many,' Merah grunted. 'It is said that the King hath a mind to go a-hunting for the purpose of killing a tiger.'

Norris knew well enough that there was no tiger in the vicinity, and that he was the person whose death the King desired to compass.

'Have a care, Merah,' he cried, with the same careless laugh on his lips. 'Have a care, for tigers have claws and teeth wherewith to guard their lives.'

All within hearing knew what the hint implied, and Norris had the pleasure of seeing approving glances bent upon him; for Malays love pluck, especially if it be garnished with a touch of swagger and a ready tongue.

Norris approached the King, and, seating himself on the

mat opposite to him, noted with satisfaction that no one was sitting within striking distance of his back. The King sat in stolid silence for some moments, with bowed head and downcast eyes, while with restless, nervous fingers he picked at the matting of woven palm leaves. His face, conforming to the habit of brown countenances in moments of strong emotion, was almost black in hue, and his jaw was tight-set as a clinched vice. All the principal *rajas* and chiefs of his Court were present, squatting reverently about their King; and Norris noticed that even their trained self-control was powerless wholly to conceal their perturbation and anxiety. For close upon five full minutes no word was spoken. Norris, who, to all appearances, was the least troubled person present, sat cross-legged in the conventional attitude, covertly observing those around him, while he patiently waited for the King to fire the first conversational shot. At last, however, as the silence threatened to become interminable, he decided himself to take the initiative.

'Men said that your Majesty desired to have speech with me,' he said. 'And for this purpose, therefore, I have come hither. If they spoke in error, I pray your leave to depart, for my belly is empty, since all the day I have gone fasting.'

The King slowly raised his head and looked Jack straight in the face, for the first time since the arrival of the white man at the place of meeting. For an instant there peeped out of the King's eyes a flash of the emotions of which he was the prey—baffled desire, endured by one whose will, even in trivial matters, had never been crossed for years; the bewilderment of rage and indignation thus occasioned; and the hate aroused by the sight of this young Englishman, who had subjected him to the unprecedented humiliation of opposition. It was not a pleasant glimpse of a human soul that this look afforded to Norris, for behind the anger there lurked an air of triumph, confident, cruel, and menacing, which told plainly that the King believed himself to hold his opponent in the hollow of his hand, and meant to use his power to repay humiliation with humiliation. It was an appreciation of this fact that caused Jack's mouth to set hard with determination, which had in it more of personal feeling than any sentiment of which he had so far been conscious in his dealings with the King. Deep down in his heart he registered a vow that, God helping him, he would do nothing that should seem, even for an instant, to justify that expression of gloating triumph in the eyes of his adversary.

'Have patience for a little space, *Tuan*,' replied the King. He spoke with that peculiar softness of voice and gentleness of manner which were characteristic of him, and which assorted so ill with his reputation for ruthlessness. 'There is indeed a trifling matter concerning which I would speak to you. It has been said by certain foolish folk that you intend to carry Ah Ku and his family away to the colony. I place no faith in a report so palpably false.'

'Did no man read to your Majesty the letter which I wrote a month or more ago giving notice of my intention in this matter?' enquired Norris. 'Had this been done, your Majesty would know that this is no vain report. If Allah be willing, to-morrow at the dawn I shall remove these people. They desire to go; they have made their desire known to me; and, moreover, they are British subjects, wherefore no man may interfere with their comings in and their goings forth.'

'How can they be British subjects?' asked the King. 'Do they not dwell in this land of Pĕlĕsu? Am I not the ruler of the country; and are not all who dwell within my dominions subject to me?'

'All who are born in Pĕlĕsu are your Majesty's subjects,' Norris replied; 'and were any such to come to me weeping and wailing, I could not succour them. But these folk are children of Hong-Kong, and, like myself, they are mere sojourners in Pĕlĕsu. They are the subjects of Her Majesty the Queen, the Most High and the Most Honourable, and as such they have the right to claim, and it is my duty to afford to them such poor protection as I can give.'

'They are indeed fortunate folk!' ejaculated the King. 'Verily the protection of yourself and of your so numerous retinue must be unto them as an impregnable fort drawn round about them.'

Jack grinned, wholly unmoved by the King's jibe.

'None the less,' he reiterated, 'to-morrow at the dawn they will leave Pĕlĕsu.'

'But that may not be. They owe me money; they are deep in my debt,' cried the King.

A slow, meaning smile spread over Jack's ugly face.

'It is indeed true that they owe you much,' he said. 'Also I pray to Allah that, in the fulness of time, that debt may be paid in full. As for any money that may be due to your Majesty, so be it that the account can be proved—for this is the first word that I have heard concerning it—the liability shall, in due course, be discharged, and for its payment I will stand surety. But was it not on account of money owing to Ah Ku that your Majesty condescended to cause certain gems to be sent to his house, gems which, doubtless through the unhandiness of those who had them in charge, were suffered to fall into the gutter?'

Jack was young, and for the life of him he could not forego the taunt. It was now the King's turn to wince. The lines about his mouth set harder than ever; he drew in his breath once or twice gaspingly, and when he next spoke his voice vibrated with suppressed anger. His courtiers watched him out of furtive, fearful eyes.

AT THE COURT OF PĚLĚSU

'I care naught for money, as you, *Tuan*, know well,' he said. 'But I bid you refrain from attempting to remove these people from Pělěsu, for I cannot suffer them to depart.'

Jack drew a sigh of ostentatious dejection.

'*Ya Allah!*' he exclaimed. 'Verily my fate is evil. When men be young they lie in the wombs of their mothers; when they be grown to full estate they lie in the womb of custom; when they are dead they lie in the womb of the earth.[1] Behold, it has ever been my wish to obey the laws and customs of this land of Pělěsu. When among the kine, I have striven to low; when among the goats, I have joined in the bleating; when among the fowls, I have crowed with the cocks;[2] but now, at last, I must abandon this my habit, for I, who am still alive, am also in the womb of custom—the custom of mine own people; and in this matter I may not conform to your will, but instead must do that which it is laid upon me to do at the behest of the great Queen whose servant I am. My liver within me is sorrow-stricken because, on this occasion, I cannot comply with your Majesty's wishes.'

In a discussion among Malays it is ever the man who can *quote*, not he who can *argue*, who carries off the palm of debate; and Norris knew that this speech, with its tags of old wise-saws drawn from the proverbial philosophy of the people, was well calculated to appeal to his audience. Also the calm determination which his words expressed had a certain moral effect upon the chiefs and courtiers, and caused the King to feel that in this contest of words he was losing, rather than gaining, ground.

'But, *Tuan*,' he screamed almost hysterically, his self-control failing him for the first time. 'But, *Tuan*, you do not understand! I have said that I will not suffer this thing to be done.'

'Pardon, Majesty,' Jack replied. 'Full well do I understand

---

[1] and [2] Malayan proverbial sayings.

your words; and it is for that reason that I am filled with sorrow. Certainly my fate is accursed, for with your wishes I can by no means comply.'

'But *I*—I and none other—am the ruler of this land of Pĕlĕsu!' cried the King.

'That is very certain,' assented Norris. 'But Ah Ku and his people are the subjects of Her Majesty the Queen, and all her folk, of no matter what degree, are free to come and go without let or hindrance, whithersoever they may desire. I, too, am her servant, to come at her call, to go at her bidding; and it is demanded of me that in all things I should obey her commands, and that I should aid her people to maintain their rights.'

'Ah, truly,' said the King, suddenly changing his tone from one of anger and excitement to the dulcet note that gives a double edge to a sneer. 'Ah, truly, I, what am I? And what is my power? I have neither men nor weapons, nor force, nor wisdom, nor skill, nor state; whereas you, *Tuan*, are indeed well equipped to carry out the orders of your so great Queen.'

'I pray your Majesty to refrain from smiting your daughter, the better to get even with your son-in-law,' said Norris, making use of the Malay proverbial saying. He spoke very quietly, but he did not like the tone which his adversary was assuming. 'I and those who follow me are few and weak. We be a little thing to swallow—like the bait that killed the shark. We are, as it were, only the shadow; but the substance that hath cast us before it is a mighty thing. To-night, O Majesty, you are all-powerful; your men are numerous, mine are few; but what profits it to discuss such matters? Our talk is not of men and weapons, but of wholly other things. I have said that I will remove Ah Ku from Pĕlĕsu, if he live till the dawn; and if I also live, this I will surely do.'

'But, *Tuan*, perchance the man will die, lacking the strength to make the journey.'

'Better so, if he die fulfilling the wish of his heart. Your Majesty's capital hath had no good effect upon the health of this man; otherwise there would have been no cause to remove him.'

'Men say that he smote his head against the lintel of his door,' said the King.

'Many folk say strange things in this land of Pĕlĕsu, knowing in their hearts that they lie,' Jack returned grimly.

'Then what say you hath caused his wounds?'

For a moment, before he replied, Jack looked the King very steadily in the eyes.

'He was stabbed, your Majesty—stabbed at the entrance to his house—stabbed within a yard or two of the spot where, nightly, members of your Majesty's own bodyguard keep watch and ward. Moreover, in spite of the darkness and the surprise, he saw and recognised those who attacked him.'

'Whom did he see?' asked the King eagerly.

'Maybe, when Ah Ku reaches the colony, the Governor may think fit to answer that question,' said Norris grimly. For the present I say nothing.'

'But what hath this to do with me?'

'Your Majesty is more wise than I,' replied Norris, making use of the conventional compliment, which bears at least two interpretations.

'You do not say that *I* slew him?'

'I do not suggest that it was the hand of your Majesty that struck the blow.'

There fell a long silence. Then the King spoke again.

'But, *Tuan*, will you not listen to reason?' He spoke almost entreatingly. 'I pray you to forego your resolve. If you so desire, take the woman Chik into your own keeping. Let her live within your house. I will do her no harm; but I cannot suffer her or her man to leave Pĕlĕsu.'

'There is a saying of the men of ancient days: '*Set not a snare, and thereafter thrust your own head into it.*' My house is a male household, and no woman could dwell therein without scandal arising. Moreover, Chik will accompany Ah Ku to the colony.'

'Is that your last word, *Tuan*?' asked the King. He was weary of dashing against this stone wall of resolution, through which no known means of persuasion had apparently the power to break.

'Yes, your Majesty. It is my last word. Moreover, I am hungry, and therefore I ask your leave to depart to my house.'

'But understand that I cannot suffer this thing to come to pass,' cried the King in a frenzy.

'*Apa buleh buat?*' (What can one do?) murmured Jack, as he rose to his feet and made his way through the squatting crowd, without attempting any more direct reply.

As he passed back to his house he called in at Che' Ah Ku's dwelling, and found his patient very feeble and sick, but feverishly anxious to find himself *en route* for the colony. Jack gave orders as to the food which was to be given to him at regular intervals throughout the night, and prescribed a certain amount of stimulant, the woman Chik listening obediently and promising to keep watch by her husband's bed till dawn. All her preparations for the coming journey were already complete.

In the *balai* of his own house Norris found Raja Haji Hamid and Raja Uteh waiting with all his followers fully armed. The little knot of perhaps thirty ragamuffins were holding themselves in readiness to run *amok* through the town, in order to avenge their *Tuan*, if aught of ill had befallen him at the hands of the King.

AT THE COURT OF PĚLĚSU

Before doing anything else, Jack set to upon a large meal of curry and rice, to which, after his prolonged fast, he did ample justice. It is a fine thing to be young and healthy, for even danger, excitement, and anxiety cannot then put a man off his food. The meal finished, he rolled a cigarette thoughtfully, and then called all his people about him. In a few words he explained to them the position in which he found himself, and added:

'There will be trouble at dawn when we seek to escort these people to the boat, and it may well be that few of those who follow me will remain alive. Therefore, think well. If there be any among you who fear the risk, you have my leave forthwith to depart, and I will give to each one a letter to show that he left me with my permission and consent. But may the curse of Allah the Most High blight the soul and body and heart and brain and vitals of anyone who to-night elects to stay with me, and who to-morrow fails me in the hour of need. Give me your answers that I may hear.'

'The *Tuan* speaks for me as well as for himself,' cried Raja Haji.

'And for me,' said Raja Uteh.

They rose up and seated themselves behind Norris on the dais. They did not wish the other Malays to regard them as men who had any choice in a situation such as this.

'*Tuan*,' said an old man acting as the spokesman of his fellows, whose eyes shone and whose teeth flashed in the lamplight, 'we be all of one mind. Behold, we have eaten your rice, and have worn garments of your giving in the days of your ease. It would not be fitting that we should desert you now that trouble hath come upon you. Therefore, not only unto death will we follow you, but, if Allah so wills it, even unto the Lake of Fire itself. Come, my brothers. Let us make ready our weapons against the battle at dawn.'

'It is well,' said Norris, though the loyalty of his people touched him nearly, making him feel at once proud and humble; and then he left them and went to his own room. He whistled to cover his emotion—whistled sadly out of tune, it must be confessed; but the music-hall air which he mangled was 'There's Another Jolly Row Downstairs', a song popular at that time which seemed to him to be grimly appropriate to the moment.

He had hardly reached his desk when the Ungku Muda and another leading chief who was known to be friendly disposed towards Norris were announced. They came from the King to try whether their persuasions could not even now cause this foolhardy strong-willed stranger to forego his purpose. Both of them were a prey to strong excitement and they did not disguise their conviction that if Norris persisted in his declared intention he and his people would die violent deaths at an early hour on the morrow.

'What profits it to talk further?' asked Norris when he had listened patiently to all that they had to say. 'If we spoke together until the dawn I could not recall my words, nor would I if I could.'

So, sorrowful and disconsolate, his visitors returned to their King.

'It is enough,' said the ruler of Pĕlĕsu to his assembled chiefs, when he had received his messengers' report. 'This white man is a *kafir* (an infidel), and it is notorious that none such has any fear of death, since a belief in a life to come and dread of the fires of the terrible place are alike denied to unbelievers, though of those very fires they are the everlasting fuel. For me, I go a-hunting; even now my boat lies ready moored at the landing-stage; but I confide this business to you, and you shall not suffer Ah Ku or the woman Chik, his wife, to leave Pĕlĕsu. Your King will be absent from the city when the deed is done, and it will, therefore, be difficult for the white man to hold him responsible for aught that may befall.'

The *rajas* and chiefs lifted up their hands, palm pressed to palm, in homage to their King.

'*Tuan-ku!*' (Majesty!) they ejaculated in choric acquiescence.

With them to hear was to obey, and no man so much as dreamed of protesting or of blaming the King for his cynical selfishness. Half an hour later, therefore, he was lying on his mat in one of his houseboats, being paddled up stream by a few of his youngest and least-tried warriors, while half a dozen young women shampooed his limbs, kneaded his body, and fanned him to sleep. The more experienced of the King's fighting-men remained behind. They were likely to be needed for the work which the morrow's dawn would witness.

VII

It was ten o'clock at night before Jack Norris sat down squarely at his desk to write the despatch which he believed was destined to be his last official report. He knew, of course, that after his death the good people of Pělěsu would seek to justify his murder by the fabrication of some lying story, ascribing that regrettable incident to causes wholly disconnected with politics. Accordingly, he was anxious that an exact version of all that had happened should survive him, and that it should have a fair chance of finding its way into the hands of the men who presently would come to Pělěsu to gather up his bones. To this end he sent one of his people for a bamboo, in the hollow of which he determined to place his letters, and he bade a small boy belonging to his household, whose tender years would probably save his life, mark well the spot where he intended to secrete this improvised envelope in the thatch of the roof. The house, being the property of the King, was pretty certain to escape destruction.

These arrangements completed, he wrote calmly and steadily, a cigarette between his lips, pausing every now and again to seek the exact word he wanted, or to listen to the 'run' of a sentence. His mind was working with more than its usual activity, and he flattered himself that his posthumous despatch would do him credit. The thought of the unusual sympathy and interest with which it would be read set him grinning, for he had in those days the quite undeserved scorn of the painstaking and plodding souls who manned the Colonial Secretariat that is commonly entertained by the young and active members of the Civil Service.

All the time that he sat writing, there lay at the back of his mind the absolute certainty of his conviction that he was only separated by the space of a few hours from a violent and ugly death; but this seemed merely to throw his thoughts upon other subjects more clearly into relief. The very near presence of death has a curiously numbing effect when the threatened man is in full possession of all his vital forces. It is possible at such times to look the king of terrors steadily between the eyes, with awe and with respect, but without dismay. It is as though for a little while fear forebore to claim its prey.

When the despatch had been drafted, revised, and finally signed, Jack began a letter to his mother. He told her the facts of the position in which he then found himself, of the certain death that awaited him at dawn, and wound up with a few simple sentences expressive of his love for her and of his gratitude for all her lifelong tenderness to him. He added a word or two of sympathy with her in the grief which his death would bring; but he was conscious throughout that he was viewing his case dispassionately and without emotion, as

AT THE COURT OF PĚLĚSU

though it were that of some third person, the pathos of whose end had no power to move him. Then he wrote a short line to his sister, the member of his family who was his especial pal. But here things were different, for his words conjured up a vision of her face, gone suddenly pale, and stained with weeping, and with an incredulous despair in those eyes that were wont to be so soft and bright. He finished his letter with a sob in his throat, and from sheer inability to go on with it. For the first time that night he felt heartily sorry for himself, and for those distant folk who loved him.

The hour was now very late, and Jack, calling one of his men to bring his soap and towels, went out to the moored bathing-raft, off which he presently took a flying header into the cool waters of the river. The swim was infinitely tonic, and Jack, much refreshed in body and mind, had just drawn himself into a sitting position on the raft when an excited voice spoke to him suddenly from the doorway of the hut behind and above him.

'*Tuan*,' it cried, 'a man hath come from the house of Ah Ku praying you to go thither speedily.'

Jack hastened to put on the jumper, drawers and *sarong* which his follower was holding ready for him, snatched up a broadsword, crammed a fez upon his head, and, bare-shod as he was, ran out of the house and down the street in the direction of the Chinaman's hut. Raja Haji and a dozen men pelted after him. Raja Uteh and the remainder stayed behind to garrison the house.

As Norris ran, there presently was borne to him on the wind of the night a shrill, despairing keening, which he knew betokened death; and on entering Che' Ah Ku's room he found Chik, flung prostrate across the corpse of her husband, wailing as only Oriental women can when freshly smitten by bereavement. Just as he was nearing the end of the last lap

Ah Ku had lost the race, which his ebbing vitality had so long been running against time, and he had died in his sleep while Chik sat tending him.

Chik screamed till she collapsed in a faint; recovered consciousness only to cast herself again across the dead body of her husband, whispering words of endearment to his deaf ears, and showering caresses upon the hands and feet and face of the dead man whom in life she had loved so faithfully. Jack knew that until the elaborate burial rites of the Chinese had been complied with there could be no thought of separating Chik from her dead, and that all idea of sending her and her children to the colony must be abandoned for the time being.

He assured himself by minute examination that there had been no loophole left open for the administration of poison or for other foul play, and that the death, which had resulted thus opportunely, was merely the natural culmination of Ah Ku's long illness. Then he turned away with his spirit suddenly relaxed from the tension to which it had been strung all through the night, and with an appreciation of the bathetical character of the end which had come to his adventure, causing something akin to disappointment in his heart.

He knew now that his difficulties were practically at an end. The mouth of the river was again open to traffic, and he would no longer be as completely cut off from all communication with his Government as he had been during the past five months. The *Bang Ah Hong* would convey to the colony a despatch from him that would speedily bring a gunboat to his aid, and in the meantime no question of removing or even of protecting Chik would arise. Even the King would not dare to molest her while she was busy performing the last rites for her dead husband. Norris also foresaw that the Government would now have no alternative but to include

Pĕlĕsu in the protectorate before the year was out. No step short of that would be regarded as sufficient to guarantee the future safety of the life and property of British subjects in that troubled land. For himself, he felt that he had played his part unflinchingly, and in his heart there was satisfaction, and even a little pride in his own steadfastness—sentiments that were oddly blended with something resembling surprise. Anyway, he was glad that, as he mentally phrased it, he had 'kept his end up'; but he realised, none the less, that the whole affair had terminated in so unsensational a fashion that no special credit would be reaped by him, when such of the facts as it would be necessary for him to report were learned by Government through his own modest account of his proceedings.

Then, on a sudden, there was borne in upon him an acute appreciation of the fact that his life had been saved in the very nick of time, and by the merest accident; and the fear of death, and of the extreme peril in which he had so recently stood—fears to which he had been a stranger all the night— assailed him unexpectedly, and shook him with a tremor that made him ashamed.

A moment later he was startled from his reverie by hearing Raja Haji Hamid, whose very presence he had forgotten, swearing softly under his breath.

'What ails you?' Jack asked.

'*Ya Allah!*' sighed Raja Haji. '*Ya Allah, Tuan!* I have dreamed the long night through that now indeed should I once more see shrewd blows given, and the red blood running in spate. It is very certain that my fate is accursed; and when I looked upon the so beast-like body of this Chinaman, whose inappropriate death hath robbed us of our play and hath marred the playing, I could in my wrath have spurned it with my foot.'

He spat noisily in the dust in token of his inexpressible disgust.

Jack laughed softly, but his ugly face wore a look of unwonted tenderness, and his thoughts were far away in sheltered England with his little sister, in whose eyes, as he saw them in imagination, the light of happiness had again been kindled.

And thus the British Government took charge of the destinies of the land of Pĕlĕsu.

From *In a Corner of Asia*, London, 1899.

THE STORY OF RAM SINGH

THE night was intensely still. The dawn-wind had not yet come to rustle and whisper in the trees; the crickets had not yet awakened to scream their greeting to the morning sun; the night-birds had gone to their rest, and their fellows of the day had not yet begun to stir on branch or twig. Nature, animate and inanimate alike, was hushed in the deep sleep which comes in this torrid land during the cool hour before the dawn, and the stillness was only emphasised by the sound of furtive, stealthy steps and cautious words whispered softly under the breath. The speakers were a band of some fifty or sixty ruffians—Malays from the Těmběling Valley of Pahang, clothed in ragged, dirty garments; long-haired, rough-looking disreputables from the wilder districts of Trěngganu and Kělantan and Běsut, across the mountain range; and a dozen truculent, swaggering Pahang chiefs, rebels against the Government, outlaws in their own land, beautifully and curiously armed, clothed in faded silks of many colours, whose splendour had long been dimmed and stained by the dirt and dampness of the dank jungles in which their owners had found a comfortless and insecure hiding-place.

A score of small dugouts were moored to the bank at a spot where the coconut-trees, fringing the water's edge, marked an inhabited village. The gang of rebels was broken up into little knots and groups, some in the boats, some on the shore, the men chewing betel-nut, smoking palm-leaf cigarettes, and talking in grumbling whispers. They had had a very long day of it. The mountain range which divides Kĕlantan from Pahang had been crossed on the afternoon of the preceding day; and save for a brief night's rest, the marauders had been afoot ever since. Ever since the dawn broke they had been making their way down the Tĕmbĕling River, forcing any natives whom they met to join their party; taking every precaution to prevent word of their coming from reaching in advance the lower country for which they were bound; paying off an old score or two with ready knife and blazing firebrand; and loudly preaching a *Sabil Allah* (Holy War) against the Infidel in the name of Ungku Saiyid. The latter was at that time the last of the Saints of the Peninsula, a man weak and wizened of body, but powerful and great of reputation, who sent forth others to do doughty deeds for the Faith, while he lived in the utter peace and seclusion of the little shady village of Paloh near Kuala Trĕngganu.

An hour or two before midnight the raiders reached a spot about three-quarters of a mile above the point where the Tĕmbĕling River falls into the Pahang, and here a halt was called. The big native house, surrounded by groves of fruit and coconut-trees, was the property of one Che' Bujang, and no other dwellings were in the immediate vicinity. Che' Bujang was a weak-kneed individual, who never had enough heart to be able to make up his mind whether he was himself a rebel or not; but he claimed kinship with half the chiefs of the raiding party, and he was filled to the throat with a shuddering fear of them all. The principal leaders among the rebels landed when Che' Bujang's *kampong* was reached, leaving the bulk of their followers squatting in the boats and on the water's brink, and made their way up to their relative's house. Che' Bujang received them with stuttering effusion, his words tripping off his agitated tongue and through his chattering teeth in trembling phrases of welcome. The visitors treated him with scant courtesy, pushing him and his people back into the interior of the house. Then they seated themselves gravely and composedly round the big ill-lighted room, and began to disclose their plans.

They were a curious group of people, these raiders who, with their little knot of followers, had dared to cross the mountain range to batter the face of the great Asiatic god Pax Britannica. The oldest, the most infirm, the most wily, and the least courageous, was the ex-Imam Prang Indĕra Gajah Pahang, commonly called To' Gajah, a huge-boned, big-fisted, coarse-featured Malay of Sumatran extraction, as the scrubby fringe of sparse, wiry beard encircling his ugly face bore witness. Before the coming of the white men this man had been a terror in the land of Pahang. The peasants had been his prey; the high-born chiefs had been forced to bow down before him; the Sultan had leaned upon him as upon a staff of strength; and his will, cruel, wanton, and unscrupulous, had been his only law. The white men had robbed him of all the things which made life valuable to him, and though he had held up his hand to the last, doing all in his power to make others run the risks that in the end he might reap the benefit, his fears had proved too strong for him, and he had turned rebel eventually because he could not believe that Englishmen would be likely to act in good faith where he knew that he would, in similar circumstances, have had recourse to treachery. He had suffered acutely in the jungles whither he had fled, for his body was swelled with dropsy and rotten with disease; and who shall say what floods of hatred and longings for revenge surged up in his heart as he sat there in the semi-darkness of Che' Bujang's house, and gloated over the prospects of coming slaughter?

To' Gajah's three sons, the three who, out of his odd score

of male children, had remained faithful to their father in his fallen fortunes, were also of the party. They were Mat Kilau, Awang Nong, and Teh Ibrahim, typical young Malay roisterers, truculent, swaggering, boastful, noisy, and gaily clad. They had no very fine record of bravery to point to in the past, but what they lacked in this respect they made up for in lavish vaunts of the great deeds which it was their intention to perform in the future.

The foremost fighting chief of the band was the Orang Kaya Pahlawan of Sĕmantan, who was also present. A thick-set, round-faced, keen-eyed man of about fifty years of age, he was known to all the people of Pahang as a warrior of real prowess, a scout without equal in the Peninsula, and a jungle-man who ran the wild tribes of the woods close in his knowledge of forest-lore. When the devil entered into him he was accustomed to boast with an unfettered disregard for accuracy which might have caused the shade of Ananias to writhe with envy, but the deeds which he had really done were so many and so well known that he could afford for the most part to hold his peace when others bragged of their valour. His son Wan Lela, a chip of the old block, who had already given proofs of his courage, sat silently by his father's side.

The last of the Pahang chiefs to enter the house was Mamat Kĕlubi, a Sĕmantan man who, from being a boatman in the employ of a European mining company, had risen during the disturbances to high rank among the rebels, and now bore the title of Panglima Kiri, which has something of the same meaning as Brigadier-General. He was a clean-limbed, active fellow of about thirty years of age, and he stated that he had just returned from Kayangan (fairyland), where he had been spending three months in fasting and prayer, a process which had had the happy result of rendering him invulnerable to blade and bullet. Three weeks later he was shot and stabbed in many places by a band of loyal Malays, which can only be accounted for by the supposition that the fairy magic had gone wrong in one way or another.

To' Gajah spoke when all were seated, and Che' Bujang then learned that an attack was to be made just before dawn upon the small detachment of Sikhs stationed in the big stockade at Kuala Těmběling. Che' Bujang had been in daily communication with these men and something like friendship had sprung up between them, but no idea of setting them upon their guard occurred to him. To do so would entail some personal risk to himself, and rather than that, he would have suffered the whole Sikh race to be exterminated.

At about three o'clock in the morning the chiefs joined their sleepy followers at the boats. The word was passed for absolute silence, and the dugouts with their loads of armed men were then pushed out into mid-stream. The stockade, which was to be the object of the attack, was situated upon a piece of rising ground overlooking the junction of the Těmběling and Pahang Rivers, and at its feet was stretched the broad sandbank of Pasir Tambang, which has been the scene of so many thrilling events in the history of this Malayan State. The Těmběling runs almost at right-angles to the Pahang, and the current of the former sets strongly towards the sandbank. The chiefs knew this well, and they therefore ordered their people to allow the boats to drift, feeling sure that without the stroke of a paddle the whole flotilla would run aground of its own accord at Pasir Tambang.

The busy eddies of chill wind, which come up before the dawn to wake the sleeping world by whispering in its ear, were beginning to stir gently among the green things with which the banks of the river were clothed. A cicada, scenting the daybreak, set up a discordant whir; a sleepy bird among the branches piped feebly, and then settled itself to rest again with a rustle of tiny feathers; behind Che' Bujang's *kampong* a cock crowed shrilly, and far away in the jungle the challenge was answered by one of the wild bantams; the waters of the river, fretting and washing against the banks, murmured complainingly. But the men in the boats, floating down the stream borne slowly along by the current, were absolutely noiseless. The nerves of one and all were strung to a pitch of intensity. Horny hands clutched weapons in an iron grip; breaths were held, ears strained to catch the slightest sound from the stockade which, as they drew nearer, was plainly visible on the prominent point, outlined blackly against the dark sky. The river, black also, save where here and there the dim starlight touched it with a leaden gleam, rolled along inexorably, carrying them nearer and nearer to the fight which lay ahead, bearing sudden and awful death to the dozen Sikhs in the stockade.

At last, after a lapse of time that seemed an age to the raiders, the boats grounded one by one upon the sandbank of Pasir Tambang, so gently and so silently that they might have been ghostly crafts blown thither from the Land of Shadows.

The Orang Kaya Pahlawan landed with Wan Lela, Mat Kilau, Awang Nong, Teh Ibrahim, Panglima Kiri, and a score of picked men at his heels, leaving old To' Gajah and the rest of the party in the boats. Very cautiously they made their way to the foot of the eminence upon which the stockade stood, flitting across the sand in single file as noiselessly as shadows. Then, with the like precautions, they crept up the steep bank till the summit was reached, when the Orang Kaya drew hastily back, and lay flat on his stomach under the cover of some sparse bushes. He and his people had ascended at the extreme corner of the stockade, and he had caught sight of the glint of a rifle-barrel as the Sikh passed down his beat away from him. The raiders could hear the regular fall of the heavy ammunition boots as the sentry marched along. Then they heard him halt, pause for a moment, and presently the sound of his footfalls began to draw near to them once more. Each man among the raiders held his breath, and listened in an agony of suspense. Would he see them and give the alarm before he could be stricken dead? Would he never reach the near end of his beat? Ah, he was there, within a yard of the Orang Kaya! Why was the blow not struck? Hark, he halted, paused, and looked about him, and still the Orang Kaya held his hand! Had his nerve failed him at this supreme moment? Now the sentry had turned about and was beginning to pace away from them upon his beat. Would the Orang Kaya never strike? Suddenly a figure started up in silhouette against the skyline behind the sentry's back, moving quickly, but with such complete absence of noise that it seemed more ghost-like than human. A long black arm grasping a sword leaped up sharply against the sky; the weapon poised itself for a moment, reeled backward, and then with a thick swish and a thud descended upon the head of the Sikh. The sentry's knees quivered for a moment; his body shook like a steam-launch brought suddenly to a standstill upon a submerged rock; and then he fell over in a limp heap against the wall of the stockade, with a dull bump and a slight clash of jingling arms and accoutrements.

In a second all the raiders were upon their feet, and, led by the Orang Kaya, waving his reeking blade above his head, they rushed into the now unguarded stockade. Their bare feet pattered across the little bit of open which served the constables for a parade-ground, and then, sounding their war-cry for the first time that night, they plunged into the hut in which the Sikhs were sleeping.

There were nine men, out of the eleven survivors, inside the hut. The jangle caused by the fall of the sentry by the gate had awakened two of them, and these threw themselves upon the rebels and fought desperately with their clubbed rifles. They had no other weapons. Their companions came to their aid, and a good oak Snider-butt was broken into two pieces over Teh Ibrahim's head in the fight which ensued, though no injury was done to him by the blow. The rush of the Sikhs was so effectual that they all won clear of the hut, and six of their number escaped into the jungle and so saved themselves. The remaining three were killed outside the hut, and Kuala Těmběling stockade had fallen into the hands of the raiders. Their greatest enemy, the loyal Imam Prang Indĕra Stia Raja, had his village some thirty odd miles lower down the Pahang River, at Pulau Tawar, and if this place could also be surprised, the best part of Pahang would be in the possession of the rebels, and a general rising in their favour might be confidently looked for. The Orang Kaya and his people knew this, and their hearts were uplifted with triumph, for they saw now that the Saint who had foretold victory to their arms had been no lying prophet.

Unfortunately for the rebels, however, all the Sikhs had not been within the walls of the stockade when the well-planned attack was delivered. Sikhs keep very curious hours, and one of their habits is to rise before the dawn breaks, and to go shuddering down in the black darkness of that chilly hour to the river's brink, there to perform the elaborate ablutions which, to the keen regret of our olfactory organs, seem ever to be attended with such lamentably inadequate results. On the morning of the attack two of the little garrison, Ram Singh and Kishen Singh, had bestirred themselves before their fellows, and were already shivering on the water's edge when the raiders arrived. It says a good deal for the admirable tactics of the latter that it was not until the attack had been delivered that the two Sikhs became aware of the approach of their enemies. Suddenly, as they stood, naked save for their loin-cloths, the great stillness of the night was broken by a tempest of shrill yells. Then came half a dozen shots, ringing out crisply and fiercely and awakening a hundred clanging echoes in the forest on either bank of the river. An answering cheer was raised by the Malays in the boats, the tumult of angry sound seeming to spring from out of the darkness in front, behind on every side of the bewildered Sikhs. The thick mist beginning to rise from the surface of the water served to plunge the sandbank upon which they stood into fathomless gloom. The ears of the two men rang again with the clamour of the fight going on in the stockade, with the shouts and yells of those who shrieked encouragement to their friends from the moored boats, with the clash of weapons, and with the sudden outbreak of the unexpected hubbub. But they could see nothing—nothing but the great inky shadows all about them into which everything seemed to be merged, and from which issued such discordant and fearful sounds.

'Where art thou, Ram-siar, my brother?' cried Kishen Singh, despairingly; and a heavy silence fell around them for a moment as his voice was heard by the Malays in the boats. Then the shouts of the enemies nearest to the two Sikhs broke out more loudly than before.

' 'Tis the voice of an infidel!' cried some—'Stab, stab!'— 'Kill, and spare not, in the name of Allah!'—'Where, where?' —and then came the crisp pattering of many bare feet over the dry, hard sand in the direction from which the Sikh had shouted to his fellow.

'Brother, I am here,' cried Ram Singh, more quietly, close to Kishen Singh's elbow. 'Alas, but we have no arms, and these jungle-pigs be many. We must tear the life from them with our hands. Oh, Guru Nanuk, have a care for thy children in this their hour of need!'

In the dead darkness both men could hear the swish of naked blades on all sides of them, for the Malays were as much baffled by the gloom as were their victims, and men struck right and left on the bare chance of smiting something. Presently the swish of a sword very near to Ram Singh ended suddenly in a sickening thud, the sound of steel telling loudly upon yielding flesh, and Kishen Singh gave a short, hard cough. The unseen owner of the weapon which had gone home raised a cry of '*Basah! Basah!* I have wetted him! I have drawn blood!' and a yell of exultation went up from a score of fierce voices. Guided by the noise, Ram Singh threw himself upon the struggling mass which was Kishen Singh rolling over and over in his death-agony, with the Malays tossing and tumbling, hacking and smiting above him. Ram Singh's left hand grasped a sword-blade, and though the fingers were nearly severed he managed to wrench the weapon from the grip of a Malay. Then, with a roar as of some angry forest-monster, he charged the spot where the tumult was loudest.

Putting all his weight into each blow, and striking blindly and ceaselessly, he fought his way through the throng in the direction from which the sound of the river purring between its banks was borne to him. The Malays fell back before his desperate onslaught, but they closed in behind him, wounding him cruelly with their swords and daggers and wood-knives, while he in his blindness did them but little injury. None the less, as the dawn began to break, Ram Singh, bleeding from more than a score of wounds, and with his left arm nearly severed, succeeded at last in leaping into one of the moored

THE STORY OF RAM SINGH

boats, and, cutting the rope, pushed out into mid-stream. There were three Malays on board the little dugout, but they quickly slipped over the side, and swam for the shore, deeming this blood-stained, fighting, roaring Sikh no pleasant foe with whom to do battle; and as they went, Ram Singh, utterly spent by his exertions and by loss of blood, slipped down into the bottom of the boat in a limp heap. To' Gajah, furious at the sight of an enemy's escape, danced a kind of palsied quick-step on the sandbank, cursing his people and the mothers that bore them to the fifth and sixth generation, and administering various kicks and blows to such among his followers as he knew would not dare to retaliate in kind. But all this exhibition of bad temper was to no purpose. The excitement of the assault and of the unequal fight in the darkness was over, and the raiders were worn out by the long journey of the preceding day and night. They were very sleepy, and their stomachs cried aloud for rice. The rank and file absolutely declined to give chase until they had eaten and slept their fill; and thus, as the day-light began to draw the colour out of the jungle on the river-banks, out of the yellow stretch of sand and the gleaming reach of running water, the dugout, in which the wounded Sikh lay, was suffered to drift rocking down the stream, until at last it disappeared round the bend a quarter of a mile below the rebel camp.

Ram Singh lay so very still that the raiders may perhaps have persuaded themselves that he was dead; but they should have made sure, for their next move must be down stream, and the success or failure of their enterprise depended almost entirely upon the village of Pulau Tawar, in which the loyal Imam Prang Stia Raja lived, being surprised as Kuala Těmbĕling had been. The rebel chiefs knew this, but it is characteristic of the race to which they belonged that they suffered the whole of their plan of action to be jeopardised rather than take the prompt measures that must have insured success, because these necessitated a certain amount of immediate trouble and exertion. Ram Singh was also aware of the enormous importance of a warning being carried to Imam Prang, and, weighed against this, the mere question of saving or losing his own life seemed to him a matter of little moment.

Although he was too weak to stand or to manage the boat, he determined to remain where he was until the current bore him to Pulau Tawar, and then, and not till then, to spread the news of the fall of Kuala Těmběling. He knew enough of Malay peasants to feel sure that no man among them would dare to help him if they learned that the rebels were in the immediate vicinity, and that he had received his wounds at their hands. Therefore he decided to keep his own counsel until such time as he found himself in the presence of the Imam Prang. He knew also that he could not rely upon any Malay to pass the word of warning which alone could save Imam Prang from death, and the whole of Pahang from a devastating little war. Therefore he determined that, dying though he believed himself to be, he must take that warning word himself. He swore to himself that he would not even halt to bind his wounds, nor to seek food or drink. Nothing must delay him, and the race was to be a close one between his own failing strength and inexorable time.

It was a typical Malayan morning. A cool fresh breeze was rippling the face of the water, and stirring the branches of the trees. The sun-light was intense, gilding the green of the jungle, deepening the black tints of the shadows, burnishing the river till it shone like a steel shield, and intensifying the dull bronze of the deep pools where they eddied beneath the overhanging masses of clustering vegetation. The shrill thrushes were sending their voices pealing with an infectious gladness through the sweet morning air; the chirp of many birds came from out the heavy foliage of the banks to the ears of the wounded man and seemed to speak to him of the cruel indifference with which Nature witnessed his sufferings. Presently his boat neared a village and the people crowding to the bathing-huts moored to the shore cried to him with listless curiosity asking him what ailed him.

' 'Tis naught, O my brothers,' Ram Singh returned, in a voice as firm and cheerful as his ebbing strength admitted.

But a woman, pointing with a trembling finger, screamed, 'See, there is blood, much blood!' and a child, catching her alarm, lifted up its little voice and wept dismally.

'Let be, let be!' whispered an old man cautiously to his fellows. 'In truth there is much blood, even as Minah yonder hath said; but let us be wise and have naught to do with such things. Perchance, if we but speak to the wounded man, hereafter men will say that we had a hand in the wounding. Therefore suffer him to drift; and for us, let us live in peace.'

So Ram Singh was suffered to continue his journey down the stream undisturbed by prying eye or helping hand. The sun rose higher and higher, each moment adding somewhat to the intensity of the heat. By nine o'clock, when but half the weary pilgrimage was done, the waters of the river, struck by the fierce slanting rays, shone with all the pitiless brilliancy of a burning-glass. The colour of all things seemed suddenly to have become merged in one blazing white tint, an aching, dazzling glare, blinding the eye and scorching the skin. The river caught the heat and hurled it back to the cloudless sky; the sound of bird and insect died down, cowed by the terrors of the approaching noon-tide; the winds sank to rest; the heat-haze, lean and hungry as a demon of ancient myth, leaped up and danced horribly, with restless, noiseless feet, above yellow sand-spits and heavy banks of jungle; and all the tortured land seemed to be simmering audibly. An open dugout, even when propelled by strong men at the paddles so that the pace of the rush through the still, hot air makes some little coolness, is under a Malayan sun more like St. Lawrence's gridiron than a means of locomotion; but when it is suffered to drift down the stream at such a rate of speed only as the lazy current may elect to travel, it quickly becomes one of the worst instruments of torture known to man. In the Malay Peninsula men have frequently died in a few hours from exposure to the sun, and this form of lingering death, which is ever ready to a *raja's* hand should he desire to inflict it, is perhaps more dreaded than any other. Ram Singh bore all this, and in comparison the pain of his seven-and-twenty wounds seemed to sink almost into insignificance. The blood with which he was covered caked in hard black clots; his stiffening wounds ached maddeningly; the clouds of flies swarmed about him, adding yet one more horror to all that he had to endure; but never for a moment did this brave man forego his purpose of keeping his secret for Imam Prang himself, and though the fever surged through his blood and almost obscured his brain, he held steadfastly to the plan which he had formed.

Shortly after noon a sudden collision with some unseen object jarred the Sikh cruelly, and wrung a moan from his lips. A brown hand seized the gunwale of the dugout, and a moment later a beardless, brown face, seamed with many wrinkles, looked down into the boat. The dull, unfeeling eyes wore that bovine expression which is ever to be seen in the countenances of those Malay peasants who can remember the evil days when they and their fellows were as harried beasts of burden beneath the cruel yoke of their chiefs.

'What ails thee, brother?' asked the face, still without any signs of curiosity.

'I have been set upon by Chinese gang robbers,' whispered

Ram Singh, lying bravely in spite of his ebbing strength. 'Help me to reach the Imam Prang at Pulau Tawar that I may make to him *rapport*.'

The instinct of the Malay villager of the old school is always to obey an order, no matter from whose lips it may come. In many places in the Peninsula you may nowadays see some youngster, who has gotten some book-learning and what he represents as a thorough insight into the incomprehensible ways of the white men, ruling the elders of his village with a despotism that is almost Russian; and the sad-eyed old men run to do his bidding with feet that step unsteadily through the weight of the years they carry, nor dream of questioning his right to command. It is the instinct of the peasantry of this race, as it is wont to be, dying hard in the face of modern innovations.

The man who had hailed Ram Singh did not even think of disputing the Sikh's order, and in a little while the dugout was racing down stream with the cool rush of air fanning the fevered cheeks of the wounded man most deliciously. An hour or two later Pulau Tawar was reached, and Imam Prang, hearing that a Sikh in trouble wished to have speech with him, came down to the water's edge, and squatted by the side of the dugout.

'What thing has befallen thee, brother?' he asked, aghast at the fearful sight before him. The dugout was a veritable pool of blood, and the great fevered eyes of the stricken man stared out at him from a face blanched to an ashen grey, more awful to look upon by contrast with the straggling fringe of black beard. The pale lips opened and shut, like the mouth of a newly landed fish, but no sound came from them; the great weary eyes seemed to be speaking volubly, but alas! it was in a language to which the Chief could find no key. Was the supreme effort which the stricken Sikh had so nobly made to be wasted? For a moment it seemed as though the irony of Fate would have it so; and Ram Singh, deep down in his heart, prayed to Guru Nanuk to give him the strength he lacked, that his deed might be suffered to bear fruit. Mightily, with the last remnants of his failing forces, the Sikh fought for speech. He gasped and struggled in a manner fearful to see, till at last the words came, and who shall say at what a cost of bitter agony?

'Dato . . . the . . . rebels . . . ' came the faltering whisper. 'The rebels . . . Kuala . . . Tĕmbĕling . . . fallen . . . taken . . . many killed . . . make ready . . . against their . . . coming . . . and behold . . . I have brought the word . . . and I die . . . I die. . . .'

His utterance was choked by a great flow of blood from his mouth, and without a struggle Ram Singh fainted away and lay as one dead.

Imam Prang was a man of action, and he had his people collected and his stockades in a thorough state of defence long before the afternoon began to wane. While Imam Prang was busily engaged in profiting by the warning thus timely brought to him, Ram Singh was tended with gentle hands and soothed with kind words of pity by the women-folk of the Chief's household. He was a swine-eating infidel, it was true, but he had saved them, and all that they held dear, from death, or from the capture which is worse than death.

So the rebels were repulsed, and were chased back to the land from whence they had come, and up and down that land, and across and across it, till many had been slain and the rest made prisoners, and at last Pahang might once more sleep in peace. And Ram Singh, who had saved the situation, was sent to hospital in Singapore, where he was visited by the Governor of the colony, who came thither in his great carriage to do honour to the simple Sikh private; and when at last he was discharged from the native ward healed of his wounds, a light post in the Pahang Police Office was found for him, where he will serve until such time as death may come to him in very truth. If you chance to meet him, he will be much flattered should you allow him to divest himself of his tunic; and you will then see a network of scars on his brown skin, which will remind you of a raised map designed to display the mountain-system of Switzerland. He is inordinately proud of them, and rightly so, say I, for which man among us can show such undoubted proofs of courage, endurance, and self-sacrifice as this obscure hero?

From *A Corner of Asia*, London, 1899.

WAN BEH, PRINCESS OF THE BLOOD

I WAS on tour. My great house-boat lolled down the long reaches of the Pahang River through the eternal forest, past the scattered villages which here and there were nicked out of the vast expanse of jungle or sat perched high and dry upon the banks of the stream. Twenty indolent Malays squatted under the palm-leaf shelter forward, and dipped their dripping paddles listlessly into the water. They chewed betel-nut, smoked cigarettes, and gossiped and laughed, all with a complete absence of hurry. Before us the white stretch of river lay extended, dazzling our eyes; on either hand near the bank the waters were stained a sombre green, upon which the reflections of the forest showed clear and shiny, as a new canvas; a marvel of vegetation shut us in on either hand, and above it on our left the distant mountains were visible as a faint blue line, hardly to be distinguished from the clouds hovering around them on the white-hot horizon.

Presently, as we neared a village, three dugouts pushed off from the bank and were paddled towards us; then there was a sound of wood striking and grating against wood, the clash of oars thrown aside, and a party of some twenty Malays trooped on board. They stepped gravely among the rowers, apologising courteously for their rudeness in thus passing sitting men, and squatted silently in the doorway of the cabin, a shapeless heap of brown faces and limbs set in a kaleidoscopic blending of gay silks and cottons. In answer to my conventional greeting they replied stolidly that the news of the village was good, but the faces of the headmen were set like the day of judgment, and the whole group was big with strange tidings and quivering with excitement.

'What ails you?' I said.

The senior headman opened his mouth to speak, but his junior dug him sharply in the ribs with his elbow, and the elder man was silent, though his lips, stained scarlet with arecanut, remained parted presenting me with an elaborate view of his tongue and his gums, with a few blackened stumps of tooth pricking up oddly here and there.

'Thy servant, this headman, is a fool,' said the younger Chief simply; 'wherefore I have become unto him a mouth. He hath neither manners nor language, nor is he skilled in speaking to white folk.'

The old man shut his mouth dejectedly, acquiescing in this pitiless verdict without a murmur or a wince. The facts stated had been dinned into his ears so frequently that he now accepted them as true with a faith which was unquestioning. Moreover, he was not without pride in the eloquence of his younger brother, and was conscious of a certain glow of reflected glory. The younger headman, looking up at me from where he was seated upon the ground, settled himself into an attitude of intense respect, and plunged forthwith into his story.

'It is not right, *Tuan*, that any person should put upon this village a shame which may not easily be covered. It is not fitting that soot should be smeared upon our faces—soot that may not be washed away. The men of old say in the words which they have bequeathed to us, "Let sparrows mate with sparrows, and the great hornbills with their own kind." Is it not so, *Tuan*?'

I grunted an assent.

'Now when the hornbills begin to mate with the sparrows, is it not fitting that we should come hither to thee, weeping and wailing, in order that our so heavy responsibility in this matter should be discharged?'

I grunted once more.

'That, then, *Tuan*, is the matter of our complaint. Is it not so?' he added, turning towards the assembled villagers.

The old headman, beaming with satisfaction at the clearness of this exposition of the case, said, 'Verily, it is so,' with immense solemnity, and the men behind him made use of similar ejaculations. The boat still slid placidly down the river, bearing the villagers farther and farther from their home. As it seemed probable that the interview would be long protracted, I called to my men to let go the anchor in midstream, and as we swung round with the current I turned once more to the villagers, and inquired, 'And what have I to do with the mating of all these bird-folk?'

The younger headman caught a twinkle in my eye, and nudging his fellows, he said smilingly, 'It is our *Tuan*; of a certainty he understandeth,' and then relapsed into silence.

'Speak on,' I said rather wearily. 'Tell me the names of the folk who have done this thing.'

'It is Wan Beh and thy servant Panglima.'

I whistled.

'Yes, it is they,' continued the younger headman; 'and we who are of his kith are filled with fear, for the matter, if it reacheth his ears, will greatly anger Underneath-the-Foot.'

'Relate the matter from the beginning,' I said.

'It is in this wise, *Tuan*. Wan Beh, who is a woman of the blood royal, as thou knowest, *Tuan*, hath been smitten with the madness because of thy servant the Panglima. He being one of the many people (*i.e.*, a commoner) cannot wed with her, and indeed he too is sore afraid, thinking by day and by night of the wrath of Underneath-the-Foot. But, *Tuan*, what can a man do when a woman is set upon winning him for her own? Moreover, Wan Beh is devoid of shame. She knoweth that she may not wed with him, and therefore she careth nothing for the eyes of folk, and pursueth him by day and by night, and hearkens not at all to the advice of the elders of her village.'

'I am her brother, *Tuan*,' said a large-limbed man who was seated in the background. 'I am her brother, the son of the same father and the same mother, and I have beaten her, and that not sparingly, no, nor once only; but she does not care for me or for my blows. She is a woman with a very hard liver.' He spoke grimly, glowering over the shoulders of the headman, and I was sorry for the erring Wan Beh. Her brother did not look a pleasant fellow to be beaten by. 'Also, *Tuan*, I am fearful lest by any chance my hand should break loose and, striking unwarily, should kill her, for my hand is apt to go far, and, moreover, is a heavy hand. Once long ago I did but slap a slave, and all the days of his life he hath gone halting.'

'Is the woman at hand?' I asked.

'Yes, *Tuan*,' said the younger headman. 'She is even now in the village; for yesternight she entered forcibly into the house of the Panglima and beat the woman his wife, so that her face bled, and thereafter she tore to shreds all the clothes of the said woman, and did not even spare her sleeping-mat, or the coverlet which she is wont to use at night-time. Then, when the woman ran screaming from the house, Wan Beh made fast the door, nor did she release the Panglima until the dawn had come. Verily this thing is a thing accursed!'

I sent for the woman, and after an hour's wait she came off to my boat in a dug-out, sitting very demurely in the stern, the Panglima following shamefacedly enough in a second canoe. His wife, much tattered and ruffled, brought up the rear, under the escort of several very angry brothers.

Though the accessories of the affair were sufficiently ridiculous, the difficulty which had arisen was in itself both troublesome and important. The Malays are among the most aristocratic of peoples, and the law which forbids the marriage of a woman of the royal stock to a commoner is by no means to be evaded. A young *raja* may marry any girl whom his fancy may select, and his children by her all inherit the rank of their father; but a woman of the blood, no matter how remote her connection with the ruling house, can wed only with one of her own clan, or with a *saiyid*, a descendant of the Prophet Muhammad. In the capital, and in the down-country districts generally this is no great hardship; for not only are *rajas* numerous, but they are mostly well to do, and so can afford to support more than one wife. In the interior, however, this law brings sadness to many lives. I have known cases of women whose rank forbade matrimony with the peasants, and who yet were so utterly alone in the world that they were forced to labour unremittingly to keep the rice-bin stocked and their backs covered with patched garments. Had they been commoners they would not have lacked men to marry and work for them, but since they were royal they had to choose between the existence of the wanton or of the drudge; and the former, in old days, usually meant that their crimes against the family pride were punished sooner or later by a violent death. These are the sort of strange anomalies which we find besetting life in Asia, and so long as a land has newly come under our control we cannot attempt to remedy an evil which has its root in the most cherished traditions and keenest feelings of the people we are called to rule. The Sultan—the 'Underneath-the-Foot' of

WAN BEH, PRINCESS OF THE BLOOD

whom the people spoke—as the head of the royal family, would regard conduct such as that of Wan Beh as a direct insult to himself and to his House. He would, I knew, consider himself most villainously ill-treated were no action to be taken to put a stop to the intrigue. He would deem the Panglima worthy of death, and would only be restrained from demanding the infliction of the extreme penalty by a knowledge of the, from his point of view, lop-sided ideas concerning justice which notoriously prevail among white folk. And yet what could I do? The law against which Wan Beh and the Panglima had sinned was to be found in no written code; it had its place only in the hearts and the traditions of the people. I could enforce nothing. If I gave an order, the parties concerned might refuse to obey it, and I should be powerless to punish them. The position was one such as no man concerned in ruling a wild people can pretend to regard with complacency; but it was necessary that I should risk a fiasco, since it would be impossible to deal with the Sultan were I to give him a cause of complaint, which he would feel to be so well founded, against the Government whose representative I was. I thought of all these things as the two women and the Panglima stepped on board the boat and passed into the cabin.

Wan Beh was a very pretty girl. Her face was a delicate oval, her hair black and abundant, her skin a light brown, clear and transparent. Her nose was slightly tip-tilted, her mouth was soft and pouting like that of a saucy child, and her magnificent dark eyes were filled to the brim with impudence. She came into my cabin, stepping lightly and gracefully, nodded to me familiarly as to an old acquaintance whose presence was somewhat of a joke, and seated herself composedly upon the bunk opposite to that upon which I was squatting. The Panglima and his injured wife, eyeing one another askance, crouched down upon the floor among the other villagers. In Asia the ruling classes are frequently good-looking. For countless generations the men have wedded with the most beautiful women in their districts, so the hereditary leaning towards comeliness is strong. Malays of royal stock have also a great deal of pride of race, and the women especially are wont to bear themselves with an insolence toward the rest of the world which is at once baffling and amusing. I looked at Wan Beh, and inwardly I laughed; for I knew that, so far as in her lay, this young lady would give me as bad a quarter of an hour as she could manage, and the encounter promised to be entertaining. Native women soon learn that white men are likely to treat them with greater courtesy than they are used to receive from their own male folk, and I regret to say that they generally take the fullest advantage of this fact.

'Well, Wan Beh,' I said, turning towards that lady, 'what is the meaning of this thing which men tell me concerning thee?'

The girl looked at me with her little head on one side. 'I have not inquired,' she said sweetly. In imagination I could hear the British matron ejaculating 'Hussy!' and I wished that I could boast her strength of mind, and her complete case-armour against feminine wiles.

'Wilt thou promise me that thou wilt return up river to thy brother's village, and live there peaceably with him, bringing no further shame upon thy people?'

'I will not!' said the girl laconically.

'Undoubtedly her liver is very hard—very hard indeed,' murmured her brother despairingly from the background.

'It matters not at all,' said I cheerfully. 'If thou wilt not do that which I require of thee, I shall be in no way inconvenienced. I shall bear thee down river with me in this big boat, thy brother yonder coming with me, and I will hand thee over to Underneath-the-Foot. Thou art of his blood, and if thou wilt not guard his honour, he, doubtless, will find means to ward it securely when thou art given over to his keeping.'

The girl looked at me with her eyes blazing. Her forehead was knitted into little hard puckers of wrath, and her hands clenched and unclenched convulsively. If her wish could have slain me I should have been as dead as a door-nail. The royal enclosure at the capital, where ladies are carefully watched and guarded, had few attractions for a Malay woman.

'I will *not* go,' cried the girl.

'One or the other,' I said quietly. 'Choose which of the two courses best pleaseth thee. I care nothing, one way or the other. I cannot suffer this shame to be put upon Underneath-the-Foot, and if thou wilt not return up stream with thy brother, thou shalt come down river with him and with me.'

'I will *not*,' cried the girl again. 'It is easy for thee to sit there giving orders, but I will not obey them. I want to live as I like, to go whithersoever I will, to dwell with whomsoever I may select, and no man shall stay me—no man, no man, no man!' And she stamped her shapely foot against the deck of the boat.

'It is well,' I said, though I felt myself to be both a bully and a brute. 'Heave up the anchor, and let us go down river. Too much time has been wasted already over this insignificant matter. Heave the anchor up there! And ye,' turning to the villagers, 'have my leave to depart.'

'Patience, *Tuan*, patience!' cried the girl, now thoroughly cowed. 'Try to have pity upon me. Behold, he is very dear to me. Suffer me to stay with him,' and her eyes were dewy with tears. The impudence had vanished completely from her face.

'What can I do?' I said. 'Thou knowest the law; I can in no wise aid thee. In truth I feel pity for thee, but thy birth will not suffer thee to wed with the Panglima, and therefore. . . .'

'I have no desire to wed with him,' cried Wan Beh, interrupting me. 'He is one of the "many-people", while I am a daughter of the *rajas*. But the madness hath come upon me, and I want him for my own. Give him to me, *Tuan*! Give him to me!' and she held out her arms to me entreatingly. She was so like a little, naughty, wheedling child, pleading for some trifle which she desired, that again I felt a brute for being so hard upon her; but the thought of the inexorable British Matron, and what she would think of such a request, nerved me anew, and eventually the weeping girl was put into a boat, under the charge of her brother and a handful of his dependents, and began the weary journey up stream, leaving the man she loved behind her.

Then I turned upon the Panglima, and poured out the vials of my wrath upon him. I was thoroughly out of temper at having had to treat so pretty a girl so harshly, and, manlike, I could not but think that the male lover was the more to blame. But the Panglima was quite frank and straightforward. He said that a great weight was lifted from off his mind by the removal of Wan Beh; that he in no way returned her love for him; that her attentions, more especially when accompanied by violence and the destruction of much valuable gear, had terrified him into a state of mind bordering upon frenzy, and that he too had beaten her without producing any tangible result. The sense of the villagers was certainly with him in the matter, and their attitude towards him one of the deepest sympathy in his affliction. They knew, and I was obliged to recognise, that the man was speaking nothing but the truth when he complained of the persecution to which he had been subjected, and expressed himself infinitely relieved at the turn which events had taken. The flaccid-looking little woman, the Panglima's wife, was evidently regarded as both more beautiful and more desirable by all the assembled Malays than the spirited young creature who had just left us in such bitter tears.

All this took place at the point where the Těmběling River joins the Jělai, the combined streams forming the Pahang, and Wan Beh's home lay five days' journey up the valley of the former stream. Around the compound, which contained her brother's house, the forest shut down inexorably; behind it, in an irregular horse-shoe, the mountains, in which the Těmběling River has its source, rose in a blue barrier, dividing the State of Pahang from its neighbours, Trěngganu and Kělantan. Past the gate of the compound the shallow waters of the stream bustled along, squabbling with the shingle of their bed, hurrying ever towards the village in which the Panglima lived secure at last from the persecutions of the poor little princess.

The girl used to sit by that river for hours at a time—her knees drawn up to her chin, her hands clasped about them, the flickering light and shadow cast by the fruit-trees behind her dappling the bright silks of her garments. Her eyes would be fixed dreamily upon the stream that flowed so ceaselessly; her forehead would be puckered with thought; her mind dwelling always upon the man who cared nothing for her, yet to her was all her world. Her people sought to arrange a second marriage for her—she had some years before been wedded to a young *raja* of the district, from whom she had been divorced after a distinctly lively twelve-month—but the girl would not listen to any such proposal. Her heart was still set upon the Panglima; walking and sleeping, her sole desire was to be with him again; if she might not win him for her own, she at least would wed with no other man. She envied the running water that sped so gaily in his direction; the folk who passed down stream on business to the village in which he dwelt; even the drifting twigs and leaves, borne along by the current, setting toward the river's mouth. Time had no power to comfort her. After months of captivity in her brother's house her memory dwelt upon nothing save that night when she had put shame away, had routed the Panglima's wife, and had made one great effort to win him for herself. She was resolutely idle, hoping thereby to induce her brother to let her go away; she was determinedly ill-tempered, as is the way of folk who are crossed in love; but her people bore all with equanimity. Their one object was to preserve their House from shame, and to avoid incurring the wrath of their powerful relative the Sultan. If these ends could be achieved they cared little what they might be called upon to endure at the hands of a girl.

Time passed away, and presently rumours began to reach the distant up-country village of trouble in the lower country. One of those obscure little wars, which in those days were for ever being fought in some corner or another of England's dominions in Asia had broken out in Pahang between the Government and one of the great territorial Chiefs, and rumour magnified the weary business into a campaign of the most magnificent description. All sorts of vague reports came to Wan Beh and to her people, and presently the news was brought that the Panglima had sided with the Government, and had been given the command of a party of friendly Malay warriors. From this moment Wan Beh's interest in the struggle was intense. She sat as of old on the bank of the river, dreaming. But when a dug-out from the lower country came round the bend below the compound she ran to the water's edge and screamed enquiries as to all that had befallen, trembling with fear lest she should hear that the Panglima was dead or wounded.

At last one day, as she sat in her accustomed place a small fleet of boats hove in sight. The craft were manned by a curious rabble of men, women, and little children; their scanty garments torn and travel-stained; their hair long, shaggy, and unkempt; their faces strained, with eyes wild with the look which comes to those who have long gone in fear of their lives at the hands of relentless pursuers. They had with them a quantity of useless gear—bundles of soiled clothes, sodden with the damp of the jungles; women's sewing-boxes, that no longer contained anything that was useful; cooking-pots which had seen better days; pillows shapeless, soggy and filthy; rolls of rotting palm-leaf mats; and other wrecks of households which had been hurriedly broken up. The only articles that were clean and well kept were the weapons of the men—the long Snider rifles, the daggers, and the spears. Wan Beh thought that she had never before seen so miserable a crowd. Some of the men were in fair condition, though their bodies were lean and spare, but many of the women and the children showed terrible signs of famine and disease. The naked ribs of the little ones stood out like the lathes upon a crate, their stomachs were horribly distended, their limbs shrunken to mere sticks of bone with ugly bosses at the joints. Hardships, exposure in the jungle, and scanty and unwholesome food had evidently worked their will upon them all. Wan Beh needed no man to tell her that these were the rebels flying before the wrath of the white men, and her heart was glad that her lover had not espoused the losing cause, although she still cherished a fierce hatred of the Europeans, which had its root in the fact that I had ordered her removal from the neighbourhood of the Panglima.

The boats drew up at the bank near the village, and several

of the Chiefs landed and strode up to the house of Wan Da, the brother who had Wan Beh in his charge. Here they loudly demanded food, and Wan Da, who found himself in a very uncomfortable position, called all his women-folk about him and bade them prepare a meal. Obediently the women set to work to cook rice and curry, but Wan Beh pushed past the curtain which shrouded the entrance to the female apartments, and cried truculently that she would not aid in doing aught for the rebels.

'My lover is your enemy,' she cried brazenly. 'He hath fought against you these many months, putting you to flight, routing you with great valour, and he did not so act that I, a Daughter of the Blood, should serve you as a menial.'

Then she spat viciously into the centre of the circle in which the Chiefs were seated and turned back into the dim interior of the house. Wan Da looked after her, and then cast a frightened glance around him at the assembled rebels. He threw his arms above his head, and suffered them to drop back limply into his lap. It was a gesture of utter despair, as of one whose patience has been sorely tried, and now found himself unable to cope with the difficulties encompassing him. Also he moaned aloud.

To' Gajah, the principal Chief among the rebels, rapped out an ugly phrase, calling Wan Beh a foul name. Then he turned to Wan Da.

'Art thou also one of these infidels?' he asked threateningly.

'May Allah remove such a thing far from me!' cried Wan Da eagerly. 'I have no part or lot with the infidels, but this sister of mine hath been glamoured by the Panglima, who is thine enemy, as he is mine also, seeing that he hath smudged soot upon the face of our folk, and even upon the countenance of Underneath-the-Foot!'

'It is well,' said To' Gajah. 'Now suffer us to eat our fill.'

The meal was soon ready and was devoured ravenously by these famine-stricken folk, with hideous sounds of sibilant guzzling. Then the rebels returned to their boats and started once more upstream. They were bound for Kĕlantan, a neighbouring independent State, where they would be safe from pursuit.

As soon as they had rounded the point, Wan Da, who was anxious to save his own skin by displaying an overflowing loyalty to the white men, sent a boat down river with four of his youths in it to bear the news to the pursuers that the rebels had made good their escape. Before doing so, however, he hung up an old pair of trousers to the branch of a tree, and fired a bullet through one leg.

'Show this to the *Tuan*,' he said to one of his men, 'and make known to them that we in our loyalty did resist the rebels even to the burning of much powder, that we bathed us in the smoke and in the bullets, Jusop yonder narrowly escaping death, since a ball passed through his trousers and, but for the luck which ever attends those who befriend the white men, had surely died from a wound. This say, that great credit and honour may be ours.' The men grinned and nodded and started upon their way.

But as ill-luck would have it, that night the Panglima came forward with a party of scouts hot-foot on the rebel track, and since he knew that much may be learned from a loving woman, he went very cautiously to Wan Da's house and aroused Wan Beh while all the rest were sleeping.

Very quietly the girl stole out of the house, and threw herself into her lover's arms, and when their first greetings were over she told the Panglima all that had passed during the preceding day. This is how it came about that, though the rebels won clear of the country and so found shelter from pursuit, Wan Da fell upon troublous times, and was too engrossed in his own affairs to be able to guard his sister with his accustomed rigour. The land was in so distracted a condition after the disturbances that no one had time to protest against the action of Wan Beh and the Panglima, and for a space the girl was happy.

A year later the Panglima was called by some private business into the district which lies at the head-waters of the Těmběling, and within a mile or two of the Kělantan boundary. Wan Beh accompanied him as far as her own village, and thence he journeyed forward alone.

Wan Beh, for the sake of old memories, sat daily at the spot upon the river's brink which had been her favourite nook during the months of her captivity, looking dreamily at the hurrying waters, and thinking ever of her lover and of the months which they had passed together. Her thoughts ran riot, now pondering on the time that was past, now peeping forward into the future, picturing happiness yet to come. The white folk were revolutionising the land, and was it not possible, she asked herself, that they might destroy the barrier that still prevented her from wedding with her lover, together with the other old landmarks and customs which they were breaking down? She hoped so now with all her heart, for she was expecting shortly to become a mother, and she longed to remove from the little life, which was already dear to her, the stain of shame. So she sat staring at the water and weaving happy dreams.

One morning some four days after the departure of the Panglima she was seated thus, when suddenly from round the bend up-stream a flotilla of rafts and dugouts came into view. It seemed to Wan Beh that she was living through once more an incident in her past life. The scene was the same as before, the same travel-stained warriors, the same bright weapons, dingy faded garments, the same air of dirt and mouldiness which comes from long living in dank jungles, the same eager eyes and lean haggard faces, but, this time, there were no women or children with the mob of warriors. The boats came from the opposite direction, and this, when compared with her recollection of them, made them seem to the girl like things reversed, as though seen in a mirror. It had all happened before, only differently, but now, she knew, the war-party was raiding, not beating an ignominious retreat.

The raiders were in a hurry, and they pressed on without halting at Wan Beh's compound, leaving her quivering with excitement. All the dreaminess had faded from her eyes, her head was erect, her nostrils dilated, her little hands clenching and unclenching convulsively, as was her habit in moments of intense emotion. The rebels who were the sworn enemies of her lover were once more upon the war-path, and if they caught the Panglima, her knowledge of their ferocity told her that his shrift would be a short one. Before the swish of the paddle-blades had ceased to sound in her ears Wan Beh had leaped into a canoe and was poling herself up-river for her life. She stood in the stern of the little dugout, the bow pricking up clear of the water, and she punted swiftly with long sweeping pushes. The current was strong, and the exertion soon caused her limbs to ache maddeningly; but she kept on, a wild fear in her heart, and her determination to save her lover deadening all other sensations mental and physical.

All that day she poled her boat through the blaze of the sun-glare, past the few scattered villages which line the banks in this part of the country, through lowering depths of forest, melancholy, impenetrable and mysterious; now halting to tug her little dugout laboriously up a rapid, now forcing it over shingles where the water worried down the shallow places noisy with anger, now gliding swiftly forward up the long smooth reaches. The sun stood in the centre of the sky beating down pitilessly on the girl's bare head, then lounged adown the slope toward the west, throwing more slanting rays, and finally dipped behind the bank of forest, to die in an inglorious twilight. Then came the darkness with the winking stars and a faint crescent moon, but still the girl punted onward bravely in spite of failing strength and flagging limbs. At midnight she at last reached her destination, a village lying up the Těmběling above the point whence the rebels had entered the valley, and she stumbled up the bank through the darkness to the house in which her lover was sleeping. In a few words she told him all, saying little enough concerning her own efforts on his behalf, and he listened calmly, chewing a quid of betel-nut with the placidity of a ruminating bull. When she had ended her recital he said no word of thanks, for that is not the custom among his people; but he at once set to work arranging his gear for a journey, and bade the two boys who were with him make ready for an immediate start. Wan Beh retired into the background, which in a Malay house is devoted to the use of the women-folk, and fell to upon a vast plate of rice, but when her lover rose to leave the house she also got up and followed him.

'Whither goest thou?' he asked.

'With thee, sweetheart,' she said simply.

'Thou can'st not,' said he shortly. 'I am going down river to pass by stealth through the body of the rebel party, for with them between me and the lower country there is surely no safety for me. If fate prove kind I shall win through without mishap, but if an evil fortune pursueth me by chance I may meet with death. On such journeys a woman is of no profit to those who bear her with them. Therefore thou can'st not come.'

Wan Beh was a young lady who, with all her faults, always

knew her own mind. She made no answer, but very deliberately she stepped into the Panglima's big dug-out and seated herself amidships. The Panglima shrugged his shoulders and grunted. Malay-like his energy was not equal to arguing the point further. 'Let her be,' he said to his two followers. 'She hath for ever made trouble for me; it is her custom. What can one do? *Kras hati ta' takut mati*—the hard heart feareth not to die! Let her be.'

So the Panglima, his two men, and Wan Beh started down the river, the Chief taking the steering-paddle, his two youths working vigorously, and the girl, snuggled down upon the bamboo decking sleeping placidly. The beat of the paddles, as they churned the water violently, made a rhythmical splashing, varied by the bump of wood upon wood regular as a heart-beat, as the paddles told loudly against the boat's side. The damp night air, as it fanned the Malays' cheeks was cold and clammy; the myriad noises of the vast forest fell upon their ears in musical cadence. Occasionally an elephant trumpeted very far away. Now and then, in the darkness of the shadows thrown by the jungle-covered banks, some unseen brute, disturbed by the passing of the boat, leaped from its drinking-pool and crashed away through the underwood. Once in a while a village was sighted, the huts showing dim outlines in the darkness, a smouldering fire making a blurred patch of scarlet, a torch in the interior of a house pricking the wattled walls with little points of light.

All night they journeyed, and the yellow dawn found them still labouring doggedly, skimming down stream many miles below the village whence Wan Beh had started on the preceding morning. At about noon they halted to feed, and learned that the rebels had passed down the river some twenty hours earlier. The little band of fugitives were gaining upon their enemy, and might hope to overtake them by nightfall.

The meal was eaten hastily, and the journey was at once continued, the Panglima and his men taking it in turn to sleep, while Wan Beh, who had dozed all night, managed the steering-paddle deftly. At dusk they again halted to eat, this time at a place which is the last village above the great flight of rapids which divides the Těmběling valley in two, and before again pressing forward they snatched a couple of hours' sleep.

When they resumed their journey they abandoned their boat, since they feared to attempt the descent of the rapids on a night so dark, and walking in single file, threaded their way through the heavy jungle which here lines the banks of the river. The insistent roar of the falls was in their ears during the whole of their trudge, mingling with the faint half-heard noises of beast and insect with which the forest vibrates all night long. They carried bamboo torches, which flared furiously, casting grotesque shadows around them, shadows which danced and capered restlessly. Against the bright glare of the flames their figures showed black as silhouettes. It took them nearly three hours to cover the five miles that separated them from the foot of the falls; for though the footpath was well marked, they were spent with the fatigue of their long journey.

At the foot of the falls they appropriated a boat which lay moored close to the village bathing-place, and again set off down stream, using laths of bamboo as improvised paddles.

It was now past ten o-clock at night, and the darkness was complete; but none the less the fugitives proceeded with the greatest caution. They did not know with any certainty where their enemy might have camped, and they expected every moment to find themselves in his midst. All around them was profoundly still. The ticking and the restless murmur of faint sound coming to them from the forest only seemed to emphasise the eerie silence. The Panglima, steering the boat with noiseless caution, was bristling all over like a dog held in leash. One of his followers was shivering with excitement, so that, from time to time, his teeth chattered against one another audibly. The other Malay sat stolidly at his paddle, making no sound, but peering into the darkness with heavy tired eyes. Wan Beh, seated erect in the middle of the boat, wore a smile upon her lips. She came of a fighting race, and the joy of the expected battle was strong upon her; also she knew that her lover was brave, and she longed to see him doing grest deeds in his own and in her defence.

Thus they glided forward upon their way, their nerves strung and tense, their hearts leaping with excitement, their tongues silent; and one by one the hours crawled by. Presently, when the chill winds which herald the dawn began to whisper to the forest, the Panglima shifted his seat in the boat uneasily.

'In the space of the cooking of a rice-pot it will be light,' he said. No one answered, and they paddled on vigorously, but as noiselessly as ever.

Just as the dawn was breaking they passed round a bend of the river, and saw before them the whole of the rebel flotilla lying moored to the banks on either hand. The Panglima caught his breath, and his men looked round to him for orders, but it was Wan Beh who gave the answer.

'Paddle!' she said. 'Paddle in the name of Allah, the Merciful, the Compassionate! We of this boat be men and the children of men; what care we for these swine of the forest? Paddle!'

'Paddle!' echoed the Panglima. In the face of this woman who loved him he dared not suffer his men to put about. So the boat sped forward through the dawn-mists and the slowly growing daylight. Soon a few indistinct figures were seen, huddled to the chin in their *sârongs* and bedcloths, on the river-bank. They gazed sleepily at the boat, as though they hardly perceived its presence; but as the grey dawn gave up to view the faces of its occupants they suddenly became thrilled with excitement. A great shouting arose; more and more figures leaped erect; there was a mighty running to and fro upon the banks on either side of the stream; arms were seized, boats manned hurriedly; and the name of the Panglima was screamed again and again in tones of hatred and menace. The fugitives, silent no longer, propelled their dug-out with feverish energy, whooping and yelling at the top of their voices, and above all the babel of sound arose the shrill treble of Wan Beh.

'Swine of the forest!' she shrieked. 'Swine, accursed swine! Get back to your jungle places lest we pen you in sties, or slit your throats, as is fitting that it should be done with swine. Swine, forest swine!'

An angry roar answered the insult, and a hail of bullets plashed into the water around the boat. Wan Beh seized a rifle and fired without aim. The bullet crashed into the tree-tops, and the recoil of the gun knocked it out of the girl's grip into the water.

'Accursed one!' cried the Panglima. 'Thou wast ever a source of trouble to me. Paddle, ye sons of evil women! Paddle!'

The men dug out the water with their laths of bamboo, and the boat rolled and leaped down stream. In the wake of the fugitives, at a distance of about a quarter of a mile, half-a-dozen canoes were dancing over the face of the waters in hot pursuit. The rowers were using the strong quick strokes which, for some inscrutable reason, the Malays call 'the dove', that kicks a canoe along as nothing else can do. In the first gleams of the early morning sun the wet blades of the paddles flashed like steel as they rose twirled high in air above the men's heads; as their points bit the water, churning it into eddies, the rowers gave vent to short fierce howls which carried far through the stillness; momentarily the pursuers drew closer to their quarry. A man in the bow of the leading dug-out shipped his paddle, snatched up a Snider rifle, and aimed a shot at the Panglima's broad back. The bullet flew wide, and the paddlers, who had stopped to watch the effect of the shot, fell to their work again with renewed energy. The man in the bow reloaded, his fellows steadied the boat for an instant, and once more the report of the rifle clanged out discordantly. Again the bullet missed the Panglima; but it passed very close to him, and a panting sound, half sob, half exclamation, came from Wan Beh. The bullet had struck her in the back of the neck, and she fell forward with her face in the water, her weight over the side capsizing the crank little craft. The dug-out was close to the jungle-smothered bank, and in a twinkling the Panglima and his two followers had swum ashore and had vanished into cover. A Malayan forest is so dense that it is impossible to distinguish the shape even of an elephant through the maze of living vegetation, though the great beast be but a dozen yards away; accordingly the Panglima and his fellows had very little difficulty in baffling their pursuers when once they had entered the jungle. They turned up at one of our camps a few days later, but Wan Beh was not with them.

'Dead, I fancy,' said the Panglima calmly, in reply to my inquiry. 'The wound in her neck had the air of a grievous hurt, though I tarried not to examine it. Also she fell into deep water, and how should one so wounded win to the shore? Of a certainty she is dead, *Tuan*. The hairs of our heads are alike in the blackness of their colour, but the fate of each one of us is a thing separate and distinct. No deed of mine could have saved her, and what did it profit anyone that I should abide with her body and lose mine own life? Moreover, the hour of my death had not yet come. I too am sorry, *Tuan*, but it is better so. She was ever a woman with a very hard liver, and had she lived she had surely worked the undoing of me and mine. Indeed it is better so.'

'I am inclined to agree with your friend the Panglima,' said an Englishman who was sitting by me when the news was brought in. He knew the previous history of the little princess, and took the view of the situation most natural to white folk. 'From all accounts she seems to have been a thoroughly bad lot.'

Those were the epitaphs pronounced over poor Wan Beh by her brown lover and a white critic; but I, who had been studying Malays almost ever since I was breeched, looked upon the whole tragedy of the girl's short life through different eyes. Had this wilful creature belonged to my own race, I should have agreed with the pitiless verdict that brought her in a hussy, and condemned her conduct as incapable of excuse or extenuation; but as she was sprung from a people whose ideas of right and wrong are far less rigidly defined than those which we boast, who have no moral education to guide them, who find in the teachings of their religion little support in the hour of temptation, I could not but see things from the point of view of the girl herself.

Her life had held but a single great passion—her love for the Panglima, who now considered that her death was in some sense a blessing in disguise. She was the daughter of a long line of princes; men who had been accustomed to regard their passions as things given to them solely to be gratified; who had never learned the hard lessons of self-control, self-discipline, self-denial. Wan Beh had inherited the natures of her forebears, their untamed desires, their vices, and their courage; but she had developed on her own account a virtue to which they were strangers—a devoted faithfulness to a single love, which kept her true to the Panglima for years, and led her in the end to risk all things, even death, if so she might serve him and be near him in the hour of danger. It was merely the accident of her rank and of her sex that prevented this poor little girl from dedicating her life to a passion which might well have been pure and holy. Had she been a man of her clan, there would have been no obstacle to marriage with a daughter of the people; had she been a woman of the villagers, not raised above them by the royal blood running in her veins, she might have been the wife of the Panglima for all her days; but Fate, that inscrutable monster upon whose broad shoulders Orientals are accustomed to lay the heaviest of their burdens, had ordered otherwise. Her very superiority in rank to the folk who lived around her, a superiority which consisted chiefly in the title she bore, stood as a bar between her and the happiness which was the birthright of so many of her friends and neighbours. The injustice of such a convention maddened her; the unchained lusts of her ancestors drove her headlong into sin; and yet, since she was a woman of the Malays, unsustained by any tradition of virtue, she took small shame in seizing by means dishonest that which might not be hers lawfully in the face of the customs of her people.

To me the tragedy of this girl's life, which would be a thing paltry and mean in a state of society such as we know, is very pitiful, very pathetic; for what can be sadder than the sight of virtue robbed of its possibilities of development, and driven by the conventions and the snobbery of man into ugly byways of vice? In a land where principle has no existence, where sin is held lightly, where the faltering feet of one who shudders on the brink of dishonour have nothing to aid or steady them, men may well suspend their harsh judgments on those who go grievously astray. Therefore I ask your pity, not your condemnation or your contempt, for Wan Beh, Princess of the Blood. Let him who is without sin amongst us cast the first stone; let us think a little how we should fare were our training and our surroundings such as went to fashion the life of this poor little princess. Then let us leave her, secure in the knowledge that

'The Lord who made her, He knows all.'

From *Bush-whacking and other Asiatic Tales and Memories*,
London, 1929

THE WEEDING OF THE TARES

ONE morning, some fifteen years ago, old Mat Drus, bare to the waist, sat cross-legged in the doorway of his house, in the little sleepy village of Kĕdondong on the banks of the Pahang River. A single long blade of *lalang* grass was bound about his forehead, to save appearances—for all men know that it is unmannerly to go with the head uncovered, and Mat Drus had mislaid his headkerchief. His grizzled hair stood up stiffly above the bright green of the grassblade; his cheeks were furrowed with wrinkles; and his eyes were old, and dull, and patient—the eyes of the driven peasant, the cattle of mankind. His lips red with the stain of the areca-nut, bulged over a damp quid of coarse tobacco, shredded fine and rolled into a ball the size of a marble. His jaws worked mechanically, chewing the betelnut, and his hands were busy with a little brass tube, in which he was crushing up a fresh quid, for his teeth were old and ragged, and had long been powerless to masticate the nut without artificial aid. The fowls clucked and scratched about the litter of trash with which the space before the house was strewn; and a monkey, of the species called *brok*, which the Malays train to pluck cocoa-nuts, sat on a box fixed to the top of an upright pole, searching diligently for fleas, with the restlessness of its kind, and occasionally emitting a plaintive, mournful cry. In the dim interior of the house, the voices of the women could be heard, amid the recurring clack of crockery; and the fresh, pure, light-hearted laugh of a very young girl rippled out constantly, the soft and tender cadence of her tones contrasting pleasantly with the harsher notes of her older companion.

Presently a gaily dressed youngster entered the compound. He carried a *kris* at his belt, and in his hand was a short sword, with a sheath of polished wood.

'O Che' Mat Drus!' cried the new-comer, as soon as he caught sight of the old man in the doorway.

'What thing is it?' asked the latter pausing in the preparation of his quid of betel-nut.

'The Chief sends greetings to thee and bids thee come on the morrow's morn to the rice-field, thee and thine, to aid in plucking the weeds from amid the standing crop.'

'It is well,' said Che' Mat Drus resuming his pounding stolidly.

'Also the Chief sends word that no one of thy household is to remain behind. The women-folk also are to come, even down to the girl Minah, who has newly wedded thy son Daman.'

'If there be no sickness, calamity, or impediment we will come,' said Mat Drus, with the caution of the Oriental.

But here a third voice took part in the conversation—a voice shrill, and harsh, and angry, which ran up the scale to a painful pitch, and broke queerly on the higher notes.

'Hast thou the heart, Kria, to bring this message to my man?' it cried. 'We both are of age, we both know and understand. The Chief shall die by a spear cast from afar, shall die vomiting blood, shall die a violent death, and thou also, thou who art but the hunting dog of the Chief.'

'Peace! Peace!' cried Mat Drus, in a voice betokening an extremity of fear. 'Hold thy peace, woman without shame. And Kria do thou tell the Chief that we will come even as he bids us, and heed not the words of this so childish woman of mine.'

'Indeed,' said Kria, 'I cannot trouble me to bandy words with a hag, but the Chief will be wroth if he learns of the things which thy woman hath spoken.'

'They matter not, the words of a woman who is childish,' said Mat Drus uneasily. 'Speak not of them to the Chief.'

'Then lend me thy spear with the silver hasp at the base of the blade!' said Kria, and when he had obtained possession of this weapon, which he had long coveted, he swaggered off to pass the word to other villagers that the Chief required their aid to weed his rice crop.

The sun stood high in the heavens, its rays beating down pitilessly upon the broad expanse of rice-field. The foot-high spears of *padi* received the heat and refracted it, while the heat-haze danced thin, and restless, and transparent over the flatness of the cultivated land. The weeders, with their *sarongs* wound turban-wise about their heads, for protection against the fierce sun, squatted at their work, men, women, and little children, the perpendicular rays dwarfing their shadows into malformed shapeless patches.

Near the centre of the field a hut had been erected, walled and thatched with palm-leaves, and the interior was gay with many-coloured hangings surrounding the mat and pillows of the Chief. Numerous brass trays containing food specially prepared for the occasion lay upon the flooring. In the interior of the Malay Peninsula, the luxury accessible to even the richest and most powerful natives is of a somewhat primitive order; but to the eyes of the simple villagers, the interior of this hut presented as high a degree of civilisation, as did the *chateau* of a French noble before '89 to the peasant who dwelt on his estate.

About noon the Chief emerged from the hut, and began a tour of inspection among the weeders, throwing a word to one or another, and staring boldly at the women, with the air of a farmer apprizing his stock. Half a dozen fully-armed youths, dressed brilliantly in many-coloured silks, followed at the heels of their master.

Mat Drus and his son Daman, with three or four women, sat weeding near the edge of the jungle, and Minah, the girl who had recently married Daman, edged her way towards her husband, as the Chief drew near.

'What is the news, Mat Drus?' asked the harsh, coarse voice of their Master.

'The news is good, O Chief,' replied Mat Drus, stopping his work, and turning submissively towards the speaker. All the rest of the little party acted in like manner, and the women-folk, squatting humbly with their men, bowed down their heads to avoid the hungry eyes of the Chief.

'Who is this child?' asked the great man, pointing to Minah.

'She is the wife of thy servant's son,' replied Mat Drus.

'Whose daughter is she?'

'She is thy servant's daughter,' said an old and ill-favoured woman, who squatted at Mat Drus's elbow.

'Verily a *salak* fruit!' cried the Chief. 'An ugly tree, thorny and thin art thou, but thou hast borne a pretty luscious fruit.'

The weeders laughed obsequiously.

'How clever are the words of the Chief!' ejaculated Mat Drus, in a voice carefully calculated to reach the ears of the man he feared. The Chief did not even condescend to glance at him.

'Sweet Fruit,' he said addressing Minah. 'Thou art thirsty with thy toil. Come to my hut, and I will give thee luscious sweetmeats to slake thy little parched throat.'

'Don't want to,' mumbled the girl.

'Nay come, I bid thee,' said the Chief.

'Go, girl,' said the mother.

'Don't want to,' repeated Minah, nestling more closely to Daman, as though seeking his protection.

'What meaneth this?' cried the Chief, whose eyes began to wax red. 'Come when I bid thee, thou daughter of an evil mother!'

'She is afraid,' said Mat Drus pleadingly. 'Be not angry, O Chief, she is very young, and her fears are great.'

'May she die a violent death!' yelled the Chief. 'Come! Wait but a moment, and thou shalt be dragged thither!'

'Have patience, O Chief!' said Daman sulkily. 'Let her be. She desires not to go.'

'Arrogant one!' screamed the Chief. 'Thou art indeed a brave man to dare to thwart me. Thou shalt aid to drag her to my hut.'

Daman leaped to his feet. Like the rest of his kindred, he had squatted humbly in the dust during all the talk—a serf in the presence of his lord—but now he stood erect, an equal facing an equal, a man defending his women-folk from one who sought to put shame upon them.

'Peace, Daman! Have patience!' cried Mat Drus nervously, but his son had no thought to spare for any save the Chief just then. His clear, young eyes looked boldly and angrily into the sodden, brutal, bloodshot orbs, set in the coarse self-indulgent face of his enemy, and the Chief faltered and quailed before his gaze. Daman's hand went to his dagger-hilt with a sounding slap, and the Chief reeled hastily backwards, nearly losing his footing, as he stepped blindly. His youths surged up around him, and the coward felt his courage returning to him, when he realised that they were at hand. No word was spoken for a little space, as the enemies eyed one another, and Minah, crouching close to Daman's mother, whimpered softly, though a thrill of love and admiration ran through her, as she marked the bearing of her husband.

Suddenly Kria, who stood somewhat to the right of the Chief, raised his arm in act to throw, and the bright sunlight glinted for a moment on the naked blade of a spear—a spear with a silver hasp, which, until lately, had been the property of Daman's father. Kria's eye sought that of the Chief, and the latter signalled to him to cast his weapon. The long spear-handle, with its shining tip, flew forward with incredible velocity, like a snake in the act of striking, but Daman leaped aside, and the weapon hissed harmlessly past him.

'Strike with the Paralyser!' cried the Chief, and at the word one of his youths ran forward, and stabbed swiftly and shrewdly at Daman with a long uncanny-looking weapon. It was a forked spear with two barbed blades of unequal length, and, after vain attempts to avoid the thrusts of his enemy, Daman at length took the point in his chest. He was now powerless, for the barbed tip could not be withdrawn, and the sharp point of the shorter blade prevented him from running up the spear, and killing his man, as has frequently been done in the Peninsula by one mortally stricken.

The women screamed shrilly, and Minah sought to run to her man's aid, but those about her held her fast, while she shrieked in an agony of horror. The weeders clustered around, murmuring sullenly, but none dared interfere, and above all the tumult sounded the harsh, coarse laugh of the Chief.

'Verily a fish at the end of a fish-spear! Watch him writhe and wriggle!' he cried. 'Do not kill him until we have had our sport with him.'

But Daman, who had never uttered a sound, was not a man to die without a struggle. He soon found that it was impossible for him to wrench the barbed spear from his breast, and seeing this, he threw his *kris* violently in the face of the man

THE WEEDING OF THE TARES 141

who had stabbed him. The snaky blade flew straight as a dart, and the tip ripped open the cheek and eye-lid of Daman's enemy. The latter dropped the end of the spear, which he had hitherto held firmly in both hands, and Daman now strove manfully, in spite of the agony it occasioned him, to wrench the blade free. This was an unexpected turn for affairs to take, and the Chief's laughter stopped suddenly.

'Slay him! Slay him!' he yelled to his men, and, at the word, Kria, who had recovered his weapon, stabbed Daman full in the throat, with the broad spear-blade. The murdered man sank to the ground with a thick, sick cough, and no sooner was he down, than the Chief's youths rushed in to wet their blades in his shuddering flesh.

Minah, wild with fear, threw herself prostrate upon the ground, seeking to shut out the sight with her tightly clasped hands, and, as she lay on the warm earth, the wailing of the women, the rough voices of the men, and the soft *swish* of the steel piercing the now lifeless body of her husband, told her that all was over.

The day waned, darkness shut down over the land, and the moon rose above the broad, still river, pale and passionless, looking calmly down upon a world which, bathed in her rays, seemed unutterably peaceful and serene. But all through that night, and for many days and nights to come, the pitiful wailing of a girl broke the stillness of the silent hours, in the neighbourhood of the Chief's compound. It was only Minah mourning for her dead, and taking more time than her friends thought altogether necessary to become accustomed to her new surroundings, as one of the household of the Chief.

Her new lord was not unnaturally annoyed by her senseless clamour; and beating, he discovered, tended only to increase the nuisance. But crumpled rose-leaves are to be met with in every bed of flowers, and the Chief had, at any rate, the satisfaction of knowing that in future the season of weeding would be a merry time for him, and that all would be conducted seemly and orderly, without any risk of his peace or his pleasure being further disturbed by rude and vulgar brawls.

From *Studies in Brown Humanity*, London, 1898.

THE FATE OF LEH THE STROLLING PLAYER

At Kota Bharu, the Capital of Kĕlantan, the Powers that be are at great pains to preserve a kind of cockeyed limping, knock-kneed Morality, which goes on all fours with their notion of the eternal fitness of things. Yam Tuan Mulut Merah—the Red-Mouthed King—did his best to discourage theft; and with this laudable intention killed during his long reign, sufficient men and women to have repeopled a new country half the size of his own kingdom. Old Nek 'Soh, the Dato' Sri Paduka, who stood by and saw most of the killing done, still openly laments that all the thieves and robbers were not made over to him, instead of being wasted in the shambles. With so large a following, he says, he might have started a new dynasty in the Peninsula, and still have had enough men and women at his disposal to enable him to sell one or two, when occasion required, if ready money was hard to come by. Nek 'Soh is a wise old man, and he probably is sure of his facts, but though his influence with his master, the Red-Mouthed King, was great in most things he never succeeded in persuading him to try the experiment. So the King continued to slay robbers, suspected thieves, and the relations and relatives of convicted or accused persons, while Nek 'Soh mourned over the sinful waste of good material, and the bulk of the population thieved and robbed as persistently and as gaily as ever.

It must be owned that these efforts at reform were not

encouraging in their results, and perhaps this is why, so long as the Red-Mouthed King, with Nek 'Soh at his side, was responsible for the government of the country, no other attempts to improve the morality of the people of Kĕlantan were made by the disheartened rulers.

At length, in the fulness of time, old Mulut Merah died, and his son, and later his grandson, ruled in his stead. Nek 'Soh continued to have a hand in the government of the country, but a younger man than he was now the principal adviser and soon the real ruler of Kĕlantan. This person bore the title of Maha Mĕntri, which means the Great Minister, and since he was young and energetic he plunged hotly into reforms which were destined, as he forecast them, to revolutionise the ways and manners of the good people of Kĕlantan. Quite oblivious of the fact that mutilation and sudden death, to which an added horror was lent by some ingenious contrivances cunningly devised with the amiable object of increasing the intensity of the pain inflicted upon the unfortunate victims, had completely failed to cure the Kĕlantan folk's innate propensity to rob and thieve, Maha Mĕntri conceived the bold idea of forthwith converting an irreligious people into fervent and bigoted Muhammadans. To this end, he insisted upon attendance at the Friday congregational prayers, even to the breaking of the heads of recalcitrant church-goers; he observed, and personally superintended the observance of Fasts; he did his best to prevent the use of silk garments by any save the women-folk, and this, be it remembered, in a country which is famed for its silk fabrics; he put down cock-fighting, bull matches, prize-fights, hunting, and the keeping of dogs—all the sports of the wealthy, in fact; and while he pried into the home of every family in the capital, with the laudable object of ascertaining whether the inmates prayed regularly at each of the Five Hours of Appointed Prayer, he

THE FATE OF LEH THE STROLLING PLAYER 145

dealt an even more severe blow to the bulk of the population by forbidding the performance of the *ma'iong*, or heroic plays, such as are acted throughout the length and breadth of the Peninsula by troupes of strolling players but which are an amusement that is specially dear to the hearts of the good people of Kĕlantan.

These plays are performed inside a small, square paddock, enclosed by a low bamboo railing, but otherwise open on all four sides, so as to give the spectators an unobstructed view of all that goes forward within. A palm-leaf roof protects the players from the sun by day, and from the heavy dews of the tropics by night; and whenever a *ma'iong* shed is erected upon a new site, the Pawang, or Medicine Man, who is also the Actor-Manager of the company, performs certain magic rites with cheap incense, and other unsavoury offerings to the Spirits, reciting many ancient incantations the while to the Demons of Earth and Air, beseeching them to watch over his people, and to guard them from harm. First he calls upon Black Awang, King of the Earth, who is wont to wander in the veins of the ground, and to take his rest at the Portals of the World; next to the Holy Ones, the local demons of the place; and finally to his Grandsire, Pĕtĕra Guru, the Teacher who is from the Beginning, who is incarnate from his birth, the Teacher who dwelleth as a hermit in the recesses of the Moon, and practiseth his magic arts in the Womb of the Sun, the Teacher whose coat is wrought of green beads, whose blood is white, who hath but a single bone, the hairs of whose body stand erect the pores of whose skin are adamant, whose neck is black, whose tongue is fluent, whose spittle is brine! All these he prays to guard his people, and then he cries to them to aid him by opening the gates of Lust and Passion, together with the gates of Desire and Credulity, and the gates of Desire and Longing, the Longing which lasteth from dawn unto dawn, which causeth food to cease to satisfy, which maketh sleep uneasy, which remembering maketh memory unceasing, causeth hearing to hear, seeing to see!

These exhortations to Spirits, which should find no place in the Demonology of any good Muhammadan, were naturally regarded as an Uncleanness and an Abomination by the strait-laced Maha Měntri; and not content with prohibiting the performances of the *ma'iong*, he made life so excessively unattractive to the actors and actresses themselves, that many bands of them trooped over the jungle-clad mountains, which divide Kělantan from Pahang, to roam the country playing for hire at the weddings and feasts of a people who, no matter what other faults they may have, cannot justly be accused of bigotry or fanaticism.

So great joy was brought to the natives of Pahang, and from end to end of the land the throbbing beat of the *ma'iong* drums, the clanging of the gongs, the scrapings of the ungainly Malay fiddles, the demented shrieks and wailings of the *sĕrunai* and the roars of hearty laughter, which greet each one of the clown's jests, made merry discord in the villages. The gates of Lust and Passion, the gates of Desire and Longing—that Longing which lasteth from dawn unto dawn, which causeth food to cease to satisfy, which maketh sleep uneasy—were opened wide that tide, and there were tales of woe brought in from many a village in the long Pahang valley. While the *ma'iong* was a-playing no one had any care for the crops, the women left their babies and their cooking-pots, and the elders of the people were as stage-struck as the boys and maidens. When the strolling actors moved forward upon their way, having squeezed a village dry of its last copper coins, many of the *kampong* folk followed in their train, cadging for their food from the people at each halting-place, enduring many hardships often enough, but seemingly unable

THE FATE OF LEH THE STROLLING PLAYER 147

to tear themselves away from the fascinations of the players and of the actresses. Many lawful wives found themselves deserted by their men, and the husbands and fathers in the villages had to keep a sharp eye upon the doings of their wives and daughters while the *ma'iong* folk were in the neighbourhood; for when once the dead monotony of their lives is broken into by some unusual occurrence, the morality of the Malay villagers, which is generally far better than that of the natives of the Capitals, quickly goes to pieces, like a wrecked ship in the trough of an angry sea.

Of all the Actor-Managers who were then roaming up and down Pahang, none were so successful both with the play-goers and with the women, as Saleh, or Leh, as he was usually called, for Malay energy is rarely equal to the effort necessary for the articulation of the whole of a proper name. In their mouths the dignified Muhammad becomes the plebeian Mat, Sulehman—our old friend Solomon—is reduced to plain Man, and a like evil fate is shared by other high-sounding, sonorous names. This is worth noticing, because it is very typical of the propensity, which the Malay can never resist, to scamp every bit of labour, no matter how light its nature, that falls to his share in this workaday world.

Leh was a man of many accomplishments. He played the fiddle, in most excruciating wise, to the huge delight of all the Malays who heard him; he was genuinely funny, when he had put his hideous red mask, with its dirty sheepskin top, which stood for the hair of his head, over his handsome, clever face, and roars of laughter greeted him at every turn; he had a keen eye for a topical joke, a form of satire much appreciated by his Malay audiences; he had a happy knack of imitating the notes of birds, and the cry of any animal; and above all he was a skilled Rhapsodist, and with that melodious voice of his would sing the wonderful story of Awang Lotong, the

Monkey Prince, which is a bastard, local version of the Ramayana, until the cocks were crowing to a yellow dawn. He travelled with me, on one occasion, for a fortnight, and I had the whole of the Folk-Tale written down, and when completed it covered the best part of sixty folios, yet Leh knew every word of it by rote, and could be turned on at any point, continuing the story every time in precisely the same words. He had learned it from an old man in Kĕlantan, and he was reputed to be the only surviving bard to whom the whole of the tale was known. In due course I sent the manuscript, with a translation, and elaborate notes to a Learned Society, where it was lost with the usual promptitude and despatch.

It was always a marvel to me that Leh escaped having some angry man's knife thrust deftly between his fourth and fifth ribs, for the natives of Pahang are wont to discourage too successful lovers by little attentions of this sort, and Leh was much loved by the women-folk, both high and low, throughout the length and breadth of the land. Perhaps he was as cunning as he was successful, for he certainly lived to return to his own country.

This was rendered possible for all the *ma'iong* people by the sudden death of Maha Mĕntri. This great and good man—the self-appointed Champion of Muhammadanism, the enforcer of Prayer, the orderer of Fasts for the mortification of the erring flesh—like some other zealous people, who in the cause of Religion have contrived to make their neighbours' lives as little worth living as possible, had one little weakness which marred the purity and consistency of his character. This was an irrepressible impulse to break the Seventh Commandment, a strange failing in a man who was so scrupulous that he would not even suffer himself to be photographed when a view of Kota Bharu, in which several hundreds of people figured, was being taken. This is but one of the startling inconsistencies which are to be remarked in the religious Oriental. Until one has become familiar with an Eastern People, it is difficult to realise how far the Letter of the Law may be pushed by a man who, all the while, is daily defying its Spirit.

The good people of Kĕlantan bore with Maha Mĕntri and his little peculiarities for a considerable time, and they might, perhaps, even have suffered him for a longer period, had it not been for the fact that his religious fanaticism, on subjects which did not happen to hit him in a tender place, had the effect of making life a more evil thing than seemed to be altogether necessary. Be this how it may, upon a certain night Maha Mĕntri was shot through the flooring of another man's house by the owner thereof, ably and actively assisted by two other men, who were entirely convinced that there was not sufficient room for them and for Maha Mĕntri upon the surface of one and the same Planet.

Everybody knew who had done the deed and the Raja would dearly have loved to take a life for a life, but the murderers were under the protection of a young prince, with whom, for political reasons, the Raja could not afford to precipitate a quarrel. Therefore he and his advisers professed to wonder very much indeed who could have been so unmannerly as to shoot Maha Mĕntri in three several places; and there the matter ended, in spite of the clamorous protests of the dead man's relatives.

Very soon the news of Maha Mĕntri's death spread through Pahang, word being brought by the trading boats lurching down the Coast, or by the sweating villagers who trudged across the mountains to bring the glad tidings to the exiles from Kĕlantan, to whose return the presence of Maha Mĕntri had hitherto been a very sufficient obstacle.

So the *ma'iong* folk packed their gear, and started back for their own country, and many men and maidens were left lamenting, when the players who had loved them strode away.

Leh went back by sea, with half a dozen broken hearts in his *gendong* (bundle), and soon after his return, he was appointed to the post of Court Minstrel, and Master of the royal Dancing Girls. For the Kĕlantan to which he came back, was a very different place from the land which he had quitted when he started out for Pahang. As soon as the worthy Maha Mĕntri had been laid in his grave, the reaction, which always follows any paroxysm of religiosity, set in in full force, and for a season Kĕlantan was a merry land for a pleasure-lover to make his home in. The Five Hours of Appointed Prayer were suffered to slip by unregarded of the people; no man troubled himself to fast more than his stomach thought fitting; and the music of the *ma'iong* was once more heard in the land.

In this new and joyful Kĕlantan, Leh found himself very much in his element. The old Pillar Dollars, which are the standard currency of the country, came rolling merrily in, and Leh was able to go abroad among his fellows lavishly clad, from the waist downwards, in a profusion of gaily-coloured silk *sarongs* and sashes, such as the souls of the Kĕlantan people love. He wore no coat, of course, for in this State that garment is never used, except by the Nobles on official occasions when strangers chance to be present.

Leh was never a man to keep all his good fortune to himself, and not only a select few of the King's Dancing Girls, but a countless troop of other dames and maidens, who should rightly have been entirely occupied with their lawful lords and masters, came in for a large share of the spoil. Given a well-set-up figure, a handsome face, gay garments, a witty tongue, and a superfluity of ready money, and a far less clever and engaging fellow than Leh, the Strolling Player, might be expected to win the facile heart of any average Malay woman. It was not long before the best-favoured half of the ladies of Kota Bharu—and that means a surprisingly large proportion of the female population of the place—were, to use the Malay phrase, 'mad' for Leh. The natives of the Peninsula recognise that Love, when it wins a fair grip upon a man, is as much a disease of the mind as any other form of insanity; and since it is more common than many manias they speak of the passion as 'madness' *par excellence*. And this was the ailment from which a large number of the ladies of Kota Bharu were now suffering with greater or lesser severity, according to their several temperaments.

This state of things naturally caused a considerable amount of dissatisfaction to the whole of the male community, and the number of the malcontents grew and grew, as the 'madness' spread among the women-folk. The latter began soon to throw off all disguise for they were too numerous for even the most extensive system of wife and daughter beating to effectually cope with the trouble. When they were not occupied in waylaying Leh; in ogling him as he swaggered past their dwellings, cocking a conquering eye through the doorways; the ladies of Kota Bharu were now often engaged in shrill and hard-fought personal encounters one with another. Each woman among them was wildly jealous of all her fellows; mother suspecting daughter and daughter accusing mother of receiving more than her fair share of Leh's generous and widely scattered attentions. Many were the scratches made on nose and countenance, long and thick the tussocks of hair reft from one another by the angry ladies, and the men beholding these impossible goings-on with horror and dismay said among themselves that Leh, the Strolling Player, must die.

He was a good man of his hands, and badly as they felt about him no one saw his way to engaging him in single combat, though enough men and to spare were ready to have a hand in the killing. At last a committee of three angry men was appointed, by general consent, and these lay in wait for Leh, during several successive evenings, in the hopes of finding him returning alone from the *ma'iong* shed.

It was on the third night of their vigil that their chance came. The moon was near the full, and the heavy, hard shadows lay across the ground, under the gently waving palm-fronds, like solid objects. The footpath which leads from the main thoroughfare into the villages around Kota Bharu branches off some twenty yards from the spot where the watchers lay concealed. The Committee of Three sat huddled up, in the blackness cast upon the bare earth by a native house just within the clustering compounds, and the vivid Eastern moonlight gave up the colour of the yellow sun-baked soil, the green of the smooth banana leaves, even the red of the clusters *rambutan* fruits on a neighbouring tree.

Presently the sound of voices, talking and laughing light-heartedly, came to the ears of the listening men, and as the speakers drew nearer, the Committee of Three were able to distinguish Leh's mellow tones. At the parting of the ways Leh turned off by himself along the footpath, the others, with whom he had been walking, keeping still to the main road. Leh took leave of them, with a farewell jest or two which sent the others laughing upon their way, and then he strolled slowly along the footpath, humming the air of Awang Lotong under his breath. The Three, in the shadow of the house, could see the colour of the gaudy cloths wound about Leh's waist, the fantastic peak into which his head-kerchief was twisted, the glint of the polished yellow wood and the gold settings of his dagger-hilt, and the long, broad-bladed spear that he carried in his hand. They watched him draw nearer and yet more near to them, still humming gently, and wearing a half smile upon his face. They suffered him to come abreast of them, to stroll past them, all unsuspicious of evil; but no pity for him was in their hearts, for they had all been injured in a deadly manner by this callous, lighthearted libertine, who now went to the death he knew not of with a smile on his face, and a stave of a song upon his lips.

As soon as Leh had passed them, the Committee of Three stepped noiselessly out of the shadow, and sounding their *sorak*, or war-cry, into which they threw all the pent-up hatred of their victim which for months had been devouring their hearts, plunged their spears into his naked brown back. Leh fell upon his face with a thick choking cough, and a few more vigorous spear-thrusts completed the work which the Committee had been appointed to perform.

They left the body of Leh, the Strolling Player, lying where it had fallen, face downwards in the dust of the footpath, and though the King did all that lay in his power to discover the secret of the identity of the murderers, and though half the women-folk in the Capital seconded his efforts to the utmost, hoping that thereby their lover's death might be avenged, the men who had planned the deed kept their secret well, so no punishment could be meted out to those who had actually brought about the destruction of the Warden of the King's Dancing Girls. But in the eyes of Malay Justice—which is a very weird thing indeed—if you cannot punish the right man, it is better to come down heavily upon the wrong one, than to allow everybody to get off scot free. The house near to which the body of Leh had been found, chanced to be tenanted only by an old crone and her widowed daughter, with her three small children, but none the less, this hut was taken as the centre of a circle of one hundred fathoms radius, and all whose dwellings chanced to lie within its circumference, whether men or women, old or young, whole or bedridden, women great with child, or babes at the breast, were indifferently fined the sum of three dollars each—a large sum for a Malay villager to be called upon to pay, and a delightfully big total, from the King's point of view, when all heads had been counted.

This new system of punishment by fine has several advantages attaching to it. In the first place it enhances the revenue of the King, which is a matter of some moment; and secondly, if you chance to have a quarrel with some one whom you are unable to get even with in any other way, you need only leave a corpse at his front door, which, in a land where life is as cheap as it is in Kĕlantan, is an easy matter to arrange. If the corpse, by any chance, should be that of a man who has done you an injury, you will kill two birds with one stone. Which is economical.

From *Studies in Brown Humanity*, London, 1898.

UMAT

THE *punkah* swings freely for a space; then gradually shortens its stride; hovers for a moment, oscillating gently, in answer to the feeble jerking of the cord; almost stops; and then is suddenly galvanised into a violent series of spasm-like leaps and bounds, each one less vigorous than the last, until once more the flapping canvas fringe is almost still. It is by signs such as these that we know that Umat, the *punkah*-puller, is sleeping the sleep of the just.

If you look behind the screen which cloaks the doorway, you will see him, and, if the afternoon is very warm and still, you may even hear his soft, regular breathing, and the gentle murmur with which his nose is wont to mark the rhythm of his slumber. An old cotton handkerchief is bound about his head, in such a manner that his bristles of hair stand up stiffly, all over his scalp, in a circular enclosure, like the trainers in a garden of young *sirih* vines. On his back he wears an old, old coat of discoloured yellow *khaki*, once the property of a dead policeman. The Government buttons have been taken away from him, by a relentless Police Inspector, and their place is supplied by thorns, cunningly arranged pieces of stick, and one or two wooden studs. The shoulder-straps flap loosely, and their use is a problem on which Umat often ponders, but which he is never able to satisfactorily solve. A cotton *sarong*—not always of the cleanest, I fear—is round Umat's waist, and, falling to his knees, supplies the place of all other lower garments. For Umat is both comfort-loving and economical, and Pahang is now a free country where a man may go clad as he likes, without fear of some ill-thing befalling him. Less than ten years ago, a man who went abroad without his trousers ran a good chance of never returning home again, since Pahang Malays were apt to think that such an one was no lover of war. Among Malays, who are the most personally modest people in the world, it is well known that no man may fight with a whole heart when, at every moment, he runs the risk of exposing his nakedness; and, in days gone by, the natives of Pahang were well pleased to display their prowess in mangling one from whom little resistance could be expected. But, in Kĕlantan, where Umat was born, few men possess trousers, and no one who loves to be comfortable wears them, when he can avoid doing so.

Below his *sarong*, goodly lengths of bare and hairy leg are visible, ending in broad splay feet, with soles that seem shod with horn; for Umat could dance barefoot in a thorn thicket with as much comfort as upon a velvet carpet.

He half sits, half lies, huddled up in a wicker-work armchair, his head canted stiffly over his right shoulder, his eyes tight shut, and his mouth wide open, exposing two rows of blackened tusks, and a fair expanse of gums and tongue stained scarlet with areca-nut. His feet are on the seat of the chair, one doubled snugly under him, with the suppleness of the Oriental, and the other supporting the knee upon which his chin may rest as occasion requires. The pull-cord of the *punkah* is made fast about his right wrist, and his left hand holds it limply, his arms moving forward and backwards mechanically in his sleep. At his feet, humming contentedly to himself, sits a tiny brown boy, dressed chastely in a large cap and a soiled pocket-handkerchief; and thus Umat dreams away many hours of his life. If his sleeping memory takes him back to the days when he followed me upon the war-path, when we went a-fishing on a dirty night, or when the snipe were plentiful, and the bag a big one, the *punkah* dances merrily, and takes a violent part in the action of which he dreams. But, if Umat's mind plays about the tumble-down cottage in my compound, which he calls 'home', and dwells upon his soft-eyed, gentle wife, Sĕlĕma, and upon the children he loves so very dearly, or if his dreams conjure up memories of good meals, and quiet sleepy nights, then in sympathy the *punkah* moves softly, sentimentally, and stops.

'*Tarek*! Pull!' comes a voice from the inner room, and Umat, awakened with a start, bursts into voluble reproaches, addressed to himself in the guttural speech of the Kĕlantan people. Then he falls asleep more soundly than ever.

If you run up the East Coast of the Peninsula, past the smiling shores of Pahang and Trĕngganu, you at last reach the spot where the bulk of the Kĕlantan river-water formerly made its way into the China Sea. The better entrance is now a mile or two farther up the Coast, but the groves of palm-trees show that the people have been less fickle than the river, and that the villages at the old mouth are still tenanted as of yore. It is here that Umat was born and bred, the son of a family of Fisher Folk, countless generations of whom have dwelt at Kuala Kĕlantan ever since the beginning of things.

If you look at Umat's round face, and observe it carefully, you may read therein much that bears upon the history of his people. The prevailing expression is one of profoundly calm patience—not that look of waiting we understand by the term, the patience which, with restless Europeans, presupposes some measure of anticipation, and of the pain of hope long deferred—but the contented endurance of one who is satisfied to be as he is; of one whose lot is unchanging, and whose desires are few. It is a negative expression, without sadness, without pain, or the fever of longing, and yet sufficiently far removed from dulness or stupidity. It speaks of long years during which Umat's forebears have laboured stolidly, have been as driven cattle before prince and chief, and yet, since the curse of knowledge that better things existed had not fallen upon them, have accepted their lot as they found it, unresisting and uncomplaining.

This is what one reads in Umat's face when it is in repose, but when emotion changes it, other things may be seen as clearly. Suddenly, his features break up into a thousand creases, the brown skin puckering in numberless spreading lines, like the surface of a muddy puddle into which a stone has fallen. A laugh like the crowing of a cock, combined with the roaring of a bull, accompanied this phenomenon, and you may then know that Umat's keen sense of humour has been tickled. It does not take much to amuse him, for, like most Malays, he is very light-hearted, and anything which has a trace of fun in it delights him hugely. Almost every Kĕlantan fishing boat that puts to sea carries its *alanalan*, or jester, along with it, for toil is lightened if men be merry, and in days gone by, Umat was the most popular man in his village. A quaint phrase; a happy repartee, not always in the most refined language; the rude mimicry of some personal eccentricity; word or two of rough chaff; or a good story; such things are his stock in trade and, this is why Umat is so well beloved by his fellows.

But he can be grave, too. As my raft whirls down a rapid, a clumsy punt sends it reeling to what looks like certain destruction. Umat's face sets hard. His teeth are clenched, his lips compressed tightly. His bare feet grapple the slippery bamboos with clinging grip, and his twenty-foot punting-pole describes a circle above his head. The point alights, with marvellous rapidity, and unerring aim, upon the only projecting ridge of rock within immediate reach, and all Umat's weight is put into the push, while his imprisoned breath breaks loose in an excited howl. The raft cants violently, and wallows knee-deep, but the danger of instant destruction is averted, and we tear through the fifty yards of foaming, boiling, rock-beset water, which divides us from the rapid's foot, without further mishap. Then, Umat's face relaxes, and his queer laugh resounds, as he chaffs the man, whose clumsiness had nearly been our ruin, with unmerciful disregard for his feelings.

His promptness to see the nature of the emergency, his ready presence of mind, his quick, decisive action, that saves us from a break-up, which, in a boiling, foaming rapid, is no pleasant experience, have little to do with Umat himself. He owes all to his kinsmen, the Fisher Folk, who have been accustomed to risk their lives on the fishing banks, amid the sandy river bars, the rocky headlands, and the treacherous waves of the China Sea, for many unrecorded centuries. Readiness to face a danger, prompt and fearless action, quick apprehension of the best means of escape, are qualities without which the race would long ere this have become extinct, and in Umat these things amount to absolute instincts.

But he can, on occasion, show pluck of quite another kind —the courage which is no mere flash-in-the-pan, born of excitement, and owing its origin to an instinct of self-preservation—that long-enduring fearlessness in the face of a danger, before which a man must sit down and wait. It is no light thing to stare death in the eyes for days or weeks together, to expect it in some cruel, merciless form, and yet to possess one's soul in patience, and to keep a heart in one's body that does not sink and quail. Yet, Umat is capable of this higher form of courage, as you shall presently hear, and though the limitations of his imagination stand him in good stead, and doubtless make the situation easier to him than it can be to the white man, cursed with the restless brain of his kind, yet one must give Umat credit for valour of no mean order. The merriment dies out of his face at such times, for, unlike my friend, Raja Haji Hamid, whose eyes were wont to dance, and whose mouth smiled cheerily when danger was afoot, Umat comes of a class to whom a gamble with death is a hated thing. The look of calm patience is in his eyes, but now he is enduring consciously, and the hard puckers in his forehead show that his nerves are tightly strung, and that there is little gladness in his heart.

But Umat's face is capable of yet another change. When his brown eyes blaze, when his face is full of excitement, and a torrent of hardly articulate words bursts headlong from his lips, you may know that Umat is angry. A tumult of wrathful sound, at the back of the bungalow, where the servants congregate, in the covered way which joins the cook-house to the main building, begins the uproar, and if you fail to interfere, some Chinese heads will infallibly be broken in several places. Knowing this, I run to the spot, and reduce my people to silence. On inquiry, it will prove to be that the cook has accused Umat of adulterating the milk, or the water-coolie, whose business it also is to make lamps smell and smoke, has charged him with purloining the oil. No words can describe Umat's fury, and indignation, if he is indeed guiltless; but he is a bad liar, and, if the charges are true, his manner soon betrays him, and his wrath fails to convince. In a little time, he will produce the bottle of lamp-oil from the folds of his *sarong*, and, laughing sheepishly, will claim that praise should be his portion, since the bottle is only half full. He takes my pungent remarks with exaggerated humility, and, five minutes later, the compound will be ringing with the songs he loves to bellow. It is not possible to be angry with Umat for long. He is so very childlike, and I, in common with many others, love him better than he deserves.

I first met Umat in 1890, when, after a year spent in Europe, I returned to Pahang, and took charge of the interior. I was very lonely. My Malay followers had been scattered to the winds during my absence in England, and I had none but strangers about me. The few European miners scattered about the district were only met with from time to time. The Pahang Malays stood aloof from us, and I found the isolation dreary enough. Pahang had had an ill name on the Coast, any time these last three hundred years, and, until the white men protected the country, few strangers cared to set foot in a land where life was held on such a precarious tenure. But, presently, the whisper spread through the villages of Trĕngganu and Kĕlantan that work found a high price in Pahang under the white men, and a stream of large-limbed Malays, very different in appearance from the slender people of the land, began to pour over the borders. On this stream Umat was borne to me, and, since then, he has never left me, nor will he, probably, till the time comes for one or the other of us to have his toes turned up to the love-grass.

Umat saw that I was lonely, and perhaps he dimly realised that I was an object of pity, for he would creep into my bungalow, and, seating himself upon the floor, would tell me tales of his own people until the night was far advanced. His dialect was strange to me, at that time and the manner in which he elided some of his vowels and most of his consonants puzzled me sorely. I could not understand the system under which *anam* (six) shrank into *ne'*, and *kĕrbau* (buffalo) became *kuba'*; but I let him talk on—for was he not my only companion?—and, in the end, I not only learnt to understand him, but actually to speak his barbarous lingo.

So Umat and I became friends, and life was to me a trifle less dreary because he was at hand. He taught me many things which I did not know, and his simple stories, told with little skill, served to enliven many an hour of crushing, overwhelming solitude.

Then came a period when trouble darkened the land, and I turned to the war-path, which to me was then so strange and unfamiliar, with Umat stamping along at my heels. He never left me all that time, and I had many opportunities of testing the quality of his courage. At last, it became necessary for me to visit a number of almost openly hostile Chiefs who, with their six hundred followers, were camped about half a mile from my stockade. I had only a score of men at my disposal, and they were needed to hold our frail fort, so it became evident to me that I must go alone. I was not altogether sorry to have the opportunity of doing so, for I knew how susceptible to 'bluff' Malays are apt to be, and I was aware that in a somewhat ostentatious display of fearlessness —no matter what my real sensations might be—lay my best hope of safety. Therefore, I armed myself carefully, and prepared to set out, though most of my Malay friends were clamorous in their efforts to dissuade me. As I started, Umat, armed with *kris* and spear, and with a set look of resolve upon his face, followed at my heels.

'It is not necessary for thee to come,' I said. 'If all goes well, there is no need of thee, and, if aught goes amiss, what profits it that two should suffer instead of one?'

Umat grunted, but he did not turn back.

'Return,' I said. 'I have no need of thee.'

I halted as I spoke, but Umat stood firm, and showed no signs of obeying me.

'*Tuan,*' he said, 'for how long a time have I eaten thy rice, when thou wast in prosperity and at ease; is it fitting that I should leave thee now that thou art in trouble? *Tuan*, where thou goest I will go. Where thou leadest I will follow after.'

I said no more, but went upon my way with Umat at my heels. I was more touched than I liked to say, and indeed his courage was of the highest, for he believed himself to be going to certain death, whereas I was backing my own opinion of the character of those with whom I had to deal, and, though the stake was a big one, I was sufficiently conceited to feel confident about the result. During the long interview with the Chiefs, the knowledge that Umat's great, fleshy body was wedged in securely between my enemies and the small of my back, gave me an added confidence, which was worth many points in my favour. We won through, and the hostile Chiefs dispersed their people, and, that night, Umat made darkness hideous by the discordant yellings with which he celebrated the occasion, and gave token of the reaction that followed on the unstringing of his tense nerves.

Later I was promoted, and Umat came with me to the Capital, and since then he has lived in a house in my compound with Sĕlĕma, the Pahang girl, who has made him so gentle and faithful a wife. It was soon after his marriage that his trouble fell upon Umat, and swept much of the sunshine from his life. He contracted a form of ophthalmia, and for a time was blind. Native Medicine Men doctored him, and drew sheafs of needles and bunches of thorns from his eyes, which they declared were the cause of his affliction. These miscellaneous odds and ends used to be brought to me for inspection at breakfast-time, floating, most unappetisingly, in a shallow cup half full of water; and Umat went abroad with eye-sockets stained crimson, or black, according to the fancy of the native physician. The aid of an English doctor was called in, but Umat was too thoroughly a Malay to trust the more simple remedies prescribed to him, and, though his blindness was relieved, and he became able to walk without the aid of a staff, his eyesight could never really be given back to him.

But Umat is sanguine, and, though he has now been blind for years, and each new remedy has proved to be merely one more disappointment, he still believes firmly that in time the light will return to him. Meanwhile, his life holds many emotions. His laugh rings out, and the compound at night-time resounds with the songs he loves to improvise, which have for their theme the marvellous doings of 'Umat the Blind Man whose eyes cannot see'. His patience has come to the rescue, and the sorrow of his blindness is a chastened grief, which he bears with little complaining. He has aged somewhat, for his sightless orbs make his face look graver, heavier, duller than of old, but his heart is as young as ever.

Though his affliction has been a heavy one, other good things have not kept aloof. One day, as I sit writing, Umat comes into the room, and presently the whole house resounds with the news that he expects shortly to become a father. Umat's face dances with delight, and excitement, and pride; but it wears also an uneasy look, which tells of his anxiety for Sĕlĕma, and another new expression which speaks of a fresh-born love for the child whose arrival he prophesies so noisily. When the latter feeling is uppermost, Umat's ugly old face is softened until it looks almost sentimental.

Umat rushes off to the most famous midwife in the place, and presents her with a little brass dish filled with smooth green *sirih* leaves, and sixpence of our money (25 cents) in copper, for such is the retaining fee prescribed by Malay Custom. The recipient of these treasures is thereafter held bound to attend the patient whenever she may be called upon to do so, and when the confinement is over, she can claim other moneys in payment of her services. These latter fees are not ruinously high, according to our standard, two dollars being charged for attending a woman in her first confinement, a dollar or a dollar and a half on the next occasion, and twenty-five, or at the most fifty cents being deemed sufficient for each subsequent event.

When Umat has placed the *sirih* leaves, he has done all he can for Sĕlĕma, and he resigns himself to endure the anxiety of the next few months, with the patience of which he has so much at command. The *pantang bĕr-anak*, or birth taboos, hem a husband in almost as rigidly as they do his wife, and Umat, who is as superstitious as are all Malays of the lower classes, is filled with fear lest he should unwittingly transgress any law, the breath of which might cost Sĕlĕma her life. He no longer shaves his head periodically, as he loves to do, for a naked scalp is very cool and comfortable; he does not even cut his hair, and a thick black shock stands five inches high upon his head, and tumbles raggedly about his neck and ears. Sĕlĕma is his first wife, and never before has she borne children, wherefore no hair of her husband's must be trimmed until her days are accomplished. Umat will not kill the fowls for the cook now, nor even drive a stray dog from the compound with violence, lest he should chance to maim it, for he must shed no blood, and must do no hurt to any living thing during all this time. One day, he is sent on an errand up river, and is absent until the third day. On inquiry, it appears that he passed the night in a friend's house, and on the morrow found that the wife of his host was shortly expecting to become a mother. Therefore, he had to remain at least two nights in the village. Why? Because, if he failed to do so, Sĕlĕma would die. Why would she die? God alone knows, but such is the teaching of the men of old, the wise ones of ancient days. But Umat's chief privation is that he is forbidden to sit in the doorway of his house. To understand what this means to a Malay, you must realise that the seat in the doorway, at the head of the stair-ladder that reaches to the ground, is to him much what the fire-side is to the English peasant. It is here that he sits, and looks out patiently at life, as the European gazes into the heart of the fire. It is here that his neighbours come to gossip with him, and it is in the doorway of his own or his friend's house, that the echo of the world is borne to his ears. But, while Sĕlĕma is ill, Umat may not block the doorway, or dreadful consequences will ensue, and though he appreciates this, and makes the sacrifice readily for his wife's sake, it takes much of the comfort out of his life.

Selema, meanwhile, has to be equally circumspect. She bridles her woman's tongue resolutely and no word in disparagement of man or beast passes her lips during all these months, for she has no desire to see the qualities she dislikes reproduced in the child. She is often tired to death, and faint and ill before her hour draws nigh, but none the less she will not lie upon her mat during the daytime lest her heavy eyes should close in sleep, since her child would surely fall a prey to evil spirits were she to do so. Therefore, she fights on to the dusk, and Umat does all he can to comfort her, and to lighten her sufferings, by constant tenderness and care.

One night, when the moon has waxed nearly to the full, Pĕkan resounds with a babel of discordant noise. The large brass gongs, in which the devils of the Chinese are supposed to take delight, clang and clash and bray through the still night-air; the Malay drums throb, and beat, and thud; all manner of shrill yells fill the sky, and the roar of a thousand native voices rises heavenwards, or rolls across the white waters of the river, which are flecked with deep shadows and reflections. The jungles on the far bank take up the sound, and send it pealing back in recurring ringing echoes, till the whole world seems to shout in chorus. The Moon which bathes the Earth in splendour, the Moon which is so dear to each one of us, is in dire peril, this night, for that fierce monster, the Gĕrhana, whom we hate and loathe, is striving to swallow her. You can mark his black bulk creeping over her, dimming her face, consuming her utterly, while she suffers in the agony of silence. How often in the past has she served us with the light; how often has she made night more beautiful than day for our tired, sun-dazed eyes to look upon; and shall she now perish without one effort on our part to save her by scaring the Monster from his prey? No! A thousand times no! So we shout, and clang the gongs, and beat the drums, till all the animal world joins in the tumult, and even inanimate nature lends its voice to swell the uproar with a thousand resonant echoes. At last, the hated Monster reluctantly retreats. Our war-cry has reached his ears, and he slinks sullenly away, and the pure, sad, kindly Moon looks down in love and gratitude upon us her children, to whose aid she owes her deliverance.

But during the period that the Moon's fate hung in the balance, Sĕlĕma has suffered many things. She has been seated motionless in the fireplace under the tray-like shelf, which hangs from the low rafters, trembling with terror of—she knows not what. The little basket-work stand, on which the hot rice-pot is wont to rest, is worn on her head as a cap, and in her girdle the long wooden rice-spoon is stuck daggerwise. Neither she nor Umat know why these things are done, but they never dream of questioning their necessity. It is the custom. The men of olden days have decreed that women with child should do these things when the Moon is in trouble, and the consequences of neglect are too terrible to be risked; so Sĕlĕma and Umat act according to their simple faith.

Later, comes a day when Sĕlĕma nearly loses her life by reason of the barbarities which Malay science considers necessary if a woman is to win through her confinement without mishap. Umat's brown face is gray with fear and anxiety, and drawn and aged with pain. He paces restlessly between the hut, where Sĕlĕma is suffering grievous things, and my study, where he pours his terror and his sorrow into my ears, and wets the floor-mats with his great beady tears. Hours pass, and a little feeble cry comes from Umat's house, the sound which brings with it a world of joy, and a wonder of relief that sends the apple lumping in one's throat, and tears rising to one's eyes. Umat, mad with delight, almost delirious with relief that the danger is over, laughing through his tears, and sobbing in his laughter, rushes to me with the news that a man-child has been born to him, and that Sĕlĕma is safe. Nightly for many weeks after, the cries of Awang—as the boy is named—break the peace of my compound during the midnight hour. The poor little shapeless brown atomy is being ruthlessly washed in *cold* water, at this untimely hour, and thereafter is cruelly held face downwards over a basin filled with live embers, whence a pungent, reeking wood smoke ascends to choke his breath, and to make his tiny eyes smart and ache fiercely. No wonder the poor little thing yells lustily; the marvel is that he should survive such treatment. But he does outlive it, and, so soon as he is old enough to leave the house, he becomes Umat's constant friend and companion. Long before the child can speak, he and Umat understand one another, and you may hear them holding long conversations on the matting outside my study-door with perfect content for hours at a time.

Love is infectious, and as Awang grows big enough to use his legs and his tongue, the little brown mite patters nimbly around his blind father, with an air which has in it something of protection. He is usually mother naked, save that now and again a hat is set rakishly upon one side of his little bullet head, and, when I speak to him, he wriggles in a most ingratiating manner, and stuffs his little hand half-way down his throat. Umat's eyes follow him constantly, and, though they are very dim, I fancy that he sees Awang more clearly than anything else on earth.

So much love cannot go for nothing, and I hope that Awang will grow up to repay his father for the devotion he lavishes upon him. But whatever gifts he may be able to bring to Umat, he can never win him back to sight, and the best that we can hope for is that, in the days to come, Umat may learn to see more clearly through Awang's eyes. Meanwhile, I think he is not altogether unhappy.

From *Studies in Brown Humanity*, London, 1898.

ON MALAYAN RIVERS

In the Jungles of the Peninsula, where the soil under foot is a rich, black loam, composed of decayed vegetation, and the damp earth is littered with brown and sodden leaves, newly shed, or partially decomposed, one may often chance upon a pale, ghost-like object, white or gray in colour, and delicately fine in its texture as a piece of fairy lace. This is the complete skeleton of a giant leaf, which once was fair, and green, and sappy, but now has rotted away, little by little, until nothing remains save the midrib, from which the spines branch off, and a mazy network of tiny veins.

If you could strip any river basin, in the Peninsula, of its forests, and could then lay bare its water-system, you would find that it presented, on a gigantic scale, an appearance very similar to that of the skeleton leaf. The main river would represent the midrib; the principal tributaries falling into it would supply the place of the branching spines; and the myriad tiny streams and rivulets, which babble and trickle through the jungles, or worm their way, slowly and painfully, through the low-lying tracts of swampy country, would be the numberless delicate veins of the leaf. All the spaces and interestices, which in the skeleton are found between midrib and spine, and spine and vein, are, in the river basin, wide tracts of forest-clad country, intersected, and cut up, across, and through and through, by the rivers and streams of the most lavish water-system in the world.

ON MALAYAN RIVERS

The dense jungles present a barrier which has very effectually resisted the encroachments of primitive men. In the valleys of the large rivers, the Malay villages cluster along the banks, and the rice-fields spread behind the groves of palm and fruit trees, but half a mile inland, the forest shuts down around the cultivated patches, like a wall about a kitchen-garden. Up-country, where the rivers are smaller, man has won an even more insecure foothold, and the tiny plots of tilled land peep from out of the masses of jungle that surround them like a bird from out of a field of standing rice. Further up river still, you will find the camps of the Sakai and Sĕmang, but even these forest-dwelling people make their homes on the edges of the streams, and thread their way through the jungles, in which they roam, by wading up and down the water-courses. Thus, it is not too much to say that only an insignificant fraction of the Peninsula has ever been trodden by the foot of man in all the long days since this old world was young. There are thousands of miles of river, in the Peninsula, whose banks have never even been camped upon by human beings, and, in country which is comparatively thickly populated, the vast tracts of jungle, lying between river and river, and between stream and stream, are as unexplored and untrodden as are the distant polar regions of the South. Thus it comes to pass, that one who would here study native life must learn his lessons, and seek his knowledge, on the banks of the rivers, and upon the water-ways of the Malay Peninsula.

On the West Coast, where the roads and railways of the White Men have partially annihilated distance, and have made travelling and transport easy, even through the densest jungle, the waterways are fast becoming deserted. The enterprising Chinese hawker still makes his way from village to village, in his patched and rotting *sampan*, for the people on the river banks need dried sea-fish, sugar, that is more than half sand, and salt, that is three-parts dirt. Also little bits of jungle produce that have escaped duty may be bought and smuggled, if a man works carefully and with cunning. Now and again, a half-empty boat sags and lolls adown the long reaches, or an old-world Chief, who prefers the cool recesses of his *prahu* to the heat and dust of a railway carriage, is punted up stream by half a dozen straining boatmen. For the rest, the river is no longer alive with crafts, as it was in the days of old, and the sleepy villager, whose patient eyes watch life indolently from the water's brink, wonders why the land has fallen to sleep since the coming of the noisy, energetic, White Men.

But in Pahang, Trĕngganu, and Kĕlantan, where men still punt and paddle and wade, as of old, the rivers are the chief, if not the only highways, and, sitting in the shade of the palm-trees on the bank, a man may watch all the world gliding to and fro. There he may see the King's boat—gay with the bright silks of swaggering youths and nobles, with men sitting on the palm-leaf roofing, and dangling their legs at the bow, to mark that their Master is aboard—steam past him, with its waving flag, amid a wild tumult of drums and yells. There he may see the heavily-laden craft, banked high with freight to the very bow, propelled up river by a dozen punters, whose clattering poles drip streams of sun-steeped water; or the yellow face of a Chinese trader, peering from under the shelter at the stern shows for a moment as a trading boat glides by. As he sits watching, the villager sees the tiny dug-out, bearing the wrinkled midwives, paddled downstream by a sweating man, who works as he has never worked before, that relief and aid may come speedily to the woman he holds dear. Or, amid the rhythmical thud of the drums, the droning of verses from the Kuran, and wild bursts of the *sorak*, another *sampan*, bright with gorgeous silks and glittering with tinsel, passes by, bearing the bridegroom and his relations to the hut where the little frightened bride awaits their coming. Or perhaps, when the heavens are bright, lying there stark in his graveclothes, carefully covered from head to foot, and surrounded by a cluster of sad-faced relations, who shield his head lovingly from the fierce sun's rays, another villager may be seen, gliding gently towards the little, shady graveyard, making his last journey on the bosom of the river by which his days have been spent. The birth, the marriage, the death, all the comings and the goings, all the sorrows and the labour, and the rest, may be seen hinted at or exemplified, if a man watch long enough on the banks of a Malayan river; for the running water, which bears them to and fro, enters more closely into the everyday life of the people, than do any of the other natural objects with which the Malays are surrounded.

The large river boats, which ply on the rivers of Kĕlantan, Trĕngganu, and Pahang, are of different builds, each one of which is in some measure peculiar to the State in which it is used. In Kĕlantan the favourite craft is one which, for some obscure reason, is called by the natives *kĕpala bĕlalang*—or the grasshopper's head. Needless to say, it resembles anything in the world more closely than it does the head of any known insect. It is long and narrow, with a short tilted puntingplatform at the bow, and the cabin consists of a bark or wooden erection, like a low, square tunnel. The decking is sunk below the waterlevel, so that the occupants of the cabin sit or lie in a deep hollow with only an inch of bamboo flooring between them and the boat's bottom. If the calking be sound, this is cool and fairly comfortable—though a man might as well lie in his coffin for all he can see of the world around him—but, if the boat leaks, as it usually does, this arrangement means wet bedding, and thereafter lumbago and rheumatism. The long narrow tunnel has no windows, and the only means of egress or entrance is by the open space at each end of the cabin. Malays of other States, who do not love the Kĕlantan people, say that this form of boat is the only one which can be used in their country, because a window would enable thieves to possess themselves of the entire property of the occupant of the cabin with too great ease and convenience. It is due to the people of Kĕlantan, however, that I should state that their ingenuity is not baffled by such a trifle as the absence of windows, for two young Saiyids, whom I once sent from the interior to Kota Bharu—the King's capital—had most of their raiment removed from between them, as they lay sleeping on board one of these boats, during the quiet night-time. This, when they awoke, seemed to them to be almost as miraculous as it was annoying, for they would certainly have been roused had the thief entered the boat, nor was the mystery explained until they found that one of their own boatpoles had been fashioned into a hook, while they slept, and that the thief had successfully fished for their property, with this cunning instrument, over their recumbent bodies. Fortunately, however, they had been provided with a professional thief by the courtesy and forethought of my good friend Dato' Lela Dĕrja, and he quickly restored their missing property, by the simple expedient of robbing the original thief, who was now lapped in peaceful slumber. For such is the custom of the land.

The boat-poles used in Kĕlantan are furnished with large crutch-handles, and, when the punters have walked up the steep incline of the forward platform, and have found bottom with their poles, they suddenly double up their bodies, from the waist, and throw the whole of their weight on to the crutch, which they wedge into the hollow of their shoulders. They rarely touch their poles with their hands, during this part of the operation, and their arms wave about, clawing the air aimlessly, as the punters step slowly down the incline, doing all the pushing with their shoulders, and deriving the power from the weight of their great, fleshy bodies. They give a melancholy, discordant, inarticulate howl each time that they take the strain, and, with their bent backs, quivering legs, and groping arms, they present the appearance of some strange quadrupeds, impaled upon spears, vainly striving to fight their way to the earth on which their forefeet cannot win a grip.

In the Trĕngganu Valley—which in some ways is one of the most curious places in the Peninsula—the river boats are inferior to those found elsewhere. This is to be explained by the fact that the great Trĕngganu River is only navigable for fifty miles from its mouth, and this waterway is therefore of less importance to the natives than are most of the wide rivers of the East Coast. In 1895, only some five hundred Malays were living in the broad tracts of country that lie above the Kĕlantan Falls. The rest of the population of the Trĕngganu Valley was wedged into the space between the rapids and the sea. To this is mainly attributable the great ingenuity and industry of the Trĕngganu Malays, for, in a land where men are very thick upon the ground, a lack of these qualities will surely result in a want of anything to eat. The banks of the Trĕngganu, from Kĕlĕmang to the mouth, are cultivated and inhabited, as are only a very few regions in the Peninsula. No produce of a bulky nature can be brought from the interior, for the slender footpath, which runs round the Falls, is the only means of communication, and all things must be carried on men's shoulders. Therefore, such things as bamboos, from which the walls, and flooring of houses, and the fences round the standing crops, are constructed, must be *planted* by the people who need them, since there is no possibility of cutting them in the neighbouring jungles, as may be done in more comfortable lands. Accordingly there are vast areas under cultivation, and a man may travel on foot from Kĕlĕmang to Kuala Trĕngganu without once leaving the string of villages that line the bank.

There is one form of boat, however, which is to be met on the Trĕngganu River, that would make a stranger fancy that this valley, which was never visited by White Men until 1895, had long been under the influence of Europeans. Clinker-built boats, beautifully fashioned from Siamese teak, and constructed with a finish and a grace of line which excel anything that the dockyards of Singapore can produce, look somewhat incongruous on the rivers of an Independent Malay State; and but for the palms upon the banks, and the paddles with which the gaily dressed natives propel these boats in lieu of oars, one might almost fancy one's self once more upon the brown waters around Chertsey.

But it is in Pahang, where the current of the river is stronger than that of any other on the East Coast, and where a boat may travel up stream two hundred and twenty miles from the mouth without let or hindrance, that the large river-craft approaches most nearly to perfection. The best constructed boats are nearly eight fathoms long, and the poling platform occupies much space forward, so as to give the punters plenty of room as they step aft, leaning heavily on their poles. At the bow and the stern, a square sheet of meshed woodwork is fixed in such a manner as to give the deck of the boat an almost rectangular surface, without diminishing the speed-power by widening her lines. The cabins are usually two in number—the *kurong* or main apartment, and *kurong ânak* or after cabin. They are roofed in with thatch, overlaid with sheets of dried *mĕngkuang* leaves, kept firmly in place by long lathes of split bamboo, lashed securely with rattan. The line of the roof forms a bold, sweeping curve, from the peak at the extreme stern to the middle of the boat. There is a slight flattening of this curve near the centre, and an even slighter rise near the forward end of the cabin; the effect being exceedingly graceful, the more so since the long sloping line is broken by a tiny, thatched perch, in which the steersman has his seat.

The Pahang Malay punts with an air, a swagger—as he does everything—and the clatter and the clash of the poles, the single recurring thud against the side, which results from the excellent time the men keep, the loud complaining creak of the rudder-rod, as the boat lurches along up stream, make a lilting, rhythmic cadence not unpleasant to listen to. And descending the river, also, when punting-poles are laid aside, and the men grasp their paddles, the splash and the beat of the even strokes, the song of the steersman in his perch, and the crashing chorus of the crew, combined with the cool current of air which the pace of the gliding boat sends rushing through the cabin, make as soothing and lazy a lullaby as a man need desire to listen to. The boatmen take a pride in displaying their skill in all kinds of 'fancy' paddling, which, while it has a pretty and graceful effect, serves also to ease their muscles by employing them in a constantly changing motion. The bow paddler sets the stroke; first, one long sweep of the blade, quickly followed by three short ones; or later, three long strokes with a short one in between. There are hundreds of combinations of long and short, each of which has its own well-known name in the vernacular, and a properly trained crew will travel all day long without rowing in precisely the same manner for half an hour together. It is marvellous how long a time Malays will sit at their paddles, without ever pausing in their rowing, and yet experience no especial fatigue or exhaustion. I remember, on one occasion, in 1894, setting a crew of five-and-twenty men to paddle down river at four o'clock in the morning. They had never worked with me before, they were not a picked crowd, and they were not men who were accustomed to row together. Yet these Malays paddled down river to Pĕkan, a distance of a hundred miles, in twenty-six hours. They never quitted their work all that long and weary time except twice, when half their number ate rice while the other half continued rowing. Once in an hour, or so, they would shift from one side of the boat to the other; but that was all the relief that they sought for their aching limbs. The time in which we did the journey was not particularly good, for the river chanced to be somewhat shrunken by drought, and we frequently ran aground. During the night, which was intensely dark, we more than once found ourselves straying from the main stream into a backwater, or *cul de sac*, and so had to paddle up river again, the way we had come, with all the weary work to do once more. Yet, in spite of all these trials to body and temper, no word of complaint, no whispered murmur of remonstrance, came from the men at the paddles. That they suffered to some extent I do not doubt, for I, who was awake all night to see that they kept at it, was dropping with fatigue long before the dawn showed grayly in the East. Towards morning, their *sorak* grew very thin and weedy and faint, and their eyes were dull and heavy, but this did not prevent them from making half a dozen spurts in the last three or four miles. To appreciate to the full the achievement of these men, you must realise what paddling is like. Personally I know of no more tiring occupation. The rower sits cross-legged on the hard decking of the boat, with nothing to support his back, and with nothing in the nature of a stretcher against which to gain a purchase for his feet. The cross-piece at the top of the paddle shaft is gripped in one hand, the other holding the shaft firmly an inch or two above its point of junction with the blade. Then the body of the rower is bent forward from the hips, the arms extended to their full length, as the paddle-blade takes the water. The arm which is uppermost is held rather stiffly, the whole strain of the stroke being taken by the hand and arm that grips the paddle near the base of the blade. When this motion has been repeated half a dozen times the lower arm begins to complain, and presently its fellow joins in the protest. Continue paddling for an hour or two, and not only your arms, but your shoulders, your back, your legs, almost every muscle in your body, will begin to ache as they have never ached before, and, though practice is half the battle, you may thus come by a sound working knowledge of what the sensations of a man must be who has laboured for more than five-and-twenty hours at the paddles. After this, it is probable that you will hesitate to join in the loud-mouthed chorus of those who tell you that the Malays are the laziest people that inhabit God's Earth.

Those people who, nowadays, rush through Perak and Sĕlangor in railway carriages can have but a poor conception of what a lovely land it is through which they are hurrying. The narrow lines, cut through the forest, are only broken, here and there, by patches of coffee-gardens, and other ranker cultivation. Here, there is nothing really distinctive of the Peninsula, and if you would see the country in its full glory and beauty, you must still keep to the river routes, which are the highways proper to the Land of the Malays. Travelling up and down the Peninsula, for a dozen years and more, one chances upon so many lovely scenes that it is not easy to decide which among them all is the most good to look upon. A hundred spots come before my mind's eye as, in spirit, I pass once more up and down the streams I love best; but just as, among a collection of beautiful pictures there must always be some which appeal to one more strongly than do the others, so, in this galaxy of Malayan scenes, I have my favourites. One is very far away, on a river called the Pĕrtang, a tiny stream of the interior, that falls into the Tĕkai, which falls into the Tĕmbĕling, which falls into the Pahang, which flows into the China Sea. The reach of river is not wide, but it is very long for an up-country stream, flowing, straight as an arrow, for a distance of nearly a mile. The bed of this river is shallow, its water running riot down long stretches of shingle, forming a succession of miniature rapids. Little sun-flecked splashes of water are thrown up by the fiery dashing of the hurrying current against the obstructions in its path, and the whole surface of the stream seems to dance, and glitter, and shimmer, as you look at it. But the distinctive feature of this reach of river, that marks it out from its fellows, is to be looked for on its jungle-covered banks. The shelving earth at the water's edge is lined with magnificent specimens of the *ngĕram* tree—a jungle giant which is probably but little known to any White Men whose work has not chanced to take them into the far interior of the Malay Peninsula. The peculiar form in which these trees grow renders them specially suitable for the river banks on which they are always found. Their trunks, which are several yards in circumference at their base, grow erect for only a few feet. Then they gradually trend outwards, leaning lovingly over the stream; and, when two of these trees grow on the opposite banks of a river facing one another, their branches not infrequently become interlaced, forming a natural arch of living greenery overhead. In this reach of the Pĕrtang, of which I speak, the banks from end to end are lined with *ngĕram* trees, and with *ngĕram* trees only. The effect is, therefore, that of a splendid arch of foliage a mile in length, like a long green tent spread above a line of dancing, joyous river. Overhead, the network of graceful, slender boughs, with their trailing wealth of gorgeous leaves, sways gently in the faint, soft breeze that seems to be for ever sweeping swooningly over the still forests of the remote interior. On either hand, the massive trunks of the *ngĕram* trees show gray, save where the vivid flecks of sunlight paint them a whiter hue, and form the sides of the avenue through which the leaping waters run. The surface of the stream itself is alive with motion and colour. The brilliant sunshine struggle, through the heavy masses of interwoven boughs, and twigs, and leaves, forcing its way amid the thick clusters of creepers and trailing orchids with which the branches of these trees are draped, throughout their entire length. Here, for near a mile, there is cool, deep shade, that would almost be gloom, were it not that the fierce Eastern sun will not suffer himself to be altogether defeated, and still finds means to dust and powder the running water with little shifting flecks of light and colour, and, here and there, to cast broad belts of glimmering brilliancy on the surface of the stream. As you glide slowly down this reach upon your raft, a great brown kite, disturbed by your approach, flaps heavily away from you, between the long avenue of the *ngĕram* trees; a brilliantly painted butterfly catches your eye, a tiny point of colour quickly fading into nothingness, as it flits adown the reach; or, perhaps, a troop of monkeys passes scurryingly across the river, from tree to tree, and, in a moment, is swallowed up in the forest. Your pleasure in gazing on the beauties of this scene will not be diminished by the recollection that they have only once before been looked upon by the eyes of a White Man, and that the place is too far removed from the beaten track for even the most energetic globe-trotter to visit it, and defile it with his unappreciative presence.

There is another spot on a river in Pahang that will always have a place in my memory; but, though a few years ago it was almost as remote from the paths of the European as is the *ngĕram* tree-reach to-day, the trunk-road across the Peninsula now skirts it closely, so that every passer-by may see it. This is the Jĕram Bĕsu, the great rapid on the Lipis River. At this point the waters of the Lipis, which have hitherto meandered through a broad green valley, dotted with nestling villages, and gay with the vivid colouring of the standing rice, suddenly become pent, in a narrow bed, between grim walls of granite. The stream above the rapid runs smooth and even, growing more oily to look upon, as it combs over, in a great curved wave, at the head of the fall. Then, in an instant, the gliding water is broken up into a leaping, whirling, tearing, fighting, roaring torrent, that dashes madly against the rocky walls that hem it in, and seem to lash it into a frenzy of rage. The rapid is only about thirty yards long, and the drop is probably about half as many feet, but the volume of pent water, that strives to force itself through this narrow channel, makes the pace furious, and gives a strength to the leaping flood which is altogether irresistible. The combing wave, at the rapid's head, first dashes itself upon a prominent, outstanding wedge of rock on the left, which the natives of the place name 'The Wall,' and when the dangers of a capsize at this point have been avoided, 'The Toad' is found waiting, near the exit from the gorge, to pick up the bits. The rock which bears this name is set in mid-stream, leaning slightly towards the hurrying current, for the rush of water upon this side of it, during countless ages, has worn away the stone. This is really the only great danger to be encountered in shooting this rapid, for the offset of the water from the other rocks is sufficient to prevent a man being dashed with any great violence against them. But with 'The Frog' this is not the case. The whole run of the current tends to drive a man into the hollow in the rock, and once there, with the weight of that mighty torrent to keep him in place, he has but a poor chance of ever getting out again. Old Khatib Jafar, who lives in the little village above the rapid, and has spent all the best years of his life in ferrying men's rafts down the fall, boasts that he has, at different times, had every rib on his right side smashed between the rafts and 'The Frog,' but he says that he has always escaped being forced under it, or he would not be there to tell of his manifold experiences.

Before long, no doubt, some energetic White Man will utilise the power of Jĕram Bĕsu for the generation of electricty, and the place will be rendered unsightly by rusty iron piping, and cunningly constructed machinery. Then, incidentally, Khatib Jafar and his brethren will lose their means of livelihood, as, by the way, they are already doing as one of the first effects of the new road. I fear that they will not be greatly comforted by the recollection that their individual loss is for the good of the greater number, or by the thought that they may in future earn their rice and fish in a manner that carries with it less risk than did their former occupation.

There is yet another place upon the banks of a Malay river —in Trĕngganu, this time—of which I shall always retain a grateful recollection. At the foot of the Kĕlĕmang Falls, a little stream flows into the wide Trĕngganu River on its left bank. It comes straight down from the hills, which, at this point, rise almost precipitously from within a few yards of the river's edge. They mount up skywards, in a series of steep ascents, and on the summit of the first of these there stands a very ancient grave, in which, tradition says, there repose the mouldering bones of a hermit of old time, who dwelt here in solitude, during his days of life, and elected to lie here through the ages, awaiting his summons before the Judgment Seat. The still forest spreads around him, the note of bird, and beast, and insect comes to lull him in his long slumbers, and the monotonous sound of the neighbouring waterfall cries 'Hush!' to the noisy world. Once in a long while the Sultan of Trĕngganu comes hither, with all his Court, to do honour to the dead Sage; now and again, villagers visit the spot in pursuance of some vow, made in their hour of need; but, for the rest, the place where the hermit lies is undisturbed by the passing to and fro of man.

From the natural terrace in the hill, upon which the grave stands, the little stream of which I speak falls in a series of cataracts to the valley below. Its source must be at a spot far up the mountain side, for its waters, when they reach the plain, are as fresh and cold as those of a highland stream in Scotland. They come dashing and leaping along, from point to point, down the steep hillside, and fall in a body upon the broad, smooth surface of an immense granite boulder, which lies at the base of the rising land.

I, and the Pahang Malays who were my companions, reached this place one morning, just when the dew had dried, after travelling without rest, during all the long hours that should have been passed in sleep. We were weary and tired to the last degree, and our eyes had that curious feverish, burning sensation in their sockets, which ever comes to one who looks out at the blazing tropic sunshine after a sleepless night. We halted to cook our rice, and we were all, I think, pretty sorry for ourselves. I longed for champagne, even at that early hour in the morning, or for any pick-me-up to make me feel equal to the long journey which we should have to make between that hour and the dawn of the next day. My Malays, too, squatted about disconsolately by the river, where they were washing their rice, and by the fires, upon which the cooking-pots were humming. One or two of their number went off into the jungle, that lay round and about us, to search for fuel, and presently one of them returned, and said that he had found a capital place for a bath. He looked so fresh and comfortable, as he stood there with the beads of water still glistening in his hair, that several of our people went in search of the place of which he spoke. They all came back in tearing spirits, loudly extolling the marvels of the bath, and at last I, too, went to try what it was like.

When I arrived, I found two or three of my people lying sprawling on the large smooth boulder at the foot of the fall, and, when they presently made room for me I crept cautiously on to the great stone upon which the stream of water from above was thudding heavily. The fall was about twenty feet in height, and the first blow of the icy water laid me flat upon the rock, and held me there breathless. It was like the most splendid combination of cold shower-bath and vigorous *massage* imaginable, and though it was not to be borne for more than a minute or two at a time, I stretched myself on the boulder, again and again, until my skin was turned to gooseflesh. Never was there a more splendid tonic, and though we did not rest again till the Eastern sky waxed red next morning, I, for one, felt no more fatigue of mind or body, after that marvellous bath.

When once a man falls a-thinking of the thousand scenes in the Malay Peninsula, any one of which it is a keen delight to look upon, it is difficult to quit the subject, and to make an end of vain attempts to picture to others some few of the things which have filled him with a pleasure that was an ample reward for the hardships of many a long and arduous journey. But the end must come, sooner or later, and perhaps, the sooner the better for how can one hope to paint in words, things that, even as one looked upon them, seem too full of varied beauty for the sight to really comprehend them? On Malayan rivers, at any rate, the eye *is* abundantly filled with seeing.

From *Studies in Brown Humanity* London 1898.

AMONG THE FISHER FOLK

THIS is a land of a thousand beauties. Nature, as we see her in the material things which delight our eyes, is straight from the hand of God, unmarred by man's deforming, a marvellous creation of green growths and brilliant shades of colour, fresh, sweet, pure, an endless panorama of loveliness. But it is not only the material things which form the chief beauties of the land in which we dwell. The ever-varying lights of the Peninsula, and the splendid Malayan sky that arches over us are, in themselves, at once the crown of our glory, and the imparters of a fresh and changeful loveliness to the splendours of the earth. Our eyes are ever glutted with the wonders of the sky, and of the lights which are shed around us. From the moment when the dawn begins to paint its orange tints in the dim East, and later floods the vastness of the low-lying clouds with glorious dyes of purple and vermilion, and a hundred shades of colour for which we have no name, reaching to the very summit of the heavens; on through the early morning hours, when the slanting rays of the sun throw long broad streaks of dazzlingly white light upon the waters of sea and river; on through the burning noonday, when the shadows fall black and sharp and circular, in dwarfed patches about our feet; on through the cooler hours of the afternoon, when the sun is a burning disc low down in the western sky, or, hiding behind a bank of clouds, throws wide-stretched arms of prismatic colour high up into the heavens; on through the hour of sunset, when all the world is a flaming blaze of gold and crimson; and so into the cool still night, when the moon floods us with a sea of light only one degree less dazzling than that of day, and when the thousand wonders of the southern stars gaze fixedly upon us from their places in the deep clear vault above our heads, and Venus casts a shadow on the grass; from dawn to dewy eve, from dewy eve to dawn, the lights of the Peninsula vary as we watch them steep us and all the world in glory, and half intoxicate us with their beauty.

But the sea is the best point of vantage from which to watch the glories of which I tell—speaking as I do in weak colourless words of sights and scenes which no human brush could ever hope to render, nor mortal poet dream of painting in immortal song—and if you would see them for yourself, and drink in their beauty to the full, go dwell among the Fisher Folk of the East Coast.

They are a rough, hard-bit gang, ignorant and superstitious beyond belief, tanned to the colour of mahogany by exposure to the sun, with faces scarred and lined by rough weather and hard winds. They are plucky and reckless, as befits men who go down to the sea in ships; they are full of resource, the results of long experience of danger, and constant practice in sudden emergencies, where a loss of presence of mind means a forfeiture of life. Their ways and all their dealings are bound fast by a hundred immutable customs, handed down through countless ages, which no man among them dreams of violating; and they have, moreover, that measure of romance attaching to them which clings to all men who run great risks, and habitually carry their lives in their hands.

From the beginning of November to the end of February the North-East monsoon whips down the long expanse of the China Sea, fenced as it is by the Philippines and Borneo on the one hand, and by Cochin China and Cambodia on the other, until it breaks in all its force and fury on the East Coast of the Peninsula. It raises breakers mountain high upon the bars at the river mouths, it dashes huge waves against the shore, or banks up the flooded streams as they flow seaward, until, on a calm day, a man may drink sweet water a mile out at sea. During this season the people of the coast are mostly idle, though they risk their lives and their boats upon the fishing banks on days when a treacherous calm lures them seaward, and they can rarely be induced to own that the monsoon has in truth broken, until the beaches have been strewn with driftwood from a dozen wrecks. They long for the open main when they are not upon it, and I have seen a party of Kĕlantan fishermen half drunk with joy at finding themselves dancing through a stormy sea in an unseaworthy craft on a dirty night, after a long period spent on the firm shore. 'It is indeed sweet,' they kept exclaiming—'it is indeed sweet thus once more to play with the waves!' For here or elsewhere the sea has its own peculiar strange fascination for those who are at once its masters, its slaves, and its prey.

When they have at last been fairly beaten by the monsoon, the fisher folk betake themselves to the scattered coast villages, which serve to break the monotonous line of jungle and shivering *casuarina* trees that fringe the sandy beach and the rocky headlands of the shore. Here under the cocoa-nut palms, amid chips from boats that are being repaired, and others that still lie upon the stocks, surrounded by nets, and sails, and masts, and empty crafts lying high and dry upon the beach out of reach of the tide, the fishermen spend the months of their captivity. Their women live here all the year round, labouring incessantly in drying and salting the fish which have been taken by the men, or pounding prawns into *blachan*, that evil-smelling condiment which has been so ludicrously

AMONG THE FISHER FOLK 189

misnamed the Malayan Caviare. It needs all the violence of the fresh, strong, monsoon winds to even partially purge these villages of the rank odours which cling to them at the end of the fishing season; and when all has been done, the saltness of the sea air, the brackish water of the wells, and the faint stale smells emitted by the nets and fishing tackle still tell unmistakable tales of the one trade in which every member of these communities is more or less engaged.

The winds blow strong, and the rain falls heavily. The frogs in the marshes behind the village fill the night air with the croakings of a thousand mouths, and the little bull-frogs sound their deep see-saw note during all the hours of darkness. The sun is often hidden by the heavy cloud-banks, and a subdued melancholy falls upon the moist and steaming land. The people, whom the monsoon has robbed of their occupation, lounge away the hours, building boats, and mending nets casually and without haste or concentrated effort. Four months must elapse before they can again put to sea, so there is no cause for hurry. They are frankly bored by the life they have to lead between fishing season and fishing season, but they are a healthy-minded and withal a law-abiding people, who do little evil even when their hands are idle.

Then the monsoon breaks, and they put out to sea once more, stretching to their paddles, and shouting in chorus as they dance across the waves to the fishing grounds. During this season numerous ugly and uncleanly steamboats tramp up the coast, calling at all the principal ports for the cargoes of dried fish that find a ready market in Singapore, and thus the fisher folk have no difficulty in disposing of their takes. Prices do not rank high, for a hundredweight of fish is sold on the East Coast for about six shillings and sixpence of our money, but the profits of a season are more than sufficient to keep a fisherman and his family in decency during the months of his inactivity. The shares which are apportioned to the working hands in each crew, and to the owners of the crafts and nets, are all determined by ancient custom. The unwritten law is clearly recognised and understood by all concerned, and thus the constant disputes which would otherwise inevitably arise are avoided. Custom—*Adat*—is the fetish of the Malay. Before it even the *Hukum Shara*, the Divine Law of the Prophet, is powerless, in spite of the professed Muhammadanism of the people. 'Let our children die rather than our customs,' says the vernacular proverb, and for once an old saw echoes the sentiment of a race.

The average monthly earnings of a fisherman is about sixteen shillings ($8), and though to our ideas this sounds but a poor return for all the toil and hardship he must endure, and the many risks and dangers which surround his avocation, to a simple people it is all-sufficient.

A fisherman can live in comfort on some three shillings a month, and wife and little ones can, therefore be supported, and money saved against the close season, if a man be prudent. The owners of boats and nets receive far larger sums, but none the less they generally take an active part in the fishing operations. From one end of the coast to the other, the capitalist who owns many crafts, and lives upon the income derived from their hire, is almost unknown.

The fish crowd the shallow shoal waters and move up and down the coast, during the whole of the open season, in great schools acres in extent. Occasionally their passage may be marked from afar by the flight of hungry sea-fowl hovering and flittering above them; the white plumage of the restless birds glints and flashes in the sunlight as they wheel and dip and plunge downwards, or soar upwards again with their prey. I have seen a school of fish beating the surface of the quiet sea into a thousand glistening splashes, as in vain they

AMONG THE FISHER FOLK

attempted to escape their restless pursuers, who, floating through the air above them, or plunging madly down, belaboured the water with their wings, and kept up a deafening chorus of gleeful screamings.

These seas carry almost everything that the salt ocean waters can produce. Just as the forests of the Peninsula teem with a life that is strangely prodigal in its profusion, and in the infinite variety of its forms, so do the waters of the China Sea defy the naturalist to classify the myriad wonders of their denizens. The shores are strewn with shells of all shapes and sizes, which display every delicate shade of prismatic colour, every marvel of dainty tracery, every beauty of curve and spiral that the mind of man can conceive. The hard sand which the tide has left is pitted with tiny holes, the lairs of a million crabs and sea insects. The beaches are covered with a wondrous diversity of animal and vegetable growths thrown up and discarded by the tide. Seaweed of strange varieties, and of every fantastic shape and texture, the round balls of fibrous grass-like gigantic thistledowns, which scurry before the light breeze, as though endued with life, the white oval shells of the cuttle-fish, and the shapeless hideous masses of dead *medusae*, all lie about in extricable [*sic*] confusion on the sandy shores of the East Coast.

In the sea itself all manner of fish are found; the great sharks, with their shapeless gashes of mouth set with the fine keen teeth; the sword-fishes with their barred weapons seven and eight feet long; the stinging ray, shaped like a child's kite, with its rasping hide and its two sharp bony frickers set on its long tail; the handsome *těnggiri*, marked like a mackerel, the first of which when taken are a royal perquisite on the Coast; the little smelts and red-fish; the thousand varieties that live among the sunken rocks, and are brought to the surface by lines six fathoms long; the cray-fish, prawns, and shrimps; and the myriad forms of semi-vegetable life that find a home in the tepid tropic sea, all these, and many more for which we have no name, live and die and prey upon each other along the eastern shores of the Peninsula.

Here may be seen the schools of porpoises—which the Malays name 'the racers'—plunging through the waves, or leaping over one another with that ease of motion, and that absence of all visible effort, which gives so faint an idea of the pace at which they travel. Yet when a ship is tearing through the waters at the rate of four hundred miles a day, the porpoises play backwards and forwards across the ploughing forefoot of the bow, and find no difficulty in holding their own. Here, too, is that monster fish which so nearly resembles the shark that the Malays call it by that name, with the added title of 'the fool'. It lies almost motionless about two fathoms below the surface, and when the fisher folk spy it, one of their number drops noiselessly over the side, and swims down to it. Before this is done it behoves a man to look carefully, and to assure himself that it is indeed the Fool, and not his brother of the cruel teeth who lies down below through the clear water. A mistake on this point means a sudden violent commotion on the surface, a glimpse of an agonised human face mutely imploring aid, the slow blending of certain scarlet patches of fluid with the surrounding water, and then a return to silence and peace, and the calm of an unruffled sea. But if it is indeed the Fool that floats so idly below them, the boatmen know that much meat will presently be theirs. The swimmer cautiously approaches the great lazy fish, which makes no effort to avoid him. Then the gently agitated fingers of a human hand are pressed against the monster's side just below the fins, and fish and man rise to the surface, the latter tickling gently, the former placid and delighted by the novel sensation. The swimmer then hitches one hand on to the boat in order to support himself, and continues the gentle motion of the fingers of his other hand, which still rests under the fin of his prey. The great fish seems too intoxicated with pleasure to move. It presses softly against the swimmer, and the men in the boat head slowly for the shore. When the shallow water is reached every weapon on board is plunged into the body of the Fool, and he is cut up at leisure.

Cray-fish also are caught by tickling all along the coast. The instrument used in this case is not the human hand, but a small rod, called a *jai*, to the end of which a rattan noose is fixed. The work is chiefly entrusted to little children, who paddle into the shallow water at points where the cray-fish are feeding, and gently tickle the itching prominent eyeballs of their victims. The irritation in these organs must be constant and excessive, for the cray-fish rub them gently against any object that presents itself, and when they feel the soothing friction of the rattan noose they lie motionless, paralysed with pleasure. The noose is gradually slipped over the protruding eyes, when it is drawn taut, and thus the great prawns are landed. Even when the strain has been taken too soon, and a cray-fish has escaped with one eyeball wrenched from its socket, it not uncommonly occurs that the intolerable irritation in its other eye drives it back once more to the rattan noose, there to have the itching allayed by the gentle friction.

Jelly-fish, too, abound on the East Coast. They come aboard in the nets, staring with black beady eyes from out the shapeless masses of their bodies, looking in the pale moonlight like the faces of lost souls, showing on the surface of the bottomless pit, casting despairing arms around their heads in impotent agony. The water which has sluiced over their slimy bodies is charged with irritating properties, such as drive a man to tear the very flesh from his bones in a fruitless attempt to allay the horrible itching. When the water dries, the irritation ceases, but at sea, and at night, when the dew falls like rain, and one is drenched to the skin by water from the nets, it is not easy for anything to become dry. Therefore one must suffer patiently till the boat puts back again at dawn.

These are some of the creatures which share with the Fisher Folk the seas of the East Coast, and hundreds of devices are used to capture them. Nets of all shapes and sizes, seine nets with their bobbing floats, bag nets of a hundred kinds, drop nets, and casting nets. Some are set all night, and are liberally sprinkled with bait. Some are worked round schools of fish by a single boat, which flies in its giant circle, propelled by a score of paddles dripping flame from the phosphorescence with which each drop of the Eastern sea is charged. Some are cautiously spread by the men in one boat, according to directions signalled to them by a second, from the side of which a diver hangs by one arm, listening intently to the motion of the fish, and judging with marvellous accuracy the direction which they are taking. Lines of all sorts, hooks of every imaginable shape, all the tricks and devices, which have been learned by hundreds of years of experience on the fishing grounds, are employed by the people of the East Coast to swell their daily and nightly takes of fish.

In the sheltered water of the Straits of Malacca, huge traps are constructed of stakes driven into the sea-bottom, and in these the vast majority of the fish are caught. But on the East Coast such a means of taking fish is forbidden by nature. A single day of monsoon wind would be sufficient to destroy and scatter far and wide the work of months, and so the Fisher Folk whose lot is cast by the waters of the China Sea, display more skill in their netting and lining than any other Peninsula Malays, for on these alone can they depend for the fish by which they live.

Their boats are of every size, but the shape is nearly the same in each case, from the tiny *kolek* which can only hold three men, to the great *pukat dalam* or seine-boat, which requires more than a score of paddlers to work her. They are all made of *chĕngal*, one of the hardest and toughest woods that is yielded by the jungles of the Peninsula. They all rise slightly at the stern and at the bows; they all are decked in with wide laths of bamboo; they all carry a mast which may be lowered or raised at will, and which seems to be altogether too tall and heavy for safety; they all fly under a vast spread of yellow palm-mat sail, the sight of which, as it fills above you, and you lie clutching the bulwark on the canting boat, while half the crew are hanging by ropes over the windward side, fairly takes your breath away; and all are so rigged that if taken aback the mast must part or the boat be inevitably capsized. But the Fisher Folk know the signs of the heavens as no others may know them, and when danger is apprehended the mast is lowered, the sail furled, and the boat headed for shore.

The real danger is when men are too eagerly engaged in fishing to note the signals which the skies are making to them. A party of Kĕlantan fisher folk nearly came by their death a year or two ago by reason of such carelessness. One of them is a friend of mine, and he told me the tale. Eight of them put to sea in a *jalak* to troll for fish, and ran before a light breeze, with two score of lines trailing glistening spoon-baits in their wake. The fish were extraordinarily active, itself a pretty sure sign that a storm was not far off, but the men were too busy pulling in the lines, knocking the fish from the hooks with their wooden mallets, and trailing the lines astern again, to spare a glance at the sky or the horizon. Suddenly came the gust, striking, as do the squalls of the tropics, like the flat of a giant's hand. The mast was new and sound, the boat canted quickly, the water rose to the line of the bulwarks, paused, shivered, and then in a deluge plunged into the hold. A cry from the crew, a loud but futile shriek of directions from the owner, a splashing of released fish, a fighting flood of water, and the eight fishermen found themselves struggling in the arms of an angry sea.

The boat, keel uppermost, rocked uneasily on the waves, and the men, casting off their scant garments, made shift to swim to her, and climb up her slippery dipping side. The storm passed over them, a line of tropic rain, beating a lashing tattoo upon the white-tipped troubled waters; then a blinding downpour stinging on the bare brown backs of the shivering fishermen; and lastly a black shadow, lowering above a foam-flecked sea, driving quickly shorewards. Then came the sun, anxious to show its power after its temporary defeat. It beat pitilessly on the bare bodies of the men huddled together on the rocking keel of the boat. First it warmed them pleasantly, and then it scorched and flayed them, aided as it was by the fierce reflection thrown back from the salt waters. For a day and a night they suffered all the agonies of exposure in the tropics. Burning heat by day, chill airs at night, stiffening the uncovered limbs of the fishermen, who now half mad with hunger, thirst, and exhaustion, watched with a horrid fascination the great fins, which every now and then showed above the surface of the waters, and told them only too plainly that the sharks expected soon to get a meal very much to their liking.

On the second day Che' Leh, the owner of the boat, urged his fellows to attempt to right her by a plan which he explained to them, but at first the fear of the sharks held them motionless. At length hunger and thirst aiding Che' Leh's persuasions, they dropped off the boat, making a great splashing to scare the sharks, and after hours of cruel toil, for which their exhausted condition fitted them but ill, they succeeded in loosening the mast, and releasing the palm-leaf sail. Long pauses were necessary at frequent intervals, for the men were very weak. At last the sail floated upwards under the boat, and by a great effort the castaways succeeded in spreading it taut, so that the boat was half supported by it. Then, all pushing from one side, gaining such a foothold as the sail afforded them, they succeeded, after many straining efforts, in righting her. Slowly and painfully they baled her out, and then lay for many hours too inert to move.

Late on the third day they reached the shore, but they had been carried many miles down the coast to a part where they were unknown. The eight naked men presented themselves at a village and asked for food and shelter, but the people feared that they were fugitives from some *Raja's* wrath, and many hours elapsed before they received the aid of which they stood so sorely in need.

The beliefs and superstitions of the Fisher Folk would fill many volumes. They believe in all manner of devils and local sprites. They fear greatly the demons that preside over animals, and will not willingly mention the names of birds or beasts while at sea. Instead, they call them all *chewch*—which, to them, signifies an animal, though to others it is meaningless, and is supposed not to be understanded of the beasts. To this word they talk on the sound which each beast makes in order to indicate what animal is referred to; thus the pig is the grunting *chewch*, the buffalo the *chewch* that says '*uak*', and the snipe the *chewch* that cries '*kek-kek*'. Each boat that puts to sea has been medicined with care, many incantations and other magic observances having been had recourse to, in obedience to the rules which the superstitious people have followed for ages. After each take the boat is 'swept' by the medicine man, with a tuft of leaves prepared with mystic ceremonies, which is carried at the bow for the purpose. The omens are watched with exact care, and if they be adverse no fishing boat puts to sea that day. Every act in their lives is regulated by some regard for the demons of the sea and air, and yet these folk are nominally Muhammadans, and, according to that faith, magic and sorcery, incantations to the spirits, and prayers to demons are all unclean things forbidden to the people. But the Fisher Folk, like other inhabitants of the Peninsula, are Malays first and Muhammadans afterwards. Their religious creed goes no more than skin deep, and affects but little the manner of their daily life.

All up and down the coast, from Sĕdĕli in Johor to the islands near Sĕnggora, the Fisher Folk are found during the open season. Fleets of smacks leave the villages for the spots along the shore where fish are most plentiful, and for eight months in the year these men live and sleep in their boats. The town of Kuala Trĕngganu, however, is the headquarters of the fishing trade, as indeed it is of all the commercial enterprise on this side of the Peninsula. At the point where the Trĕngganu river falls into the sea, a sandy headland juts out, forming a little bay, to which three conical rocky hills make a background, relieving the general flatness of the coast. In this bay, and picturesquely grouped about the foot of these hills, the thatched houses of the capital, and the cool green fruit groves cluster closely. Innumerable fishing crafts lie at anchor, or are beached along the shore; gaily-dressed natives pass hither and thither, engrossed in their work or play; and the little brown bodies of the naked children fleck the yellow sands. Seen across the dancing waves, and with appearance of motion which, in this steaming land, the heat-haze gives to even inanimate objects, this scene is indescribably pretty, shining and alive.

But at dawn the prospect is different. The background is

the same, but the colour of the scene is less intense though the dark waves have rosy lights in them reflected from the ruddy sky of the dawn. A slowly paling fire shines here and there upon the shore, and the cool land breeze blows seaward. Borne upon the wind come stealing out a hundred graceful, noiseless fishing smacks. The men aboard them are cold and sleepy. They sit huddled up in the stern, with their *sarongs* drawn high about their shoulders, under the shadow of the palm-leaf sail, which shows dark above them in the faint light of early morning. The only sound is the whisper of the wind in the rigging, and the song of the forefoot as it drives the water before it in little curving ripples. And so the fleet floats out and out, and presently is lost on the glowing eastern sky-line. At sundown the boats come racing back, heading for the sinking sun, borne on the evening wind, which sets steadily shorewards, and at about the same hour the great seine-boats, with their crews of labouring paddlers, beat out to sea.

So live they, so die they, year in and year out. Toiling and enduring, with no hope or wish for change of scene. Delighting in such simple pleasures as their poor homes afford; surrounded by beauties of nature, which they lack the soul to appreciate; and yet experiencing that keen enjoyment which is born of dancing waves, of pace, of action, and of danger, that thrilling throb of the red blood through the veins, which, when all is said and done makes up more than half of the joy of living.

It was not always so with them, for within the memory of old men upon the Coast, the Fisher Folk were once pirates to a man. The last survivor of those who formed the old lawless bands was an intimate friend of mine own. When I last saw him, a day or two before his death in 1891, he begged that I would do him one final act of friendship by supplying him with a winding sheet, that he might go decently to his grave under the sods and the spear-grass, bearing thither a token of the love I bore him. It was a good shroud of fine white calico bought in the bazaar, and it cost more than a dollar. But I found it very willingly, for I remembered that I was aiding to remove from the face of the earth, and to lay in his quiet resting-place, the last Pirate on the East Coast.

From *In Court and Kampong*, London 1897.

UP COUNTRY

It has been said that a white man, who has lived twelve consecutive months in complete isolation, among the people of an alien Asiatic race is never wholly sane again for the remainder of his days. This, in a measure, is true; for the life he then learns to live, and the discoveries he makes in that unmapped land, the gates of which are closed, locked, barred, and chained against all but a very few of his countrymen, teach him to love many things which all right-minded people very properly detest. The free, queer, utterly unconventional life has a fascination which is all its own. Each day brings a little added knowledge of the hopes and fears, longings and desires, joys and sorrows, pains and agonies of the people among whom his lot is cast. Each hour brings fresh insight into the mysterious workings of the minds and hearts of that very human section of our race, which ignorant Europeans calmly class as 'niggers'. All these things come to possess a charm for him, the power of which grows apace, and eats into the very marrow of the bones of the man who has once tasted this particular fruit of the great Tree of Knowledge. Just as the old smugglers, in the Isle of Man, were wont to hear the sea calling to them; go where he may, do what he will, the voice of the jungle, and of the people who dwell in those untrodden places, sounds in the ears of one who has lived the life. Ever and anon it cries to him to come back, come back to the scenes, the people, the life which he knows and understands, and which, in spite of all its hardships, he has learned to love.

The great wheel of progress, like some vast snowball, rolls steadily along, gathering to itself all manner of weird and unlikely places and people, filling up the hollows laying the high hills low. Rays of searching garish light reflected from its surface are pitilessly flashed into the dark places of the earth, which have been wrapped around by the old-time dim religious light, since first the world began. The people in whose eyes these rays beat so mercilessly, reel and stumble blindly on in their march through life, taking wrong turnings at every step, and going woefully astray. Let us hope that succeeding generations will become used to the new conditions, and will fight their way back to a truer path; for there is no blinking the fact that the first, immediate, and obvious effects of our spirit of progress upon the weaker races tend towards degeneration.

Ten years ago the Peninsula was very different from what it has since become, and many places where the steam-engine now shrieks to the church bells, and the shirt-collar galls the perspiring neck, were but recently part and parcel of that vast 'up country', which is so little known but to the few who dwell in it, curse it,—and love it.

> I sent my soul through the invisible,
> Some Letter of the After-Life to spell,
> And Presently my Soul returned to me
> And whispered 'Thou thyself art Heaven or Hell.'

So sings the old Persian poet, lying in his rose garden, by the wine-cup that robbed him of his Robe of Honour, and his words are true; though not quite in the sense in which he wrote them. For this wisdom the far-away jungles also teach a man who has to rely solely upon himself, and upon his own resources, for the manner of his life, and the form which it is to take. To all dwellers in the desolate solitude, which every white man experiences, who is cast alone among natives, there are two 'up countries'—his Heaven and Hell, and both are of his own making. The latter is the one of which he speaks to his fellow race-mates—if he speaks at all about his solitary life. The former lies at the back of his heart, and is only known to himself, and then but dimly known till the time comes for a return to the Tents of Shem. Englishmen, above all other men, revel in their privilege of being allowed to grumble and 'grouse' over the lives which the Fates have allotted to them. They speak briefly, roughly, and gruffly of the hardships they endure, making but little of them perhaps, and talking as though their lives, as a matter of course, were made up of these things only. The instinct of the race is to see life through the national pea-soup fog, which makes all things dingy, unlovely, and ugly. Nothing is more difficult than to induce men of our race to confess that in their lives —hard though they may have been—good things have not held aloof, and that they have often been quite happy under the most unlikely circumstances, and in spite of the many horrors and privations which have long encompassed them about.

Let us take the Hell first. We often have to do so, making a virtue of necessity, and a habit is a habit; moreover, our pains are always more interesting than our pleasures—to our neighbours. Therefore, let us take the dark view of up-country life to start upon. In the beginning, when first a man turns from his own people, and dwells in isolation among an alien race, he suffers many things. The solitude of soul—that terrible solitude which is only to be experienced in a crowd—the dead monotony, without hope of change; the severance from all the pleasant things of life, and the want of any substitutes for them, eat into the heart and brain of him as a corrosive acid eats into iron. He longs for the fellowship of his own people with an exceeding great longing, till it becomes a burden too grievous to bear; he yearns to find comradeship among the people of the land, but he knows not yet the manner by which their confidence may be won, and they, on their side, know him for a stranger within their gates, view him with keen suspicion, and hold him at arm's length. His ideas, his prejudices, his modes of thought, his views on every conceivable subject differ too widely from their own, for immediate sympathy to be possible between him and them. His habits are the habits of a white man, and many little things, to which he has not yet learned to attach importance, are as revolting to the natives, as the pleasant custom of spitting on the carpet, which some old-world *Rajas* still affect, is to Europeans. His manners, too, from the native point of view, are as bad as his habits are unclean. He is respected for his wisdom, hated for his airs of superiority, pitied for his ignorance of many things, feared for what he represents, laughed at for his eccentric habits and customs, despised for his infidelity to the Faith, abhorred for his want of beauty, according to native standards of taste, and loved not at all. The men disguise their feelings, skilfully as only Orientals can, but the women and the little children do not scruple to show what their sentiments really are. When he goes abroad, the old women snarl at him as he passes and spit ostentatiously, after the native manner when some unclean thing is at hand. The mothers snatch up their little ones and carry them hurriedly away, casting a look of hate and fear over their shoulders as they run. The children scream and yell, clutch their mothers' garments, or trip and fall, howling dismally the while, in their frantic efforts to fly his presence. He is Frankenstein's monster, yearning for love and fellowship with his kind, longing to feel the hand of a friend in his, and yet knowing, by the unmistakable signs which a sight of him causes, that he is indescribably repulsive to the people among whom he lives. Add to all this that he is cut off from all the things which, to educated Europeans, make life lovely, and you will realise that his is indeed a sorry case. The privations of the body, if he has sufficient grit to justify his existence, count for little. He can live on any kind of food, sleep on the hardest of hard mats, or on the bare ground, with his head and feet in a puddle, if needs must. He can turn night into day, and sleep through the sunlight, or sleep not at all, as the case may be, if any useful purpose is to be served thereby. These are not things to trouble him, though the fleshpots of Egypt are very good when duty allows him to turn his back for a space upon the desert. Privations all these things are called in ordinary parlance, but they are of little moment, and are good for his liver. The real privations are of quite another sort. He never hears music; never sees a lovely picture; never joins in the talk and listens lovingly to conversation which strikes the answering sparks from his sodden brain. Above all, he never encounters the softening influence of the society of ladies of his own race. His few books are for a while his companions, but he reads them through and through, and cons them o'er and o'er, till the best sayings of the best authors ring flat on his sated ears like the echo of a twice-told tale. He has not yet learned that there is a great and marvellous book lying beneath his hand, a book in which all may read if they find but the means of opening the clasp which locks it, a book in which a man may read for years and never know satiety, which, though older than the hills, is ever new, and which, though studied for a lifetime, is never exhausted, and is never completely understood. This knowledge comes later; and it is then that the Chapter of the Great Book of Human Nature, which deals with natives, engrosses his attention and, touching the grayness of his life, like the rising sun, turns it into gold and purple.

Many other things he has to endure. Educated white men have inherited an infinite capacity for feeling bored; and a hot climate, which fries us all over a slow fire, grills boredom into irritability. The study of oriental human nature requires endless patience; and this is the hardest virtue for a young, energetic white man, with the irritable brain of his race, to acquire. Without it life is a misery—for

> It is not good for the Christian's health
>   To hurry the Aryan brown,
> For the Christian riles and the Aryan smiles
>   And he weareth the Christian down;
> And the end of that fight is a tombstone white
>   With the name of the late deceased,
> And the epitaph clear, A fool lies here
>   Who tried to hustle the East.

Then gradually, very gradually, and by how slow degrees he shudders in after days to recall, a change comes o'er the spirit of his nightmare. Almost unconsciously, he begins to perceive that he is sundered from the people of the land by a gulf which *they* can never hope to bridge over. If he is ever to gain their confidence the work must be of his own doing. They cannot come up to this level, he must go down to the plains in which they dwell. He must put off many of the things of the white man, must forget his airs of superiority, and must be content to be merely a native Chief among natives. His pride rebels, his prejudices cry out and will not be silenced, he knows that he will be misunderstood by his race-mates, should they see him among the people of his adoption, but the aching solitude beats down one and all of these things; and, like that eminently sensible man, the Prophet Mohammed, he gets him to the Mountain, since it is immovable and will not come to him.

Then begins a new life. He must start by learning the language of his fellows, as perfectly as it is given to a stranger to learn it. That is but the first step in a long and often a weary march. Next, he must study, with the eagerness of Browning's Grammarian, every native custom, every native conventionality, every one of the ten thousand ceremonial observances to which natives attach so vast an importance. He must grow to understand each one of the hints and *doubles ententes*, of which Malays make such frequent use, every little mannerism, sign and token, and, most difficult of all, every motion of the hearts, and every turn of thought, of those whom he is beginning to call his own people. He must become conscious of native Public Opinion, which is often diametrically opposed to the opinion of his race-mates on one and the same subject. He must be able to unerringly predict how the slightest of his actions will be regarded by the natives, and he must shape his course accordingly, if he is to maintain his influence with them, and to win their sympathy and their confidence. He must be able to place himself in imagination in all manner of unlikely places, and thence to instinctively feel the native Point of View. That is really the whole secret of governing natives. A quick perception of their Point of View, under all conceivable circumstances, a rapid process by which a European places himself in the position of the native, with whom he is dealing, an instinctive and instantaneous apprehension of the precise manner in which he will be affected, and a clear vision of the man, his feelings, his surroundings, his hopes, his desires, and his sorrows —these, and these alone, mean that complete sympathy, without which the white man among Malays is but as a sounding brass and as a tinkling cymbal.

It does not all come at once. Months, perhaps years, pass before the exile begins to feel that he is getting any grip upon the natives, and even when he thinks that he knows as much about them as is good for any man, the oriental soul shakes itself in its brown casing, and comes out in some totally unexpected and unlooked-for place, to his no small mortification and discouragement. But, when he has got thus far, discouragement matters little, for he has become bitten with the love of his discoveries, and he can no more quit them than the dipsomaniac can abandon the drams which are killing him.

Then he gets deep into a groove and is happy. His fingers are between the leaves of the Book of Human Nature, and his eager eyes are scanning the lines of the chapter which in time he hopes to make his own. The advent of another white man is a weariness of the flesh. The natives about him have learned to look upon him as one of their own people. His speech is their speech, he can think as they do, can feel as they feel, rejoice in their joys, and sorrow in their pains. He can tell them wonderful things, and a philosophy of which they had not dreamed. He never offends their susceptibilities, never wounds their self-respect, never sins against their numerous conventionalities. He has feasted with them at their weddings, doctored their pains, healed their sick, protected them from oppression, stood their friend in time of need, done them a thousand kindnesses, and has helped their dying through the strait and awful pass of death. Above all, he *understands*, and, in a manner, they love him. A new white man, speaking to him in an unknown tongue, seems to lift him for the time out of their lives. The stranger jars on the natives, who are the exile's people, and he looking through the native eyes which are no longer strange to him, sees where his race-mate offends, and in his turn is jarred, until he begins to hate his own countrymen. Coming out of the groove hurts badly, and going back into it is almost worse, but when a man is once well set in the rut of native life, these do not disturb him, for he is happy, and has no need of other and higher things. This is the exile's Heaven.

As years go on the up-country life of which I write will become less and less common in this Peninsula of ours, and the Malays will be governed wholly by men, who, never having lived their lives, cannot expect to have more than a surface knowledge of the people whose destinies are in their hands. The Native States will, I fancy, be none the better governed, and those who rule them will miss much which has tended to widen the lives of the men who came before them, and who dwelt among the people while they were still as God made them.

And those who led these lives? The years will dim the memories of all they once learned and knew and experienced; and as they indite the caustic minute to the suffering subordinate, and strangle with swaddlings of red-tape the tender babe of prosperity, they will perchance look back with wonder at the men they once were, and thinking of their experiences in the days of long ago will marvel that each one of them as he left the desert experienced the pang of Chillon's prisoner—

> Even I
> Regained my freedom with a sigh.

From *In Court and Kampong*, London 1897.

'OUR TRUSTY AND WELL-BELOVED'

SIR PHILIP HANBURY-ERSKINE, G.C.B.,G.C.M.G.—whose other titles, in the liberal type of the Royal Commission, which that day had been read before the Legislative Council, had filled up many lines of print, 'Our trusty and well-beloved Philip Hanbury-Erskine', as the said Commission had it— was pursued by the twin devils of restlessness and insomnia. Old memories—memories that mocked his present eminence —tore at the heart of him; and after sundry vain attempts to read, first a turgid official report and subsequently a frivolous French novel, he slipped from under his mosquito-net, and paddled barefoot on to the wide verandah that flanked his bedroom.

Leaning over the balustrade, he looked forth upon the sleeping capital of his kingdom. The throne which he had that day ascended had been for many years the Mecca of his pilgrimage, the goal of his ambitions, the dream of a man to whom hard toil of a practical kind had left scant space for dreaming. From the verandah upon which he stood aided by the eminence upon which Government House was set, he looked in bird's-eye fashion over the town that lay sleeping about his feet. The ethereal moonlight of south-eastern Asia spread its glamour all about, blurring and softening details, but revealing essentials as clearly as the light of day could do. Against the distant skyline the wooded cones of a little archipelago seemed to float like giant lotuses upon the surface of the glittering sea; nearer inshore the lights of moored shipping were points of garish, crudely-red fire against the black bulks of the hulls; immediately before them big stone buildings huddled closely together as though striving for standing-room marked the offices and godowns the stores and shops of the business quarter of the town.

Sir Philip's eye passed casually over all these things—though each one of them held for him memories of a half-forgotten youth—and drawing farther inland, dwelt upon the packed yet straggling native quarter, which, beginning where the solid edifices devoted to toil and trade had their ending, covered closely some ten square miles of alluvial flat, and broke up, just as a wave sprays against a rock, around the foot of the hill upon which Government House had its stand. Far away to the right, the bungalows of the European population gave a hint of their presence by glimpses of tiled roofs embowered in clustering vegetation.

Although the town was sleeping, from the restless native quarter there came a low, monotonous buzz and hum, that was as a familiar music in Sir Philip's ears. The pulsing of native drums, faint as a heart-beat, but instinct with a wild, half-savage unrest, came to him fitfully, like a voice crying from the past, and set his nerves tingling. The subtle scent of an Eastern bazaar—which is compact of spice and garlic and fruit, and of warm, voluptuous humanity—was borne to him, faint and enervating, upon the sauntering breezes of the night, awakening old thoughts, old memories, old desires, with a vividness that is possible only when an appeal is made to us through our sense of smell. Sight and sound and scent—each one of them so strangely, so startlingly familiar; each one of them an experience that belonged to a dim and distant past—whipped Sir Philip with a sudden craving for freedom and for youth; pricked him with an unfettered recklessness; rowelled him with a passionate hatred for the ordered present with its conventions, its formalities, its duties, its burdens, its petty responsibilities; and held forth to him as a lure the delight of one 'crowded hour of glorious life' down there in the seething ant-heap of native life—one more hour. only one, such as had been his of old.

He was a thick-set but active man, somewhat below middle size, with coarse black hair and dark, piercing eyes. He bore his fifty years more lightly than many men his juniors by a decade bore the burden of their age; and to-night memory and association had awakened in him the recklessness, the impetuosity and something of the divine, audacious folly of youth. He was quivering like a terrier as he stood there gazing out into the night, inhaling with fierce eagerness the scents that were borne to him from the bazaar; and his grasp upon the verandah-rail tightened till the iron seemed to eat into his palms. It was to him as though he were holding on with might and main to the conventional, respectable, iron-bound realities that hem in the life of a high Colonial official; yet he held on to them, mechanically, instinctively, reluctantly —for of a sudden these things were revealed to him as harassing trivialities that were of nothing worth.

He had left this land on promotion three-and-twenty years before; and in leaving, it had always seemed to him, he had left behind him also his youth. Since then, in uncounted quarters of the Empire, he had served in this post or the other, garnering unsought honours by the way, dealing with problems of various degrees of interest, complexity, difficulty, or dulness; and climbing ever higher, higher in the Colonial hierarchy, until now, in the fulness of time, his dearest, his only steady, ambition had been gratified, and he had returned at last to the land in which his first years of toil had been spent, to rule over it as Governor. All through those years, in climates good and bad—climates whose unvarying heat had tanned his face to a dull, colourless brown—the attainment of this position had ever nestled somewhere at the back of his mind as a cherished hope. Now that hope had been realised, and Philip Hanbury-Erskine, loosing his hold on the verandah-rail, threw passionate hands aloft, and broke out into the oldest and surely the bitterest of all human cries, '*O vanitas vanitatum*! Which of us has his desire, or, having it, is satisfied?'

He had won back his kingdom; but the cruelty of convention still withheld from him a taste of his vanished youth. Should it? Must it? To the devil with conventions and respectabilities!

He had loosed his hold on the verandah-rail, and with it his grip upon the staid and straitened path, in the rut of which the feet of a Colonial Governor should rest. He passed into his bedroom with a furiously beating heart, and presently youth and memory had wrought their miracle. Sir Philip Hanbury-Erskine passed, I have said, into his bedroom, but the man who presently emerged therefrom was not, to all outward seeming, Sir Philip Hanbury-Erskine. One distinguished potentate had dropped for the nonce out of the Colonial Office List: one unconsidered entity the more had been added to the seething, shifting, brown thousands of the native quarter.

As he slipped over the rail of the ground-floor verandah—using in his exit from his own house as much caution as a thief might have adopted in effecting an entrance—he laughed to himself with a light-hearted recklessness that had not visited him for years. His staid, official self had been left among the tumbled bed-sheets and the cast-off pyjamas in his room upstairs, and with it had remained the burden of advancing age.

Once free of the house and within the shelter of the black shadows cast by a clump of palms, he stamped his bare feet into the cool fragrance of the dew-drenched grass, and with difficulty restrained a shout of exultation. He was young again—young, young, young! He was going back to 'his own people', as he had always affectionately called them—the people among whom his youthful days had been spent; the people whose language, thoughts, and hopes and fears had of old been as his own. He was about to dip once again into the secret wells of native life, to hear the old sounds, smell the old smells, experience the old sensations, and for a brief hour to forget that he was one upon whose shoulders Fate had imposed the burden of official greatness, with all its dwarfing, soul-stunning conventionalities. For years—such long, long weary years—he had not been suffered to be natural, to be himself—even to be a Man. Instead, he had been only an Official, only the temporary holder of a given post—one who was so much in the public eye in the little worlds wherein he had laboured, that his every action, his every opinion, almost his every chance word, had been regarded as legitimate subject for comment and for criticism. Now, just for once, before it was too late, before his should have become a figure too familiar in the place for such wild pranks to be possible, he would steal from the hampering fictions wherewith his life was beset one little hour of freedom absolute, of unshackled individuality, of manhood and of youth.

It is one of the many astounding facts of Asia that two sets of human lives, the white and the native can coexist side by side in a single locality, each almost completely ignorant of the other, each barely touching its neighbour on the outside edges, and then only at rare intervals. Yet the man who is, as it were, amphibious—to whom the *terra firma* of solid

British convention and the deep waters of Oriental life are alike familiar—finds himself stepping from one to the other at will and with an appalling suddenness. Philip Hanbury-Erskine had in the days of his youth been one of these rare amphibians; and even now his memory held the key which can unlock the gates that are barred so jealously against all but a handful of his countrymen. Within half an hour of the time that had seen him leave the outer shell of His Excellency the Governor the G.C.B. and the G.C.M.G. and all the rest of it, in a discarded heap upon his bedroom floor, Europe and its memories had been thrust into the obscure distance, and he was back once more in the old, old East.

His bare feet puddled the dust of the roadway, already set with the impressions of countless unshod feet; his eyes dwelt lovingly upon the string-bedsteads placed in the five-foot ways before the native shops, and upon the white figures stretched corpse-like upon them; the throbbing beat of drums, each thud and lilt of which held for him its inner meaning, came to his ears, the half-savage cadences keeping time to his own unrest; the reek—the old, familiar reek—of an Asiatic bazaar, pungent, penetrating, enervating, voluptuous, pervaded the stillness of the night, and he opened wide his nostrils and snuffed it in lovingly because it awoke in him such wild visions of the past.

Noiselessly as a shadow he flitted along the broad road—flanked by native shops and by the sleeping, white-clad figures aping the likeness of the dead—and presently turned down a narrow alley on his left, where old and dilapidated houses leaned helplessly on one another's shoulders, as though overcome with weariness, their roofs nearly joining ragged hands across the crooked fairway.

'Deplorably insanitary,' was the comment of Sir Philip. 'Homey, homey, homey!' cried the new-born man in him.

'Unchanged by a hair's breadth in a quarter of a century! As it was in the beginning, is now, and ever shall be! Asia, my Asia!'

He groped his way down the straitened passage, for the bulging roofs overhead nearly excluded the moonlight, and paused presently to take his bearings.

'This must be the place,' he murmured to himself. 'I wonder if it is unchanged too. I'll try.'

He crept into the shadow, and drew near to a door sunken below the level of the alley, and rapped upon its panel with the knuckles of his hand. He rapped seven times with 'dots' and 'dashes', much as a telegraph operator manipulates his instrument; and a moment later the door shuddered and creaked, and then drew cautiously backward for the space of a few inches.

'*Salam Aleikum!*' said a creaking, nasal voice.

'*Aleikum salam!*' returned Sir Philip mechanically.

'Whither comest thou?' pursued the voice.

'I come,' said Sir Philip—and in a flash the old jingling formula, which he had not thought upon for years, recurred to his memory—

' I come from the forests that know no paths,
  From the waters that hold no fish;
  From the place where the wild kite veers and sails,
  Where the man-apes drink as they swing from the
                                         boughs,
  Where no Law runs and where men are free!'

'Enter, Brother,' said the voice, and the door stood wide.

Philip had no need for the flaring torch which the woman who had opened to him held high above her head. The narrow passage down which they were walking, with its meaningless twists and turns, was to him at that moment the most familiar thing in all the world, though his feet had not trodden it for a quarter of a century. It gave presently upon a big square room, the centre of which was filled by a raised platform or dais, covered with thick carpets, upon which near a dozen natives, men and women, were seated playing cards. The only light in the place was shed by *damar*-torches fixed in heavy wooden stands. The players glanced up at the approach of the new-comer.

'Peace be upon this house and upon all who sit therein!' said Philip from the doorway.

'And upon thee peace!' came in answering chorus from the card-players.

'This be a Brother who hath strayed far,' piped the woman, indicating Philip with a gesture that had in it something of proud proprietorship. 'His password is that of the forest!'

The players laid down their cards and stared at Philip.

'That password hath not been used for twenty year and more,' declared an old man who sat among them. 'Say, little Brother, whither hast thou been, that thy password dates from the days of long ago?'

'I have been far,' said Philip; 'far, very far—farther than eye can see, farther than horse may gallop, farther than bird can fly! Listen! Even my mother-tongue hangs awry upon my lips!'

'Didst thou incur the sentence of Bombay?' asked the man quite simply. 'Bombay', in the vernacular, stands for 'transportation'.

'Yes,' said Philip, with a sullen nod; and he felt that he spoke the truth.

'What thing led thereto?' pursued his interrogator.

'Certain services I rendered to the Kompani,' said Philip, again with perfect truth. In these lands, where the memory of 'Old John Company Bahadur' still lingers, the Government continues to be known among the natives by the ancient title.

'The Kompani hath a long arm and a longer memory,' said another of the card-players. 'Art wise to return, my friend?'

'Of my wisdom Brother, I am by no means assured,' said Philip, feeling that he and Truth were indeed walking hand-in-hand to-night. 'But thou knowest the saying: "A golden rain in a stranger's land and a pelt of hail in the land of thy fathers; yet dearer ever must thine own land be." To-night, I am feeling, according to the saying of the men of old, as feels the eel when it wins back to its mud-hole, the *sirih*-leaf to its vine, or the areca-nut to its twig!'

'And behold, there be yet another returned this day,' piped the woman who had let him in. ' "Tuan Iskin" we were wont to call him in the old days and now he is the Tuan Gubnor who is set to rule over all our land!'

'Of old he had a man's tongue in him,' said one of the card-players, a lithe, clean-limbed, sharp-featured fellow of about Philip's own age, extravagantly dressed in silks of many hues, and armed, in defiance of the white men's law, with a native *kris* of wonderful workmanship. 'He and I were as brothers, close in friendship as is the quick and the nail; and the word passed amongst us that he was one of the Faithful.'

'In very truth he was,' screamed the woman, who had now seated herself on the edge of the dais. 'Else, had he been an unbeliever, would I, Si-Bedah, have loved him?'

Philip Erskine, half hidden among the wavering shadows, looked keenly first at the man, then at the woman; and as he looked their faces came up through the mists of memory and grew plain to him, much as the face of a diver grows plain to the sight as it comes upward through still waters. Raja Sulong was the name of the man, he recalled—a roistering young scion of a royal house whose recklessness, extravagance, and courage had passed in those days into a byword. The woman—he would never unassisted have recognised her—was Bedah, the dancing-girl, of old the cause of much 'madness', as the emphatic vernacular phrase has it, to the love-lorn youths of the city. In those days she had been a dainty creature with bright eyes, sleek flower-decked hair, soft, delicately-tinted yellow cheeks, and a wondrous grace of movement. Now she was a hag, no less; for a quarter of a century brings old age to womanhood that blossoms prematurely before the teens are reached.

'But he did not love thee, mother,' sneered one of the other women present—'or so men say.'

'He did! He did!' screamed the woman who had of old been Bedah. 'But he was not fashioned in the mould of common men. He loved me, but I was what Fate had made of me—a woman of the bazaar! He had no appetite for *sisa*—the scraps that remain when others have had their fill; wherefore he threw me to the dogs—such dogs as you, and you, and you!' And with a furious gesture she indicated several of the men present.

'Better such "dogs", as thou namest us, than a white man!' said one, and he turned aside to spit as a token of his unutterable disgust.

'Yet is he the only *man* that I have ever known,' yelled the woman, her voice rising in tremulous, discordant sharps and flats. 'He was full of pity and of compassion, like Allah's self, the Merciful, the Compassionate. To him women-folk were not oxen to be yoked for the service of man, their master, but queens; and as a queen he treated me—*me*, Bedah, the dancing-girl of the bazaar! I loved him and he loved me; but owing to the devil of perversity within him, never did our love know happiness. Yet had I rather been loved once after a fashion such as his than a thousand times by you—men of monstrous passions and dwarfish souls. Now hath he come back to rule over this our land, and you, who prate sedition against the Kompani and hatch clutches of addled plots, have a care, I say, have a care, for ye have now to deal with a Man!'

An angry growl broke from several of the men, and the old woman, drawing deeper into the shadows, fell to mumbling to herself as her emotions simmered away.

'To-morrow I go to him,' said Raja Sulong, 'and he will receive me brotherly for the sake of old days. The pig-folk of the Kompani are in sore doubt anent the free tribes of the frontier, for their minds are divided as to the quarter whence the threatened raid will come. They think, poor deluded ones, that this said raid will be like unto its forerunners—a police stockade surprised, a few slaughtered Sikhs sent screaming to the Terrible Place, some fifty villages in flames, and then retreat. They know not that the eve of the Great Combat is at hand, that the *Jehad* which shall see the extermination of the Infidel' (all present spat in unison at the word) 'draws hourly more near, and that the Holy One of Paloh hath promised victory, final and everlasting, to the Children of the Prophet. Say, Brother,' he continued, turning towards the shadow in which Philip had his seat, 'hast thou also a mind to take a hand in this game of hazard which we are about to play, with men's lives for the dice and kingdoms for the stakes?'

'Allah aiding me,' said Philip from the darkness in deep, guttural tones, 'I too will take some little part in the said game!'

'And the plan, the plan?' said a youngster eagerly. 'Hath all been thought out with wisdom and with strategy?'

'Judge ye, then; judge!' said Raja Sulong; and while the rest of the party gathered about him, he proceeded, by means of the contents of a match-box, some cards, and bone counters to produce a rough map of the area which would be involved in the coming rising. Philip, watching keenly, heard the old names of men and places crop up one after the other; and though sprinkled among them there were a few which were to him unfamiliar, in half an hour he found himself in possession of the whole of the Raja's scheme.

'And to-morrow,' that worthy concluded triumphantly, 'I go to Tuan Iskin, who now hath been made Governor over us, and he will receive me in brotherly fashion for the sake of old memories. Then shall I fill his ears with false rumours and vain report; and he, reposing in me much confidence, will order all things as we, who have framed this plan, would elect that they should be ordered. In this is plainly to be discerned the finger of Allah, the Merciful, the Compassionate, who is mindful ever of his children.'

Philip rose to his feet and stepped forth very deliberately into the full glare of the *damar*-torches.

'What doth it profit to wait for the morrow?' he asked, in a soft and even voice. 'Speak now, friend, that he whom you name Tuan Iskin may hear.'

The recklessness that had been upon him that evening, as a veritable demoniacal possession, had mastered him now. Prudence had bidden him depart as he had come, undetected; but prudence he had thrown to the winds. He knew that he had but to follow her wise counsels, and presently he would find himself safe within the walls of Government House, where, armed with the authority that belongs to rulers, he would be able to baffle utterly the paltry schemes that had been laid bare for his inspection. But to-night, for a little space, he had promised himself, he would put off the things of his authority and would pass down, for the only, for the last time, into the world of men, to be there just a man among his fellows. If he were to defeat Raja Sulong and his conspiracies, he would compass his end unaided by powers external to himself. Therefore he rose and spoke, and waited with a tense, quivering excitement, that was all pleasurable, to see what would result.

For an instant those who heard him sat in stunned silence; then the room buzzed like a hive into which a stone has been flung. Men and women sprang to their feet—the former feeling for their weapons, the latter screaming their fear. Torches and brass ewers were overturned; bare feet scuttered and stamped; voices a-thrill with excitement gave vent to fierce ejaculations, though their tones were sunken to prudent whispers; and the flickering light of the unextinguished torches glinted upon the blades of knives held in nervous, eager hands.

A clutch fell upon Philip's arm, and he was drawn back against one of the immense bevelled pillars that stood at each corner of the dais; someone, crouching upon the floor at his feet, thrust a naked *sundang*—the stout Malayan broadsword —into his hand; and the voice of the hag, who of old had been Bedah the dancing-girl, whispered to him to be wary.

The solid wooden pillar that protected his back from all possibility of assault filled him with a splendid confidence.

'Speak now, friend, if thou hast a mind to speak,' he said, and a laugh of sheer exultation broke from him. He had promised himself freedom from trammelling conventions, he had promised himself a revival of the memories of his youth. His wildest hopes had never suggested the possibility of a rough-and-tumble such as now was imminent, a situation such as this, which belonged to what had so long seemed a closed chapter of his history. Of old, too, life had spread inviting vistas ahead of him: now he had explored them and found them empty. His supreme indifference to the event, let what would befall, steeled him with a new courage. He was having a moment of big emotions, and the rest mattered not at all.

A breathless silence had fallen upon the room, out of which there presently emerged a voice that cried, 'He is a dead man! He hath mastered our secrets! He must die!'

'Hold! Hold!' cried other voices.

Suddenly there was a scuttering rush made at him by three or four men, and Philip, swinging his broadsword, heard the flat of the blade tell loudly upon the faces of his opponents. He had as yet no occasion to use the edge, for two men went down and climbed painfully out of harm's way, while their fellows drew back into the darkness. 'Well struck, but why didst thou not *slay?*' piped Bedah at his feet.

A loud knocking came suddenly from the outer door, and a hushed silence followed on its heels. The knocking came again more insistent than before, blent with the rough voice of a white man demanding admittance in sadly mispronounced Malay.

'The police, the police!' whispered half a dozen voices, and the last torch was extinguished, while bare feet pattered hastily across the mat-strewn floor.

Heavy blows were falling now upon the outer door. The police were breaking it in.

'Come, heart of my heart,' whispered Bedah; and holding his hand in hers, she led him down from the dais and into some by-passage of this human rabbit-warren. Still clutching his broadsword, he followed blindly through the intense darkness; and as the shouts of the police and the hammering upon the yielding door grew faint in the distance, he found himself being led out into the moonlight.

The passage gave upon a narrow alley—the identity of which came back to Philip's memory, as so many identities had recurred that night—and as Philip and his guide emerged through the straitened doorway a lithe figure flung itself upon them, the moonlight glinting on a bared blade. Philip saw in a flash the nervous, muscular arm upraised, the snake-like *kris* poised aloft, the fierce face of Raja Sulong—with flaming eyes, hair flying backward wildly, and tilted prominent chin—and knew that the broadsword he was himself raising in his defence was stayed, as weapons are arrested in a nightmare, by the lintel of the door.

With a grunt from Raja Sulong the *kris* descended, and Philip, feeling his impotence, nerved himself to receive the blow; but with a shrill scream Bedah threw herself upon him, and the snaky blade was buried in her back. Philip, freeing himself from her grip, leaped clear of the doorway, and concentrating all his strength and all his fury in a single stroke, brought the broadsword down upon the head of Raja Sulong, cleaving it to the cheek-bones. The man's body dropped limply across the body of the woman.

Philip, kneeling on one knee, turned Bedah on her side, and laid a hand above the region of her heart. No faintest throb responded. Stooping low above her, he kissed her reverently, and rising, turned and left her.

'A life for a life,' he murmured, 'and his was taken in self-defence, and hers was given for me. God forgive me this night's work, for never shall I forgive myself!'

The dawn was breaking greyly as Sir Philip Hanbury-Erskine was born once more into the official world of which he is still by no means the least distinguished ornament.

Next day, clothed and in his right mind, he wrote the famous Minute forecasting the plan of campaign which the natives were about to adopt in the threatened frontier rising—the Minute upon which rests the almost superstitious belief of his subordinates in his prescience and understanding of native character. Later, as in duty bound, he bade the police make diligent search for the author of the double murder reported to have occurred upon the previous night in an alley of the native city. Later still he opened a charity bazaar, and made a speech so strikingly appropriate to the occasion that it has been pirated and sold widely for the benefit of uninventive country vicars.

And when the day was ended, in the dead unhappy night, he told himself that old age had come upon him in the space of a single hour.

From *Malayan Monochromes*, London, 1913.

Other Oxford Paperbacks for readers interested in South-East Asia, past and present

Cambodia

Angkor: An Introduction
GEORGE COEDÈS

Angkor and the Khmers
MALCOLM MacDONALD

Indonesia

An Artist in Java and Other Islands of Indonesia
JAN POORTENAAR

Bali and Angkor
GEOFFREY GORER

Coolie
MADELON H. LULOFS

Flowering Lotus: A View of Java in the 1950s
HAROLD FORSTER

Forgotten Kingdoms in Sumatra
F. M. SCHNITGER

The Head-Hunters of Borneo
CARL BOCK

The Hidden Force*
LOUIS COUPERUS

A House in Bali
COLIN McPHEE

In Borneo Jungles
WILLIAM O. KROHN

Indonesia: Land under the Rainbow
MOCHTAR LUBIS

Island of Bali*
MIGUEL COVARRUBIAS

Islands of Indonesia
VIOLET CLIFTON

Java: Facts and Fancies
AUGUSTA DE WIT

Java: The Garden of the East
E. R. SCIDMORE

Java Pageant
H. W. PONDER

Javanese Panorama
H. W. PONDER

The Last Paradise
HICKMAN POWELL

Makassar Sailing
G. E. P. COLLINS

The Malay Archipelago
ALFRED RUSSEL WALLACE

The Outlaw and Other Stories
MOCHTAR LUBIS

Rambles in Java and the Straits in 1852
'BENGAL CIVILIAN' (CHARLES WALTER KINLOCH)

Rubber
MADELON H. LULOFS

Six Moons in Sulawesi
HARRY WILCOX

Soul of the Tiger*
JEFFREY A. McNEELY
and PAUL SPENCER WACHTEL

Sumatra: Its History and People
EDWIN M. LOEB

A Tale from Bali*
VICKI BAUM

The Temples of Java
JACQUES DUMARÇAY

Through Central Borneo
CARL LUMHOLTZ

Tropic Fever
LADISLAO SZÉKELY

Twilight in Djakarta
MOCHTAR LUBIS

Twin Flower: A Story of Bali
G. E. P. COLLINS

Unbeaten Tracks in Islands of the Far East
ANNA FORBES

Yogyakarta: Cultural Heart of Indonesia
MICHAEL SMITHIES

Malaysia

Ah King and Other Stories*
W. SOMERSET MAUGHAM

Among Primitive Peoples in Borneo
IVOR H. N. EVANS

An Analysis of Malay Magic
K. M. ENDICOTT

The Best of Borneo Travel
VICTOR T. KING

Borneo Jungle
TOM HARRISSON

The Casuarina Tree*
W. SOMERSET MAUGHAM

The Field-Book of a Jungle-Wallah
CHARLES HOSE

The Gardens of the Sun
F. W. BURBIDGE

Glimpses into Life in Malayan Lands
JOHN TURNBULL THOMSON

The Golden Chersonese
ISABELLA BIRD

Illustrated Guide to the Federated Malay States (1923)
C. W. HARISSON

Malay Poisons and Charm Cures
JOHN D. GIMLETTE

My Life in Sarawak
MARGARET BROOKE, THE RANEE OF SARAWAK

Natural Man
CHARLES HOSE

Nine Dayak Nights
W. R. GEDDES

Orang-Utan
BARBARA HARRISSON

The Pirate Wind
OWEN RUTTER

Queen of the Head-Hunters
SYLVIA, LADY BROOKE, THE RANEE OF SARAWAK

Saleh: A Prince of Malaya
SIR HUGH CLIFFORD

Six Years in the Malay Jungle
CARVETH WELLS

The Soul of Malaya
HENRI FAUCONNIER

They Came to Malaya: A Travellers' Anthology
J. M. GULLICK

Wanderings in the Great Forests of Borneo
ODOARDO BECCARI

The White Rajahs of Sarawak
ROBERT PAYNE

World Within: A Borneo Story
TOM HARRISSON

Philippines

Little Brown Brother
LEON WOLFF

Singapore

Main Fleet to Singapore
RUSSELL GRENFELL

The Manners and Customs of the Chinese
J. D. VAUGHAN

Raffles of the Eastern Isles
C. E. WURTZBURG

Singapore 1941–1942
MASANOBU TSUJI

Thailand

Behind the Painting and Other Stories
SIBURAPHA

The English Governess at the Siamese Court
ANNA LEONOWENS

The Kingdom of the Yellow Robe
ERNEST YOUNG

A Physician at the Court of Siam
MALCOLM SMITH

The Politician and Other Stories
KHAMSING SRINAWK

Temples and Elephants
CARL BOCK

To Siam and Malaya in the Duke of Sutherland's Yacht *Sans Peur*
FLORENCE CADDY

Travels in Siam, Cambodia and Laos 1858–1860
HENRI MOUHOT

Vietnam

The General Retires and Other Stories
NGUYEN HUY THIEP

*Titles marked with an asterisk have restricted rights.

Introduction to Amazon AWS

How to Get Started With Amazon Web Services

Eric Frick

Published by Eric Frick 2023

Last Update August, 2023

Copyright

Copyright © 2023 Eric Frick.

While every precaution has been taken in the preparation of this book, the publisher assumes no responsibility for errors, omissions, or for damages resulting from the use of the information contained herein.

Foreword

Hello, and welcome to the exciting world of cloud computing. I specifically designed this book to be the companion book to the video course that I have hosted on my website. You might think of this as the lab manual for the course. You can get more out of this book by reviewing the accompanying videos in the web-based course.

You have free access to this course by purchasing this book. I included the link to this course in the Appendix of this book. Thank you for purchasing this book, and welcome to the class!

Contents

Copyright	**2**
Foreword	**4**
Contents	**5**
1.0 Introduction	**8**
1.1 Course Overview	10
1.2 Amazon AWS Overview	16
1.3 AWS Free Account	22
1.4 The AWS CLI	36
2.0 Cloud Concepts	**43**
2.1 What is Cloud Computing?	44
2.2 The History of Cloud Computing	47
2.3 What Are the Advantages of Cloud Computing?	56
2.4 The Limitations of Cloud Computing	61
2.5 Cloud Service Models	66
2.6 The Economics of Cloud Computing	71
2.7 The AWS Well Architected Framework	76
2.8 Cloud Concepts Quiz	82
3.0 Amazon AWS Core Services	**84**
3.1 What is Amazon EC2?	88
3.2 How to Create a Virtual Machine Using Amazon AWS	97
3.3 What is Amazon S3?	119
3.4 Deploying a Website on Amazon S3	128
3.5 Amazon Relational Database Service (RDS)	140
3.6 How to Create a Database in Amazon RDS	146
3.7 Amazon Cloud Watch	150
3.9 AWS Lambda	155
3.9 How to Build a Lambda Function	160

4.0 Security and Account Management	**163**
4.1 What is IAM?	164
4.2 IAM Hierarchy	171
4.3 IAM Roles	175
5.0 Billing and Pricing	**180**
5.1 AWS Pricing Models	181
5.2 AWS Account Structures	187
6.0 Cloud Career Information	**191**
6.1 Top Cloud Jobs and Salaries	192
6.2 Top AWS Certifications for 2023	195
Chapter 7 Summary	**199**
7.1 Course Summary	200
7.2 About the Author	201
7.3 More From Destin Learning	202
7.4 Destin Learning YouTube Channel	204
Appendix	**205**
A.1 Access to Online Course	205
A.2 Cloud Concepts Quiz Answers	206

Eric Frick

1.0 Introduction

Hello, and welcome to the book! This book is the first part of a series that is an introduction to cloud computing concepts. I have based these books on courses that I have taught online to entry-level students on various web platforms. I designed this course to give you some of the theory behind cloud systems and some practical experience using a real cloud system, like Amazon AWS.

I assume for this book and course that you are a complete beginner and have no previous experience

Introduction to Amazon AWS

with cloud computing. You will need a computer with a web browser to view the videos and access Amazon AWS. Also, you will need a valid credit card to sign up for your trial Amazon AWS account. Amazon will not charge you for the use of this account, but they require this for registration.

I wrote this book for absolute beginners and kept the material to a reasonable length, so you can quickly get up to speed with cloud computing and see if it interests you for study further. I also wanted to mix in some of the theory and definitions of cloud computing, along with some practical, hands-on exercises, so you can not only read about systems, but actually learn to use them in practice.

Eric Frick

1.1 Course Overview

Welcome to the **Introduction to Amazon AWS** course! In this course, you will learn about the basics of cloud computing and how to get started with Amazon AWS. Amazon is the world's leading cloud computing platform and is offering more and more services each month. In this course, I will explain the key concepts of each area and then reinforce those concepts with hands-on exercises. I am a firm believer in learning by doing. I have organized this course to be modular, so you can take one concept at a time and work on the material at your own pace.

I recommend reading the material first to give yourself an excellent overview and background on the topic. Next, follow up by watching the videos, in the online course, that also include demonstrations. This may take some extra time, but it will also help you retain the information.

Course Objectives:

By the end of this course, you will:
- gain a solid understanding of cloud computing and the AWS ecosystem.
- explore AWS's major services, their use cases, and how they interact.
- master key concepts, such as virtualization, networking, security, and scalability in the cloud.
- learn to create and manage virtual servers, databases, storage, and more using AWS services.
- understand AWS's pricing models and strategies for cost optimization.
- develop hands-on skills by working with real-world scenarios and practical examples.
- build a strong foundation for AWS certification exams, if desired.

Course Modules

This book and course are grouped into the following Modules/Chapters.

Eric Frick

Introduction

In the introduction of this book, you will learn about AWS's history, market position, and key services. I will also show you how to set up a free account with Amazon AWS and how to navigate the AWS console. This section concludes with a brief introduction to the AWS command line.

Cloud Concepts

In this chapter, we will look at the fundamentals of cloud computing. We will first start off with a definition of cloud computing and then follow up with a brief history of cloud computing. Next we will look at the advantages and limitations of cloud computing. Following this we will look at how cloud systems are deployed by defining cloud service models. This chapter then concludes with a look at the Amazon AWS well architected framework.

Introduction to Amazon AWS

Amazon Core Services

In this chapter, I will introduce you to the core services of Amazon AWS. After this introduction we will examine each of these core services:

- Amazon EC2 and Virtual Servers:
    - Create, configure, and manage Amazon EC2 instances.
    - Explore instance types, storage options, and security considerations.
- Amazon S3 and Data Storage:
    - Master Amazon S3 for object storage and distribution.
    - Learn about storage classes, data management, and common use cases.
- Amazon RDS and Databases:
    - Set up and manage relational databases using Amazon RDS.
    - Explore supported database engines, benefits, and use cases.
- Amazon Lambda and Serverless Computing:
    - Discover serverless architecture and create AWS Lambda functions.
    - Learn to respond to events and execute code without managing servers.

Eric Frick

Security and Account Management

An important part of any system is security and access management. With Amazon AWS, this is Identity and Access Management (IAM). In this section, we will learn about the basic features of IAM and how roles are used to provision access to services for users.

Billing and Pricing

In this section, we will learn the basics of how AWS prices for services are determined and how to estimate the cost of services using the AWS Price Calculator.

Who Should Take This Course

I designed this course for beginners aiming to learn about cloud computing and AWS from scratch. I also designed it for Developers, System Administrators, and IT professionals seeking to expand their AWS skills. Individuals pursuing AWS certifications can also benefit from this course.

Summary

This book and course combine insightful content, practical demonstrations, and hands-on exercises to ensure a comprehensive learning experience. Each module provides clear explanations, real-world examples, and step-by-step instructions to help you grasp complex concepts and apply them practically.

Get ready to unlock the power of Amazon AWS and harness its capabilities to build scalable, reliable, and innovative solutions. Let's get started and learn the basics of Cloud Computing and Amazon AWS!

Eric Frick

1.2 Amazon AWS Overview

Amazon Web Services (AWS) is a subsidiary of Amazon.com, founded in 2006. It emerged as a response to Amazon's own need for scalable and flexible infrastructure to support its rapidly growing e-commerce platform. AWS started by offering basic cloud computing services and has since evolved into a comprehensive suite of over 200 services covering computing, storage, databases, analytics, machine learning, and more. AWS's innovative approach to cloud computing revolutionized the IT industry, paving the way for businesses to scale and innovate without the constraints of traditional on-premises infrastructure.

Market Position

AWS is widely recognized as a global leader in cloud computing services. It holds a substantial market share in the cloud industry and continues to dominate the market along with other major players, like Microsoft Azure and Google Cloud Platform. Its early entry, extensive service offerings, and focus on innovation have solidified its position as a go-to choice for organizations of all sizes seeking reliable, scalable, and cost-effective cloud solutions.

Major Services Offered

AWS offers a comprehensive range of cloud services across multiple domains. The following list of services is not exhaustive, but gives you some of the highlights of the hundreds of services they offer.

Compute: Amazon EC2 (virtual servers), AWS Lambda (serverless computing), AWS Elastic Beanstalk (application deployment and management)

Storage: Amazon S3 (object storage), Amazon EBS (block storage), Amazon Glacier (long-term archival)

Eric Frick

Databases: Amazon RDS (relational databases), Amazon DynamoDB (NoSQL database), Amazon Aurora (high-performance database)

Networking: Amazon VPC (virtual private cloud), Amazon Route 53 (DNS), AWS Direct Connect (dedicated network connection)

Analytics: Amazon Redshift (data warehousing), Amazon EMR (big data processing), Amazon QuickSight (business intelligence)

Machine Learning and AI: Amazon SageMaker (ML platform), Amazon Polly (text-to-speech), Amazon Rekognition (image and video analysis)

Security: AWS Identity and Access Management (IAM), AWS Key Management Service (KMS), Amazon GuardDuty (threat detection)

IoT: AWS IoT Core (Internet of Things), AWS IoT Analytics (data analysis), AWS Greengrass (edge computing)

Application Integration: Amazon SQS (message queue), Amazon SNS (notification service), AWS Step Functions (workflow automation)

Introduction to Amazon AWS

Regions and Availability Zones

AWS operates a global network of data centers in geographic regions around the world. Each region consists of multiple Availability Zones, which are physically separated data centers with redundant power, networking, and cooling. AWS operates in multiple regions, including North America, Europe, Asia, South America, and more.

The following is a map of Amazon AWS regions:

○ Regions
○ Coming Soon

I should note that this is constantly changing as Amazon is adding more regions every year. A key advantage of having regional data centers worldwide is to locate services closer to the end user, which improves performance and reduces network latency.

Eric Frick

Key Customers

AWS serves a diverse customer base ranging from startups to enterprises and public sector organizations. Some of its key customers include:

- Netflix
- Airbnb
- NASA
- General Electric (GE)
- Samsung
- BMW
- Siemens
- Johnson & Johnson
- Pfizer
- Capital One

AWS's customer base spans various industries, demonstrating its ability to cater to a wide range of use cases and requirements.

Summary

In summary, Amazon Web Services (AWS) has played a pivotal role in transforming how organizations consume and manage IT resources. With a rich history, a robust portfolio of services, a global presence, and a reputation for innovation, AWS remains a frontrunner in the cloud computing industry, enabling businesses to accelerate their digital transformation journeys. For the latest information, I recommend visiting the official AWS website. (https://aws.amazon.com)

Eric Frick

1.3 AWS Free Account

This section describes how to sign up for a free Amazon AWS account. Once you sign up, you can use their cloud services from the web console.
In your web browser, Navigate to the AWS Web Page http://aws.amazon.com/free.

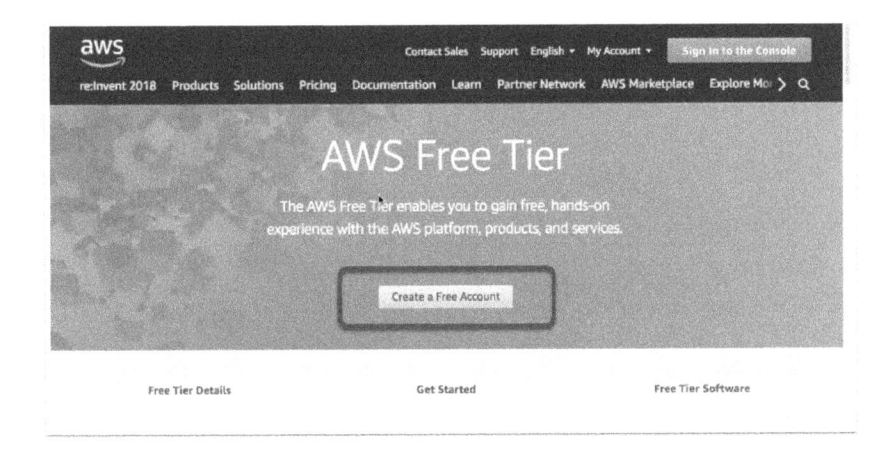

Introduction to Amazon AWS

Read About the FREE Tier

Next, read about the features of Amazon's free service tier. This trial period lasts for 12 months. It does have limitations on the number of computer hours you can consume and the size of the virtual servers you can provision. These free services change from time to time, so scroll through the list to see the complete details.

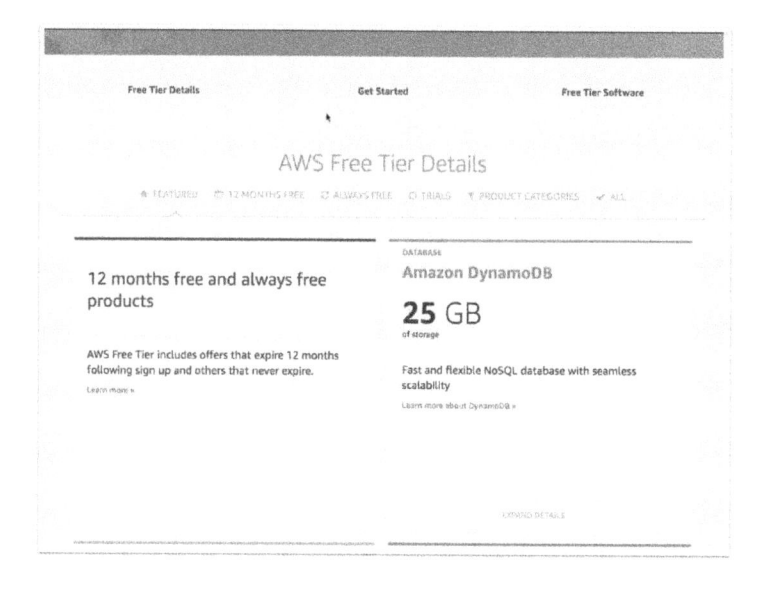

Eric Frick

Click on the Free Tier Button to Get Started

After you have reviewed the list of free services, click on the *Create a Free Account* button to begin the registration process.

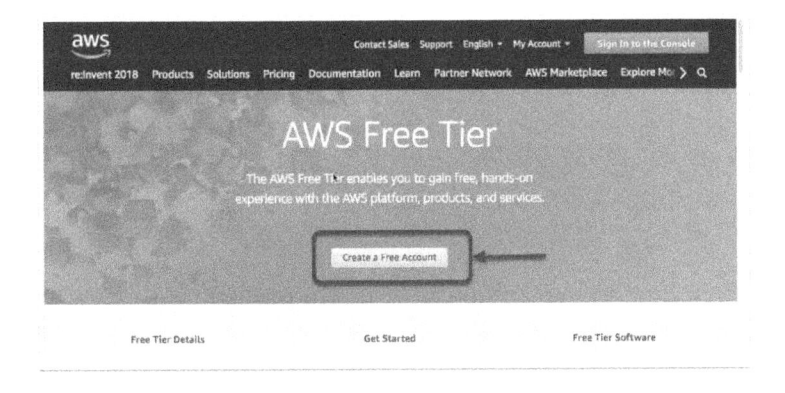

Introduction to Amazon AWS

Create Your Login Credentials

Enter your email address and your desired password for your account. You will also have to enter an account name. Click the *Continue* button once you have completed entering this information.

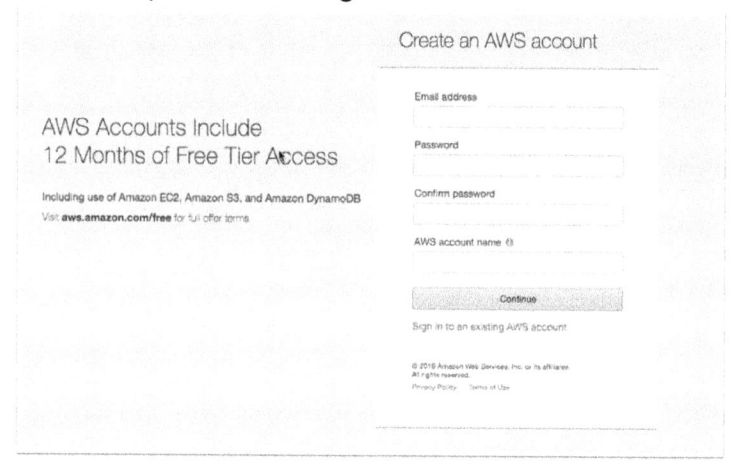

Eric Frick

Enter Your Contact Information

Next, enter all of your account information. Select whether this is a company or personal account. After filling this in, enter the captcha code and check that you have read the terms and conditions. After completing this, click the *Create Account and Continue* button.

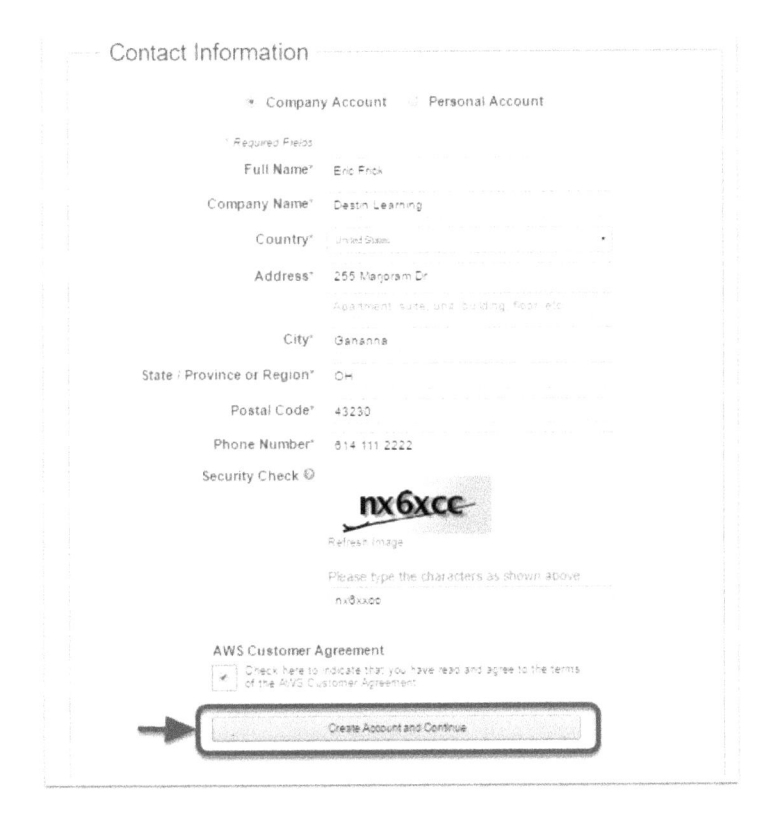

Introduction to Amazon AWS

Enter Your Payment Information

Now, enter your credit card information and select the *Continue* button. Even though this is a free account, they still require a credit card number, in case you use resources outside the free tier. This account will allow you to use resources outside the free ones, and Amazon does an excellent job of letting you know when you are going to use resources outside the free tier. We will see this in a later chapter, when we create a virtual machine with a free account.

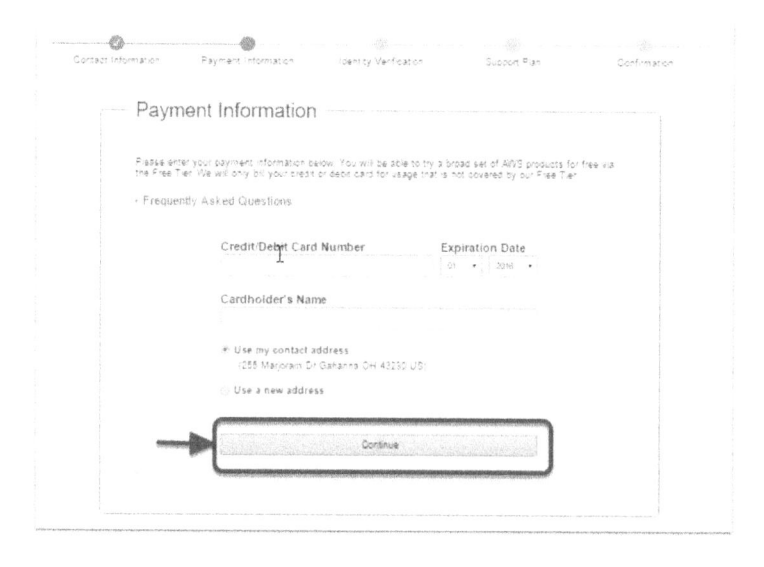

Eric Frick

Verify Your Identity

Next, enter your cell phone number for an identity verification check.

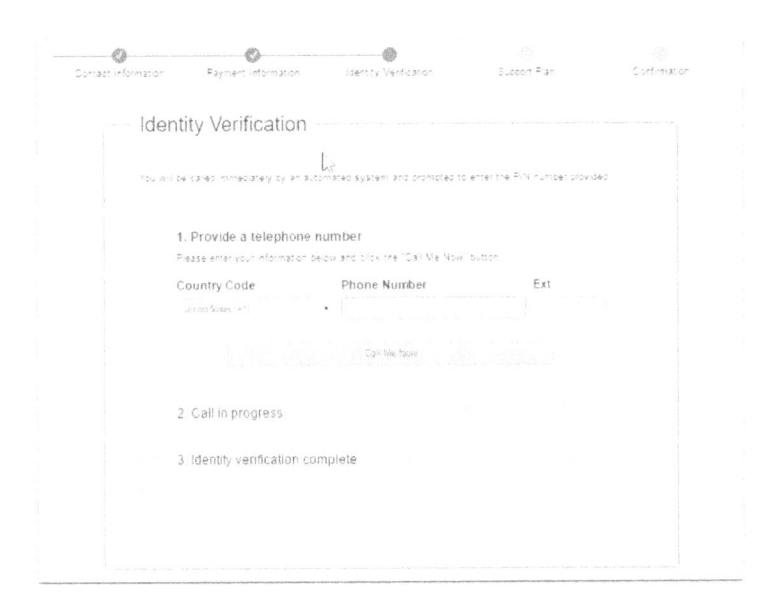

Introduction to Amazon AWS

Enter Your PIN

Identity Verification

You will be called immediately by an automated system and prompted to enter the PIN number provided.

1. Provide a telephone number ✓

2. Call in progress
Please follow the instructions on the telephone and key in the following Personal Identification Number (PIN) on your telephone when prompted.

PIN: 5180

If you have not yet received a call at the number indicated above please wait. This page will automatically update with what you need to do next.

3. Identity verification complete

Eric Frick

Complete the Verification

Next, click the *Continue to select your Support Plan* button.

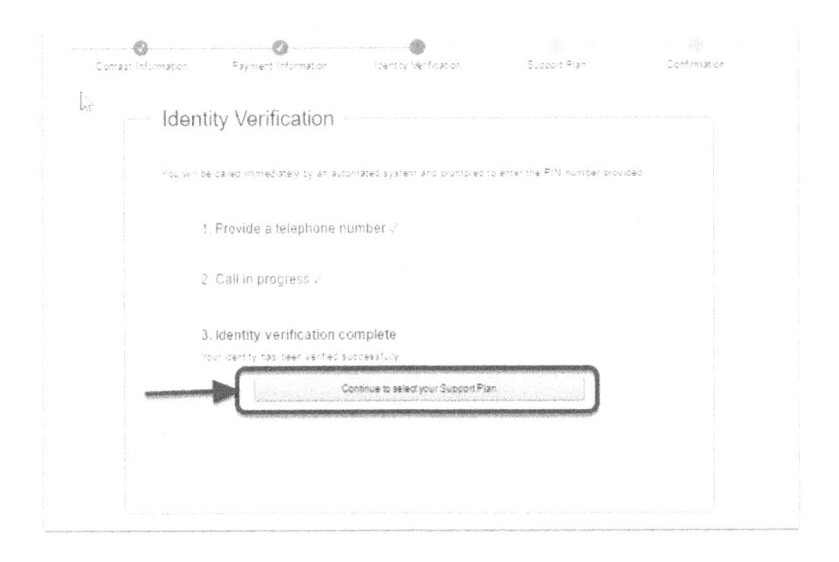

Introduction to Amazon AWS

Select Your Support Plan

Select the *Basic* support plan, which Amazon includes for free. The other plans are paid support plans you can upgrade to later, if you need them. For just getting started with the platform, the basic plan is all you need.

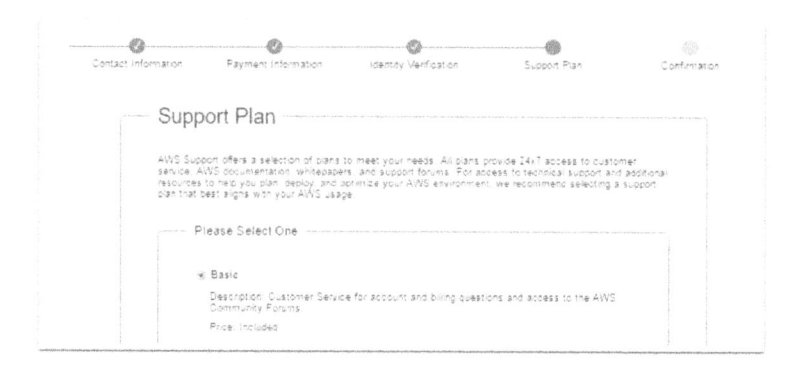

Eric Frick

Complete Your Selection

After selecting the basic plan, click the *Continue* button to move to the next step.

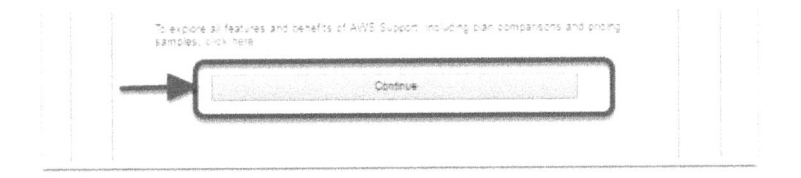

Wait For Your Verification Email

Wait for your verification email. Once you have received this, you can then sign into your account and use AWS. Click the *Sign in to the Console* button to use your new account.

Introduction to Amazon AWS

Log Into Your New Account

Enter your email address and password, and then click the *Sign in using our secure server* button to log in.

Eric Frick

You Are Now Logged In

Now that you are logged in, you can use AWS services. Click on the *EC2* icon to get started. We will cover this in more detail in later lessons. Once you are finished using the service, click on the menu, under your name, to log out.

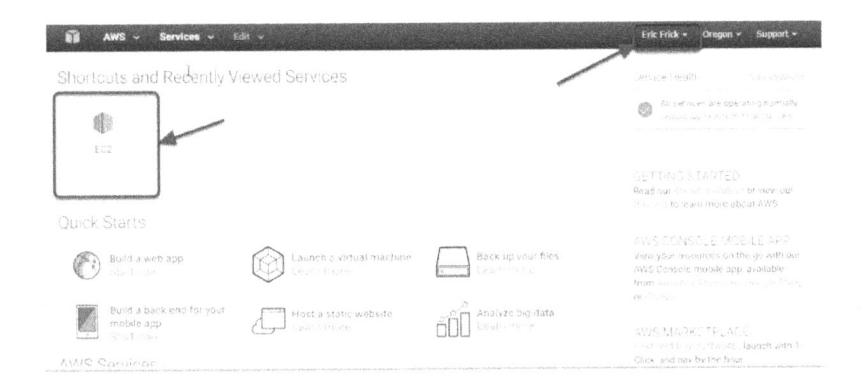

Introduction to Amazon AWS

Summary

Now that you have your AWS account, you will be able to access cloud services. The AWS system is easy to navigate and has a built-in search to help you find the services you are looking for. There is also a command line interface that you can use if you prefer not to access the services through the use of the web screens. In this course, we will concentrate on the web interface, since it is more user friendly for beginner users.

1.4 The AWS CLI

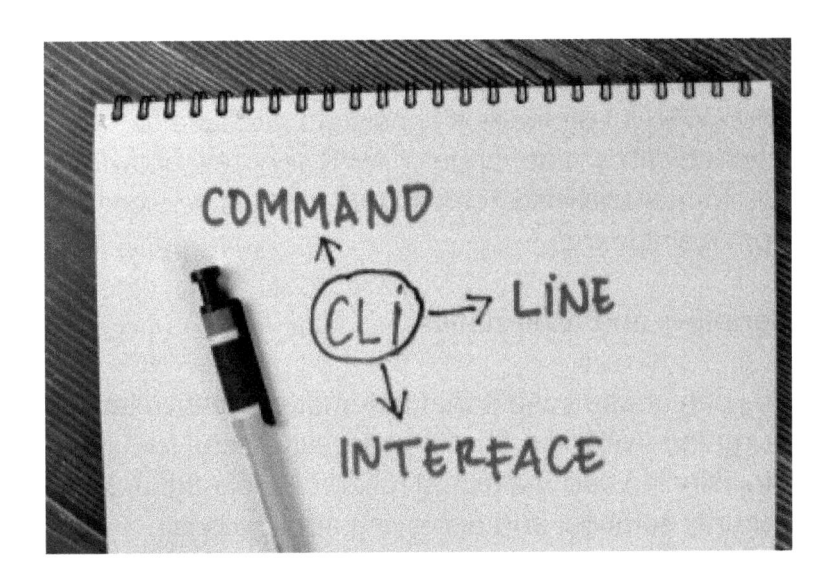

The Amazon Web Services (AWS) Command Line Interface (CLI) is a powerful tool that enables users to interact with AWS services and resources directly from the command line. It provides a command-based interface for managing and automating various aspects of your AWS infrastructure. Whether you're a developer, administrator, or DevOps professional, the AWS CLI offers a convenient and efficient way to manage your cloud resources.

Introduction to Amazon AWS

Key Features and Benefits

Unified Access to AWS Services

The AWS CLI provides a consistent interface to interact with a wide range of AWS services, allowing you to manage resources across multiple services from a single tool.

Scripting and Automation

You can create scripts that automate repetitive tasks using the AWS CLI. This is especially useful for provisioning and managing resources, configuring security settings, and deploying applications.

Flexibility

The AWS CLI gives you the flexibility to work from any terminal or command prompt, making it suitable for both local development environments and remote servers.

Integration with Other Tools

The AWS CLI can be easily integrated with other tools and systems, making it an essential component of continuous integration and continuous deployment (CI/CD) pipelines.

Eric Frick

Secure Authentication

The AWS CLI supports multiple methods of authentication, including access keys, temporary security credentials, and AWS Single Sign-On (SSO).

Common AWS CLI Commands

Here are some commonly used AWS CLI commands and their purposes:

```
aws configure
```
Set up your AWS credentials and configure default settings for the CLI.

```
aws s3 ls
```
List the contents of an S3 bucket.

```
aws ec2 describe-instances
```
Retrieve information about EC2 instances.

```
aws lambda list-functions
```
List your Lambda functions.

```
aws rds create-db-instance
```
Create an Amazon RDS database instance.

```
aws cloudformation create-stack
```
Create a CloudFormation stack.

Eric Frick

Usage Examples

- List S3 Buckets:

```
aws s3 ls
```

- Retrieve EC2 Instance Information

```
aws ec2 describe-instances
```

- Create an S3 Bucket you must include the bucket as part of the input.

```
aws s3api create-bucket --bucket my-bucket-name
```

- Invoke a Lambda Function:

```
aws lambda invoke --function-name my-function-name output.json
```

- Deploy a CloudFormation Stack:

```
aws cloudformation create-stack --stack-name my-stack --template-body file://template.json
```

Best Practices

Use Named Profiles

Instead of using root user credentials, create named profiles with specific permissions for different use cases.

Practice Least Privilege

When creating IAM roles or users for CLI access, follow the principle of least privilege and grant only the necessary permissions.

Keep Credentials Secure

Avoid hardcoding your access keys in scripts. Instead, use environment variables, configuration files, or temporary credentials.

Regularly Update the AWS CLI

Keep your AWS CLI up to date to benefit from the latest features, bug fixes, and security enhancements.

Leverage Output Formats

Use different output formats (such as JSON, YAML, or text) to customize the output of AWS CLI commands.

Eric Frick

Summary

The Amazon AWS CLI is a versatile tool that simplifies and streamlines the management of your AWS resources. It's an essential component for developers and administrators looking to automate tasks, integrate with other tools, and efficiently manage cloud infrastructure from the command line.

2.0 Cloud Concepts

In this chapter, I will cover some of the fundamental concepts of cloud computing. These concepts are core to cloud computing systems and are common no matter which cloud provider you are using. We will first look at the definition of cloud computing and what differentiates cloud systems from traditional computing systems. Following that, we will look at a brief history of cloud computing and some of the underlying developments that allowed for the creation of today's public cloud systems. Next, we will look at the fundamental advantages and limitations of cloud computing. Finally, we will round out the discussion with a presentation of cloud service models.

Eric Frick

2.1 What is Cloud Computing?

Cloud computing delivers computing services to remote users over a network. Private clouds are services that are intended to be utilized by a single organization. Both private or public networks can deliver these services. Public clouds provide computing services over the Internet and are generally available to anyone with a credit card. Public cloud service providers deliver these services via massive shared data centers. These shared data centers allow cloud service providers the ability to offer services that smaller, private companies could not afford to build in their own data centers. Pictured above is one of Microsoft's Azure data centers.

Cloud computing has its roots in some of the early mainframe services offered to customers in the pre-2000 era. Many early services provided a paid service that users could consume remotely. However, network infrastructures, during that era, limited the number of services that the infrastructure could provide to remote users. Salesforce.com was one of the early pioneers of Software as a Service (SAAS) in 1999. These types of services enabled many companies to implement CRM (Customer Relationship Management) systems quickly.

In 2006, Amazon launched some new services called, Infrastructure as a Service (IAAS). They have since followed up with a large number of cloud services. Microsoft Azure began its cloud services in 2010. Since then, the leading IT companies now have their own cloud service offerings. The following diagram predicts that the cloud computing market is projected to reach $127 billion by 2017. Figure 3, from Forbes, describes the dramatic growth of cloud-based systems by different areas. I will define these areas later in this chapter.

Figure 3 Forecast: Global Public Cloud Market Size, 2011 To 2020

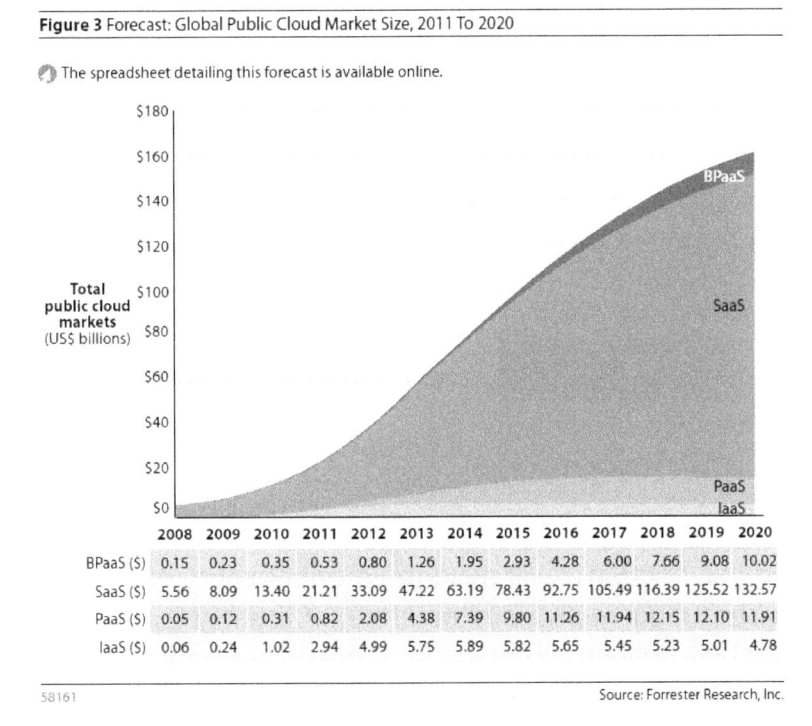

The spreadsheet detailing this forecast is available online.

	2008	2009	2010	2011	2012	2013	2014	2015	2016	2017	2018	2019	2020
BPaaS ($)	0.15	0.23	0.35	0.53	0.80	1.26	1.95	2.93	4.28	6.00	7.66	9.08	10.02
SaaS ($)	5.56	8.09	13.40	21.21	33.09	47.22	63.19	78.43	92.75	105.49	116.39	125.52	132.57
PaaS ($)	0.05	0.12	0.31	0.82	2.08	4.38	7.39	9.80	11.26	11.94	12.15	12.10	11.91
IaaS ($)	0.06	0.24	1.02	2.94	4.99	5.75	5.89	5.82	5.65	5.45	5.23	5.01	4.78

Source: Forrester Research, Inc.

Figure 3 Global Public Cloud Market Size 2011 to 2020 (http://www.forbes.com/sites/louiscolumbus/2015/01/24/roundup-of-cloud-computing-forecasts-and-market-estimates-2015/#41cd412c740c)

2.2 The History of Cloud Computing

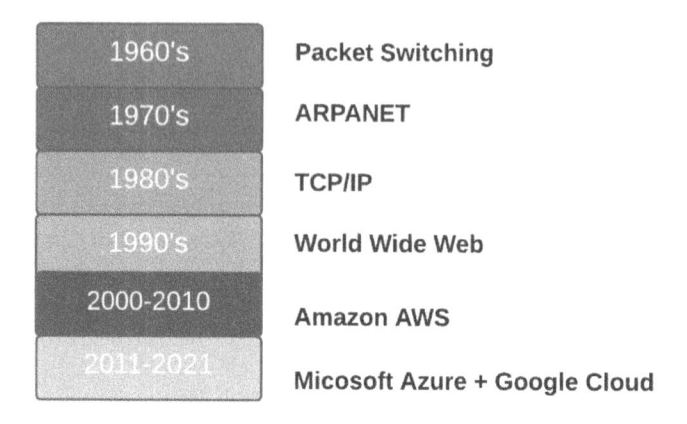

1960's	Packet Switching
1970's	ARPANET
1980's	TCP/IP
1990's	World Wide Web
2000-2010	Amazon AWS
2011-2021	Micosoft Azure + Google Cloud

In this section, I will describe a brief history of cloud computing. I will focus on some of the key technologies that pre-dated cloud computing, but provided the key components that cloud computing depends on today in order to operate.

Eric Frick

Packet Switching

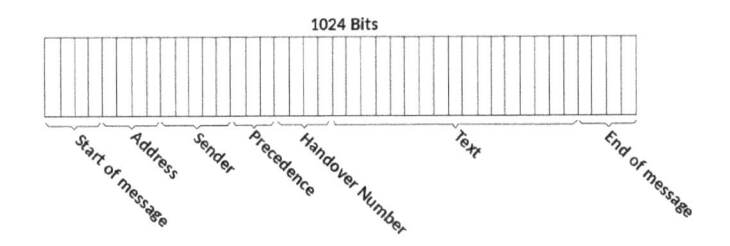

```
                          1024 Bits
```

Start of message | Address | Sender | Precedence | Handover Number | Text | End of message

In the early 1960s, several groups researched packet switching as a way to allow computers to communicate with each other. Until that time, circuit switching had been the preferred method for computer communications. Through the work of several research groups at MIT, the Rand Institute, and the National Physical Laboratory in England, they developed some of the basic concepts that the Internet uses today.

The block message, pictured above, was suggested by Paul Baran in 1964, and published during his initial research on packet switching. This concept was later referred to as a packet and was incorporated in the initial designs of ARPANET. This design was a radical departure from using dedicated circuits and expensive hardware. At the time, this concept was met with a large amount of skepticism from the engineering community.

Introduction to Amazon AWS

ARPANET

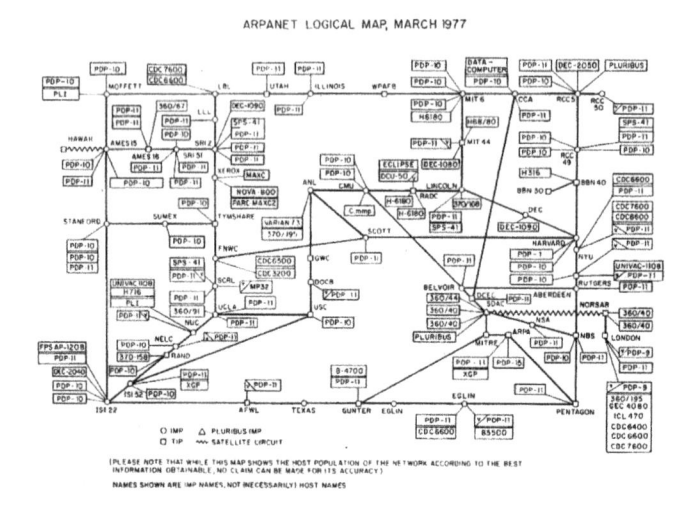

ARPANET LOGICAL MAP, MARCH 1977

In the late 1970s, work that was sponsored by the Defense Advanced Research Project Agency, or DARPA, developed a network of computers called ARPANET (Advanced Research Projects Agency NETwork). This effort developed a method for different computers to communicate with each other. This research included computers from both military installations and research universities. In the early 1980s, the project grew from an initial handful of machines, to hundreds. The structure and growth of ARPANET provided the basic model for our current Internet.

Pictured above is a map of the ARPANET computers from March 1977. At that time, this was a

Eric Frick

state-of-the-art network, and it was growing rapidly. ARPANET continued to be used for research and development until it was decommissioned in 1990.

TCP/IP

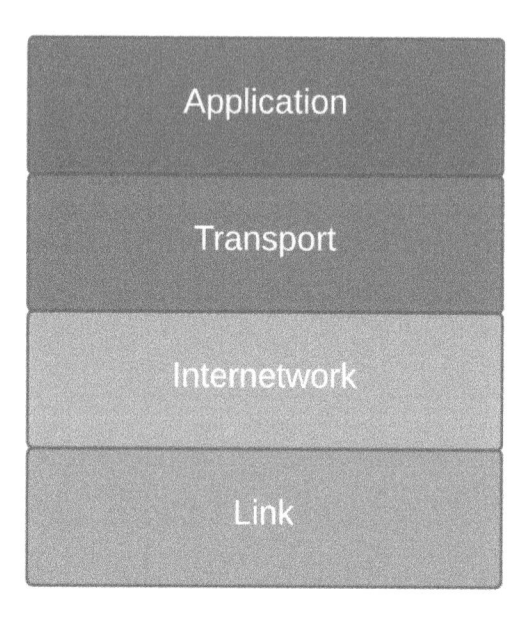

[Diagram: stacked layers — Application, Transport, Internetwork, Link]

The underlying protocol the Internet uses today, for network traffic, is called TCP/IP. It stands for Transmission Control Protocol/Internet Protocol. While working for the Defense Advanced Research Project Agency, two scientists, Vint Cerf and Bob Kahn, developed TCP/IP. They migrated the ARPA network to this protocol and eventually migrated the entire system in 1983. TCP/IP eventually became the standard for all military networks. Following this success, they published their work in the Request for Comments (RFC) standards. This allowed TCP/IP to move into the public domain. This work provided the basis for the networking standards we still use today.

The figure displayed above is the basic architecture of TCP/IP. It is a layered architecture, which allows for the flexibility of this protocol. The design of this protocol has been so successful that it has been in widespread use on the Internet since the 1990s.

World Wide Web (WWW)

Paul Clarke, CC BY-SA 4.0
<https://creativecommons.org/licenses/by-sa/4.0>,
via Wikimedia Commons

Tim Berners-Lee (pictured above), who worked at CERN, the European Organization for Nuclear Research, invented the World Wide Web, or WWW, in the 1989-1990 time frame. CERN and Tim Berners-Lee developed the first web server. This was driven by the need for researchers around the world to share information. After the first web server was developed, CERN published instructions on how other institutions could set up their own web servers. These instructions resulted in several hundred other institutions hosting their own web servers. In 1993, CERN opened the code, for the web servers and the browser, to the public domain, making the software freely available. Once the software was in the public domain, it provided the basis for the explosive growth of the World Wide Web, followed by the Internet.

Amazon Web Services is Launched

In 2006, Amazon launched Amazon Web Services. This service was a unique and innovative offering for the marketplace at the time. Amazon initially offered two key services:

- Amazon S3 - Simple Storage Service
- Amazon EC2 - Elastic Cloud Compute

These are still two key services on the platform today. We will cover these services in more detail later in this book. Amazon has consistently added more and more services since the initial launch, and today offers hundreds of cloud services.

In 2010, Amazon migrated all of its internal operations to AWS, and then began to concentrate on growing their business. Since they were first in the market, Amazon has had a consistently large lead in the market. Over time though, Microsoft has been aggressively growing their cloud business and is threatening to overtake AWS for the lead.

Competitors Enter the Space

Soon after the launch of AWS, several large competitors entered the scene. In 2010, Microsoft launched Windows Azure and began to educate their existing customers about the advantages of cloud-based systems. In 2014, Microsoft renamed the service to Microsoft Azure. Since that time, they have been investing heavily in this offering and are a close, second place competitor to AWS. Many analysts believe that Microsoft, at some point, will become the number one cloud service.

Google launched their first cloud offering in 2011. The first service they offered was their App Engine service. Currently, they are in third place, in terms of market share, behind Amazon and Microsoft.

Eric Frick

2.3 What Are the Advantages of Cloud Computing?

Cloud computing has revolutionized the way businesses and individuals use and manage technology resources. By offering a wide range of services over the internet, cloud computing provides numerous advantages that contribute to increased efficiency, scalability, flexibility, and cost savings. Here are some key benefits of cloud computing:

Cost Efficiency

Cloud computing eliminates the need for upfront capital expenses for hardware and infrastructure. Instead, it operates on a pay-as-you-go model, allowing organizations to only pay for the resources they consume. This reduces the financial burden and allows for more predictable budgeting.

Scalability and Flexibility

Cloud services can scale up or down based on demand. This elasticity allows businesses to quickly adapt to changing workloads, ensuring optimal performance during peak times, while avoiding over-provisioning during periods of lower demand.

Rapid Deployment

Cloud services can be provisioned and deployed rapidly, often in a matter of minutes. This enables faster time-to-market for applications, products, and services, giving businesses a competitive edge.

Global Accessibility

Cloud computing provides access to resources and applications from anywhere with an internet connection. This is especially valuable for remote work, enabling collaboration and productivity across geographic locations.

Disaster Recovery and Business Continuity

Cloud providers offer robust data backup, redundancy, and disaster recovery solutions. This ensures that data is secure and recoverable in the event of hardware failures, outages, or other unforeseen disruptions.

Automatic Updates and Maintenance

Cloud service providers manage the underlying infrastructure, including software updates and security patches. This frees up IT teams from routine maintenance tasks, allowing them to focus on strategic initiatives.

Resource Optimization

Cloud services allow dynamic allocation and reallocation of resources based on workload demands. This leads to efficient resource utilization and reduced energy consumption, contributing to environmental sustainability.

Innovation and Agility

Cloud computing provides a platform for experimentation and innovation. Developers can easily access a variety of services to build, test, and deploy new applications quickly.

Global Reach

Cloud providers have data centers distributed worldwide, enabling businesses to reach a global audience without the need for setting up physical infrastructure in multiple regions.

Security and Compliance

Leading cloud providers invest heavily in security measures, including data encryption, identity and access management, and compliance certifications. For many organizations, using cloud services can enhance security compared to on-premises solutions.

Collaboration and Sharing

Cloud-based tools and applications facilitate seamless collaboration by allowing multiple users to access and edit documents and projects simultaneously, regardless of their location.

Reduced IT Overhead

Cloud computing reduces the need for organizations to maintain extensive IT infrastructure and staff, leading to lower operational costs and a more efficient use of resources.

Eric Frick

Summary

Cloud computing has reshaped the way businesses operate, enabling them to be more agile, innovative, and cost-effective. By leveraging the advantages of cloud computing, organizations can focus on their core competencies, streamline operations, and remain competitive in an increasingly digital landscape.

2.4 The Limitations of Cloud Computing

While cloud computing offers numerous benefits, it's important to be aware of its limitations and considerations before fully embracing this technology. Understanding these limitations can help businesses make informed decisions about which workloads and applications to migrate to the cloud. Here are some common limitations of cloud computing:

Network Dependency

Cloud computing heavily relies on a stable and high-speed internet connection. If the network connection is slow, unreliable, or experiences outages, it can impact the performance and accessibility of cloud-based applications.

Latency and Performance

Some applications with high performance requirements or real-time data processing might experience latency issues when running in the cloud due to the distance between the user and the cloud data center.

Data Transfer Costs

Moving large amounts of data to and from the cloud can incur significant data transfer costs, particularly if data needs to be migrated frequently or in large volumes.

Data Security and Privacy Concerns

Storing sensitive data in the cloud raises concerns about data security, compliance, and privacy. Organizations need to ensure that proper encryption and security measures are in place to protect their data.

Vendor Lock-In

Once an organization's infrastructure and applications are deeply integrated with a specific cloud provider's services, it can become challenging and costly to migrate to another provider or back to on-premises solutions.

Downtime and Outages

While cloud providers offer high availability, no service is immune to outages. Businesses need to be prepared for potential downtime and have contingency plans in place.

Limited Control Over Infrastructure

Cloud customers have limited control over the underlying infrastructure, as it is managed by the cloud provider. This can hinder customization and optimization for specific requirements.

Compliance and Regulatory Issues

Some industries have strict compliance and regulatory requirements that may impact the feasibility of using certain cloud services. It's crucial to ensure that the chosen cloud provider meets industry-specific standards.

Legacy Applications

Some legacy applications might not be compatible with cloud environments due to dependencies on specific hardware or software configurations.

Data Residency and Jurisdiction

Depending on the cloud provider and the region where data is stored, data residency and legal jurisdiction issues might arise, impacting data sovereignty and compliance.

Example of an Application Unsuitable for Cloud Computing

A prime example of an application that might not be suitable for cloud computing is a high-frequency trading platform used by financial institutions. Such platforms require extremely low latency to execute trades in real time. The milliseconds saved by having the trading servers colocated with the exchange's servers can significantly impact profitability. In this scenario, the network latency introduced by cloud infrastructure could be detrimental to the platform's performance.

Due to the unpredictable nature of network latency in cloud environments, a high-frequency trading platform might be better suited to an on-premises infrastructure with specialized networking and hardware optimizations to achieve the required ultra-low latency.

Summary

Understanding these limitations helps organizations make informed decisions about which workloads to migrate to the cloud and which ones are better suited for on-premises or hybrid solutions.

2.5 Cloud Service Models

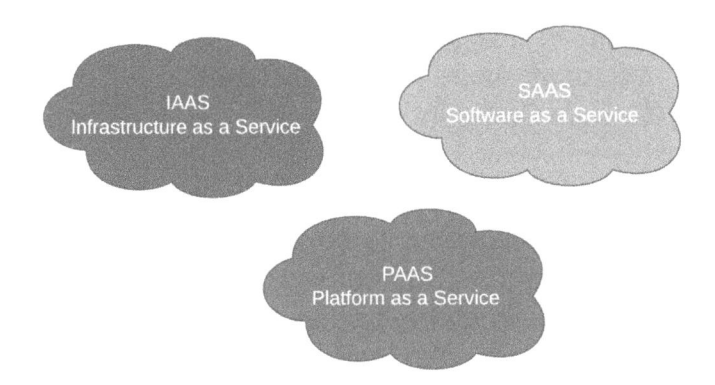

IAAS
Infrastructure as a Service

SAAS
Software as a Service

PAAS
Platform as a Service

Cloud computing offers a range of service models that cater to different business needs and levels of control over infrastructure and management. These service models provide varying levels of abstraction, allowing organizations to choose the most suitable approach for their applications and workloads. The three major cloud service models are:

Infrastructure as a Service (IaaS): IaaS provides virtualized computing resources over the internet. It offers the most control and flexibility among cloud service models. With IaaS, users can rent virtual machines, storage, and networking components on a pay-as-you-go basis. The users are responsible for managing the operating system, applications, and data.

Examples of IaaS products:

- Amazon EC2 (Elastic Compute Cloud)
- Microsoft Azure Virtual Machines
- Google Compute Engine

Platform as a Service (PaaS): PaaS provides a platform that allows developers to build, deploy, and manage applications, without worrying about the underlying infrastructure. It offers a higher level of abstraction compared to IaaS. PaaS solutions come with pre-configured environments, runtime frameworks, and development tools.

Examples of PaaS products:

- Heroku
- Google App Engine
- Microsoft Azure App Service

Eric Frick

Software as a Service (SaaS): SaaS delivers software applications over the internet on a subscription basis. Users access the software through a web browser, and the provider handles all aspects of maintenance, security, and updates. SaaS is the most user-friendly and least resource-intensive cloud service model.

Examples of SaaS products:

- Salesforce (customer relationship management)
- Google Workspace (collaboration and productivity tools)
- Microsoft 365 (office productivity suite)

Advantages and Considerations for Each Service Model:

IaaS:
- **Advantages:** Offers full control over infrastructure, suitable for custom environments and legacy applications. Ideal for businesses that need more control over their IT environment.
- **Considerations:** Requires more management and maintenance, compared to higher-level models. Users are responsible for patching, security, and scaling.

PaaS:
- **Advantages:** Streamlines application development and deployment by abstracting infrastructure management. Enables developers to focus solely on code and features.
- **Considerations:** Offers less customization and control compared to IaaS. Not suitable for applications with unique infrastructure requirements.

SaaS:
- **Advantages:** Requires minimal IT management. Provides easy access to software applications without the need for installation or maintenance

- **Considerations:** Offers the least control over the software itself. Customization options are limited compared to PaaS or IaaS.

Choosing the Right Service Model:

Selecting the appropriate cloud service model depends on factors such as the complexity of your application, desired level of control, and available resources. Organizations might use a combination of service models to meet different requirements and achieve a balance between flexibility and convenience. Understanding the strengths and limitations of each service model is crucial for making informed decisions about cloud adoption.

2.6 The Economics of Cloud Computing

One of the major considerations fueling the explosive growth of cloud computing is the economic advantages of migrating on premise services to the cloud. Cloud-based systems are cheaper from a startup standpoint and allow teams to field systems more rapidly. Let's look at a simple example and the details from a cost and time to market perspective. In this scenario, the equipment that is needed is a 64 Gigabyte server with a 1 terabyte hard drive. I did not include any other equipment such as networking gear, etc. to keep the example simple.

Eric Frick

For this example, I got pricing data from a traditional equipment provider, Dell Inc., and data from the AWS cost calculator online to compare what it would cost to buy a physical server and then to provide an equivalent server online. The table below presents the summary information of what I found.

Dell Server vs AWS EC2 Server

Initial Purchase On Premise
- PowerEdge R740xd2 Rack Server
- 64 GB Memory
- 1TB Sata Drive
- Cost $9,465.37

Initial Purchase Cloud (AWS Ohio Region)
- x2gd.xlarge
- 64 GB Memory
- 1TB Sata Drive
- Cost $0.00

Shipping Time On Premise Dell
- 30 Days (from website)

Shipping Time Cloud (AWS Ohio Region)
- Less than 30 minutes to provision

Operating Cost On Premise Dell
- $833.33 per month

Operating Cost Cloud (AWS Ohio Region)
- $252.63 per month

Eric Frick

Initial Purchase

For the initial purchase of the physical server, I went to the Dell web page and configured a daily middle of the road server and configured it with a 1TB SATA drive and 64 Gb of RAM. The purchase price of this server is $9,465.37. Compared to configuring an equivalent server in AWS, there is a $0 startup cost. You simply need to have an account with AWS and then configure and launch the server. You will then pay for the server by the hour that you use it. With one server, this cost might not make an enormous difference to a large corporation, but it would make a significant difference for a project that requires 50 or 100 servers.

Shipping Time

When I configured the server on the Dell website, it listed an approximate 30 day time from order to delivery. Based on my experience in ordering hardware, this is a typical turnaround time for a server manufacturer. In contrast, there is no shipping time for the cloud-based solution at AWS. You simply need to configure the server and it will be up and running in just a few minutes. This is an enormous advantage of cloud-based deployments; you can provision resources almost instantly. When a company is in a highly competitive environment, this time savings can represent a huge competitive advantage.

Operating Cost

Calculating the ongoing operating cost is difficult since it depends on the environment that the equipment is operating in. As an example, I assumed for the on-premise machine that the company spends $ one million annually supporting a data center of 100 machines. I then allocated a proportional monthly cost to this server, which came out to $833.33 per month to support this server. For the cost for the AWS server, I quoted the monthly cost from the AWS cost calculator to run this server in the Ohio region. Even if my on-premise calculations are way off, you can see from this example how affordable the cloud solution is, compared to operating your own data center.

Summary

Although this is a very simple example, you can see the significant advantages that cloud computing offers in terms of purchase cost, time to market, and ongoing operating expenses.

Eric Frick

2.7 The AWS Well Architected Framework

In this section, we will describe the Amazon AWS Well Architected Framework. According to Amazon, the framework is the following: "The AWS Well-Architected Framework helps cloud architects build secure, high-performing, resilient, and efficient infrastructure for a variety of applications and workloads." You can visit their website at the following address: https://aws.amazon.com/architecture/well-architected

Introduction to Amazon AWS

The Amazon AWS Well-Architected Framework is a set of best practices and guidelines for designing and building secure, high-performing, resilient, and efficient infrastructure for applications and workloads on the Amazon Web Services (AWS) cloud platform. It serves as a comprehensive reference to help cloud architects, solution designers, and developers create reliable and scalable systems that align with AWS's core principles.

The Well-Architected Framework consists of five key pillars, each addressing a specific aspect of designing and operating well-architected systems on AWS. These pillars provide guidance and considerations for making informed decisions throughout the entire lifecycle of a system, from design and implementation to ongoing maintenance and optimization.

Eric Frick

Operational Excellence

This pillar focuses on the ability to run and monitor systems effectively, gain insights through various operational data, and continuously improve processes and procedures. Key considerations include:
- Defining operational procedures and automating processes to reduce manual intervention.
- Developing mechanisms for monitoring applications, infrastructure, and performance metrics.
- Responding to incidents and issues with well-defined procedures and effective incident management.
- Learning from operational events and using that knowledge to drive continuous improvement.

Security

The security pillar emphasizes the implementation of effective security measures to protect data, systems, and assets. It includes:
- Designing security controls to protect against unauthorized access, data breaches, and other potential security threats.
- Applying the principle of least privilege, ensuring only necessary permissions are granted.

- Implementing encryption for data at rest and in transit.
- Regularly reviewing and updating security policies and practices to address emerging threats and vulnerabilities.

Reliability

Reliability focuses on the ability of systems to recover from failures and continue to function as intended. Key aspects include:
- Designing for fault tolerance by distributing workloads across multiple availability zones and regions.
- Implementing automatic scaling to handle varying workloads.
- Regularly testing failure scenarios and disaster recovery plans.
- Monitoring the health of systems and using automated recovery mechanisms to maintain reliability.

Performance Efficiency

This pillar addresses the optimization of system resources to ensure efficient performance. Considerations include:
- Selecting appropriate instance types and sizes to meet performance requirements.
- Optimizing storage solutions to balance cost and performance.
- Using caching mechanisms and content delivery networks (CDNs) to enhance response times.
- Continuously monitoring performance metrics and optimizing resources as needed.

Cost Optimization

Cost optimization involves designing systems to achieve the desired outcomes while minimizing costs. This includes:
- Choosing the right pricing models and payment options for services and resources.
- Implementing resource tagging and tracking to allocate costs accurately.
- Regularly reviewing and optimizing resource utilization to eliminate waste.
- Automating cost control mechanisms and using tools to monitor spending patterns.

Summary

By adhering to these five pillars of the AWS Well-Architected Framework, organizations can create cloud-native solutions that are secure, reliable, efficient, and cost-effective. Regularly reviewing and aligning with these best practices ensures that systems remain well-architected as they evolve over time, fostering a culture of continuous improvement and innovation.

2.8 Cloud Concepts Quiz

1) Which company is the leading cloud computing vendor in the cloud market today?
    a. Microsoft
    b. Oracle
    c. Amazon
    d. IBM

2) What is one of the primary benefits of SaaS?
    a. You are free to modify the software as needed
    b. You can choose the version of the software you would like to use
    c. The system is an end-to-end solutions that the vendor maintains for you
    d. None of the above

3) What is IaaS?
    a. Internet Awareness Service
    b. Infrastructure as a Service
    c. Intelligent Advertising Agent Service

4) What is Amazon's cloud system called?
    a. Amazon AWS
    b. The Amazon Cloud System
    c. The Amazon Personal Cloud

Introduction to Amazon AWS

5) Office 365 is an example of?
   a. IaaS
   b. PaaS
   c. SaaS
   d. None of the above

6) Having direct physical access to servers is an advantage to cloud computing.
   a. True
   b. False

7) Paying for only the cloud services and resources you are actually using is referred to as?
   a. Pay as You Go
   b. Utility Computing
   c. All of the above

8) The ability to easily scale systems up and down easily is referred to as?
   a. Autogen
   b. Elasticity
   c. Utility computing
   d. None of the above

9) The following are advantages of cloud computing?
   a. You can quickly provision resources
   b. You only pay for what you use
   c. Your systems are highly available
   d. All of the above

3.0 Amazon AWS Core Services

Amazon Web Services (AWS) Core Services are fundamental building blocks of the AWS cloud platform. These services provide the essential components required for creating and managing various cloud resources and applications. AWS Core Services are widely used as the foundation for building scalable, reliable, and cost-effective solutions. Here are some key AWS Core Services:

Introduction to Amazon AWS

Amazon Elastic Compute Cloud (EC2): EC2 offers resizable compute capacity in the cloud. It allows users to provision and manage virtual machines (instances) with different configurations, operating systems, and applications.

Amazon Simple Storage Service (S3): S3 provides scalable object storage for storing and retrieving data, such as files, images, videos, and backups, with high durability and availability.

Amazon Virtual Private Cloud (VPC): VPC allows users to create isolated networks within the AWS cloud, providing control over IP addressing, subnets, routing, security groups, and network gateways.

Amazon Relational Database Service (RDS): RDS offers managed relational database instances for popular database engines like MySQL, PostgreSQL, SQL Server, Oracle, and MariaDB.

Amazon Identity and Access Management (IAM): IAM enables users to control access to AWS resources by defining and managing user identities, permissions, and authentication.

Amazon CloudWatch: CloudWatch provides monitoring and management for AWS resources, allowing users to collect and track metrics, set alarms, and gain insights into application and infrastructure performance.

Amazon Route 53: Route 53 is a scalable domain name system (DNS) web service that translates human-readable domain names into IP addresses, routing users to AWS resources.

Amazon Simple Notification Service (SNS): SNS offers a publish-subscribe messaging service that enables communication between distributed applications, services, and microservices.

Amazon Simple Queue Service (SQS): SQS provides a fully managed message queuing service for decoupling components of a distributed application and enabling asynchronous communication.

Amazon CloudFormation: CloudFormation allows users to define and provision AWS infrastructure as code using templates, automating the deployment of resources and applications.

Amazon Lambda: Lambda is a serverless computing service that lets users run code in response to events without managing servers. It's often used for event-driven architectures and microservices.

Amazon Elastic Load Balancing (ELB): ELB distributes incoming application traffic across multiple targets (EC2 instances, containers, IP addresses) to ensure high availability and improved application performance.

Amazon Simple Email Service (SES): SES provides a cloud-based email sending service for sending transactional, promotional, and marketing emails.

Amazon CloudFront: CloudFront is a content delivery network (CDN) service that securely delivers data, videos, applications, and Application Programming Interfaces (APIs) to users globally with low latency and high transfer speeds.

Summary

These Core Services form the foundation of AWS, providing the necessary infrastructure and tools to create, deploy, and manage a wide range of cloud-based solutions. While this list covers some of the essential services, AWS offers many more specialized services for various use cases and industries.

Eric Frick

3.1 What is Amazon EC2?

Elastic Cloud Compute is AWS's virtualization service. EC2 was released in 2006 and has had many features added since that time. Pricing is based on the size and type of machine you configure. You only pay for what you use. Pricing is by the hour. (Partial hours are billed by what you actually consume) EC2 offers many tools and features, which make it very flexible for managing online servers. EC2 is one of AWS's most popular services.

In this section, we will look at some of the attributes of the EC2 service and some of the advantages it offers over servers that run in your datacenter. We

Introduction to Amazon AWS

will also look at the cost models that are available for this service.

Advantages of EC2

You can quickly provision new servers to fulfill new demands. (within minutes) This, as opposed to buying and installing physical hardware that might take weeks, or even months, to complete. Also, you can provision servers with software already installed. When you order physical hardware, you will have to install and configure software, from scratch, on a brand new machine.
You can quickly backup machines, while they are running, using snapshots. This is a quick and easy way to recover from unplanned problems. In the traditional model of a datacenter, backups are often done by special purpose software. Restoring from these backup images is often a long and difficult process.

You can easily develop your own custom server images. This is done through a mechanism called AMI (Amazon Machine Interface). By using this, you can develop custom images that will support your operations. You can use this as a base image, with specific software installed on your server. By doing this, you can then deploy new servers with a custom configuration already installed. This will result in a huge saving of labor on future deployments.

Eric Frick

You only pay for what you use. Machines that are shut down do not incur runtime charges, only storage costs. Storage costs are really cheap in the cloud. As such, you pay almost nothing for a server that is shut down. Many applications that run in a datacenter are only needed at specific times. For these types of applications, you can turn on the server when you need it and shut it down when not needed. This technique can result in significant savings.

Once machines are no longer needed, you can simply delete them. This allows you to spin up a machine for a special project, then get rid of them once the project has been completed. If you were doing this with dedicated hardware in your own datacenter, you would be stuck with either finding another use for the computer, or trying to dispose of it somehow.

Cost Model

EC2 supports several cost models for various types of applications
- On Demand
- Spot Instances
- Savings Plan (Long Term Commitment)
- Dedicated Host

On Demand: The on-demand model is the most expensive of the four models described here. There is no upfront cost or commitment required. You simply pay by the hour based on the size of the machine, the configuration, and the regions the machine is located in.

Spot Instances: Next on the list are spot instances. If you have an application that needs to be run periodically and the exact time of the day it runs is not critical. This is a good model for these types of applications. You can run these during off times, when the cost of using the servers is a much lower hourly rate.

Savings Plan (Long Term Commitment): If you know you will have an application running long term, you can sign a longer term commitment to lower your operating cost. This is a good option from a resource utilization perspective, for applications that are stable.

Dedicated Host: This last option is an offering where you can get dedicated hardware for your environment to run applications. This option requires a specified term for the contract.

Introduction to Amazon AWS

On Demand Cost Example

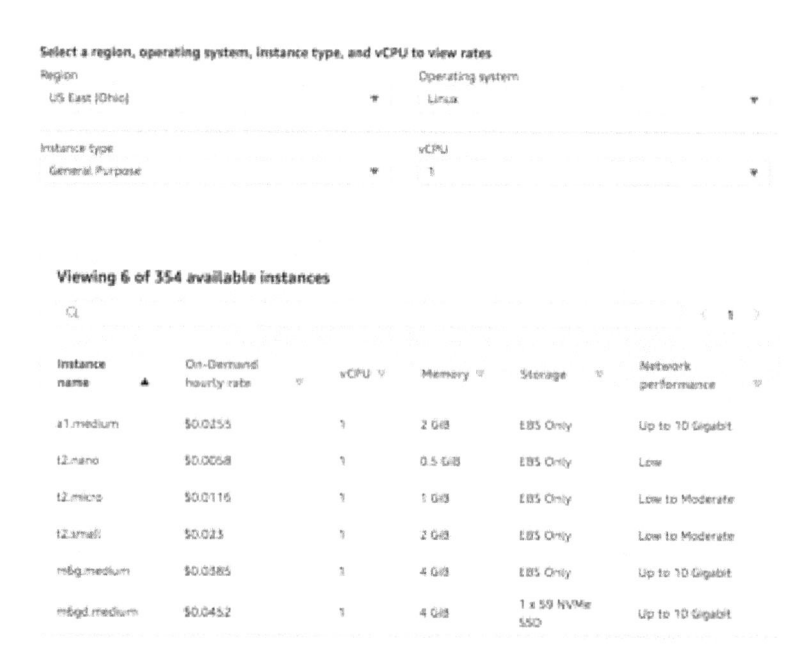

Select a region, operating system, instance type, and vCPU to view rates

Region: US East (Ohio)
Operating system: Linux
Instance type: General Purpose
vCPU: 1

Viewing 6 of 354 available instances

Instance name	On-Demand hourly rate	vCPU	Memory	Storage	Network performance
a1.medium	$0.0255	1	2 GiB	EBS Only	Up to 10 Gigabit
t2.nano	$0.0058	1	0.5 GiB	EBS Only	Low
t2.micro	$0.0116	1	1 GiB	EBS Only	Low to Moderate
t2.small	$0.023	1	2 GiB	EBS Only	Low to Moderate
m6g.medium	$0.0385	1	4 GiB	EBS Only	Up to 10 Gigabit
m6gd.medium	$0.0452	1	4 GiB	1 x 59 NVMe SSD	Up to 10 Gigabit

The example above describes the hourly pricing for Linux instances in the Ohio region, based on memory and CPU configurations.

Source: https://aws.amazon.com/ec2/pricing/on-demand/

Eric Frick

Migration Tools

There are several migration tools available that can make migrating your on-premise servers to the AWS Cloud much easier. The diagram below briefly describes some of these tools.

Migration Evaluator - tools to plan for migration

AWS Migration Hub - single source location to track migration projects

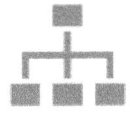

AWS Prescriptive Guidance - a resource that describes best practices

Introduction to Amazon AWS

Amazon Lightsail

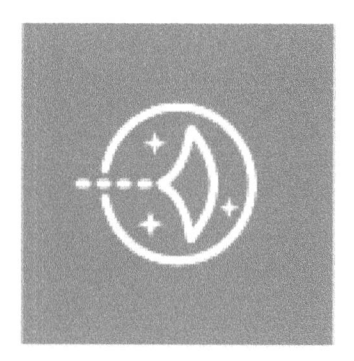

Amazon Lightsail

Although this is not part of the EC2 service, it is closely related. Amazon Lightsail is a simplified consumer grade service for virtualization. It offers preconfigured server packages for popular configurations that you can pick from a menu. Lightsail servers have low-cost options that are billed monthly. Packages include network options, such as static IP addresses.

Eric Frick

Summary

Amazon EC2 offers a way for organizations to migrate their on-premise servers to the cloud. EC2 is highly flexible and cost effective. It offers the distinct advantage that you only pay for what you use. Amazon Lightsail offers a simplified version of the service for consumer and smaller applications.

Introduction to Amazon AWS

3.2 How to Create a Virtual Machine Using Amazon AWS

Now that you have your account with Amazon AWS, I will describe how you can quickly create a virtual server, in the cloud.

Navigate to the AWS Homepage

Go to https://aws.amazon.com. Click the *Sign in to the Console* button to log in.

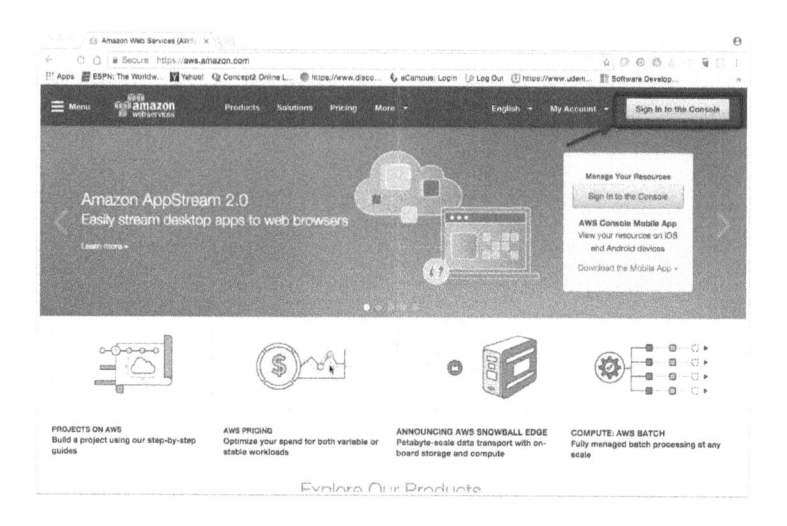

Eric Frick

Log into Your Account

Use the username and password you chose to sign up for your account.

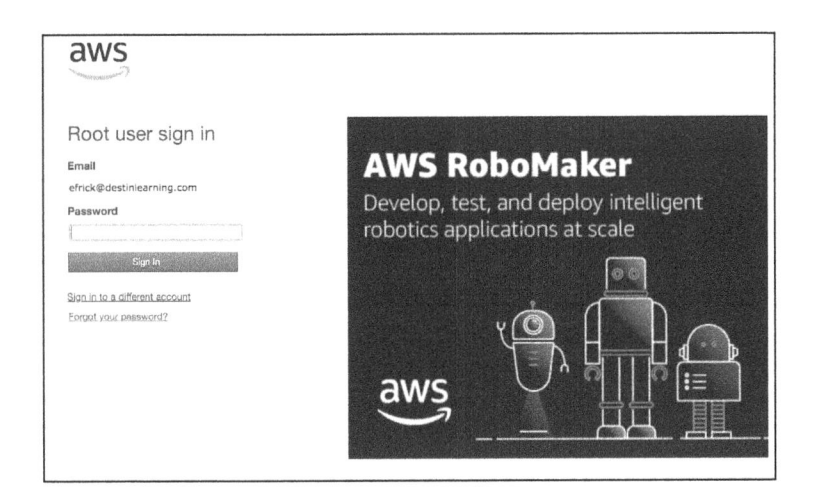

Navigate to the Services Page

Click the *Services* link in the upper left-hand portion of the screen.

Introduction to Amazon AWS

Click the EC2 Link

Once the services are displayed, click the *EC2* link to bring up the pages used to manage virtual machines.

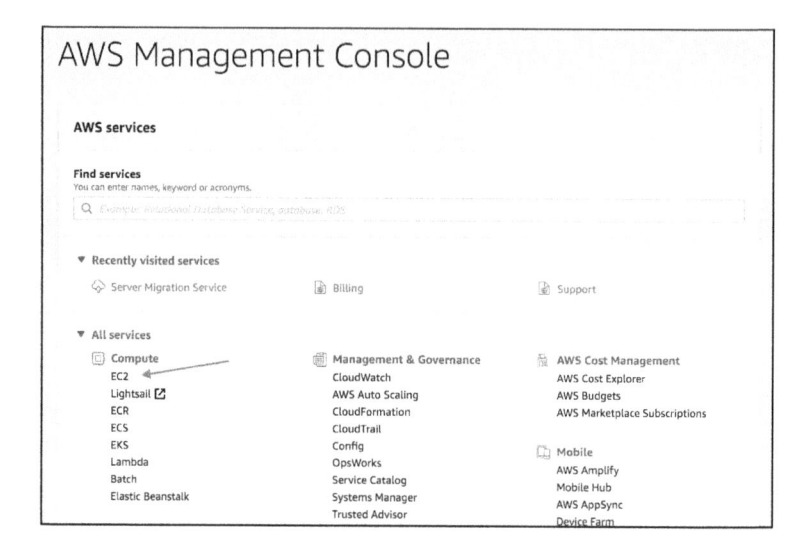

```
AWS Management Console

AWS services

Find services
You can enter names, keyword or acronyms.
Q  Example:  ...

▼ Recently visited services
   Server Migration Service        Billing                         Support

▼ All services
   Compute                      Management & Governance       AWS Cost Management
     EC2   ←                      CloudWatch                    AWS Cost Explorer
     Lightsail                    AWS Auto Scaling              AWS Budgets
     ECR                          CloudFormation                AWS Marketplace Subscriptions
     ECS                          CloudTrail
     EKS                          Config                      Mobile
     Lambda                       OpsWorks                      AWS Amplify
     Batch                        Service Catalog               Mobile Hub
     Elastic Beanstalk            Systems Manager               AWS AppSync
                                  Trusted Advisor               Device Farm
```

Eric Frick

Navigate to the Instances Page

Click the *instances* link, to the left, to open the EC2 instance manager page. On this page, you will see the list of machines you already have running, if you have any, and you will have the option of creating a new one there.

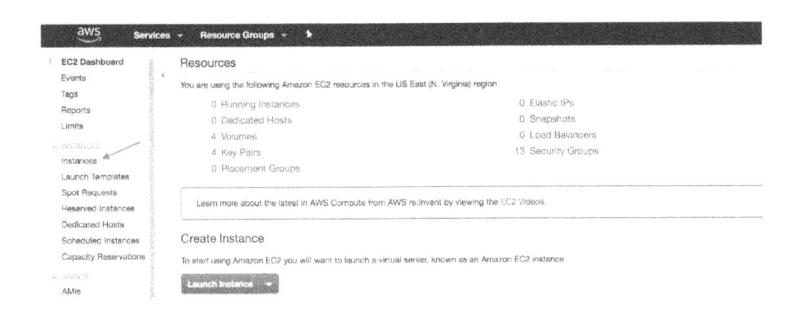

Introduction to Amazon AWS

Click the Launch Instance Button

Once this page has opened, you can review the status of any other machine in your account. Here, I already have several virtual machines created. In your case, you will have a brand-new account, and there will be no machines listed. Once this page has loaded, click the *Launch Instance* button.

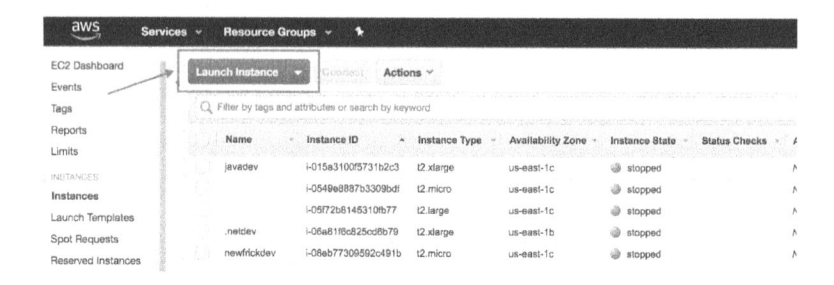

Eric Frick

Select the Instance Image

Scroll through the list and select the instance you would like to create. Here, I will use the Microsoft Windows Server 2016 Base image. Notice, the instance types that are free tier eligible, have a label indicating that.

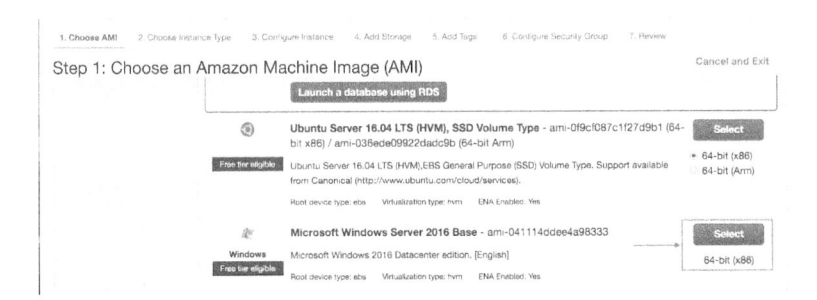

Introduction to Amazon AWS

Choose an Instance Type

This page should default to the t2.micro, which is a small, but free machine to operate. The other types listed are larger machines for which you will incur costs for using. If this computer is not fast enough for your task, you can upgrade later, on the fly. One of the significant advantages of cloud computing is the ease with which you can add resources to your projects. For this exercise, accept the default by clicking the *Review and Launch* button.

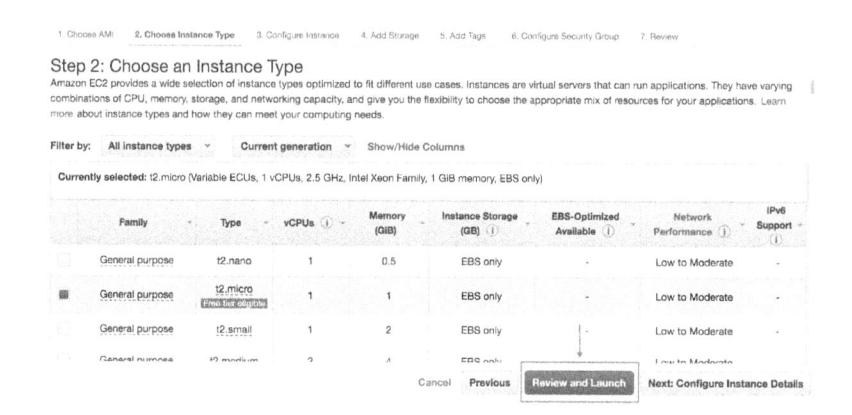

Eric Frick

Launch your Virtual Machine

At this point, you are ready to launch your new virtual machine. The system will warn you about your security group, and that it could be made to be more secure. Do not worry about that for this exercise, since it is only a development computer. If you want to use this to store more personal data later, I would recommend locking this down at a later time. Click the *Launch* button to continue.

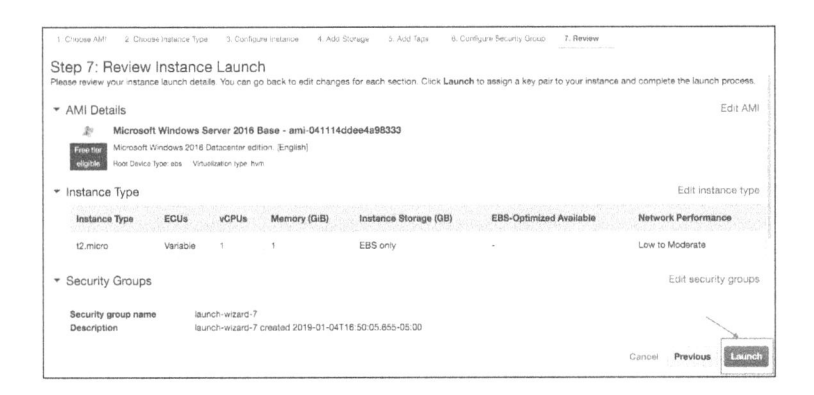

Introduction to Amazon AWS

Select the Key Pair for Your Machine

You must have a key to launch a new machine. You can use that key later to retrieve the password. Select *Create a new key pair*, and assign a name for that key. Once you have entered the name, you must download the key and store it on your local computer. You will need this key later, to retrieve the password for your new virtual machine. Click the *Download Key Pair* button.

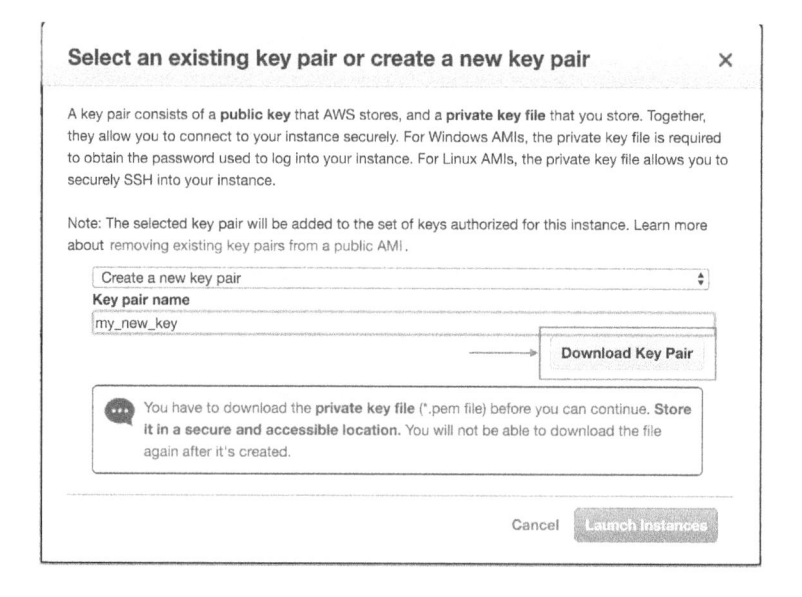

Note Where Your File is Stored

You will need this file later, so look in your browser window to note the file location.

```
my_new_key.pem                                        ×
https://console.aws.amazon.com/ec2/v2/downloadKeyPair

Show in Finder
```

Introduction to Amazon AWS

Click the Launch Instances Button

Now that you have your key file, click the *Launch Instances* button to begin the build process.

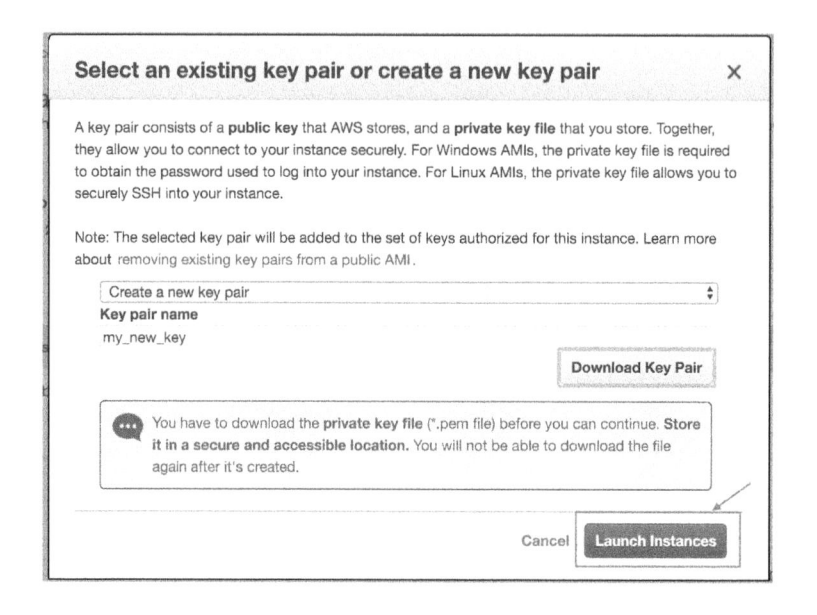

Select an existing key pair or create a new key pair

A key pair consists of a **public key** that AWS stores, and a **private key file** that you store. Together, they allow you to connect to your instance securely. For Windows AMIs, the private key file is required to obtain the password used to log into your instance. For Linux AMIs, the private key file allows you to securely SSH into your instance.

Note: The selected key pair will be added to the set of keys authorized for this instance. Learn more about removing existing key pairs from a public AMI.

Create a new key pair
Key pair name
my_new_key

Download Key Pair

You have to download the **private key file** (*.pem file) before you can continue. **Store it in a secure and accessible location.** You will not be able to download the file again after it's created.

Cancel **Launch Instances**

Eric Frick

Check the Launch Status

This window will alert you to the status of your new instance. Click the *View Instances* button, at the bottom of the page, to return to the instances management page.

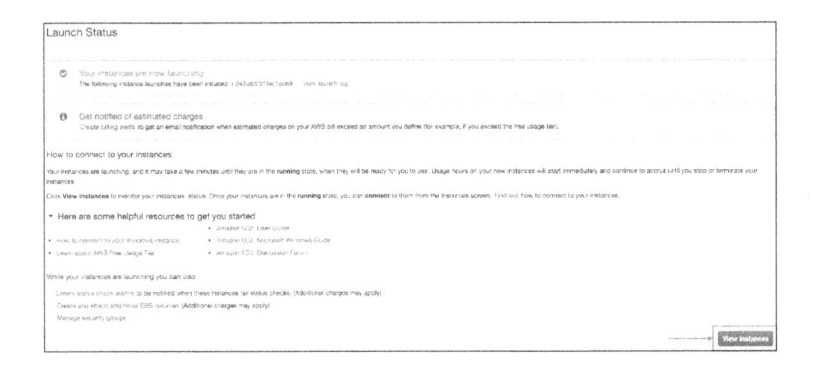

Check Your New Instance Status

When you return to this page, you will see the status of your new server. Once the round indicator turns green, your new machine has been created and is running.

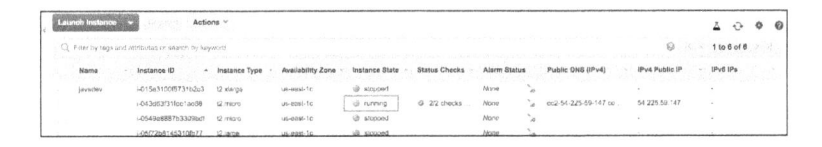

Introduction to Amazon AWS

Get the Windows Password

Right-mouse-click on your new server, and select *Get Windows Password* from the menu.

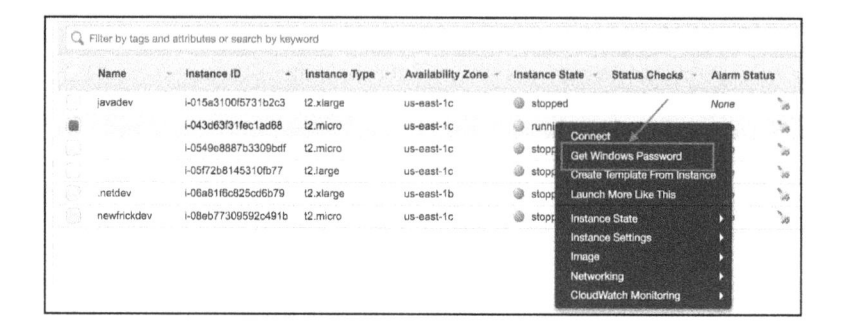

Eric Frick

Select the Key File

Once this window comes up, select the *Choose File* button, and then select the key file you created in the previous step.

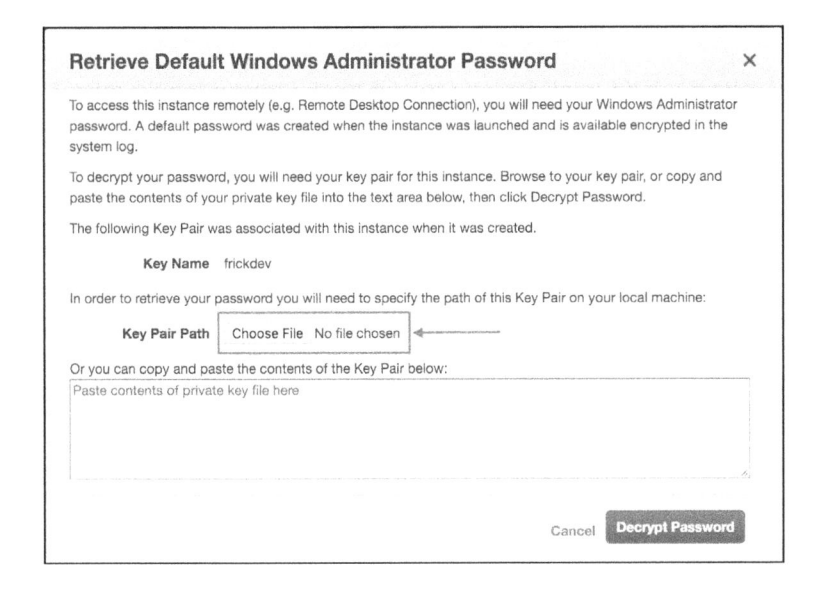

Retrieve Default Windows Administrator Password

To access this instance remotely (e.g. Remote Desktop Connection), you will need your Windows Administrator password. A default password was created when the instance was launched and is available encrypted in the system log.

To decrypt your password, you will need your key pair for this instance. Browse to your key pair, or copy and paste the contents of your private key file into the text area below, then click Decrypt Password.

The following Key Pair was associated with this instance when it was created.

Key Name   frickdev

In order to retrieve your password you will need to specify the path of this Key Pair on your local machine:

Key Pair Path   [Choose File   No file chosen]

Or you can copy and paste the contents of the Key Pair below:

Cancel   **Decrypt Password**

Open the Key File

Navigate to where you stored your key file, select the file, and click the *Open* button.

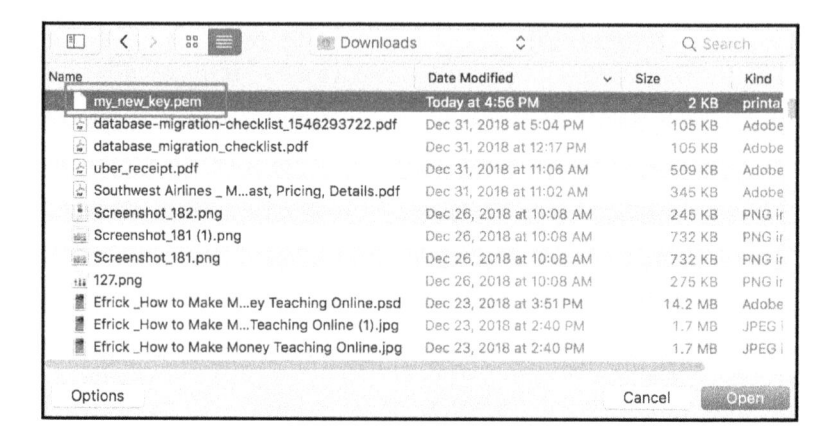

Eric Frick

Click the Decrypt Password Button

Once the key file has been loaded, click the *Decrypt Password* button to get your Windows system password.

Introduction to Amazon AWS

Note Your New Password

The system has assigned a new password to you. You can view this at the bottom of the window. Record this so you can use it in the next step. (You can highlight the password, copy it, and paste it into a text file on your system to make it easier to manage, or you can write it down.) Click the *Close* button when you finish recording your password.

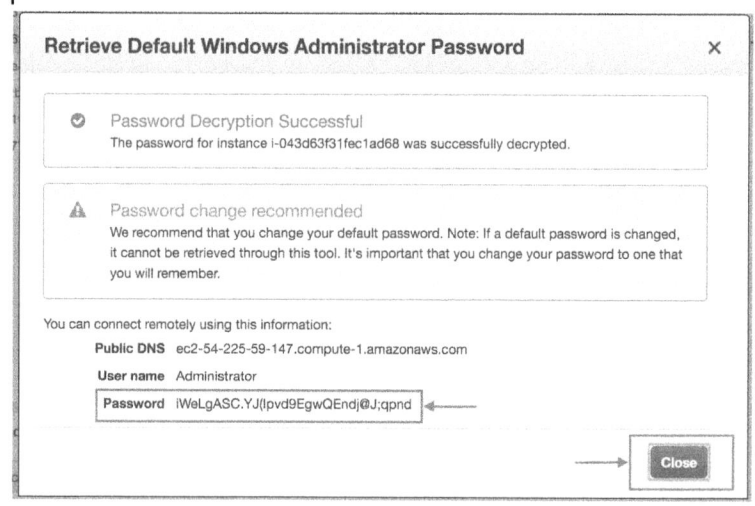

Retrieve Default Windows Administrator Password   ✕

✓ Password Decryption Successful
   The password for instance i-043d63f31fec1ad68 was successfully decrypted.

⚠ Password change recommended
   We recommend that you change your default password. Note: If a default password is changed, it cannot be retrieved through this tool. It's important that you change your password to one that you will remember.

You can connect remotely using this information:
   Public DNS   ec2-54-225-59-147.compute-1.amazonaws.com
   User name   Administrator
   Password   iWeLgASC.YJ(lpvd9EgwQEndj@J;qpnd   ⬅

                                                              [Close]

Eric Frick

Click the Connect Button

Now that you have your password, you can connect to your running computer. Right-mouse-click on the running computer line and click the *Connect* link, in the menu.

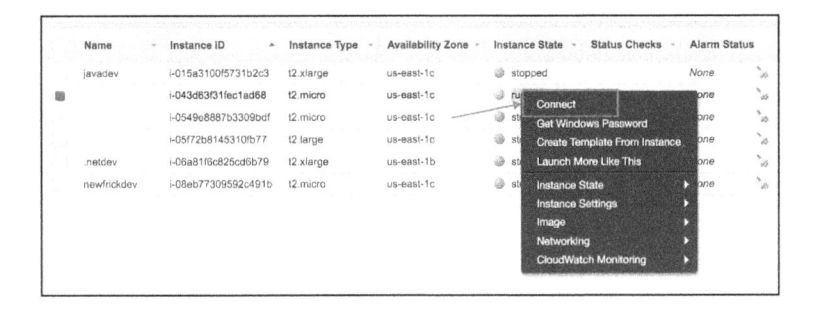

Introduction to Amazon AWS

Download the Remote Desktop File

Click the *Download Remote Desktop File* button, so you can use the remote desktop to log into your new computer.

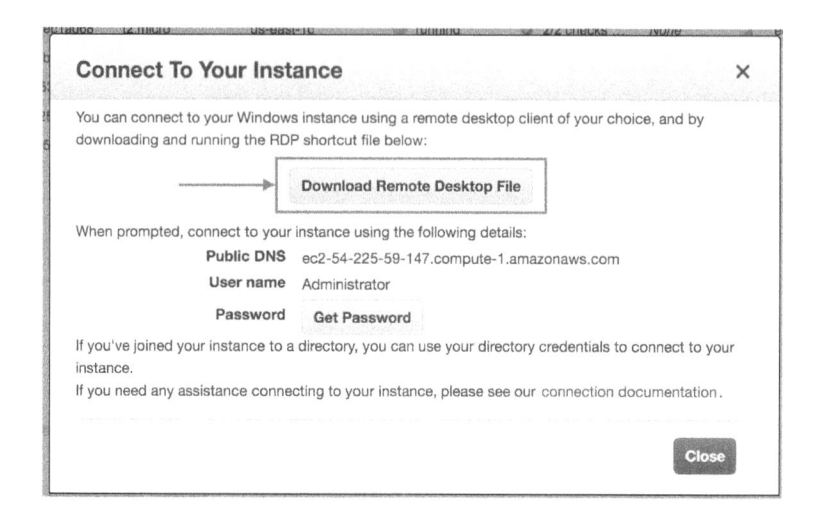

Eric Frick

Navigate to the Remote Desktop File

Once the file download completes, open the directory where the file is. Double click on the file to open the remote desktop software. Note, you must have remote desktop software installed on your computer. Windows PCs should have this software already installed. It is a free download from Microsoft and is also available for the Mac in the App Store. You can get this from the following link for Mac:

https://itunes.apple.com/us/app/microsoft-remote-desktop-10/id1295203466?mt=12

Here is the link for the Windows version of the software, in case you need it:
https://www.microsoft.com/en-us/p/microsoft-remote-desktop-preview/9nblggh30h88?activetab=pivot:overviewtab

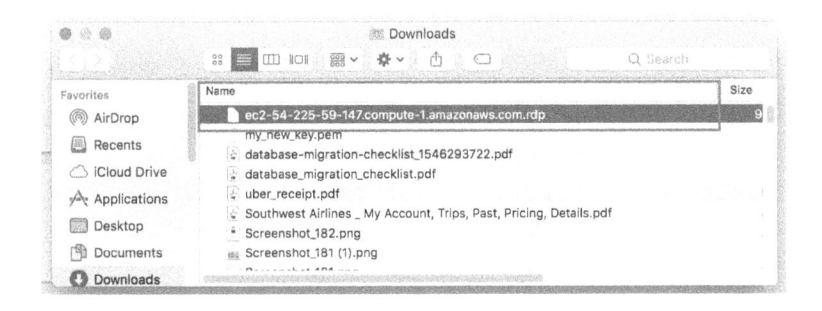

Introduction to Amazon AWS

Log Into Your New Machine

Use the password you recorded in the previous step. (It is long and difficult to type the first time.) After you log in, you can use standard Windows commands to reset the password to something that is easier for you to manage. I recommend pasting the password into a document and then printing it out to log in the first time. The password is complicated to write down correctly.

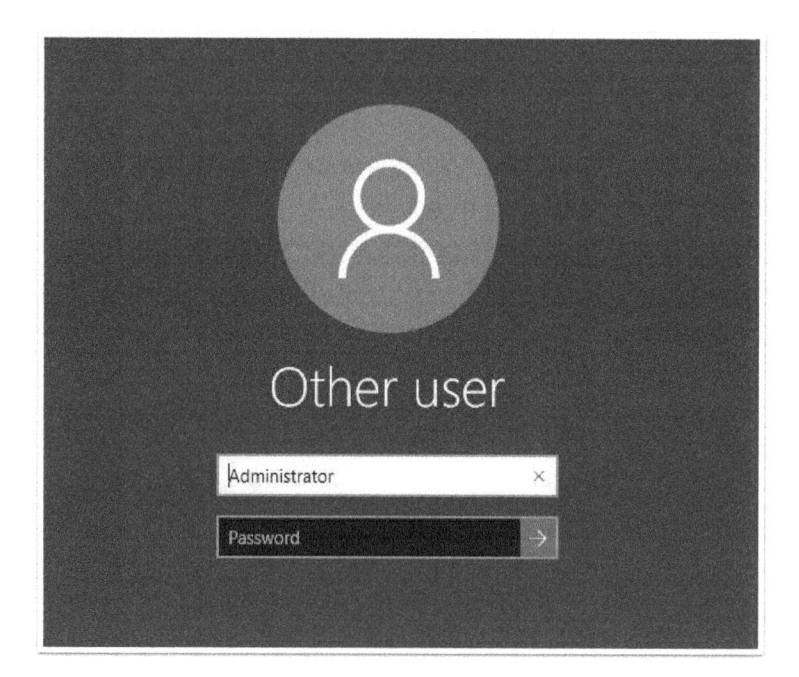

Eric Frick

You Should Now Be Logged In

If all goes well, your computer is running, you should now be logged in, and you can use your computer for anything you want. Even though this is a free tier computer, you only have a limited number of free hours, so shut it down when you are not using it. You can either shut it down from the server, or from the Amazon command line.

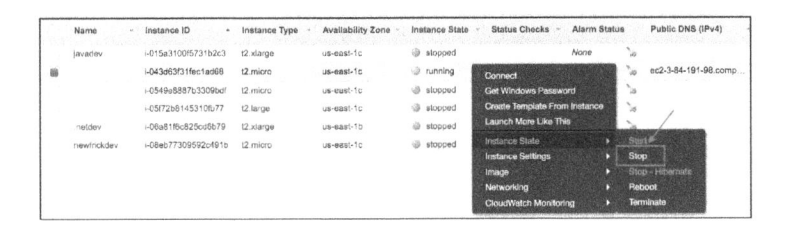

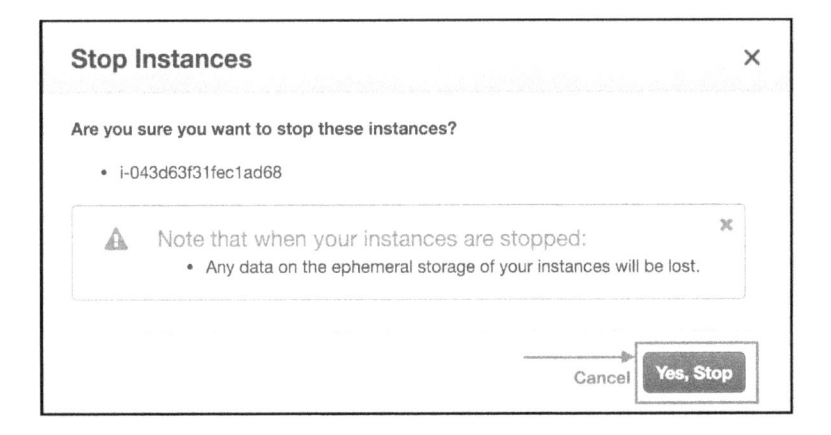

Name	Instance ID	Instance Type	Availability Zone	Instance State	Status Checks	Alarm Status	Public DNS (IPv4)
javadev	i-015a310015731b2c3	t2.xlarge	us-east-1c	stopped		None	
	i-043d63f31fec1ad68	t2.micro	us-east-1c	running			ec2-3-84-191-98.comp...
	i-0549e8887b3309bcf	t2.micro	us-east-1c	stopped			
	i-05f72b8145310fb77	t2.large	us-east-1c	stopped			
netdev	i-06a81f6c825cd6b79	t2.xlarge	us-east-1c	stopped			
newinckdev	i-08eb77309592of91b	t2.micro	us-east-1c	stopped			

Menu items: Connect, Get Windows Password, Create Template From Instance, Launch More Like This, Instance State ▶ (Start, Stop, Stop - Hibernate, Reboot, Terminate), Instance Settings, Image, Networking, CloudWatch Monitoring

Stop Instances ✕

Are you sure you want to stop these instances?

- i-043d63f31fec1ad68

⚠ Note that when your instances are stopped:
- Any data on the ephemeral storage of your instances will be lost.

Cancel **Yes, Stop**

3.3 What is Amazon S3?

Amazon S3

Amazon Simple Storage Service (Amazon S3) is an object storage service that provides highly scalable and reliable storage for a wide range of data types, including documents, images, videos, backups, and more. With a simple interface and robust features, Amazon S3 serves as a cornerstone of many cloud-based applications and architectures. It's designed to offer durability, availability, security, and cost-effectiveness, making it suitable for diverse use cases across industries.

Eric Frick

Benefits of Amazon S3

Scalability: Amazon S3 scales effortlessly to accommodate any volume of data, from a few gigabytes to petabytes, or more. This scalability ensures that organizations can store and retrieve data without worrying about storage limitations.

Durability and Reliability: S3 boasts exceptional durability, safeguarding data against hardware failures, errors, and even the loss of an entire data center. Data stored in S3 is automatically replicated to multiple Availability Zones within a region.

Availability: By distributing data across multiple Availability Zones, Amazon S3 ensures high availability. This design minimizes downtime and offers consistent access to data.

Security: Amazon S3 provides robust security features, including server-side encryption, client-side encryption, access control lists (ACLs), and bucket policies. This ensures data confidentiality and compliance with security regulations.

Versatility: S3 is a versatile storage solution. It supports a wide variety of data types, making it suitable for everything from simple file storage to complex data analytics and machine learning projects.

Data Management: S3 offers features for data lifecycle management, versioning, and cross-region replication. These features allow users to automate data movement and retention policies.

Cost-Effective: The pay-as-you-go pricing model means that users pay only for the storage and data transfer they use. S3 offers various storage classes to optimize costs based on data access patterns.

Eric Frick

Storage Classes in Amazon S3

S3 Standard

Ideal for frequently accessed data, including frequently updated content, analytics data, and content distribution.

S3 Intelligent-Tiering

Automatically moves objects between two access tiers based on changing access patterns, optimizing costs without sacrificing performance.

S3 One Zone-IA

Offers cost-effective storage for infrequently accessed data that can be stored with reduced availability. Data is stored in a single Availability Zone.

S3 Glacier

Designed for long-term data archival with retrieval times ranging from minutes to hours. Ideal for data that is accessed infrequently but needs to be retained.

S3 Glacier Deep Archive

Provides the lowest-cost storage for data archiving, with retrieval times ranging from 12 to 48 hours. Suited for long-term retention of rarely accessed data.

S3 Outposts

Extends S3 storage to on-premises environments using AWS Outposts, enabling hybrid cloud scenarios.

Eric Frick

Common Use Cases for Amazon S3

Data Backup and Recovery: Organizations use S3 to create backups of critical data for disaster recovery and compliance purposes.

Data Lakes and Analytics: S3 is often a foundational component for building data lakes, where large volumes of raw and processed data are stored for analysis using tools like Amazon Redshift or Athena.

Web Hosting and Content Distribution: S3 can host static websites and serve as a content repository for content delivery networks (CDNs), accelerating content distribution globally.

Application Data Storage: Developers use S3 to store application assets such as images, videos, user-generated content, and configuration files.

Archival and Compliance: S3 Glacier and Glacier Deep Archive are used to store data that needs to be retained for compliance reasons or long-term archiving.

Big Data and Machine Learning: S3 is a preferred storage solution for big data analytics and machine learning projects, storing datasets that are processed

Introduction to Amazon AWS

by services like Amazon EMR and Amazon SageMaker.

Log Storage and Analysis: S3 is used to store logs generated by applications, servers, and network devices. Analyzing these logs can provide insights into system performance, security, and user behavior.

Eric Frick

Detailed Use Case

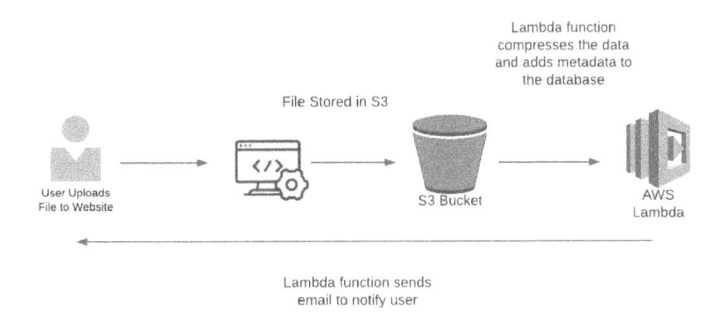

```
                    File Stored in S3         Lambda function
                                              compresses the data
                                              and adds metadata to
                                              the database

  User Uploads                          S3 Bucket        AWS
  File to Website                                        Lambda

                         Lambda function sends
                         email to notify user
```

The use case above describes a typical scenario in which S3 can interact with other services. In this scenario, a user uploads a file to a website. From there, it is stored in an S3 bucket. Once it is uploaded to S3, a Lambda function is triggered that compresses the file and tags it with metadata. When this function has completed, it sends an email notification back to the user.

Amazon S3's combination of reliability, scalability, security, and versatility have made it a fundamental building block for modern cloud-based applications. Its diverse storage classes cater to a wide range of data access patterns and business requirements, ensuring that organizations can store, manage, and retrieve their data efficiently and cost-effectively.

3.4 Deploying a Website on Amazon S3

In this section, I will show you how to deploy a website on Amazon S3. There are several advantages of hosting websites on Amazon S3. These advantages include:

- It is simple to use.
- It is very inexpensive to use for hosting.
- You can easily integrate with CloudFront.
- This process can easily be automated via scripts.

In the next few pages, I will cover the step-by-step details of how you can host a simple website.

How to Build a Simple Website with Amazon S3

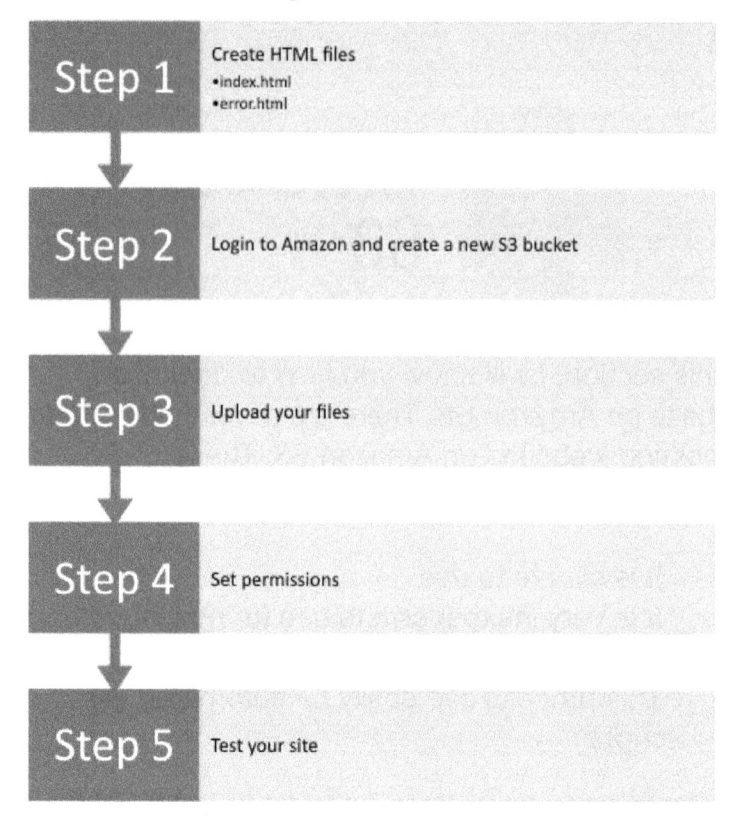

Step 1: Create HTML files
- index.html
- error.html

Step 2: Login to Amazon and create a new S3 bucket

Step 3: Upload your files

Step 4: Set permissions

Step 5: Test your site

Eric Frick

Step 1 Sample HTML Files

The following are listings of two sample HTML files we can use for building the world's simplest website on Amazon S3. You can use any files you wish, I used these for simplicity.

index.html

<html>
<h1>This is our test website for Amazon S3</h1>
<p> Hello World!</p>
</html>

error.html

<html>
<h1>OOPS an error has occurred!</h1>
<p> This is our test S3 website.</p>
</html>

Step 2 Create an S3 bucket

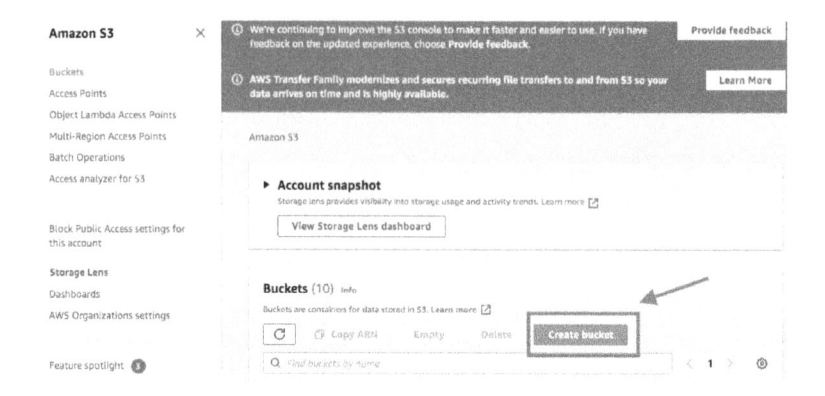

First, navigate to the S3 service page in AWS. Once you are there, click on the *Create Bucket* button that I indicated above.

Eric Frick

Step 2 continued

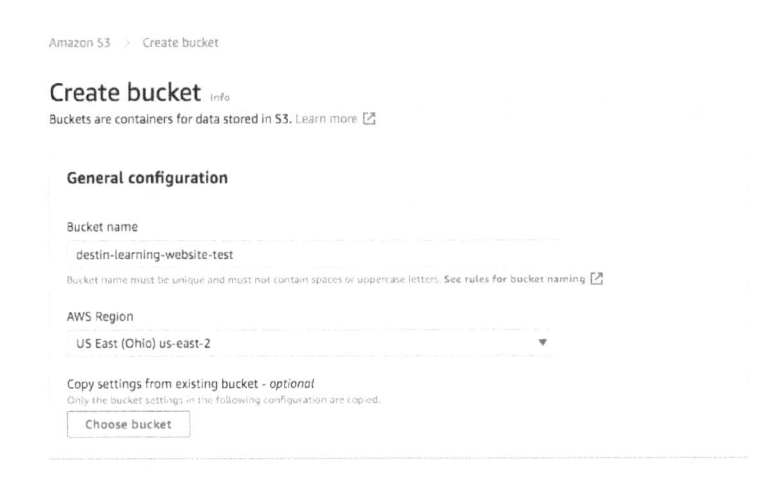

Amazon S3 > Create bucket

Create bucket Info
Buckets are containers for data stored in S3. Learn more

General configuration

Bucket name
destin-learning-website-test
Bucket name must be unique and must not contain spaces or uppercase letters. See rules for bucket naming

AWS Region
US East (Ohio) us-east-2

Copy settings from existing bucket - *optional*
Only the bucket settings in the following configuration are copied.

Choose bucket

Select a name for your bucket, as in the following screenshot. Please note that the name for your bucket must be unique. Uncheck
the **Block *all* public access selection.** Also, check **I acknowledge that the current settings might result in this bucket and the objects within becoming public.**
Once you have completed this, click the *Create Bucket* button.

Step 2 continued

| | destin-learning-website-test | US East (Ohio) us-east-2 | Objects can be public | October 16, 2021, 15:29:47 (UTC-04:00) |

Next, click on the bucket you just created to get access to its contents and settings. Since this is probably a brand new account for you, there will only be one bucket in the list.

Eric Frick

Step 3 Upload Your Files

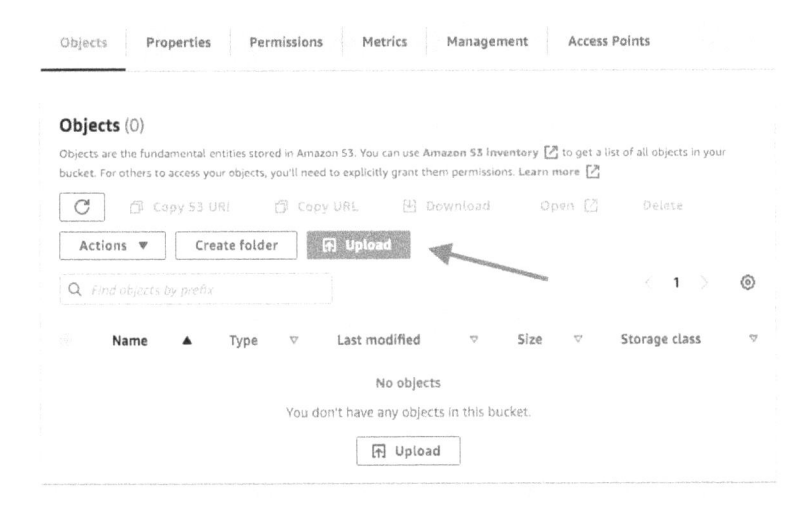

After you have opened your bucket, you will see the following screen. Click on the *Upload* button to upload your two HTML files.

Introduction to Amazon AWS

Step 3 Upload Your Files - continued

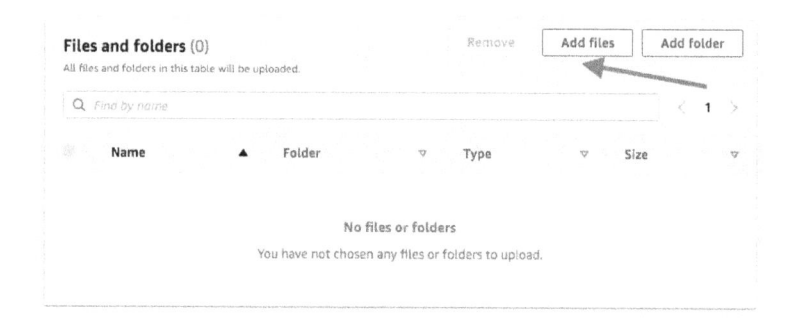

Click on the *Add files* button to upload the two html files (index.html and error.html).

Step 3 Upload Your Files - continued

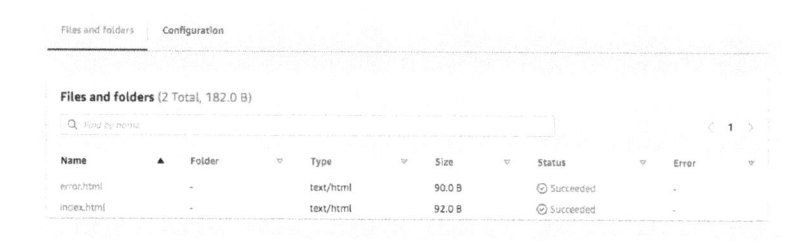

You should now see the files listed in your S3 bucket. Next, click the *Close* button to return to the bucket summary screen.

Eric Frick
Step 4 Set Permissions

destin-learning-website-test

Objects | Properties | Permissions | Metrics | Management | Access Points

Under the properties tab, scroll down to the bottom of the page and edit the Static website hosting settings.

Static website hosting
Use this bucket to host a website or redirect requests. Learn more.

Static website hosting
Disabled

Edit

Step 4 Set Permissions - continued

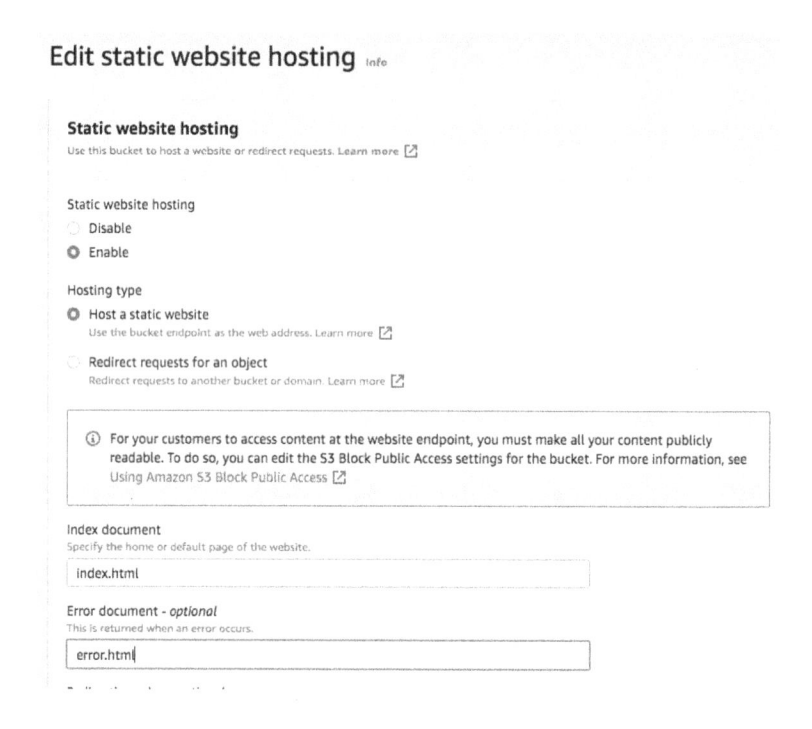

Edit static website hosting Info

Static website hosting
Use this bucket to host a website or redirect requests. Learn more

Static website hosting
- ○ Disable
- ● Enable

Hosting type
- ● Host a static website
  Use the bucket endpoint as the web address. Learn more
- ○ Redirect requests for an object
  Redirect requests to another bucket or domain. Learn more

ⓘ For your customers to access content at the website endpoint, you must make all your content publicly readable. To do so, you can edit the S3 Block Public Access settings for the bucket. For more information, see Using Amazon S3 Block Public Access

Index document
Specify the home or default page of the website.
[index.html]

Error document - *optional*
This is returned when an error occurs.
[error.html]

Enter in the file names for the index and error files, and then click the *Save changes* button.

Step 4 Set Permissions - continued

Add the following under the Bucket policies. Substitute the bucket name with your bucket name in this configuration setting.

```
{
"Version":"2012-10-17",
"Statement":[{
"Sid":"PublicReadGetObject",
"Effect":"Allow",
"Principal": "*",
"Action":["s3:GetObject"],
"Resource":["arn:aws:s3:::destin-learning-website-test/*"]
}]
}
```

Step 5 Test Your Website

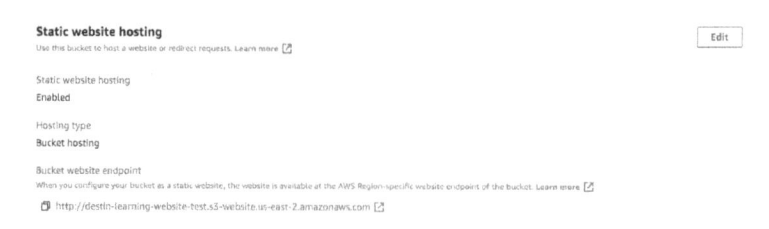

Static website hosting
Use this bucket to host a website or redirect requests. Learn more

Static website hosting
Enabled

Hosting type
Bucket hosting

Bucket website endpoint
When you configure your bucket as a static website, the website is available at the AWS Region-specific website endpoint of the bucket. Learn more
http://destin-learning-website-test.s3-website.us-east-2.amazonaws.com

Edit

Click on the URL displayed at the bottom of the Static website hosting section, and you should see your new website. You should now see the following in your browser.

Not Secure | destin-learning-website-test.s3-website.us-east-2.amazonaws.com

This is our test website for Amazon S3

Hello World!

Summary

I have shown you how simple it is to set up a website using Amazon S3. Although these were simple HTML files, you could replace these with any HTML files and your website will instantly be live worldwide. Try playing around with this to see what you can create.

Eric Frick

3.5 Amazon Relational Database Service (RDS)

Amazon Relational Database Service (RDS) is a fully managed database service provided by Amazon Web Services (AWS). It simplifies the setup, operation, and scaling of relational databases, allowing developers and businesses to focus on application development, instead of database management tasks. RDS supports multiple database engines, offers automated backups, high availability, and security features, making it a popular choice for hosting and managing databases in the cloud.

Benefits of Amazon RDS:

Fully Managed: Amazon RDS handles routine database tasks such as provisioning, patching, backups, monitoring, scaling, and failover, freeing developers from administrative tasks.

Automated Backups: RDS offers automated backups and database snapshots, allowing point-in-time recovery and reducing the risk of data loss.

High Availability: RDS provides built-in, high availability options, such as Multi-AZ deployments that replicate data across multiple Availability Zones to ensure data durability and failover.

Scalability: RDS allows you to easily scale your database resources vertically (compute and memory) and, in some cases, horizontally (read replicas) to accommodate changing workloads.

Security: RDS supports network isolation using Amazon Virtual Private Cloud (VPC), encryption at rest with keys you manage, or AWS Key Management Service (KMS), and security groups for access control.

Performance Monitoring: Amazon RDS provides metrics and monitoring through Amazon CloudWatch, allowing you to track database performance and set alarms for specific thresholds.

Database Engine Flexibility: RDS supports a variety of popular database engines, including MySQL, PostgreSQL, Oracle, SQL Server, and MariaDB, allowing you to choose the engine that best fits your application's requirements.

Automatic Software Patching: RDS automatically applies patches and updates to the database engine software, ensuring security and performance improvements without downtime.

Supported Database Engines in Amazon RDS:

MySQL: A popular open-source relational database management system known for its speed, reliability, and ease of use.

PostgreSQL: An open-source, object-relational database system known for its advanced features, extensibility, and strong adherence to SQL standards.

MariaDB: A community-developed, open-source fork of MySQL that focuses on performance, scalability, and security.

Oracle: A widely-used commercial relational database system known for its robust features, security, and support for large-scale enterprise applications.

SQL Server: Microsoft's relational database management system with comprehensive features, security, and integration with Microsoft tools.

Aurora: Amazon Aurora is a MySQL and PostgreSQL-compatible relational database engine built for the cloud, offering high performance, durability, and scalability.

Use Cases for Amazon RDS:

Web Applications: RDS is commonly used to host databases for web applications, providing a managed environment that scales seamlessly with changing user demand.

E-Commerce Platforms: E-commerce sites benefit from RDS's high availability, scalability, and automated backups to ensure seamless shopping experiences.

Business Applications: RDS supports commercial database engines like Oracle and SQL Server, making it suitable for hosting business-critical applications.

Data Warehousing: Amazon RDS can be used to build data warehouses with engines like PostgreSQL and MySQL, supporting analytics and reporting.

Content Management Systems: CMS platforms use RDS to manage content and user data efficiently, ensuring fast response times and high availability.

SaaS Applications: RDS is a solid choice for hosting databases for software-as-a-service (SaaS) applications, offering multi-tenant capabilities and easy scalability.

Introduction to Amazon AWS

Summary

Amazon RDS simplifies database management, reduces administrative overhead, and provides reliable and scalable database solutions for various use cases, whether you're a small startup, or an enterprise-level organization.

3.6 How to Create a Database in Amazon RDS

Creating an SQL database in Amazon RDS involves a few steps, including selecting the database engine, configuring the database instance, setting up security, and defining other parameters. Below are instructions on how to create an Amazon RDS SQL database using the AWS Management Console:

Step 1: Log into the AWS Management Console: Navigate to the AWS Management Console (https://aws.amazon.com/console/) and sign in with your AWS account credentials.

Introduction to Amazon AWS

Step 2: Open Amazon RDS Dashboard: Search for "RDS" in the AWS Management Console search bar and select *Amazon RDS* from the results.

Step 3: Choose "Create Database": Click the *Create database* button to start the process of creating a new database instance.

Step 4: Select Database Creation Method:
- Choose *Standard Create* to set up a new database instance with default settings.
- Choose *Easy Create* for a simplified setup with recommended configurations.

Step 5: Choose Engine Options:
- Select the database engine you want to use (e.g., MySQL, PostgreSQL, SQL Server).
- Choose the edition and version that best suits your needs.

Step 6: Specify DB Details:

- Enter a unique DB instance identifier.
- Set a master username and password for the database.
- Define the DB instance size and storage allocation.

Step 7: Configure Advanced Settings:
- Configure additional settings such as VPC, subnet group, availability zone, and storage autoscaling (if needed).

Step 8: Database Authentication:
- Choose the authentication method for your database:
    - "Password Authentication" for traditional username and password authentication.
    - "IAM Database Authentication" for using AWS Identity and Access Management (IAM) roles to authenticate.

Step 9: Network & Security:
- Configure security group settings to control network access to the database.
- Choose whether the database should be publicly accessible or not.

Step 10: Additional Configuration:
- Set up database maintenance preferences, including backups, maintenance window, and backup retention period.

Step 11: Monitoring & Maintenance:
- Enable or disable automated backups and configure the backup window.
- Set up CloudWatch monitoring and specify if you want to enable Enhanced Monitoring.

Step 12: Create Database: Review the configuration details and click the *Create database* button to initiate the creation of your SQL database.

Step 13: Wait for Creation: The database creation process may take a few minutes. You can monitor the progress on the RDS dashboard.

Step 14: Access Database: Once the database is created, you'll find its endpoint and connection details in the RDS dashboard. You can use these details to connect to your SQL database using your preferred client application or programming language.

Summary

These steps outline the process of creating an SQL database using Amazon RDS through the AWS Management Console. Remember to follow best practices for security, performance, and data management as you configure and use your database instance.

Eric Frick
3.7 Amazon Cloud Watch

Amazon CloudWatch is a monitoring and management service provided by Amazon Web Services (AWS). It enables users to collect and monitor metrics, collect and store log files, set alarms, and automate actions based on specific conditions. CloudWatch helps organizations gain insights into the performance and health of their applications, services, and resources within the AWS environment.

Benefits of Amazon CloudWatch:

Centralized Monitoring: CloudWatch provides a centralized platform to monitor various AWS resources, including EC2 instances, RDS databases, Lambda functions, and more, giving users a holistic view of their infrastructure.

Real-Time Metrics: CloudWatch collects real-time metrics, such as CPU utilization, network traffic, and disk I/O, allowing users to understand resource consumption and detect anomalies.

Custom Metrics: Users can publish custom metrics to CloudWatch, enabling monitoring of application-specific performance metrics and business Key Performance Indicators (KPI).

Automated Alarms: CloudWatch Alarms enable users to set up alarms based on defined thresholds of metrics. These alarms can trigger notifications or automated actions to maintain optimal performance.

Log Collection and Analysis: CloudWatch Logs allow users to collect, store, and analyze log data generated by applications and AWS resources. This helps with troubleshooting and understanding application behavior.

Dashboards: Users can create customized dashboards to visualize and monitor metrics, logs, and alarms in a single view, facilitating quick decision-making.

Scaling and Automation: CloudWatch can be used to trigger automatic scaling of resources based on metrics, ensuring optimal resource utilization and cost efficiency.

Application Insights: CloudWatch Application Insights provides deep insights into applications running on AWS, identifying issues and recommending remediation steps.

Integrations: CloudWatch integrates with other AWS services, allowing users to take actions based on monitored data. For example, triggering an AWS Lambda function when a certain metric threshold is breached.

Introduction to Amazon AWS

Common Use Cases for Amazon CloudWatch:

Resource Monitoring: CloudWatch helps monitor resource usage, performance, and health of AWS resources, including EC2 instances, RDS databases, S3 buckets, and more.

Auto Scaling: CloudWatch triggers auto scaling of resources based on predefined metrics. For example, scaling out a fleet of EC2 instances during peak traffic.

Application Performance: Users can monitor the performance of their applications by tracking latency, error rates, and other relevant metrics.

Operational Insights: CloudWatch Logs can be used to analyze logs and troubleshoot issues, enabling quick identification and resolution of operational problems.

Cost Optimization: CloudWatch metrics provide insights into resource utilization, helping organizations identify over-provisioned or underutilized resources to optimize costs.

Security Monitoring: CloudWatch can be used to monitor security-related metrics and set up alarms for suspicious activity, enhancing the security posture of AWS resources.

Eric Frick

Custom Application Metrics: Users can publish custom metrics from their applications to CloudWatch, allowing them to monitor application-specific performance metrics.

Performance Optimization: CloudWatch insights can guide users in optimizing application and infrastructure performance by identifying bottlenecks and inefficiencies.

Summary

Amazon CloudWatch serves as a powerful tool for monitoring, analyzing, and acting on data generated by AWS resources and applications. By providing real-time visibility, automation, and insights, CloudWatch empowers organizations to maintain a reliable, performant, and efficient cloud environment.

Introduction to Amazon AWS

3.9 AWS Lambda

Amazon AWS Lambda is a serverless computing service that enables developers to run code in response to events without managing servers. With Lambda, developers can focus on writing code and building applications while AWS takes care of provisioning and scaling the necessary infrastructure. Lambda is designed to support event-driven architectures and microservices, making it a key component in building scalable and efficient cloud-based applications.

Benefits of AWS Lambda:

Serverless Computing: Developers can write and deploy code without worrying about server provisioning, scaling, or management. AWS Lambda automatically handles the infrastructure.

Pay-as-You-Go Pricing: Lambda follows a pay-per-use model, charging only for the compute time used. This cost-efficient approach eliminates the need to pay for idle resources.

Automatic Scaling: Lambda scales seamlessly based on the incoming workload. It automatically provisions resources to handle the event traffic, ensuring high performance and availability.

Event-Driven Architecture: Lambda is designed to respond to a variety of events, such as HTTP requests, database changes, file uploads, and more, making it well-suited for event-driven architectures.

Wide Language Support: AWS Lambda supports multiple programming languages, including Node.js, Python, Java, Go, Ruby, .NET Core, and custom runtimes using the Runtime API.

Integration with AWS Services: Lambda integrates seamlessly with other AWS services, enabling easy building of serverless applications using services like Amazon S3, DynamoDB, SNS, and more.

Microservices: Lambda facilitates the development of microservices by allowing each function to perform a specific task. This modular approach promotes flexibility and maintainability.

Automatic Monitoring and Logging: Lambda provides built-in CloudWatch integration for monitoring and logging, allowing developers to track function performance and troubleshoot issues.

Eric Frick

Common Use Cases for AWS Lambda:

Data Processing: Lambda can process and transform data in real-time as it flows through the system. For instance, resizing images upon upload, performing data validation, or applying data enrichment.

Real-Time File Processing: Lambda can process files as they are uploaded to services like Amazon S3, enabling scenarios such as video transcoding or generating thumbnails.

Event-Driven Backend: Developers can use Lambda to build event-driven backends that respond to HTTP requests, authentication events, database changes, and more.

Chatbots and Voice Assistants: Lambda can be used to build chatbots and voice assistants that respond to user interactions and perform actions based on natural language input.

IoT Data Processing: Lambda can process data from Internet of Things (IoT) devices, performing real-time analytics, triggering alerts, or storing data in databases.

Introduction to Amazon AWS

Data Analysis: Lambda can be used in conjunction with analytics services to process, analyze, and visualize data in real-time, providing insights for decision-making.

Automated Workflows: Lambda functions can orchestrate and automate workflows across multiple services, enhancing efficiency, and reducing manual intervention.

Webhooks and APIs: Lambda can serve as a backend for webhooks and APIs, processing incoming requests and triggering actions.

Summary

AWS Lambda revolutionizes the way developers build applications by allowing them to focus solely on the code and functionality while offloading infrastructure management to AWS. With its ability to scale on-demand and respond to a wide range of events, Lambda enables the creation of highly scalable, flexible, and efficient, serverless applications

3.9 How to Build a Lambda Function

Creating a simple Lambda function in C# involves setting up a function that responds to an event, defining the code logic, and configuring the necessary permissions. Here are step-by-step instructions on how to do this:

Step 1: Log in to AWS Console: Navigate to the AWS Management Console (https://aws.amazon.com/console/) and log into your AWS account.

Step 2: Open AWS Lambda Dashboard: Search for "Lambda" in the AWS Management Console search bar and select *Lambda* from the results.

Step 3: Create a New Function: Click the *Create function* button to create a new Lambda function.

Step 4: Configure Function Details:
- Choose *Author from scratch*.
- Enter a unique function name.
- Choose a runtime: Select *.NET Core* as the runtime.
- Choose the execution role: Either create a new role with basic Lambda permissions or choose an existing role.

Step 5: Create Function: Click the *Create function* button to create the function.

Introduction to Amazon AWS

Step 6: Write the C# Code: In the function's detail page, you'll find the code editor. Replace the existing code with a simple C# function. For example, let's create a Lambda function that responds to an S3 object creation event:

```csharp
using System;
using Amazon.Lambda.Core;
using Amazon.Lambda.S3Events;
using Amazon.S3;
using Amazon.S3.Util;

[assembly: LambdaSerializer(typeof(Amazon.Lambda.Serialization.Json.JsonSerializer))]

namespace SimpleLambdaFunction
{
    public class Function
    {
        private IAmazonS3 S3Client { get; }

        public Function()
        {
            S3Client = new AmazonS3Client();
        }

        public void FunctionHandler(S3Event evnt, ILambdaContext context)
        {
            foreach (var record in evnt.Records)
            {
                var bucket = record.S3.Bucket.Name;
                var key = record.S3.Object.Key;

                Console.WriteLine($"New object created in bucket '{bucket}', key: '{key}'");
            }
        }
    }
}
```

Step 7: Configure Trigger:
- Under "Add triggers," click *Add trigger*.
- Choose *S3* as the trigger type.
- Select the bucket you want to use for testing.
- Choose *All object create events*.
- Click *Add*.

Step 8: Save and Deploy: Click the *Deploy* button to save and deploy your Lambda function.

Step 9: Test the Lambda Function:
- After deployment, you can test the function by manually creating an object in the specified S3 bucket. Check the CloudWatch logs for function output.

Congratulations! You've successfully created a simple Lambda function in C# that responds to S3 object creation events. This example demonstrates the basic structure of a Lambda function. You can expand on this foundation by integrating with other AWS services, handling more complex events, and incorporating error handling.

Summary

Remember that this is a basic example. In real-world scenarios, you'll need to consider security, error handling, logging, and best practices for maintaining and managing Lambda functions.

4.0 Security and Account Management

Eric Frick

4.1 What is IAM?

Amazon Web Services (AWS) Identity and Access Management (IAM) is a powerful service that enables you to securely manage user identities, control their access to AWS resources, and maintain a robust security posture within your cloud environment. IAM allows you to establish fine-grained access policies, centralized user authentication and authorization, and ensure compliance with the principle of least privilege.

Key Concepts of AWS IAM

The following are some of the key concepts of the IAM system. They provide the foundation for identity services for AWS.

Users and Groups: IAM allows you to create individual user accounts for each person who requires access to your AWS resources. Users can be organized into groups, simplifying the assignment of permissions based on job roles or responsibilities.

Roles: Roles are a secure way to delegate permissions to entities outside your AWS account, such as applications or services. Roles are often used to enable cross-account access, or to allow AWS services to interact securely with resources.

Policies: IAM policies are JSON documents that define permissions. These policies can be attached to users, groups, or roles, specifying which actions are allowed, or denied, on specific AWS resources. Policies are the building blocks of IAM's access control mechanism.

Authentication and Authorization: IAM provides both authentication (verifying the identity of users) and authorization (determining what actions they're allowed to perform). This dual-layered approach ensures that only authenticated and authorized users can access AWS resources.

Multi-Factor Authentication (MFA): IAM supports MFA, adding an extra layer of security to user sign-ins. MFA requires users to provide two or more verification factors: something they know (password) and something they possess (MFA device).

Identity Federation: With identity federation, users can sign in to AWS using credentials from their organization's identity provider (e.g. Microsoft Active Directory). This allows for centralized management of user identities and credentials.

Benefits of AWS IAM

In this section we will explore the benefits of IAM and the features it provides to ease the administration of cloud-based systems using AWS.

Security: IAM helps you implement the principle of least privilege, ensuring users have only the permissions they need to perform their tasks. This minimizes the risk of unauthorized access or data breaches.

Granular Control: IAM enables precise control over who can access specific resources and what actions they can perform. This fine-grained control enhances security while maintaining flexibility.

Centralized Management: IAM provides a central point for managing user identities and access across AWS services. This streamlines administration, reduces complexity, and improves overall security hygiene.

Audit and Compliance: IAM logs all user activity, allowing you to monitor and audit actions taken by users. This aids in compliance with regulatory requirements and helps detect potential security issues.

Eric Frick

Ease of Use: IAM integrates seamlessly with other AWS services, making it straightforward to manage access to resources as your infrastructure scales.

Introduction to Amazon AWS

Setting Up a User Account in IAM

Let's walk through a simple example of setting up a user account in IAM:

Sign in to the AWS Management Console: Log into your AWS account using your credentials.

Navigate to IAM: From the AWS Management Console, search for "IAM" in the services search bar and click on the *IAM* service.

Create a New User: In the IAM dashboard, click on *Users* from the left-hand menu, then click the *Add user* button.

Specify User Details: Enter a user name for the new user. You can choose to give the user programmatic access (for API/CLI access), AWS Management Console access (for web-based access), or both.

Set Permissions: On the permissions page, you can either add the user to an existing group with predefined permissions, or attach policies directly to the user. Policies can be AWS-managed policies or custom policies that you create.

Review and Create User: Review the user's settings and permissions, then click *Create user*.

Access and Secret Keys (Optional): If you enable programmatic access for the user, you'll be prompted to download the user's access and secret keys. These keys are needed when interacting with AWS services using the AWS Command Line Interface (CLI) or SDKs.

Finish: Once the user is created, you'll see a summary page with the user's details, permissions, and other information.

By setting up a user account in IAM and managing permissions through groups and policies, you can ensure that your AWS resources are accessed and used securely and according to your organization's requirements. IAM plays a crucial role in maintaining a strong security posture in your AWS environment.

Summary

In summary, AWS Identity and Access Management (IAM) is a fundamental component of securing your AWS environment. By following best practices and utilizing IAM's features, you can establish a strong foundation for managing user identities and access permissions, mitigating risks, and maintaining the highest levels of security within your cloud infrastructure.

4.2 IAM Hierarchy

The Identity and Access Management (IAM) hierarchy in Amazon AWS consists of several key components that work together to define and manage user identities, permissions, and access to AWS resources. Understanding this hierarchy is essential for effectively configuring access controls and maintaining security within your AWS environment. Here are the components of the IAM hierarchy, along with detailed definitions:

Eric Frick

Root Account

The root account is the highest level of access in an AWS account. It is created when you first set up your AWS account. The root account has unrestricted access to all AWS resources and services within the account. However, it's recommended to use the root account only for initial setup tasks and administrative actions that cannot be performed by other IAM users or roles.

IAM Users

IAM users represent individual identities within your AWS account. Each user is associated with a unique set of credentials (username and password or access keys) and can have specific permissions granted through policies. IAM users are the basis for access control in AWS, and they allow you to provide different levels of access to different individuals.

IAM Groups

IAM groups are collections of IAM users. Instead of assigning permissions directly to individual users, you can assign permissions to groups, which simplifies access management based on roles or job responsibilities. IAM users can belong to multiple groups, and by adding or removing permissions from a group, you can affect the access of multiple users simultaneously.

IAM Roles

IAM roles are similar to users but are not associated with permanent credentials. Roles are used to grant permissions temporarily, typically for services or applications that need to access AWS resources. Roles are assumed by entities (such as AWS services, applications, or users from different AWS accounts) to obtain temporary security credentials for accessing resources.

IAM Policies

IAM policies are JSON documents that define permissions. Policies specify which actions are allowed or denied on specified AWS resources. These policies can be attached to IAM users, groups, and roles. Policies can be inline (defined directly in the IAM entity) or managed (created and attached separately).

Resource-Based Policies

Resource-based policies are policies that are attached to AWS resources, such as S3 buckets or Lambda functions. These policies define who can access the resource and what actions they can perform on it. They are distinct from IAM policies, which are attached to users, groups, or roles.

Permission Boundaries

Permission boundaries are an advanced feature that allows you to set the maximum permissions that an IAM entity (user or role) can have. This allows you to delegate administrative control over specific IAM entities while limiting the extent of their permissions.

Service Control Policies (SCPs)

SCPs are used in AWS Organizations to set permissions on accounts within an organization. SCPs allow you to control what AWS services and actions can be accessed by the accounts, helping to enforce compliance and security standards across the organization.

Summary

Understanding the IAM hierarchy and its components is crucial for designing a secure and well-managed AWS environment. By structuring users, groups, roles, and policies effectively, you can achieve granular control over access permissions, minimize security risks, and ensure compliance with best practices and regulatory requirements.

4.3 IAM Roles

IAM roles in Amazon Web Services (AWS) are a fundamental security feature that enables temporary access to resources. Unlike IAM users, roles don't have permanent credentials associated with them. Instead, they provide a way to delegate permissions to trusted entities, such as AWS services, applications, or users from different AWS accounts. IAM roles are essential for ensuring secure access to resources without compromising long-term security.

Key Concepts and Benefits of IAM Roles

Temporary Permissions: Roles grant temporary permissions to perform actions. When an entity assumes a role, it receives temporary security credentials that are valid for a specified duration, limiting the exposure of long-term credentials.

Cross-Account Access: Roles are often used to grant access across AWS accounts. This is especially useful for third-party applications or services that need to interact with resources in another AWS account.

Service Integration: AWS services can assume roles to access other services. For example, an EC2 instance can assume a role to access an S3 bucket without needing to manage access keys directly on the instance.

Security and Least Privilege: By assigning permissions to only the roles that need them, you adhere to the principle of least privilege, reducing the risk of unauthorized access.

Best Practices for Using IAM Roles

Avoid Using Root User Credentials: Instead of using the root account's credentials, use roles whenever possible to grant temporary permissions.

Limit Permissions: Assign the minimum necessary permissions to roles based on the principle of least privilege. Regularly review and refine permissions to ensure ongoing security.

Use Roles for AWS Services: When AWS services need to interact with each other, use roles to grant necessary permissions, avoiding the use of static access keys.

Enable MFA for Assume Role: Require multi-factor authentication (MFA) for users to assume roles, adding an extra layer of security.

Rotate Role Credentials: Rotate role credentials periodically to minimize the risk of misuse.

Use Conditions: Apply conditions to role policies to further restrict access based on specific conditions, such as time of day or source IP.

Commonly Used IAM Roles

- **Amazon EC2 Instance Role:** Allows EC2 instances to access other AWS services securely without the need for access keys. Commonly used to grant permissions for services like S3, DynamoDB, or AWS Systems Manager.
- **Lambda Function Role:** Enables AWS Lambda functions to access resources like S3 buckets or databases securely. This role is specified when creating a Lambda function.
- **Cross-Account Role:** Used to grant access to resources in one AWS account from another AWS account. Commonly used in scenarios involving AWS Organizations or third-party applications.
- **Federated User Role:** Used in identity federation scenarios where users from an external identity provider (such as Active Directory) assume a role to access AWS resources.
- **Service Role:** Allows AWS services to assume a role to access other services. For example, an Amazon Redshift cluster may assume a role to access data stored in an S3 bucket.

Summary

IAM roles are a powerful mechanism for managing permissions in AWS while maintaining security and adhering to the principle of least privilege. By following best practices and understanding the roles available, you can enhance the security posture of your AWS environment and streamline the management of permissions across your resources.

Eric Frick

5.0 Billing and Pricing

In this chapter, we will look at some of the basic financial aspects of AWS. Specifically, we will look at the AWS pricing models and AWS account structures. Cloud computing can save an organization a significant amount of time and money if you manage it properly. Conversely, you can also run up a big bill in a hurry if you are not managing your resources properly. In this chapter, we will look at the foundation that the billing and pricing structures that AWS is based on.

5.1 AWS Pricing Models

Amazon Web Services (AWS) offers a variety of pricing models to accommodate different use cases and customer needs. Understanding these pricing models is essential for effectively managing costs while leveraging the rich array of AWS services. Let's delve into the main AWS pricing models:

Pay-as-You-Go

The pay-as-you-go pricing model is the most flexible option. Customers are charged based on actual usage of AWS services, with no upfront costs or long-term commitments. This model is suitable for variable workloads and projects where usage fluctuates.

Reserved Instances (RIs)

Reserved Instances allow customers to commit to a specific instance type in exchange for a lower hourly rate compared to on-demand pricing. RIs are available in three payment options:

Standard RIs: A balance between upfront payments and hourly rates.

Convertible RIs: Flexibility to change instance types later for better optimization.

Scheduled RIs: Available within specific time windows, ideal for predictable workloads.

Savings Plans

Savings Plans provide a flexible option to receive discounts on compute usage across different instance families, sizes, and operating systems. This model offers more flexibility than RIs, as it applies to a broader set of services.

Spot Instances

Spot Instances allow customers to bid on unused Amazon EC2 instances, offering substantial cost savings. However, these instances can be terminated if the Spot price exceeds the bid or if capacity is needed elsewhere.

Dedicated Hosts

Dedicated Hosts provide physical servers dedicated to your use, offering increased visibility into instance placement. This model is useful for regulatory or licensing requirements.

On-Demand Instances

This model allows customers to pay for compute capacity by the hour or second, with no upfront commitment. On-Demand Instances are suitable for short-term projects, applications with variable workloads, and testing environments.

Eric Frick

Data Transfer Pricing

AWS charges for data transfer between AWS services and the internet. Costs vary based on data volume and whether the transfer is within or outside the AWS ecosystem.

Using the AWS Pricing Calculator

The AWS Pricing Calculator is a powerful tool that helps customers estimate their monthly AWS costs. Here's how to use it:

Access the Calculator: Visit the AWS Pricing Calculator webpage (https://calculator.aws/).

Configure Services: Choose the AWS services you plan to use and specify configuration details such as instance types, storage, and data transfer.

Enter Usage: Input estimated usage, such as the number of hours instances will run or the amount of data transfer.

Eric Frick

Review Estimates: The calculator provides cost estimates based on your inputs, allowing you to see how different choices impact your costs.

Save or Share: You can save, print, or share the cost estimate for reference or further analysis.

Summary

Amazon AWS offers diverse pricing models that cater to a wide range of usage patterns and customer requirements. The pay-as-you-go model provides flexibility, while Reserved Instances, Savings Plans, and Spot Instances offer opportunities for cost optimization. The AWS Pricing Calculator empowers users to estimate costs accurately, aiding in budgeting and decision-making. Selecting the right pricing model based on your workload characteristics is crucial for maximizing the value of AWS services while managing costs effectively.

5.2 AWS Account Structures

Amazon Web Services (AWS) offers a versatile account structure that allows organizations to effectively manage resources; access control; and billing across different departments, teams, and projects. Understanding AWS account structures is crucial for optimizing resource allocation, security, and cost management within your cloud environment.

AWS Account: At the core of the AWS account structure is the AWS account itself. An AWS account serves as a container for your cloud resources, services, and configurations. Each account has a unique ID and is associated with a single email address. Accounts are billed separately and can have different access controls and resource setups.

Eric Frick

AWS Organizations: AWS Organizations is a feature that helps you manage multiple AWS accounts. Organizations enable centralized billing, resource sharing, and simplified administration across your accounts. Organizations consist of the following key components:

- **Root Account:** The initial account you create when setting up AWS Organizations. It acts as the management account for the organization and can have multiple member accounts linked to it.
- **Member Accounts:** Accounts linked to the root account within the organization. These accounts can be used to manage specific projects, departments, or teams. Member accounts can have independent resources, users, and policies.

Organizational Units (OUs): OUs provide a way to group and organize member accounts within an AWS organization. OUs help you create a logical structure to manage resources, policies, and permissions. OUs can represent departments, projects, or any other organizational structure that suits your needs.

Service Control Policies (SCPs): SCPs are a form of permission management within an AWS organization. They allow you to set granular access controls for member accounts and OUs. SCPs define which AWS services and actions are allowed or denied at the organizational level, ensuring consistent security and compliance across accounts.

Cross-Account Access: Cross-account access enables members of one AWS account to access resources in another account. This is useful for sharing resources securely, such as granting access to centralized log storage or backup services.

AWS Identity and Access Management (IAM) Roles: IAM roles enable users or services in one account to assume temporary permissions in another account. This helps in reducing the need for sharing long-term credentials and enhances security.

Resource Tagging: Tagging resources with metadata allows for easier resource management and cost allocation. Tags can provide insights into the purpose, owner, or department associated with each resource.

AWS Resource Groups: AWS Resource Groups help you organize and manage resources based on tags and attributes. They provide a way to view and monitor resources that meet specific criteria, across accounts and regions.

AWS Billing and Cost Management: AWS provides consolidated billing, which allows you to combine the usage and billing information of multiple accounts under a single payer account. This is especially useful for organizations with multiple accounts to manage costs and optimize spending.

Eric Frick

Summary

Understanding the AWS account structure, including Organizations, OUs, SCPs, and cross-account access, empowers you to design a well-organized, secure, and cost-effective cloud environment. By leveraging these features, you can efficiently manage resources, access controls, and handle billing across your AWS accounts while maintaining a clear organizational hierarchy.

Introduction to Amazon AWS

6.0 Cloud Career Information

In this chapter, I have included some brief information about careers in cloud computing. In the first section, I have included some information from a recent survey about the top cloud jobs and associated salary information. Following that, I have included some information about the top cloud certifications that are in demand in the market today.

Eric Frick

6.1 Top Cloud Jobs and Salaries

The cloud computing market continues to grow at an amazing rate. The demand for trained cloud personnel remains strong and currently there is a shortage of trained personnel. To give you an idea of the top jobs that are in demand, I have included some data from Randstad Research, which lists some of the most in-demand cloud jobs for 2021.

Top Cloud Jobs

Cloud Job	Average Salary
Cloud engineers	$132,866 USD
DevOps developers	$137,830 USD
.NET developers	$131,070 USD
Machine-learning engineers	$137,513 USD
Security analysts	$124,892 USD

Eric Frick

I have included the link to the Randstadt site below, if you would like to see further details:

https://www.randstadusa.com/job-seeker/best-jobs/best-jobs-tech/#cloud_engineer

Introduction to Amazon AWS

6.2 Top AWS Certifications for 2023

As cloud computing continues to shape the IT landscape, Amazon Web Services (AWS) certifications have become highly sought after by professionals and organizations looking to validate their expertise in cloud technologies. AWS certifications not only showcase proficiency in various cloud services but also often lead to increased job opportunities and higher earning potential. Here are some of the top AWS certifications for 2023, along with their average annual salaries:

AWS Certified Solutions Architect - Professional: This certification is designed for experienced solution architects who design and deploy dynamically scalable, highly available, fault-tolerant, and reliable applications on AWS. Average Annual Salary: $150,000 - $170,000

AWS Certified DevOps Engineer - Professional: This certification is ideal for individuals with advanced experience in provisioning, operating, and managing distributed application systems on the AWS platform. It focuses on implementing and managing continuous delivery systems and methodologies. Average Annual Salary: $140,000 - $160,000

AWS Certified Machine Learning - Specialty: With a growing emphasis on machine learning and AI, this certification is tailored for individuals who design, implement, deploy, and maintain machine learning solutions for a variety of business problems. Average Annual Salary: $130,000 - $150,000

AWS Certified Security - Specialty: As security remains a paramount concern, this certification targets professionals who have a deep understanding of securing applications, data, and systems on the AWS platform. Average Annual Salary: $130,000 - $150,000

AWS Certified Data Analytics - Specialty: For professionals working with data analytics, this certification validates expertise in designing, building, securing, and maintaining analytics solutions on AWS. Average Annual Salary: $120,000 - $140,000

AWS Certified Solutions Architect - Associate: A foundational certification, it's designed for individuals with experience in designing distributed systems and applications on the AWS platform. Average Annual Salary: $110,000 - $130,000

AWS Certified Developer - Associate: For developers, this certification focuses on designing, developing, and deploying cloud-based applications using AWS services. Average Annual Salary: $105,000 - $125,000

AWS Certified SysOps Administrator - Associate: This certification is tailored for systems administrators and focuses on deploying, managing, and operating scalable, highly available, and fault-tolerant systems on AWS. Average Annual Salary: $100,000 - $120,000

Eric Frick

Summary

It's important to note that salaries can vary based on factors such as location, experience, industry, and the specific job role associated with the certification. AWS certifications not only enhance your technical skills but also provide a tangible credential that can help you stand out in a competitive job market and negotiate a higher salary. As the cloud computing industry continues to grow, AWS certifications are expected to remain valuable assets for IT professionals seeking career advancement.

Chapter 7 Summary

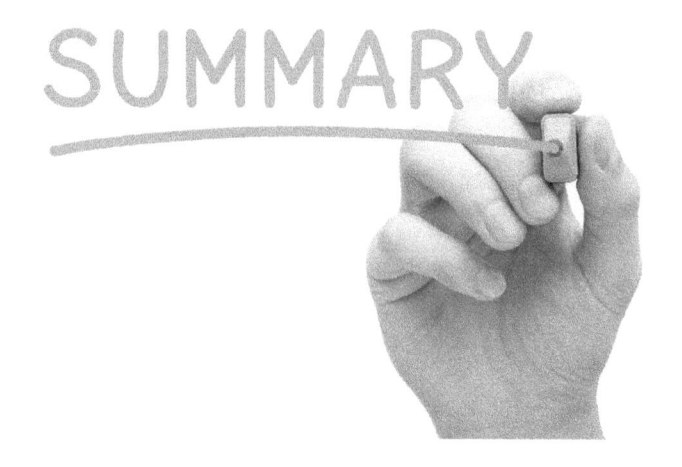

In this chapter I will wrap up the material for this book. I will present a brief summary of the course and follow up with some more detailed information about me and how you can contact me if you are interested. I have also included some links to my additional publications, as well as additional material on my YouTube channel.

Eric Frick
7.1 Course Summary

Thank you so much for reading this book. I hope it has given you a good start on your journey to learn more about computer science and cloud computing. As I mentioned in the introduction, this book is part of a series of books designed to train entry-level software developers. If you have suggestions for improvements for this book, please contact me, as I would love to hear from you. Also, please leave a review for me, so I can continually make this book better. Thank you again, and I hope to see you again soon.

7.2 About the Author

Eric Frick

I have worked in software development and IT operations for 30 years. I have worked as a Software Developer, Software Development Manager, Software Architect, and as an Operations Manager. Also, for the last five years, I have taught evening classes on various IT related subjects at several local universities. I currently work as a Software Development Manager and an IT Instructor. In 2015, I founded destinlearning.com, and I am developing a series of books that can provide practical information

Eric Frick

to students on various IT and software development topics.

If you would like to connect with me on LinkedIn, here is the link to my profile: https://www.linkedin.com/in/efrick/

Also, if you have any questions or comments about this book you can contact me directly at:

sales@destinlearning.com

7.3 More From Destin Learning

Introduction to Amazon AWS

Thank you so much for your interest in this book. I hope it has given you a good start in the exciting field of Information Technology. If you would like to learn more about software development, you can check out my book, The Beginner's Guide to C#. You can learn more by clicking on the link below.

https://www.destinlearning.com

Eric Frick

7.4 Destin Learning YouTube Channel

You can see more on my YouTube channel, where I am continuing to post free videos about software development and information technology. If you subscribe to my channel, you will get updates as I post new material weekly.

https://youtube.com/destinlearning

Appendix

A.1 Access to Online Course

By purchasing this book, you will also receive free access to the video version of this class on my website. You can access this class by using the following link:

https://www.destinlearning.com/courses/introduction-to-amazon-aws?coupon=AWSFREE2023

If you have any difficulties signing up, please contact me at sales@destinlearning.com and I will send you a coupon code. Thank you again for purchasing this book. If you have any feedback, please contact me. I want to make this book and course the very best they can be.

Eric Frick

A.2 Cloud Concepts Quiz Answers

1. C
2. C
3. B
4. A
5. C
6. B
7. C
8. B
9. D

Milton Keynes UK
Ingram Content Group UK Ltd.
UKHW020910201123
432908UK00020B/2954